Love hurts

Cheryl's mom leaned closer. "Didn't she tell you?"

"Tell me what?" Dave wondered if she could hear the fear he suddenly felt.

"Cheryl's married."

"Married." The word hit like a boulder on his chest. How could one word hurt so much?

"Yes, she's married and has a little girl."

Dave felt as if his whole world died right then. Nothing in his life had ever pained him like this.

"Can't believe it." Dave shook his head. He stood before he said anything he would later regret.

It's too late, he thought, remembering the engagement ring, the kisses, and everything they had with each other.

It's too late now . . . for everything.

Love Lost and Found

True Stories of Long-Lost Loves—
Reunited at Last

CAROLYN CAMPBELL

BERKLEY BOOKS, NEW YORK

LOVE LOST AND FOUND

A Berkley Book / published by arrangement with
International Locator

PRINTING HISTORY
Berkley edition / August 2000

The Penguin Putnam Inc. World Wide Web site address is
http://www.penguinputnam.com

ISBN: 0-425-17627-4

BERKLEY®
Berkley Books are published by The Berkley Publishing Group,
a division of Penguin Putnam Inc.,
375 Hudson Street, New York, New York 10014.
BERKLEY and the "B" design
are trademarks belonging to Penguin Putnam Inc.

PRINTED IN THE UNITED STATES OF AMERICA

10 9 8 7 6 5 4 3 2 1

To my aunt Margaret Scott,
who lost the love of her life at a young age and
carried on with courage

First Love Forever Remembered

Chapter One

Cheryl Harmon pried apart the slats in her venetian blinds. She stared out her bedroom window. The boy was moving in next door. He and his father would live in her parents' rental property. His name was David Patterson. She heard his friends call him Davey. Now he and his loud-talking friends would be right in the next yard. They might cross her own front lawn on their way down to the corner store. Just the thought brought an unfamiliar tingling to her insides, along with a trace of fear. What was this feeling?

For months the congregation held Pentecostal prayer meetings at Davey's house, because his mother was bedridden with cancer and couldn't ride to the church. During that time, Cheryl hardly heard the preacher. Her eyes and thoughts traveled to Davey. She was fascinated by the thick, mahogany-brown hair that draped his head in shiny waves. His slim, yet square shoulders, with sharp shoulder blades that Cheryl could see through the starched white shirt. Those penetrating blue eyes, a deep slate color, like a flower on one of Mama's china plates. And now he would live right next door. Last week Cheryl heard Mama say that maybe Davey and his daddy needed a fresh start, away from sad memories that hovered over the home where his mama died. Too, the rental house was smaller, now that there was just the two of them.

How would it be to have your mama die? Just the thought was painfully, frighteningly sad. Once, after prayer meeting,

Cheryl glimpsed a pale, thin woman with the same mahogany-colored hair as Davey lying in a bed off the main parlor where the meeting was held. The bedroom door was left open so she could hear the sermon, and the choir singing afterward. Her eyes were closed, yet there was a slight frown about her face. Now she was gone. Did he still cry over her?

Cheryl peered out the window and studied Davey as he stood next to her father. Davey's face held a hopeful look as if he wished the sadness in their lives would now begin to lift. Cheryl's heart thudded. She couldn't take her eyes off him. At the same time she couldn't say what glued her gaze to the window. She inhaled, and watched her breath condense as white steam on the glass.

"Cheryl! Cheryl Harmon! Have you gathered them chicken eggs yet? And I haven't heard that piano!"

It was Mama's voice. Cheryl knew this was way too late to be standing here, still in her nightgown. She scrambled for her white T-shirt and pair of jeans at the same time she heard Mama's feet tramp up the stairs.

"You're not even dressed," Mama accused.

Cheryl frantically slid her jeans up her legs. "I-I'm almost ready."

"Your breakfast is nearly cold. I was going to take you to town with me."

"I'll go to town."

"Not if your chores aren't done. And look how late it is—what's gotten into you this morning?" Mama peered down into Cheryl's face with a worried look. "Are you sick?" Mama clamped a viselike hand around her forehead.

"No, you're not going this morning. I'll take Margaret and Joe instead. You may stay home and gather your eggs."

"Oh, please, Mama!" Cheryl's plea sounded hollow, even to her own ears. She couldn't let Mama know she really wanted to stay here and see what was happening to Davey. "I want to go."

"You have a clock in here. You knew what time it was. Now if I come back and your bed is made and your chores are done, maybe we'll go to the grocery store."

"Okay." Cheryl looked down. Suddenly she felt Mama's

hand under her chin, lifting it so Mama could look into her eyes.

"He's a year older than you are, isn't he? Just turned fourteen?" Mama asked.

"Who?"

"That boy you been gawkin' out the window at . . ."

"Oh, Mama . . ." Cheryl felt a blush warm her face.

"Now, don't you be lookin' out the window all the time. He'll see you, just like I did. He'll know you got a crush on him."

"I do not!" Cheryl snapped, too fast and too loud to convince Mama.

To Cheryl's surprise, Mama walked over and peered through the slats, just the way Cheryl had moments earlier.

"Look lost, don't they, just the two of them like that. Even though poor Ruth was sick so long . . ." Mama seemed to be talking to herself rather than Cheryl. But then she turned abruptly. "Hurry now, and get them eggs done. Or I'll make you go to town with the rest of us. . . ."

Mama smiled at her. Cheryl hurried to slide her T-shirt over her head.

Davey thought he waited just about forever for his dad and the landlord to finish talking. They looked at the house and talked about how big it was and where the school was and how close everything was to the church. Now they were standing out by the barn. The barn was tall and painted red and surrounded by acres of lush green fields. Davey looked around and saw that the farm seemed to stretch as far as he could see. He looked back to see his dad and the landlord shaking hands.

"Sure sorry about your wife," said the landlord. He laid a hand on his dad's shoulder.

Dave watched Dad shake his head, the wrung-out, vacant look on his face. "Yeah." He shook his head. "Nothing worse than cancer—"

The landlord patted Dad on the back, then stopped and abruptly fished in his pocket. "Hey. I almost forgot. Here's the key. Rent due on the fifth."

Suddenly Davey saw a girl peek around the edge of the

barn. Golden blond hair like the honey-colored heart of an oak tree. Blue eyes like an afternoon lake. Her eyes matched the cornflower color of the simple, handsewn dress she wore. As Davey drank in the sight of her, she stared back at him with a look that he thought might be surprise or curiosity. Davey held his breath. She had skin as light and pure as cream. His heart pounded and he knew that she was the most beautiful person he had ever seen in his whole life. Somehow, the sight of this girl grabbed his mind and wouldn't let go. He felt tongue-tied. He tried to swallow but felt a lump in his throat. Good thing no one expected him to talk right then. His dad and the landlord were busy jawing about grain futures and plumbing in the rental property.

Then her father saw her. He smiled and walked over, grabbing her around the neck in a wrestling hold, her hair flowing over his arm.

"This here's my best baseball player. My Cheryl Lynn. Can pitch it clear across there—" Her dad's big arm pointed across the field.

Davey followed the direction of the man's broad fingers, but only for a second. Then his eyes met the girl's. A smile flickered across her face. Man, those eyes were big. And blue as the sky.

"Show me how you can pitch," Davey said. He was surprised to hear his own voice.

The girl shrugged, then turned away. She doesn't want to talk to me, Davey thought. Seconds later, though, she emerged from the barn with a ball. She glanced at him only briefly, then let the ball fly, high in the air, way over all of their heads, and clear across the field.

He watched her run after the ball, and without thinking he ran after her. She was fast, he realized as he fought to catch up with her.

She threw the ball to him.

He tossed it back.

She threw again.

He had to remind himself not to look at her face, so he'd see when the ball was coming. He reached out his arms and caught, automatically. Then he threw it back to her.

"Play catch?" he asked her. She nodded, and both of them stepped back.

They threw the ball until his dad said it was time to go home.

"See ya?" Davey asked.

The girl nodded and looked down.

As he and his dad walked away, Davey looked back. The girl was still tossing the ball into the air and catching it. She didn't miss once.

Two days later Cheryl was standing in the field with her brothers and sisters picking butter beans when someone cuffed her on the arm. She looked up to see Davey Patterson, his deep blue eyes smiling at her. When she looked at his face, it was as if soda pop were fizzing dizzily inside of her.

"Play again?" Davey asked, slamming the softball against his hand.

Cheryl nodded. She stepped back and the boy threw the ball to her. She leaped, caught it, and looked at him with satisfaction before throwing it back.

"Teams!" her brother Kevin shouted from the corner of the field.

All seven of her brothers and sisters ran from where they were working and dropped their baskets to join the game.

"Captains—me and Steve—" Kevin said, nodding at her brother.

"I get Cheryl," said Steve.

"Tommy," said Kevin.

"Kathy," said Steve.

Cheryl stared at Davey throughout this familiar ritual. Wasn't anyone going to pick him? Finally he stood alone, while the other eight of them grouped in two camps of four.

"We get him," Cheryl said, gulping with the bravery of her statement. Davey turned, gave her a quick grin of gratitude, then nodded shyly. She watched his Adam's apple move. Later, in the first inning of the baseball game, she was glad she picked Davey for their team. Her reason was simple: He could play good. Maybe he was even almost as good as she was, she thought, watching him hit the ball and run all the way to second base. When it was her turn, she hit a long shot,

hard into the outfield. Though she longed to see Davey's re-
action, she didn't dare look at him; instead she looked out at
Kevin chasing the ball as she ran, her short, agile legs moving
her past second, third, and finally home.

Someone ruffled her hair. She looked up at Daddy.

"Back to the chores now, kids," he said.

She watched her brothers and sisters head on out to the
fields. Davey walked across the lawn and home.

It was a week later, when she was shucking oysters in the
field, that she saw him again. He was walking toward her,
and she looked down as their eyes met. But as he got closer,
Cheryl sprang to her feet and called out, "Race ya!"

"Where?"

"That tree over there—" Cheryl pointed across the expanse
of green field to the huge oak, where she often climbed with
Kevin and Steve. It was a long run. She breathed fast at even
the thought of trying to outrun Davey.

"Okay," Davey said instantly, bending over, poised to head
out. "On your mark—"

"Get set!" Cheryl yelled.

"Go!" Davey screamed. Cheryl took a deep breath and
flung every ounce of energy she had into running. She moved
her legs like pistons, feet hardly touching the grass as she
propelled herself forward. Her eyes refused even to glance to
the right where Davey ran beside her. She couldn't let the
look of him throw her off the path.

Hearing his feet behind her she surged onward, forcing the
quick rhythm of her run. She began to pant. An ache started
in her side. She forced herself to stare at the tree, which
seemed impossibly far off. The field stretched farther than she
ever remembered.

Now she could see him, nearly beside her, arms swinging,
legs striding nearly as fast as hers. She pushed herself past
the new ache starting in her leg and forged on, legs still
pumping, now feeling as if they had pins inside.

She gulped as he suddenly raced up beside her. She tried
to shove him aside with her hand, but he angled away, off to
the right. Seconds later he was beside her again. Cheryl drew
in a thin, fast breath, urging her legs onward to the last
stretch.

With a final gasp she hurled herself sideways against the tree, slamming into it with a jarring thud. Then she fell, spent, on the ground. She struggled to sit up, sagging limply against the trunk of the tree. Gasps racked her rib cage. Her breath came in deep, aching pants. Tears blinked from her eyes.

"I won—" she gasped.

"You pushed me—doesn't count."

"You were running into me—" she panted, "—tryin' to knock me down."

"No—I was winnin'—so you pushed me—"

"I was ahead the whole time." Cheryl frowned and gulped in another breath. "You weren't even close." This wasn't exactly true. Her conscience gave a twinge. Davey was even with her part of the way, but she won, Cheryl decided.

"Race you again . . . rematch," he was saying.

Could she run another step? Could she even breathe?

Two more gasping pants. "Tomorrow," she said. "Same time."

"No fair. Can't chicken out. Let's do it *now*. Back to where we started."

What could she say? That her muscles were screaming? That there wasn't an ounce of air left in her entire body? He would say she was a 'fraidy cat. Leaning into the tree, she inched her way to standing, hair hanging in her face and sweat dripping off her forehead. Her lungs felt as if they were on fire. A muscle in her right leg twitched.

"On your mark—" he said, already leaning down and poised.

"Get set," she gasped halfheartedly, mentally fighting to reach inside herself for whatever tiny residue of energy might be left.

"Go!" he yelled, and she forced her aching legs into the motions of running. This time he was beside her from the start. The thought of him winning gave her an adrenaline rush, and she plunged onward, matching him pace for pace. He was right beside her.

She closed her eyes in concentration. Could she even finish this? Her feet hit the dirt. Clouds of dust rose. The barn seemed so far away. Her throat filled with a scraping ache.

Both legs held full-length pains, and were heavy, as if her bones were made of metal.

She dropped back a step, saw his hair and T-shirt were bathed in sweat. Resisting the impulse to grab his arm, she propelled herself past him with a single lunge. Seconds later their hands each hit the crackling wood of the barn, his fingers slightly under hers.

"Tie!" she yelled, an aching shout that throbbed in her throat.

"No, my hand hit first."

"Tie goes to the runner—" she said, "and I'm a runner."

"Rematch!" he yelled again. "Best of three!"

"Tomorrow—" She waved a hand and started walking away. She waited for his protest, but when he didn't speak, she finally looked back.

He was staring at her.

"Tomorrow," he agreed.

She nodded, not halting in her retreat to the house.

The next day her legs ached with stabbing pains from muscles she never knew she had. He beat her in the first race that day. Limbered up, she won the second round. Soon they were outside together daily, in more foot races, baseball games, long jumps, kick the can, and anything they could find.

"Get set," he said as the two of them prepared to start another race.

"Hey, you—boy." Cheryl looked up at the deep voice she somehow didn't recognize. It was her father, dressed as always in his overalls, the lopsided straw hat on his head.

Davey leaned back, out of his racing stance. "Yes, sir?" he said humbly.

"Come help us fix this fence over here—and we got a ton of them butter beans—"

Was her dad mad at the two of them? Cheryl couldn't tell. Something about her father's voice was different. There was a tone in it she had never heard before. While Davey and her dad fixed the fence, Cheryl picked butter beans, hardly noticing as hundreds of the rounded green lengths fell through her fingers. Every time she looked up, she saw that Davey was looking at her.

After that, whenever she was outside, Cheryl looked for

Davey. And most of the time he was there. There were more foot races, ball games. Yet right in the middle of the game, her dad always called out. "Long as you're here, boy—" were his first words whenever he asked Davey to do something for him. Shuck oysters. Pick beans. Feed the chickens. And Davey always went along without a word. Yet whenever Cheryl looked back, he was always stealing a look at her.

One day their hands brushed, and she swore he squeezed her fingers briefly, then let go. After a month or so he started coming over to their house after dinner, carrying his guitar. His eyes looked shyly away as his full, rich voice reached out and somehow wrapped around her heart.

"Davey's Cheryl's boyfriend," her little sister Margaret proclaimed at the dinner table one night, red ringlets jangling as she bounced in her kitchen chair.

"He is not," Cheryl protested.

"Is too. I saw you holding hands—" Margaret called out.

"Did not!" Cheryl shot back quickly, at the same time a hot blush spread across her cheeks.

"I saw you," Margaret chanted. "And when you were sitting on the porch you were looking at each other all lovey-dovey like this—" Margaret fluttered her eyelashes, fingers propped seductively along her chin.

"We weren't doing anything. He was just singing. He's just our neighbor."

"Uh-huh, he's your boyfriend."

Flustered, Cheryl couldn't think of an answer. She blushed again at the horrified look on Daddy's face. Mama shook her head.

"I saw you, too," Mama said.

Margaret collapsed with giggles until her face was as red as Cheryl's.

"He only touched my fingers for a second," Cheryl insisted. About five precious seconds.

"I saw you sitting on the couch. You sat way too close to him. Leave at least one foot between . . . or more. I should be able to sit down between you," Mama said.

"I don't want to be rude. He'll think I don't like him. Like he's got cooties or something—"

"See, see!" Margaret shouted. "He's her boyfriend! I told you! You saw her, too."

"Cheryl's too young to have a boyfriend," Mama replied, giving Cheryl a warning frown.

Cheryl couldn't respond. How could she say that when Davey's fingers touched hers, a tingling sensation sped up her arm and settled somewhere around her heart? And that when he sang to her, she felt her heart beating inside her chest. She never wanted the song to end. She felt like someone on TV. Just the same as those actors who stared at each other a long time before they started to kiss.

No, she couldn't admit that to somebody in a million years.

How did Margaret guess? Eight years old, and she already figured out what Cheryl was trying to understand herself.

Chapter Two

Months later there was the day when, somehow, they ended up alone by the tree.

"Race you," Cheryl called out, the way she always did.

But Davey shook his head.

"I'll get a head start," she began to run. "I'll win."

A minute later Davey caught up with her, grabbed her hand, and swung it.

"What are you doing?" Cheryl frowned. "I said 'race you' fair and square. Didn't take no head start."

"I don't want to race. . . ." he said. There was a tone in his voice that scared her a little. She saw him look around them at the fields, which were rarely, blissfully empty. No Margaret staring at them as if they were two hyenas. No Dad coming up with an endless list of chores. Just the two of them.

"Come here—" Davey said, pointing to the chicken house. He still didn't let go of her hand. Now he swung their two hands together.

Cheryl looked at him. Her mind filled with curious puzzlement. She let him lead her inside the chicken house. Was he mad at her for something?

"Sit—" he said, pointing to the stool Mama sometimes used if it was her turn to gather eggs.

Cheryl sat. Her tongue sat like a stone in her mouth. What could Davey possibly want to talk to her about?

He kneeled down, then sat in the gravelly dirt of the

chicken house. His back touched the chicken wire. Chickens around them mumbled softly, picked at the feed on the floor. Cheryl watched their jerky, yet precise movements. She couldn't look at Davey, only a foot away.

"Cheryl?" he asked, as if this could be somebody else sitting only ten inches from him.

"Yeah?" She glanced up quick, then realized his blue eyes were too close to look at without getting embarrassed. She dropped her eyes to the dirt.

"I wanna ask you out on a date. . . ."

Cheryl couldn't speak. Her heart thudded with nervous excitement. Finally she forced out the apologetic words. "I can't go out on dates. You know. Pentecostal." Her face flushed again. Davey ought to know. He was Pentecostal, too.

"I just meant the movies. Jerry Lewis. *The Nutty Professor.*"

She shook her head. "Can't date until I'm sixteen."

"What about just the park? Could we go to the park for a picnic? Maybe just a ball game?"

She didn't want to say no again. And they played ball games at the park all the time anyway. "Maybe," she said. "I'll have to ask Mama."

This wasn't like some movies. Cheryl was dressed in jeans, not a satin formal. She hadn't combed her hair that morning. Yet she sensed her heart was beating as fast as Doris Day's ever did. She was looking off to the left, into the back of the chicken house, where there were weathered boards that leaked shafts of sunlight. Chickens pecking at feed. Piles of straw. She was thinking she could sit here just about forever. Then Davey kissed her.

Sweet, intense pleasure. She melted into his arms, felt his hand stroke her hair while his other arm held her waist. His kiss filled her with heat, and she kissed him back. This is how I want it to be when I get married, she thought. I want to marry Davey. I want to be with him for the rest of my life. Her heart was clanging away now. She was surprised Margaret, Mama, and Daddy couldn't hear it back at the house. All the weeks of staring at each other, longing for him to take her hand like he did before, all piled up into the electricity that filled her like Fourth of July firecrackers going off. She clung to Davey, her breath rushing.

His arms were still around her when he said, "Don't tell Margaret about this."

She felt herself grinning. "I won't."

"Or your daddy, either."

She didn't answer. Instead, she concentrated on the soft cotton of his shirt, the light breeze of his breath ruffling her hair, his hand against her face.

"Don't tell them. Just ask if we can go out on a date. To the park."

"They don't let me go anywhere at night."

"Not at night. After morning chores."

Inner doubts nagged at her. "I'm afraid they'll say no," she agonized, abruptly backing away to give him a warning look.

His eyes met hers before his arms enveloped her waist again. "Don't worry. Just ask like you always do. Don't tell them anything's different."

"I don't want them to guess it's a date"—she finally looked up—"or they'll say we can't ever go again."

"Just say it's a ball game," he reassured, kissing the warm hair at her forehead before patting her shoulder. "Just ask and let me know. I gotta get home now," he said, hugging her once again before he backed away.

"I'll try," she said simply. She watched him brush the straw off himself, smooth his rumpled hair with a hand.

Then suddenly he glanced up. His blue eyes aimed straight at hers. "I love you, Cheryl. . . ."

She gulped. "I love you, too, Davey." A lump filled her throat.

Then she turned and ran out of the chicken house before her heart burst. She ran faster than any race—across the field and home.

When she rushed into the house, Mama looked at her curiously, gazing at her panting frame.

"Can we—go to the park?"

Mama paused. "Who is 'we'?"

Cheryl gulped in a burst of air. "Davey Patterson and me—"

She saw Mama take a long, measuring look at her. "Yes.

You may go if you take all of your brothers and sisters with you."

"Oh, Mom—" The protest was out before she could stop it.

"You must not want to go to the park that badly," her mother said airily, turning back to her embroidery and half-looking at *General Hospital* on TV.

Davey loved her. He was sure Cheryl didn't know how beautiful she looked when she told him they'd have to take every single kid in the family with them to the park. She didn't know he'd take the whole city with them if she'd just keep on looking at him like that. After a while he understood that this was just one of her Mama's tactics. Like if they sat together on the couch, she'd tell them to sit farther away. Once she even sat between them, totally unruffled as she finished another French knot in her embroidery. If she saw them hold hands, she ordered them to stop. Once she came in the front room when Cheryl had her hand on his cheek. Davey thought his face would boil like a pot of chicken noodle soup. But her mama just said, "What would your daddy say if he saw you like that?" What would Cheryl's father say if he knew about the five or six kisses in the chicken house? Davey didn't want to find out. It was after the sweetest-tastin' kiss ever that Davey decided he couldn't wait another minute to let Cheryl know what his plans were.

He looked down at her—all blue eyes and fair skin—and said, "I'm going in the service."

She looked at him as if he had thrown cold water on her. "What are you talkin' about?"

"It's for us, baby. For our life later."

He saw that she was trembling. She shook her head in disbelief. "How can that be? I won't see you. You'll be so far away."

"I'm going to make some money. I'm saving up so we can be together."

"But what if you get killed?"

"I won't if I go now ... it's peacetime."

"But what if you never come back."

He put his arm around her. "That's why I need to go now.

I'll go get this done while you finish up high school. Then I can be with you when I get back."

Now a sob escaped her and he saw she had tears. "I can't let you go. . . ."

"Write to me." He squeezed her shoulder. "Write to me every lousy day, after school. And I'll write you back every night. I promise." He kissed her again. He felt his heart swell and wondered if he really could leave. He would marry her tomorrow if she wasn't fifteen.

She shook her head. "You can't."

"I'm already enlisted. It's that simple. . . ." He squeezed her shoulder again, then kissed the top of her head.

"Cheryl—" It was her Mama's voice, calling out across the fields.

"Now we gotta get outa here." David dropped his arm from her shoulder. "Or they won't let us even write. And I won't get to see you when I come home on leave."

Cheryl was stunned. Her heart hammered. How could he tell her he was leaving—his voice all calm like that? Didn't he know how he made her feel inside?

Chapter Three

The paper looked like an award certificate—but it said $50.00. Cheryl knew this wasn't regular money. It wasn't a check. What was Davey sending to her? This couldn't be German money. All the writing on it was in English.

"It's a savings bond," her dad said to her when she showed it to him later in the day. "Cash it in now and you'll get twenty bucks. Save it and you get fifty. He's trying to give you some money to save."

Her dad's gaze was penetrating as he handed the paper back to her. "That's quite a gift for somebody who's just the girl next door."

Cheryl nodded. Mama knew about the other packages, but she didn't tell Daddy. The first package was big and heavy. It held pots and pans. Then there was a china set. And an eight-day clock, that ran more than a week if you wound it up all the way. More savings bonds followed the first one. Another bond arrived every two weeks. And Cheryl sat down, every day, after school and wrote back to Davey, who told her to call him Dave now that he was in the army.

Dear Dave,
I made a home run at school. I wish you could have seen it. Bases were loaded. I slid into home base and skinned the back of my leg. But I was so happy, I cried. And that same day I heard that song that reminds me

of you. I was picking butter beans and I had my tran-
sistor next to me. "Unchained Melody," by the Righ-
teous Brothers. It's still my favorite. Do you ever listen
to your radio over there? Do you have a TV? We
watched the Beatles on Ed Sullivan *last week. If you*
were here, I'd want you to ask me to go to the prom.
Do you know exactly when your leave is yet? Oh, yeah,
thank you for the clock. And the savings bonds. I have
them saved in a metal box under my bed. Mom says I
have to go to sleep now. We have achievement tests at
school tomorrow. My family misses you at the ball
games.

> *Love,*
> *Cheryl*

Did she have any idea how he looked for the letter every day? Dave knew that after lunch, as regular as clockwork, her pink stationery envelope with the flowers down the side would be waiting in his slot. Could she guess how it brought him close to her? He'd read the letter—maybe three or four times—and while he savored each sentence, it was as if he wasn't stuck here in the barracks. For just those few brief moments he was back home, in the open fields, feeling the sun at his back and his arm around her shoulder. Getting a letter every day was like they weren't really apart.

And he hoped she knew that all the things he sent were for her to save until they got married. It was all stuff to set up a house. The dishes. The pots and pans. The savings bonds. Dave folded the letter, slid it into the envelope, and put it in the footlocker with the others. Then he headed out to the PX for a Coke. He was looking at a deck of playing cards and then a first-aid kit. Those didn't seem like the kind of thing he wanted to send to Cheryl. After all, he could buy those at the five-and-ten back home.

He was just about to leave when he saw them. A wedding ring set. Diamonds so sparkling and bright. The rings themselves were gold as shiny as the polished brass fireplace back home. They reflected beams from the lightbulb above them.

It was a good thing he got paid that day and just happened to have his paycheck already cashed. The money was sitting—

as if it were waiting—in his wallet. Dave bought those rings, thinking he'd need to write a really romantic letter to go with them. He could say that the pots, pans, and dishes were only the warmup, and this was the gift he really wanted to give her. Or he could wait, until he went home on leave again. He kept the rings hidden in his footlocker, under all the letters and some civilian clothes and his own savings bonds.

As the days passed, he imagined what they'd say when they saw each other during his leave. He imagined a first real date when he drove Cheryl to a restaurant dinner followed by a movie at the theater in town. Their first date would be followed by others—picnics, ball games, and parties. After her high school graduation, there would be a wedding in the Pentecostal church. He pictured Cheryl in a white, lacy wedding dress, her long blond hair cascading over her back the way it did the first time he saw her. Thinking about their future made the time pass fast, and sometimes he could almost forget how long they'd been apart.

Cheryl was walking home from school when Gary approached her. He just started walking along beside her. She knew him from being in the same grade, the way you know about a hundred kids' names but nothing else. She glanced to the side and saw him walking next to her.

"Hey, Cheryl, I wanted to ask you. Will you go to the movies with me?"

"Oh, I can't date."

"Why not?"

"Pentecostal. . . . and my mom says no."

"Can I come to your house and visit?"

I have a boyfriend, Cheryl wanted to say, but curiosity confused her. Why was this guy talking to her? "You don't even know me," she said.

"I've seen you around . . . wanted to ask you out for a long time."

She walked along silently, with Gary trooping along next to her.

"Your boyfriend left you, didn't he?"

"He's just in the army, he's not gone."

"Can I at least call you?" Gary asked. He stopped and

waited. When she didn't answer, he said, "Okay. I'm calling you tonight."

"I don't know what my mother will say—" Cheryl called out without looking back.

Gary called that night, and two nights later. When she talked to him, Cheryl realized how lonely she was. She missed Davey. He left so quickly, and as much as she hated to admit it, it was hard to keep the closeness going with just letters about what was going to happen *someday*.

Gary kept calling, and she finally said she would go to the park with him. Then he called again. And again. They went to the park several times together. And each time all her brothers and sisters accompanied them. Then one day something happened. One moment they were standing at the park with all her brothers and sisters around her, and the next they were behind a tree and he was kissing her. Cheryl felt a surge of emotion—sadness, loneliness, and confusion. She kissed him back, searching the moment for any remnant of the same exhilaration she felt when Davey kissed her. She waited as he kissed her again. And felt absolutely nothing.

"We're going steady," he said to her as they sat alone together in his car later that day. It sounded like an order, or a demand. He didn't wait for her response before he kissed her again. Seconds later he took his red-stoned class ring and slid it onto her finger. It felt big and heavy, and she truly didn't want to wear it.

"I'm in love with you—" he said. These weren't words she expected to hear. She herself was puzzling out whether she felt anything at all for him. She was his girlfriend, he'd told her lots of times. Now he said he loved her. She just wanted to climb out of the car and run into her house and lock the door forever. She didn't tell him she loved him, but she did let him kiss her again.

He walked her to the door and kissed her once again. After she was safe inside the house and he was whistling as he walked back to his car, she wondered what she should do. Maybe this all would just go away. People broke up all the time, she comforted herself. If he wanted to go steady with her today, he might get mad at her tomorrow. This might not be as permanent as it felt right now. He was just a guy who moved fast. But if this relationship was going to be okay, and her life was going to be all right, why did she feel this inner sense of total, absolute panic? She took off his class ring and put it in her top drawer with her nylons. But it was a long time before she could fall asleep that night. She thought of Davey and wished he'd never left.

The next day, when it came time to write to Davey, she found she couldn't even take the pen out of her desk. She felt too guilty about seeing Gary when Davey was so far away and they were supposed to be married someday. Writing to him and pretending everything was the same made her heart hurt. A sick, sour feeling wound its way through her insides as she closed the desk drawer and left the room without looking back. The next day she tried to write again but tore the letter up. After a few days it was easier to not even think about writing. Besides that, Gary now called her every day.

Chapter Four

For the first day or two Dave thought maybe Cheryl was sick or something. He came back to the barracks for lunch and looked in the mailbox like always, and it was empty. Stark, barren, empty—just a metal slot in a bank of other metal slots. He tried to think of a reason why she couldn't write that day. Maybe schoolwork? Maybe her family went on a vacation? His mind fought against the really bad things—that she was hurt, or mad, or never wanted to see him again. How could she stop writing after that great time they had on leave? Couldn't she tell he loved her?

There were nights when Dave almost picked up the phone. He would think, Screw the cost. But it wasn't the money that stopped him from calling; he was scared—scared about what Cheryl would say. Could he survive if she said she never wanted to see him again? What if he found out she never loved him? That the feelings were all his—all in his mind? Could he stand it? Would it be easier just to back away, try to forget about her and go on? He sat back against his bunk, shifted against the scratchy, gray army blanket. He sat there nearly an hour, until someone shouted, "Lights out."

Why didn't he just write another letter? He had to admit it came down to pride. First her letters were there and then they were gone. The fact that they stopped suddenly—with no more words from her—sent him a strong message. She didn't want to write to him. Not just now, anyway. And somehow,

Dave couldn't force himself to ask, "What's going on here? Don't you love me anymore?"

He hated to admit it, but he was too afraid to find out the answer now, here, while he was thousands of miles away and couldn't do anything about it. Somehow, it seemed less scary to wait until he got home and they had time to sit down together and talk about all of this. Then, if there was a problem, he could discuss it with her. They could work things out. It would be too easy for her to tell him in a letter that she never wanted to see him again. She could write him out of her life and he couldn't say a word back to her. Better wait and hope until he could see her, Davey reasoned. Still, waiting was hard.

The sick, sad feeling of longing for Davey hovered over Cheryl as she numbly continued to go out with Gary. She half-hoped her feelings for Gary would change and, at the same time, subconsciously wondered if she would somehow escape the relationship someday.

Then there was the night when the kissing didn't stop. Gary and Cheryl were at the park again. They were alone; all the kids were far off on the swings at the other side of the hill. She pushed him away at first, trying to seem playful, but he grabbed her, and like all the other times, she waited to feel what she felt with Davey. And when Gary's hand slid to her breast, she didn't fight back because she was too numb and dead inside. Shell-shocked. They weren't supposed to be doing this—what was Gary thinking? But she was too embarrassed and mortified to say a word. No one—in the Pentecostal church or anywhere else—ever told her a boy would want to do stuff like this.

"I can't—" she finally said.

"I love you—"

"But we shouldn't—"

"Come on, baby—we're in love. It's all right."

Why couldn't she say she didn't love him? Why couldn't she tell him to stop? Was it that she didn't want to hurt his feelings? It was easier to keep quiet, to numb herself, to hope it would all somehow go away. But she was scared—too panicked even to cry. And as if she was outside of her body, she watched Gary do things to her that she knew were wrong. She felt as if she was visiting her life . . . and hoped that she could somehow go back to the way things were.

The day she went to the doctor, Cheryl debated wearing Gary's class ring backward, so that it would look like a gold wedding band. She lifted her hand with the ring up in front of the bathroom mirror. With a sigh, she decided that her hand looked even more forlorn and bare than ever with the too-big ring drooping down like that. She wished she could somehow erase this day from her life. But at the same time she knew she could wait no longer to find out if her biggest fear was true.

She chose the doctor out of the phone book. Dr. Rasmussen's office was all the way across town, requiring a long bus ride. Cheryl left school early in the afternoon, without stopping to check out at the office. She was upset enough to be sick, that was for sure. How did all this happen to her?

As she sat on the bus and scenery slid past, it was as if the life she always planned for herself was speeding farther and farther away.

No one in the doctor's office spoke or looked up when she entered. Cheryl had never felt more alone or more vulnerable in her life as she walked up to the nurse's desk, listening to the hollow, vacant click of her heels on the tile floor.

"How can I help you?" the nurse asked. When Cheryl couldn't answer, the nurse persisted, shades of impatience entering her voice. "What are we seeing you here for today?"

Cheryl lowered her voice to a near-whisper, leaned close to the desk. "My period is late, and—"

"Are you pregnant?" The nurse spoke in a perfectly loud voice.

Cheryl shook her head fiercely. This time her whisper sounded like a frantic hiss. "I don't know," she said. I hope not, she thought. I'm only sixteen.

"Take a seat in the waiting room."

Waiting room was right, Cheryl decided as she read three magazines, drank four times from the water fountain, and used the rest room twice.

Finally the icy nurse led her to an appointment room. The

doctor didn't even look at her to see if she wore a ring. His tone was brusque. "How can I help you?"

Let me start this year over, she thought. Let me finish school. Let me write to Davey again. She took a deep breath. "I'm really worried. . . ." she finally admitted. "I missed my period."

The doctor looked at her now. He saw a young girl that was fresh-faced, pale, and as slim as a string. "Is there any possibility of pregnancy?"

Cheryl nodded. She dropped her eyes to the bland, dark green leather of the examining table. She heard the doctor sigh above her. "I'll give you an exam," he said. "Then I'll send a urine sample to the lab."

She willed her mind away, back to the days of ball games and green fields, as the doctor prodded her body.

"Call tomorrow morning." No emotion in the doctor's voice. He released a weary sigh, stood, and backed away from the table. She heard resignation in his words. "I'll take the sample to the lab tonight." She felt him stare at her. What did all this mean?

Cheryl lay awake all night, paralyzed with worry. She knew there was homework she should do, household chores that she let slide. But now her future life hung in the balance. What would the laboratory say?

Cheryl called the lab first thing the next morning, feeling as if she'd lain awake with worry for days. The phone rang five times before someone answered.

"Hospital lab."

"My name is Cheryl Harmon. I'm calling about my test results," she whispered, even though she was alone in the house.

"What type of test?"

She swallowed. "Urine sample . . ."

"For *what*?"

Cheryl paused. She closed her eyes quickly. "Pregnancy."

A frustrated sigh. "One moment." The phone slamming down on the counter. Cheryl waited tensely, drumming her fingers on the schoolbook in her lap. The book she couldn't force herself to open even though the quarter was ending and final tests were next week.

"The results are here. . . ."

"They're there. . . ."

"Yeah . . . right here."

"Well . . ." What could she say now? "Is everything okay?"

A quick pause. "It looks fine. The rabbit died."

"That means . . ."

"Congratulations. You're pregnant. Go ahead and tell your husband to break out the cigars."

The lab technician hung up without a response from Cheryl. I don't have a husband, she thought as the full implications of her plight hit home. Her life was over. She couldn't go out to the yellow school bus the next morning and be the girl she was before. She had no husband. No Davey. No future. No life.

Cheryl thought of Davey again and again that night. What would he say if she called him now? She was almost sure—but this was a painful almost—that he would say he would take her baby. That they would get married anyway. That she could be with him. She sighed and sat back against the headboard of her bed. But maybe he would say no. He had every right to be furious with her and hate her for the rest of her life. He would probably get as angry with her as she was angry with herself. The thought of writing him now was so painful that she put it out of her head.

Instead, the last person Cheryl wanted to see was the one person she had to talk to now. She'd ducked Gary's calls for three days until finally she phoned him.

Words fought wearily from her throat. "I have to see you," she said.

"Okay, I guess . . ." he said tonelessly. "After school? The park?" There was a leer in his voice that filled her with fury.

"Anywhere—" she said simply. "Let's just get it over with."

"Mad at me again, huh? Well, okay babe, whatever you say."

"The park. I don't care where."

When she saw Gary at a distance, approaching her, Cheryl wished she could run away.

"What are you mad about this time, babe?" he asked her,

his voice a mixture of boredom and frustration.

"I'm not mad—I'm just totally blown away. My life is over. I can't believe this happened."

"What do you mean?"

"I'm *pregnant*—what else would it be?" She was angry with him, but part of her felt that this was mostly—if not all—her fault.

"Hey, I'm sorry, babe. But I'll marry you."

"Don't do me any favors." A huge sob welled up inside her.

"What other choices do you have?"

"None," she admitted. Not that she could think of right now, anyway.

"It won't be that bad," he said.

I'm not so sure, she thought.

"Come on—hurry up!" Gary yelled at her from the car as she stood at the pay phone. She couldn't believe this was her wedding day. They decided to run away a week after the day they met in the park.

"I can't go unless I call them," Cheryl balked.

"Well, then, hurry up!"

"The line's still busy—"

"Can't you call them tomorrow?"

"They'll be worried sick when I don't come home tonight—"

"I can't believe you. We can't even get five blocks away, and you have to call home—"

"My dad was asleep when I left! I couldn't tell him then."

"You couldn't wake him up to tell him you're getting married?"

Before she could answer, the call went through and someone picked up the line.

"Hello?"

Her father's voice. Her own heart pounding. "Daddy?"

"Cheryl? You're late for dinner, honey. Fried chicken."

She closed her eyes and spoke. "I'm not coming home, Daddy."

A pause, then concern in Daddy's voice. "Where are you? You sound like you're on a pay phone."

She swallowed. "I am, Daddy. I need to tell you that I'm not coming back today. Gary and I are getting married."

"You can't do that—you come home right now."

"I can't come back, Daddy. It's too late." Her voice broke as she thought of her baby, who needed two parents. To her surprise, she heard Daddy turn to Mama.

"This is *your* fault!" Daddy screamed at Mama. "You let her have boyfriends too early, and this is what happened."

"Daddy—" Cheryl tried to interrupt, but he didn't hear her.

"What are you talking about?" Mama's bewildered voice.

"You let her have boyfriends—and now she's getting married—"

"Oh, no—" Was Mama crying?

"You wouldn't listen to me—"

Reluctantly Cheryl hung up in the middle of her parents' argument.

She climbed in the car next to Gary, who sped off without a word.

"That'll be twenty-five dollars." The justice of the peace held out his hand to Gary, who turned to Cheryl with a shrug.

"I'm broke," Gary said.

Humiliation, sadness, and anger filled her. She frowned with embarrassed fury. "Gary. You knew it cost money for the license."

"Mighta known, but didn't have any to bring. . . ."

"Then what are we doing here?"

"Look—" Gary leaned in close to the justice of the peace. "She's pregnant, you know. We need to get married now. Is there any way you can—"

The man shook his head. "No exceptions. If I let everyone try that—"

Cheryl fought to swallow her anger at both of them. "Look, is there any way you could issue the license now . . . and then we could bring you a check?"

"No," he said simply. "Paying the fee is the first step. I don't fill out the first line of the form until the money is in my hand."

They argued all the way home.

"I can't believe you—" Cheryl said.

"Well, I didn't have the money."

"Twenty-five dollars? You can't even get twenty-five dollars?"

"No. I start working after school's out. Don't you have any money someplace?"

Gary's words caught at her heart. Yes, she did have some. Money she promised herself she'd never touch. Unless . . .

"Well—I do have some savings bonds."

"Where did you get those?"

"I just . . . have them."

"Why didn't you bring them this morning?"

Because they're not yours, she thought. They're Davey's and mine, for the life we were going to have together. The life that is gone now.

"Let's go get them. We can make it before the license bureau closes."

She started to cry as he drove to her house. Then, making him wait downstairs, she went upstairs to her room. When she realized her parents weren't home, she took a few minutes to say good-bye to the life that might have been. She lifted the pots and pans out of the box, and ran her hand over the surface of a cream-colored dinner plate. She touched the face of the clock. Then she reached in the top drawer of her dresser and drew out the savings bonds, all ten of them. They felt like limp flowers in her hand. It was a feeling that stayed with her as they drove to the license bureau with the bonds on her lap.

Davey, I'm sorry, she thought. I didn't mean for this to happen. I'd give anything if I could turn the clock back.

Chapter Five

After the wedding Cheryl's thoughts focused on the fact that she was carrying a baby within her body. She took vitamins, ate healthy, and tried to picture the child she would soon hold in her arms. It gave her aching heart a place to go, she realized; if she could think only of her baby and not of all the losses in her life, she could survive. She could only look forward because it hurt so much to look back. These were simple things she could do right, at a time when she felt as if everything had gone so terribly wrong.

"I'm sorry this happened," she said once to Mama as they drove to the doctor's office.

Her mother looked at her.

"I wish I could go back. . . ."

"It's done now," Mama said, in a quiet, torn voice. She sighed. "Let's just try to look forward to the new baby." She reached out and squeezed Cheryl's fingers. Cheryl was grateful for her mother's understanding and all her support. But Cheryl didn't let Mama know the real reason why she always needed her mother to give her a ride to the doctor. Gary already told her that no wife of his was going to get a driver's license. His excuse was that he didn't want her to get hurt. Though she wasn't old enough to get a license now, no matter how old she got, Mama and Daddy would always have to come and pick her up. They were all she had. Gary didn't like her to have friends and even told her he didn't trust her brothers and sisters. He had no reason—it was just how he felt. He also wanted her to stay home. She had to make excuses to Mama and Daddy about how she rarely visited in the six months since she got married.

Sitting in Mama's car, Cheryl sighed in desperation. What could she do about all of this now?

Weeks later the pain started thin, like a cramp easing its way into the rounded lump of her stomach. Yet instantly she knew this was a different sensation from the occasional aches she'd felt all these months.

The pain grabbed again. It lasted longer—and hurt a little more—than the first time.

By now she and Mama knew Dr. Rasmussen's office well. They knew which waiting room table held the new magazines and that you didn't need to take a magazine back in the examining room with you, because new magazines often found their way back there, too.

But today there wasn't time for any of that. Mama walked up to the nurse's desk. "This is an emergency. My daughter is having her baby."

The nurse yawned. "Please have a seat in the waiting room, and I'll let the doctor know you're here."

"There isn't time. She's about to give birth. . . ."

"I'll tell him. The average first time labor is at least eight hours. . . ."

"Not in my family. We go fast—please . . ."

Now the nurse stood. "I'll tell him, but I need to tell you that your daughter will be more comfortable if you help her to relax."

Mama pounded her hand on the desk. "She's having labor pains. It's her first baby. How can she relax?"

The nurse sighed. She waved them off with a dismissive hand. "I'll tell him."

It was less than a minute before the nurse returned. "He'll check you now," she said.

The doctor was already in the examining room, glaring at Cheryl and Mama with a look of impatience. "This has thrown off my schedule. I can tell you there is nothing to worry about."

Cheryl climbed on the table without being asked. She tried

to numb herself to both the doctor's irritation and Mama's urgency. Dr. Rasmussen's hands were rougher than usual, but she fought not to notice.

The room was silent. "Go home. Go back to bed. There's no way you're having this baby any time soon," the doctor said abruptly with an annoyed sigh.

"I tell you, she needs to go to the hospital," Mama insisted.

"Call me tomorrow if she keeps having pains . . . late this afternoon, maybe . . . at the earliest."

The doctor left the room.

"Hurry and get dressed," Mama said quickly.

Another pain racked Cheryl. She held still and waited for it to subside.

"I'll tie your shoes. . . ." Mama said, leaning over. Then she put her arm around Cheryl's shoulder and led her to the car.

They drove several blocks before Cheryl noticed they weren't heading home.

"Mama? What are you doing?"

"We're going to the hospital."

"But he didn't say we could—"

"We'll call him when we get there." Mama gritted her teeth and with a determined set to her jaw drove across town.

The pains felt like knives stabbing her insides. Cheryl gripped the dashboard. "It hurts so bad. . . ."

Mama was speeding, weaving the car in and out of traffic. "I hope we make it, girl. And he wanted you to go home!" Mama shook her head in frustration.

They surged into the emergency room parking lot. Mama grabbed an orderly by the shoulder. Before Cheryl could walk to the emergency room door, five or six nurses brought out a gurney and helped her lie down. A nurse who emerged from the building asked her, "Did the doctor send you here?"

"No," Cheryl gasped. Another pain jabbed her. This one struck on the heels of the last pain, all of them blending together until it seemed there was no relief.

"Then what makes you think you are in labor?"

"Pains—so many of them . . . all together."

In the emergency room the first nurse who checked her said, "She's dilated. At least to six . . . I'd say seven."

A second nurse bent to check. "Mercy!" she said. "The head—it's right there!"

"Do I have to go home?" Cheryl asked weakly.

"Yeah, sure." A nurse patted her on the back. The two nurses laughed lightly together.

"The only place you're going, ma'am, is the delivery room."

Chapter Six

"Kevin?" Although he was still nervous, Dave felt good just hearing Cheryl's brother's voice.

"Hey, is this who I think it is?" Kevin paused only a second, then started laughing. "Where are you? What are you doing back here?"

"Home on leave. What ya up to tonight?" Dave could hear the TV in the background.

"Not much. Just hanging out here at the house. Come on over if you want."

Dave paused. He felt his heart hammer a couple of times. "It's all right if I come on over?"

"Sure, we're just watching the game."

"Haven't seen good basketball since I've been overseas."

"If you hurry, you might make it for the third quarter."

"Be there in a few minutes," Dave managed. He hung up, then he combed his hair, staring into the mirror for a long time. He put on aftershave, all the while telling himself there was a reasonable explanation for no letters arriving. Maybe she just had a lot of homework. Maybe he said something dumb that made her mad and he needed to apologize. Maybe he even got mixed up on whose turn it was to write next. The thought nagged him that they weren't really taking turns. She was writing every day. And now she wasn't writing any day—ever. He figured he'd waited long enough. After all this time he just had to find out now.

He put on his leather jacket, ran his hand over his hair once more, and headed out with a sigh. He felt more apprehensive about just going over to her house than he had about jumping out of a plane during training, but he had to know. He couldn't go back to Germany and keep looking for letters.

Kevin opened the back door after the first knock. "Hi, guy," he said, cuffing Dave lightly on the arm. He led Dave to the dimly lit kitchen, where the basketball game blared from a small television set sitting on the counter. Dave's heart still pounded as he sat with Kevin and half-watched the game, his thoughts roaring around inside. In a way, it felt as if he'd never left town, never been half a world away. It was like if he hadn't gone in the service, this same night would still happen with the two of them sitting here, alone in the kitchen with an arena full of ball players somewhere far off.

Then a light went on in the hall. He heard footsteps heading his way. The thought that this could be Cheryl, coming down the hall to see him, was almost enough to make him faint. He held his breath.

It was her mom. She walked into the kitchen and switched on the bright overhead light.

"Hi, ma'am," Dave said, hoping she couldn't see his smile waver.

"Wondered who was down here. Never guessed it would be Davey Patterson. How you been, kid? It's been a month of Sundays! What are you doing here?"

"Home on leave, ma'am."

"Well, at least Kevin had the manners to offer you a root beer—even if he did try to ruin your eyes!"

Dave laughed with her, beginning to feel relaxed.

"So you're home for a week? Week and a half?"

"Four days, ma'am."

"Four days! Bet your dad's glad to have you back."

Dave nodded as an overwhelming urge filled him. This was it. He could wait no longer. If her mom wasn't going to tell him anything, then he'd have to ask to find out. "Uh—I was wondering if I might see Cheryl while I was here."

There was a second or two while everything held still before her face folded with concern. "Davey . . ." She leaned in closer, looked into his face with the same expression you'd use with a kindergarten boy who skinned his knee. "Didn't Cheryl tell you?"

"Tell me what?" He could hardly force the words out. He wondered if she could somehow hear the sudden fear he felt.

"Cheryl's married."

"Married." The word hit like a boulder on his chest. How could one word hurt so much?

"Yes, she's married and has a little girl."

Dave felt as if his whole world died right then. Nothing in his life ever pained him quite like this. "You're kiddin'," he managed.

"No. Didn't she send you an announcement?"

He shook his head numbly.

"I told her to write and send you an announcement. They didn't have a reception or anything, but I gave her plenty of cards to send out."

"I didn't get anything."

Cheryl's mom shook her head. "I'm real sorry, Davey. She said you two were writing real regular there for a while . . . but then you stopped."

The words thrust themselves out of his mouth. "I didn't stop. She did."

"Oh . . . well . . . I told her to tell you. I didn't really know what the status was between you two. But I'll get after her for you, don't you worry. That was a rude thing she did."

Davey could only shake his head. *Rude*. As if rude could begin to come close to how Cheryl ended his life by marrying someone else. Though he felt like throwing his root beer bottle against the wall and swearing up a blue streak, he sat silently with Kevin until the fourth quarter ended.

Then he said, "I'd better go."

Kevin held an awkward look. "Sorry about all that. Man, I coulda told ya. Didn't know you didn't know."

"Can't believe it." Dave shook his head. He stood before he said anything he would later regret. With an offhanded nod to Kevin, he walked out of the house, shutting the door a little harder than he needed to. When he looked back, he saw that Kevin and Cheryl's mom were watching him out the window.

It's too late, he thought, remembering the ring, the savings bonds, the kisses. It's too late now for everything.

It was a soothing, balmy summer night. Cheryl held Melissa in her arms until the infant's china-doll eyelids closed. The baby uttered a small, sweet-smelling breath as Cheryl laid her in the bassinet next to the bed where she and Gary would sleep later that night. Cheryl sat on the bed and sighed. She entertained thoughts of lying down, but then something about the warm night drew her outside. She walked noiselessly down the stairs of the house she shared with her in-laws, then sat on the porch steps. The royal blue sky was dotted with a sea of stars, and the air was filled with a comforting breeze. The grass and shrubs around her were a mute gray-black. She sat for what seemed like a long time, drinking in the silent stillness.

She didn't hear the phone ring. Just the front door opening and Frank, her father-in-law, interrupting her thoughts.

"Here, Cheryl—for you." He tossed the phone at her. Her hands reached, and even as she grabbed for it, the receiver clattered against the cement step.

Frank swore, then swung the front door almost shut, nearly cutting off the phone cord. She heard his heavy feet tramp up the stairs. Who would call her this late? Gary would be home in an hour. Why on earth would he phone her now?

She breathed in the warm, breezy air. "Hello?" she said, more tired than curious.

A long pause. She heard someone breathe. The caller didn't speak.

"Hello?" Her voice sounded clear and sharp in the empty darkness.

The caller breathed a sigh that somehow caught her attention.

"Who is this . . . ?" Her voice slower, more cautious.

"Cheryl?"

Chills down her spine. It really couldn't be, could it? She'd never forget Dave's voice in a million years.

"This is she," she said, her voice barely audible.

A cross between a sigh and a hum. "I found you?"

"Yes . . ." Her heart beating fast. Words and emotions a jumble in her brain.

"Hi, baby. I wouldn't have called you, but I'm right by where you are."

"In Clarksville?"

"Close. Twenty minutes away . . ."

She gasped.

"Driven by again and again. . . . Just couldn't wait any longer to talk to you—"

"Why didn't you stop by?" Her voice rose sharply, then she felt chills of panic. She turned and glanced back at the gray and silent house.

"You're a married woman—and you didn't even tell me. Made your mama do it—"

"I—" She felt herself blush in the dark. "I was embarrassed. I didn't know what to say . . . I felt so bad. . . ."

"Can I come see you?"

A rush of panic . . . and tinglings of desire ran through her. "Sometime, maybe. When my husband's gone. . . ."

"It's gotta be now . . . tonight. I'm leaving the state."

"Oh, Davey . . ."

"I won't be here after tonight. It's now or nothing."

Her heart—and the world—stopped for an endless moment. Then her heart started beating fast. Cheryl ran a hand across her hair. She swallowed quickly, shifting on the porch as he said, "Are you happy, honey?"

"I don't know," she said finally, shrugging with no one to see the movement.

"You ever think about me?"

"Sure. . . ."

"Really? What do you think about?"

She glanced backward to see if anyone in the house was standing by the door listening, or even sitting on the living room couch. From here, the inside of the house looked black and empty. His words danced on her spine, and she closed her eyes in bliss. "Thought I'd never see you again in my whole life. What ya doin', phonin' me here?"

She heard him inhale. He shuffled around in the background. "I still miss you. And now I'm right here, close." His words went straight to her heart.

"Well, I'm married now."

"But you said you still think about me. . . ."

At his words her throat caught. "I shouldn't, though. I should stop right now. . . ." She waited a moment, then admitted softly, "But I can't forget those days." A sudden tear worked its way onto her cheek.

"I'll be right there," he said quickly, and she thought she heard the phone hang up.

"Wait!" she called out. "You can't—"

"Yes, I can. I know right where you are. Be there in ten minutes."

"You can't. This isn't my house."

"Well, whose house is it?"

"My in-laws. We live here. Don't think they'd like—"

"I don't need to come in the house. Meet me out front."

"Davey—" she hissed.

"I'm heading out right now. Be there in twenty minutes, tops."

"In the back," she said, panicking, thinking quickly of how Frank and Lila's bedroom window faced the front of the house. "I'll be out back."

"Gotcha." She swore she could hear the smile in his voice seconds before he hung up the phone.

She dashed inside to check on Melissa. Standing over the bassinet, she bent suddenly, touched her cheek to the warm, round rosy one. She kissed Melissa's forehead, then the top of the tiny round head that still smelled like Baby Magic lotion. Stepping backward, she stared at the gray outline of the bassinet until she reached the doorway. Then she eased the door closed so slowly that the only sound was a tiny click.

She paused at Frank and Lila's door, listening to the rumble of Frank's snore and Lila's thin, even breathing beside him. Cheryl fought the realization that all eight of Gary's family members were here in this house, and any of them could wake up at any moment. She stepped down the stairs on tiptoe, her heart pounding with the thought that maybe Davey was already outside waiting. But the darkness appeared as seamless as when she waited on the front porch moments earlier. The only sound was her own footsteps as she trudged around the back and stood by the air conditioner. At least it wasn't cold, she reasoned. She could stand here all night and not feel a single chill—except the rising tingles inside at the thought that Davey was almost here. Or was he kidding?

Seconds, then minutes crawled by. Was this whole thing a joke? Did he just want to see if he could heat up her heart so she'd be forced to face the fact, that yes, she still loved him? That three years later her heart still thudded at the thought of even looking at him at a distance? She didn't dare recall those long-ago kisses under the sheltering roof of Daddy's chicken house, the sun peeking at them through cracks in the weathered boards. She sighed, stared out into the night. There wasn't a sound. She closed her eyes. Breathed and waited. She wondered if she should check on Melissa just once more.

Then the car sound. Was she imagining it? Was that an engine, far off, but moving closer? She stood, stared out into the night. For a moment there was only thick, navy-blue darkness.

But then her heart caught at the sight of headlights, turning the corner at the far end of the street. She held her breath.

Her heart pounded harder as chills rushed through her. Suddenly scared, she backed away and leaned hard against the house trying to make herself disappear. The car stopped in front of the house next door. The car seemed to idle for eternity before someone turned the key and the engine died with a soft purr.

She heard a man's smooth whistle in the dark. Soft, like a whisper. Cheryl leaned out slightly. Her neck craned cautiously. Then a wave of emotion surged through her as she saw Davey. Her eyes drank in the sight of him. T-shirt draping his wide shoulders, the same thick dark hair, the same lithe easy gait of an athlete.

Davey stopped in front of the house, put his hand to his brow, and peered out.

Cheryl held stock-still, suddenly wanting him to have to search to find her.

"Cheryl? That you, baby?" he called out softly. Oh, no. Did someone hear that?

She nodded at him, suddenly shy. "Yeah," she barely whispered.

He walked toward her. She glimpsed his grin in the dark. Her heart thudded stronger as he drew close. There he was, in real life, just like the pictures her mind created in her dreams. She stared and waited. Seconds later he wrapped his arms around her and she felt the delicious warm solidness of his chest against hers. He kissed her ear sloppily.

"Baby—" he said.

She closed her eyes in sheer bliss.

Then he kissed her lips, and tingles filled her body, from the crown of her head to the tips of her toes. She kissed him back, knowing she would relish this moment for the rest of her days. She promised herself she would memorize each sensation of touch, would store them up for the dark days that seemed to surely lie ahead. His tongue found hers, and his hands caressed her back. She leaned in to him, wished she could stay here for all eternity.

There was a sound from inside the house. A sound, and then the light on in Frank and Lila's room.

"Oh." She caught her breath, forced herself out of his grasp, and backed way.

His lopsided grin caught at her heart. Memories of those days, staring at each other across the field. "I love you, baby," he said tearfully.

Her voice trembled. "I love you, too. With all my soul. But you've got to leave."

"Leave? Why?"

She sighed.

"Let's go somewhere. Come with me—"

She closed her eyes in determination. "I love you, Davey. But you don't know. I'm married and I have a baby girl."

"Go get her. Get her and we'll leave."

"But I'm going to have another baby."

"So what? Let's just head out."

Could she? For the tiniest second her brain filled with the thrill of possibility. She would be with Davey, again, at last, like she dreamed so many times since she was only twelve years old.

"I can't—" Where did her voice come from? "I'm a wife, and I have to stay here."

The look on his face was like hunger. "You can, babe. I'm telling you. Just walk out of here with me right now."

"Go—" she said, waving him away with her hand. "Go before I get in trouble."

His face fell. Some of the certainty died from his voice. "I'll bring ya back if you don't want to stay."

Cheryl couldn't look at him. She shook her head furiously. "The light's on upstairs. They'll be down here in a second. You'll get us both in trouble."

As if in denial of her words, the light went out upstairs. Total darkness again.

"Go on, Davey," she pleaded. "I love you to pieces, but you can't mess up my life. Thing is, I got a kid and another on the way. I have to stay married."

He rocked on his heels. "You'll call me?" He thrust the words out through the dark. "If you ever want me to come back, you'll let me know."

She nodded, and her heart skipped a beat. "Promise," she said, relief pouring over her in waves.

"I'll wait to hear from you—you know that."

She couldn't speak. *Don't go,* said a voice inside her. *Take me with you.*

"Good night, ma'am," he said softly, tipping his baseball hat at her while she watched him, wanting to call him back with every fiber of her being.

"Good night," she managed.

"Tell your hubby hello for me," he spat, suddenly slapping his hat against the house and trudging away.

Her eyes followed him, drinking in every detail. The fluid movement of his legs, the confident set of his shoulders. That thick, gorgeous dark hair and those penetrating blue eyes. Her nostrils still memorized the delicious male smell of him.

The car door closed, ripping away at her insides. She held the rim of the air conditioner, determined not to run and grab the car door handle, scream at him that yes, she wanted to go.

The car engine sputtered and started. He drove away through the night, her screams echoing inside of her.

Come back. Come back. Yes, I'll always love you.

Chapter Seven

The night she saw Dave stayed in Cheryl's mind as if it were literally engraved there. She replayed their encounter again and again in her mind. She could still feel the electric sensation of being in his arms, the warm comfort of his cheek against hers, that kiss—just like the one that stayed in her memory ever since that day in the chicken house. She recalled the memory again and again—even when there were times that it hurt too much and left her with an aching longing. After a while she rationed her reminiscences, and only let herself think about him on really low days, and one other special day each year.

That special day was today. Another new phone book. Cheryl closed her eyes quickly and held the book on her lap. The pages were tight and smelled fresh, as if the ink were just barely dry. Each year the book got thicker. Each year, she still held hope.

Taking a breath, she flipped to the *P*'s.

Patterson.

She ran her finger along the list of first names. Bradley. Charles. Elizabeth. John A. John William. Pat.

No David Lee Patterson. Where did he go when he disappeared into the night?

She read every first name and every address, just to see if there was some sort of connection.

Nothing. She just had to wait until next year.

• • •

It was three years after he last saw Cheryl when Dave's co-worker set him up with Sandra. They went out bowling and to the movies. She wasn't Pentecostal, like Cheryl. She could stay out late on real dates, and sit next to Dave on the couch. He was standing on her porch one night, when she leaned up and kissed him, just like that. Her lips warm and ready.

"I love you," she said, her long hair tickling his cheek.

"I love you, too—" he said, thinking he said it too soon. Too easy.

They dated more as months passed. After a while it felt as if they'd seen every movie and ball game there was. Played lots of miniature golf.

"Will you marry me?" he asked one night, just to see how it sounded.

"Sure, Dave . . ." she said.

But she wasn't Cheryl.

Eight months later it was over. The taste of failure was bitter in Dave's mouth.

"I'm leaving—" Sandra said.

"What's the matter?" Dave asked, feeling more helpless than he could imagine.

"You don't know?" She thrust at him. "You really, honestly don't know."

"No," he said. "Everything's okay. I've just been working hard."

"Working!" She actually slapped her hand against the bedroom wall. "That's what being married means?"

"I'm supporting us. . . ." he said, but his words died out vaguely.

"You don't care about me . . . you don't love me."

"I'm here . . . I come home every night. . . ."

"Like that's everything. Like that's all I need."

Dave traveled all over Texas, New Mexico, Kansas, Oklahoma, Indiana, and Illinois. Seemed as if there were oil rigs all the way around the world. Best part was the people. Taught him everything they knew right from the beginning. So now he knew how to drill, and just might end up being the boss one day.

"I'm heading out—" he called down the hall to Jenny.

He heard her feet rush to him. "Already . . ." She frowned, leaned to hug him. "Thought you were here for the weekend."

"I wish—" he said, patting the top of her blond head.

"Had a surprise for you and everything. Can't ya stay until Sunday?"

"Gotta get those first wells drilled by Monday."

"I bought a roast—" she said, leaning up and pressing her cheek against his.

He shifted to extricate himself, aware of time passing. "Put it in the freezer. I'll be back in two weeks."

"That's so long—can't you be here next weekend?"

"I'll try," he said, knowing he couldn't make it.

"I can't wait until then," she said, smiling suddenly. Rosy cheeks with dimples. "I have to tell you something."

He waited. He knew the sink needed fixing and the car needed an alignment, but everything would have to wait. "I'll be back," he said, and her face fell.

"You can't leave until I tell you this," she said, wrapping her arms around him.

He leaned close, felt her breath tickle his ear. She giggled quickly, and he sensed her tremble with laughter as he held her in his arms. Suddenly her lips against his ear. "I'm pregnant, Dave. You're not just leaving me. You're leaving a baby behind. . . ."

This marriage lasted eight years.

"I can't leave Cammy. She's my daughter, too, you know." Dave struggled with the bitter sadness that filled his throat. He glanced at Jen's angry face.

"Can't leave? All you ever did was leave. . . ."

"I came back home whenever I got done with a rig."

"What, ten days out of a month?"

"It's my work, Jen."

"You enjoy it too much. You'd rather be there than with us."

"They can't drill all the wells in the same place. I have to go where the oil is. Then I come back."

"The lawyer says you can come back two weekends a

month to see her. For once, I'm going to say when you're coming and going."

"Jen, the kid's only seven. Don't put her through this now."

"She's been through it her whole life. Where have you been?"

"I won't leave my daughter." Dave raised his voice. "You can't keep her away from me."

"We'll see how much you visit. I can hardly wait."

Filled with fury, Dave rushed out of the house to where his waiting bags were packed in the car. Cammy, he thought. My little girl. As he drove through the Indiana twilight, his mind went back to the last time he saw Cheryl, and he suddenly remembered her words. *My baby,* she said. *I can't leave my baby.*

I know how you felt that night, he wanted to tell her now. I know why I couldn't make you leave him and go with me. But although he understood, he still missed her and he wished she were here now.

Chapter Eight

As soon as the girls left for school, Cheryl crept stealthily out of the house. Although no one was home, she eased her way down the front steps silently. She climbed in the car and turned the key. The engine spun to life. She was aware that every second of this drive was illegal, yet at the same time, she felt utterly, airily free. It was the first time she was ever alone in a car.

The line at the Division of Motor Vehicles was long. People of all ages stood like wilted flowers in the ovenlike July heat. Yet Cheryl hardly felt the time pass as she read the driver's handbook again and again, just the way she had every night after Gary was asleep. She thought that if she closed the book and tried hard enough, she could recite every word.

Yet her fingers shook with nervousness as she filled out the application. Name. Address. Social Security number. When she reached the section that said past traffic violations, she paused. It was almost impossible to get a ticket when your husband wouldn't even let you drive.

Cheryl watched the examiner score her written test. The woman in a starched white shirt wearing a badge scanned the paper. After flipping the page over and scanning the back, she said, "Passed. One hundred percent. That doesn't happen very often. Congratulations."

Cheryl knew her eyes were misty. She swallowed hard. "Thank you."

She moved over for the eye test. She read the letters TKPRSNI and the next line, EYFLHGZ.

The man monitoring the eye test frowned. "Read that second line again," he ordered.

She did, and he waved her along.

Now for the road test. The examiner, a small greasy-looking man in a tan DMV shirt, climbed into the passenger seat beside her. He glanced at the clipboard in his hand, then ordered, "Surrender your previous license to me—"

Previous license? What was this? Flustered, Cheryl shook her head. "I don't have one."

"Wait a minute—you're what? Twenty-five years old?" The man looked at her accusingly. He held his cupped hand out, waiting for her to drop the license into it.

A drop of sweat crawled down Cheryl's side. "I-I don't have one."

"It's illegal to keep two licenses. I have to take your first one before I can give you the test."

Cheryl shuddered. She took a deep breath. "This is my first driver's license."

"Are you kidding me? How do you get to work? What about the grocery store?"

"My husband drives me."

"Is there some kind of legal problem? An arrest warrant? Felony conviction? If there is, I need to know. I can't give you the test without a supervisor's approval."

"No—he just won't let me drive."

"Who? Your husband?"

Cheryl nodded, as afraid as if Gary were actually sitting beside her now.

The man turned his head and exhaled. "Let me get this straight. Is there going to be trouble with you being here today?"

Cheryl sighed. "I hope not."

"Look, lady. I'll give you the test. But I don't want any of this coming back on me."

Somehow Cheryl found her voice. "I need to drive," she said. "I need to get a job and go to church by myself."

"You need a life, lady," said the man. "Okay . . . drive down there—to the yield sign. Show me what yield means."

Cheryl's heart pounded as she followed the man's instructions. Turn left. Make a quick stop. Cross the railroad tracks. She saw the examiner write silently on the clipboard. "Okay," he said, with a sigh. "Pull over to the right and stop fast."

Cheryl drove, her foot stepping heavy on the brake. She flung the examiner back against the seat.

"Look, lady—" he said. "I'm not supposed to get involved with anything like this. Give 'em the test and that's it. But I gotta say, you got a big problem, and I don't know if getting a license is going to take care of it. But I'm passing you. I'm giving you that."

"Thank you," Cheryl said, a tear on her face.

"Just don't let me read about you in the newspapers."

"I won't," she assured him, trembling with elation and excitement as he handed her the paper. Vehicle operator's permit. Valid for five years. Now she could actually drive. Sweet, warm tears fell on her summer blouse as she drove on home.

"I'm going to work." Cheryl stood in back of where Gary sat at the kitchen table. Dinner was over, all the dishes were in the sink, and the only task left was to wipe off the kitchen table. She kept her voice soft and even, as if she were saying she was about to run to the corner store for a loaf of bread.

Gary sighed angrily. "What?"

Her voice fought wearily against his rage. "I got a job."

"No way is my wife going to work. We already went over this like, a million times."

"We need the money. You've been out of work four months." Cheryl's breath felt tight in her chest.

"Aw, get off me. I hurt my back. I'll get workman's comp as soon as I'm through physical therapy."

She hated the bile that rose in her throat and the edge of fear that crept into her brain. Cheryl inhaled. "But no money has been coming in for four months. Besides, I want to work."

"No wife of mine is gonna work." Anger brought him out of his seat. He turned and she saw naked rage in his eyes.

"It's for our family. To keep up with the bills." She held her breath in hopes that Melissa and Brooke, who were watching TV with friends downstairs, could not hear their raised voices.

"Let the bills stack up! Who cares! I'll pay 'em when I get better."

She took another breath. "It's been a long time since you looked in the checkbook. We're already two months behind on the gas and electric."

"Two months isn't that bad! I'll get it paid! Leave me alone!" He took a step toward her and pointed a threatening finger.

She fought to keep her voice as emotionless as possible. "I got warning notices from both of them. They'll shut the power off if I don't pay."

He shook his head. "Take it out of savings."

"There's enough to catch us up with the arrears. But not enough to pay the current bill."

Now he slammed his fist against the closed refrigerator door. "Okay. You win. Work a few weeks. Get the bills paid—but then quit or I'll quit for you."

She nodded meekly, hoping her bland expression would mask the anger that boiled inside her. But their eyes met and he somehow caught her fury.

"Women don't belong in offices!" Gary shouted, punctuating each word with a stab of his finger against her shoulder. "I know what goes on. There's too much temptation for the men. Pretty soon somebody ends up in bed. My wife's not going to do that."

Cheryl knew better than to respond. No matter what she said, Gary would continue to rage until he was spent. She only nodded meekly.

"No night shifts, either." He was still shouting.

"They close at five."

"And no business trips . . ."

"I'm only a file clerk . . . all I do is put files in cabinets."

"Then keep them there . . . keep your hands there, too."

She could hardly keep from hitting him, could hardly stay in the room one more second. But she made herself walk slowly out of the room and upstairs to choose her clothes for the first day of work. She ironed the navy blue skirt she wore to church, then selected a white blouse with long sleeves and a high collar, along with new nylons that she eased out of their cardboard sleeve. That night, lying in bed beside Gary's restless snore, she stared at the gray ceiling and prayed to survive his wrath until she could leave the house the next morning.

Cheryl started as a file clerk for State Life and Casualty—ninety-five dollars a week, and she felt rich until she paid the bills they owed. After State, there was a bigger company—and a raise of six dollars a week. In three years she graduated to the death claims desk—processing claims of accidents where people died. Needing a change from reading about death all day, she transferred to a sheet metal company as a billing clerk.

She was filling the paper clip holder on her desk when she jumped with surprise to see that Maxine was standing beside her. The supervisor's low voice brought chills to her spine—both because she wanted to do the right thing so badly and because Gary still had her paranoid about working outside the home.

"Where are the invoices?" There was no hint of emotion in Maxine's neutral tone.

"I filed them all."

"All of them? For the whole month?"

Cheryl nodded. "And the miscellaneous, too."

"But you need to go on break now."

"No, I already went."

Maxine gave her a look she couldn't decipher. It could be anger, disbelief, or incredulity. Cheryl watched Maxine pause, stand back, and fold her arms. Her voice remained as fluid and neutral as ever. "I have something else for you to do—since you are so efficient." The words stung even though they were toneless. Cheryl was left wondering if she was in trouble as Maxine left the room.

She tidied her desk, squaring papers, tossing out memos, and polishing the hardwood desktop with the can of Pledge she kept in her bottom drawer. Half an hour crept by before Maxine returned carrying a cardboard box.

"These are the company checking accounts. They need to be balanced by the end of the week. With this big conference coming up, I ran out of time."

She set the box on Cheryl's desk. Cheryl cautiously peered

over the edge and saw that it held ledgers and checkbooks. Her shock overcame her shyness. "You want *me* to balance those?"

"You may work on these each day until the mail comes." Maxine paused. "I've watched you. You're methodical."

"Methodical." Cheryl ran the word over her tongue. It didn't sound bad, although she really had no idea what it meant.

"Yes. Starting today, work on these until the mail arrives. At that point, please let me know where you stand on this task."

Cheryl watched Maxine leave the room.

She opened the first ledger. It listed expenditures.

Another volume said accounts payable. There was one for accounts receivable, too. Payroll. She opened all the ledgers and began to write. When she looked up again, it was an hour and a half later. Oh, no. She didn't start the mail. How would she finish by the time she was supposed to leave today? She rushed to Maxine's office.

As usual, the supervisor's face was expressionless.

"The mail!" Cheryl exclaimed. "It's got to be here by now."

"About an hour ago."

"You're kidding—how did I miss it?" Would Maxine change her mind about Cheryl now? Would she no longer be considered "meticulous" or whatever that word was?

The voice was cool. "The ledgers and the accounts. Are they still on your desk?"

"Yes, I think I've finished with them. . . ."

"Finished?"

Was that a hint of surprise or irritation? Cheryl couldn't tell. She nodded shyly. "I think so," she ventured.

"Bring them to me . . . never mind. I'll send someone for them."

Oh, no, Cheryl thought. She thinks I've messed it up so bad she doesn't even want to look at me. She rushed to open the mail and sort the correspondence—invoices, payments, orders. While she went through the familiar filing procedures, she half-listened for one of the thunderous shouts Maxine was famous for. Envelope after envelope entered the right slot with the help of her shaking fingers. She took a five-minute break—rather than fifteen—and came back to open the last pile of letters.

"Cheryl?" The voice that emerged from Maxine's office was cool. Cheryl couldn't tell if it hid anger.

"I'm just finishing the last section of mail," she responded quickly.

A heavy pause. "Come here, please."

Oh, no. Her heart sank. What did she do wrong now?

"I'm really almost finished with the mail," she said, entering Maxine's doorway, "and—"

Cheryl stopped when she saw that the ledgers and checkbooks were spread out on Maxine's desk.

"Sit down, please." Maxine turned away from her and coughed into her hand.

Suddenly nothing could jerk words loose from Cheryl's lips. What possible excuse could she give if she'd balanced the accounts completely wrong?

"I appreciate the time you took to work on the accounts," Maxine said.

"Was anything at all right?" Cheryl hated herself for this spontaneous interruption.

Maxine raised her chin a millimeter. "Absolutely."

"Did I *balance* the accounts?"

Maxine looked off to the side. "To the penny," she said. "One hundred percent exact."

But Cheryl still worried. "So you called me in here to—"

Maxine stared at her coolly, frowned. "As you may or may not know, there is a position open for a payroll clerk. Normally, we prefer some college training. But with the skills you demonstrated today, I'm satisfied with your qualifications. The position of payroll clerk is now yours."

Cheryl was stunned. She never even dreamed of applying. The position paid half again as much as she made now.

She swallowed. "Thank you," she said.

"Please go finish the mail now," Maxine said, with what Cheryl thought might be the vague trace of a smile. "You may begin your new position tomorrow."

Chapter Nine

Another day hot as blazes with the dry wind leaving him parched. At least they finished the rig today. Another drilling job done. Next week he'd have twenty-three years as a roughneck. Sometimes Dave wondered if he could somehow total up all the wells he'd drilled and make them all in one place, if he would drill clear through the world and come out in China or Japan or Italy or someplace like that. He knew this earth was a pretty big place, but still, he'd drilled one heck of a lot of holes. Maybe he could make it clear around the world, if there were some way he could lay the wells end to end. His eyelids drooped, and he leaned back against the chair in the Oklahoma City Holiday Inn.

Someone knocked at the door, jarring him out of a deep sleep.

"Hey, Patterson. What you doin' in there? We been standin' out here twenty minutes waitin'."

It was the guys. He scrambled to sit up straight. "No way, five minutes tops."

"You don't know"—a break for laughter—"we heard you snorin' away. Sawin' logs like crazy." He heard a couple of the guys snort, then break into guffaws.

"I was just combin' my hair. I'm coming right now," he called back, rubbing his eyes with his hands.

"Yeah—sure," Norm called out with a sarcastic laugh. "Combin' his hair," he said in a high falsetto voice.

Dave pushed the door open. The bar was right across the street from the hotel. The air-conditioned air in the dark place brought him back to life. This bar was filled with pinball machines, rows of shiny, clean glasses, and beer lights, some of which flickered. He'd been in this place a million times—same bar different city. Week after week, bar after bar, they all began to look the same.

Tonight was just another night like all the others, but something about that song on the jukebox caught his attention. What was it? Singer sounded sort of like Shania Twain, but it wasn't. Patty Loveless. That was it. Loveless . . . how appropriate.

He listened to the words of the song. "Don't toss us away," sang the voice.

Unbidden, Cheryl appeared in his thoughts as he sensed the song could be about the two of them. How did they let go of each other? What happened? He hadn't told any of the guys yet that he and April were separated. He wasn't quite a three-time loser yet, but it didn't look good. What good reason could he give for breaking up after fourteen years? It was the same old reason, tried and true: April wasn't Cheryl.

The papers Cheryl left on top of the pile on her bureau weren't in the same order as this morning. If Gary were going to search her things, he could at least be a bit more careful. The fact that she brought home every penny she earned didn't ease his suspicions. He still didn't trust her. No matter how many raises she got, no matter how many outstanding service awards she brought home, he still thought the office was a hazardous place for her to be. Why didn't he trust her? What could she do? How could she escape? She worried for the girls, who were growing up under his control, as much as she agonized for herself. But maybe later . . . when the girls were grown. Maybe later . . . someday, far away, she could leave. . . .

The call came in the late afternoon, after a shift at St. Mark's Hospital, where she now worked in billing, thanks to a great recommendation from Maxine. It was fun now to look back and remember that first day with the ledgers—she had no idea then that she'd someday be responsible for an entire hospital's budget. Insurance funds. Donations. Research monies. All of it went across her desk . . . millions of dollars.

Gary was a little late for dinner, but not unusually so. Sometimes he didn't get in until six. Cheryl never suspected him of infidelity the way he always suspected her. She shrugged and lifted the receiver. It was probably one of his friends on the phone.

"Hello?" Cheryl pushed her hair back behind her ear.

"Mrs. Slater?" Something about the voice sounded official. Clinical. Something about this voice made her hold still and wait, with her breath held.

"This is she. . . ."

"Mrs. Cheryl Slater . . . Gary Slater's wife?"

"Yes . . . this is Cheryl. . . ." Who was this?

"Mrs. Slater, this is the emergency room at Holy Cross Hospital. Your husband was admitted earlier today . . ."

"Oh . . . " Chills ran down her back. "He tries to be careful. Every step of the way. But he's in heating and air conditioning. It's hard not to lift things—"

"I don't know what you're referring to—"

"It's hard not to lift things in the business he's in . . . that's how he got his first back injury. I thought that probably—"

"Oh . . . I see. . . . I strongly doubt that this is connected. . . ."

"Really?" Cheryl shivered. What was going on?

"Ma'am, I need to let you know. Your husband had a heart attack at work. He was rushed to the emergency room here and is now resting comfortably. You may want to . . ."

Her knees gave way. She thought of how hard Gary worked, how—in spite of the problems—they had made a home together for more than twenty-five years. A home she thought was safe for Melissa and Brooke until they both grew up and moved out. They were all safe, as long as she didn't make him jealous.

"I—"

"He's in intensive care now. You may visit any time after five-thirty until eight."

The words all sounded so unreal. This couldn't be happening in her life. "When was it? What was he doing?"

"That's not in the chart, ma'am. You'll have to ask the doctor."

"Let me speak to the doctor."

"He's already left. Try calling tomorrow."

She felt like falling on the floor in a heap. Instead, she finished the dinner, and then, without eating anything, drove to the hospital.

She was stunned. Seeing him now made her realize how alive Gary used to be. Physical. Quick. Now he lay completely still.

She sat beside his bed for an hour before she picked up the phone. With a sigh, she dialed the familiar number.

Two states away in her own house, Melissa answered the phone. "Hello?"

"It's me, Mel."

"Mama? What time is it back there?"

"Not that late . . . almost eight." She paused. "I need to tell you about Daddy."

"What's wrong?" Melissa asked quickly.

Cheryl paused. "He's in the hospital."

Melissa sighed. "After the last time he got hurt, I just knew something would happen to him at work."

"They said this wasn't related to his work."

"What do you mean? What happened?"

"He had a heart attack."

"Oh, Mama. I just knew. I just knew something would happen. The way he lifts heavy things. Do you want me to fly there? I could get on standby."

"Not yet." Cheryl waited. "Why don't I let you know as soon as I talk to the doctor?"

"Mama, I could get there right away—"

"I'll call you. I'll try to find out something and call you back."

She hung up the phone and sat silently at Gary's bedside before phoning Brooke at her apartment. As opposed to Melissa's anxious worry, Brooke's concern took the form of terrified silence.

"Are you still there?" Cheryl asked.

"I'm here. I just can't believe it. Daddy was the man of steel." Brooke sobbed.

"I know. Maybe he still is. Let's hope so."

When neither of them could think of anything else to say, Cheryl said, "Let me call you back, honey."

"Okay." Brooke sniffed. "Call me."

Cheryl asked a nurse if she could talk to the doctor, but he'd gone home hours earlier.

She didn't know how long she sat at Gary's bedside and waited. Then she went home. After work, for many days afterward, she came and sat and waited. She noticed every detail about his face—the way his hair fell like lank ropes across his forehead, the wrinkles in his forehead and around his eyes . . . the stillness of his lips.

Cheryl sat for hours by the side of the hospital bed, waiting for a word from him. She kept imagining that someday she would walk in his hospital room and find the old Gary, sitting up in bed and asking her to account for what she'd done that day. Her world felt loose and free without his constant monitoring. In a way, it was a relief—in another it was as if a protective wall had suddenly crumbled underneath her. It all just felt so unreal.

Cheryl never knew she'd miss the steam and force that was Gary—the energy, spit, and vinegar that were what made him a man. At least when he was angry, I knew he was alive, she thought; that his brain and his body and everything was working. She remembered one time when she thought that living with Gary was like living with a Great Dane in the house. It was as if he took up a lot of space with his presence always felt, his feet heavy, shoulders broad and voice commanding.

Because his presence was so strong, its absence was equally powerful. For a long time after his first heart attack, she fought the realization that she was actually doing everything. Earning the living. Taking care of the yard. Doing all the laundry and every stitch of housework. There wasn't any time to stop and think. It was long after work one evening, when she'd finished the dishes and the house was quiet, that the thought came to her: I can take care of myself. I don't need anyone. I can manage everything all on my own.

But then another thought filtered through, teasing, taunting her. So why are you sitting here now, with the new phone book on your lap. Why are you even going to look?

Heart fluttering and hands shaking, she opened the pages. No use pretending she needed to look for anything else.

Patterson. Again, there was no Dave. No David. One D. L. that she already called once, three years ago, in a furtive moment, to discover that D. L. Patterson was Darlene Louise Patterson.

Davey's gone, she thought. Gone forever. Maybe dead, maybe miles away, but gone from here. Away from me.

She closed the book and tiptoed back to the bedroom, where Gary lay asleep. I could never leave him now, she thought. He needs me the way he never did before. He can't possess me like he always tried to do—but he needs me. And there's no way I could be any place but here.

Sometimes Dave looked back on the first day he drilled a well and wondered how he got brave enough. He was young, Dave decided, with no idea of the pressure that lay beneath the earth.

Today, Dave was concentrating on his drilling, like always, when he felt a slight tremor in the drill. A different pressure. It lasted only a second, but it was enough to make him shiver. His worry died down as more minutes passed. Then, suddenly, everything blew. The whole rig exploded. Metal. Earth. Oil. He flew through the air and didn't know whether he landed or not. Everything went black.

The phone rang late, long after he fell asleep. "Daddy?"

Cammy's voice, as familiar as his own breathing. Dave sat up a little in the bed. It was still hard for him to believe that she was phoning him from her own home, two states away, where she now had a husband, Scott. How did the time pass so fast?

"How you doin', sugar?"

"I'm fine, Daddy. But what about you?"

"Fair to middlin'. That old rig didn't get me yet."

"But it tried hard. It almost got you."

"No—I'm too tough." He tried to laugh, but everything hurt.

"I want you to come here, Daddy . . . and stay with me and Scott."

"I'm not taking any trips for a while." At least until I can get out of bed, he thought, with a silent chuckle.

"No, Daddy. Scott and I . . . we'll come get you."

"Now, I'm all right. I don't need no nursemaid."

"You shouldn't be alone."

"Do you know how much I've been alone in my life, girl?"

"Too much. Way too much. We'll be there Saturday morning—"

"Hey, wait a minute—" he said, but Cammy had already hung up. He shook his head.

Dave sat on Cammy's couch and counted all the states where he drilled. Fifteen states. Thirty-five years. It seemed like all the way around the world and back. But now Cammy spoiled him. As if he didn't know how to cook a hamburger or wash a shirt by himself. When she and Scott left for work, though, he did everything. Cleaned the kitchen. Washed all the clothes—his and theirs. It would be hard to tell somebody else how much he loved Cammy. As much as the sky and all the stars and every planet and every grain of sand on earth.

He'd tell Cammy and Scott that he needed to go back home, he decided. Heck, he was strong enough. Look at what his job title was: Roughneck. Did that sound like somebody who needed a baby-sitter? But at the same time it was hard to think about going away again. Here he was, right in the middle of what he always wanted. He was finally living with the most precious person in his life—his little girl.

Where were Cheryl's girls? he wondered. All grown up for sure. Maybe Cheryl had grandkids.

Maybe she didn't even remember who he was.

Chapter Ten

The call came at midnight.

"Cheryl Slater—"

Why did panic edge into her mind at those two words?

"Mrs. Slater?" the voice repeated, more determined this time.

She wondered: If she didn't answer, would everything be all right? But then she cleared her throat and sat up. "Yes . . . this is Cheryl."

"I'm telling you—come up here now. Your husband is much worse."

Her throat felt stuck, but she forced herself to speak. "I'll be there . . . right away. Just need to get dressed."

She didn't call the girls. The pantsuit she wore to work that day still lay languidly on her dresser, and she slid it on—the soft comforting fabric felt familiar against her skin. She didn't even look at the clock and hardly noticed that the sky outside was blacker than any night she ever remembered.

When Cheryl reached the hospital, she raced to her husband's room, then entered quietly. Gary couldn't talk or move. She felt the warmth of his skin, touched a place on his arm where there weren't any tubes or wires.

She sat and waited, tense inside, yet helplessly motionless on the cool, leather hospital chair. Hours passed. The sun turned the black sky to royal blue, then light blue. Her eyelids fluttered. She dozed, with no idea how many minutes passed

on the clock. She shifted on the chair, opened her eyes, and
saw that it was daylight now.

Gary was looking at her.

"Gary!" she said, forcing a smile. She stood, took his hand,
looked into his eyes.

He saw her. She knew it. With their eyes locked, she
straightened his covers and ran her hand across his forehead
and cheeks. She was gazing into his eyes when it happened.

Something changed. The spark of recognition left his eyes.
A vacant calm filled his expression. Suddenly Gary was looking at nothing. He was gone. Chills filtered from her shoulders
to her toes. She pushed the button to page the nurse.

Weeks passed. Months. Gary was part of her, Cheryl realized.
The sheer number of years they spent together. The memories
they shared. She felt as if she were wounded, even though
she'd often felt that way when he was alive. My history is
my history, she thought. It isn't perfect. But it's mine. The
feeling came over her again and again that she could survive
alone. Night after night she returned from work, cooked her
dinner, did household chores, and read or watched TV. She
was self-sufficient. The knowledge was calming, if not fulfilling.

As the months passed, her thoughts of Davey seemed less
forbidden—although the memories remained as delicious as
ever. As she sensed that her thoughts of Davey would probably never completely subside, she knew that there was only
one way to set her mind at ease. She would find him . . . or
at least find out about him. She would somehow discover
what happened to him after that final night they saw each
other. . . .

Once she made her decision, her determination overrode
her inclination to keep Davey a secret. After a lot of soul-
searching, she decided to tell Melissa, who was older, more
open about her feelings, and more likely to understand. If
Melissa told Brooke . . . well, she'd have to deal with that
when it happened.

It was a year after Gary died. Visiting Cheryl's house, Melissa was sitting on the couch, watching TV. It was hard to
believe her daughter was thirty.

Cheryl gazed at Melissa, held the picture of Dave behind her back.

"Hey, Mel—" Cheryl's voice sounded high and strange to her own ears.

Melissa looked up and frowned slightly.

"I need to tell you about something," Cheryl said, knees bending slightly as she rocked back and forth with nervousness. Her heart began to pound. What was she doing? How would Melissa take this?

"Yeah?" said Melissa, her gaze already back on the television.

"Before I was married to your daddy—" Cheryl began, and at these words, Melissa met her gaze. "I was engaged to somebody else."

"You never told me . . ." Melissa said. "I thought there was just Daddy."

Cheryl shook her head. She forced her words out past the sudden lump in her throat. "No—before I met your daddy, I was going with someone named Dave."

"Dave?" Now Melissa stood up. "Do you mean Davey? The one you told me you played baseball with?"

Cheryl nodded.

"But wasn't he your friend? Lived in that rental place of Grandpa's?"

"That's the one. But he was more than a friend. We planned on getting married."

"Then how come you didn't? Why did you get married to Dad?"

Cheryl felt a blush descend over her entire body. Chills erupted at her shoulders, and her cheeks warmed. Her lip quivered.

"I know why," Melissa said triumphantly. "You were pregnant with me. I figured it out one time."

Cheryl looked away, out the basement window, to where her red car was parked, waiting for her to drive it to the Winn-Dixie that night for the part-time job she worked after the hospital.

"Yeah, Mom. I knew it. You got married in October, and I was born in June." Melissa counted on her fingers, the same way Cheryl had a million times back when she was seventeen.

"Eight months. You were already pregnant. You had to get married."

Embarrassed, Cheryl covered her reddened face with her hand. "It all happened so fast. We started dating, and then I got pregnant, and—"

"You stayed with Daddy all your life, just because of me."

"No—" Cheryl protested, while her inner voice screamed that it was true.

"Me and Brooke, then. You stayed for us."

"Your daddy needed me. He got sick, back when—"

"I remember all that time he stayed in bed . . . all those years."

"He couldn't help it. He was sick. And he loved you girls—don't ever think for a minute that he didn't."

Melissa flung out, "But you didn't love him!"

"I was young," Cheryl protested lamely. "Way too young to get married."

"But you said you were already engaged before. . . ."

Cheryl paused. A balance seemed to weigh. It was now or never.

"Well, not officially. None of that 'get down on his knee and propose to me' stuff—but we always planned on getting married."

Melissa's smile was smug. "I think you still like him, Mom."

Cheryl blushed. The words leaked out. "Maybe I do. . . ."

"Why don't you call him up?"

"Melissa!"

"Really, Mom."

Cheryl saw that her daughter's eyes were guileless and clear. "I can't," she said, her throat filling.

"Yes, you can."

"No—I really can't. I don't know where he is. I saw him last in 1966."

"Hey. I was born by then. I was a baby."

"You were. He knew about you. He came to see me one night. He told me to get you, and we'd all go off to-gether. . . ." Cheryl's mind drifted.

"More romantic than Dad," Melissa interrupted.

"I don't know. I can't say what would have happened."

"But you'd like to know, wouldn't you?"

Cheryl felt another blush warm her face. Finally she remembered the framed photo she held behind her back. "Do you want to see his picture?" she asked her daughter.

Melissa nodded, and Cheryl held out the picture. What did she expect Melissa to say? That he was good-looking? That he looked young in the photo? That he had lots of dark hair? Her daughter surprised her.

"I'll find him, Mom. On the Internet. It'll take me about ten minutes."

"No—"

"Yes, Mom. I want you to be happy."

"I am—"

"Like you haven't been in a long, long time."

"I don't know where he is now—I don't know what kind of guy he is. He could be a criminal . . . a drug addict."

"But he was a nice guy before. Wouldn't hurt to look."

"I knew him when he was a teenager. Way back. Don't know him now."

"I remember—you played baseball."

"And ran races . . . he helped Grandpa and me pick butter beans and shuck oysters. But that was a long time ago. He was only thirteen. He probably doesn't remember."

"I'm sure he remembers. How could he forget?"

"And he could be married. With twelve kids and twenty grandkids."

"Don't you want to know, Mom? Come on. You want me to look."

She couldn't deny it. "Go ahead," she said, walking out of the room and leaving Melissa seated at the computer.

As days passed, she wondered if Melissa found anything. She didn't want to sound eager enough to ask.

Weeks flew by, then months. Now that Melissa and Brooke knew her secret and were searching themselves, she felt no guilt in consulting an outsider who could possibly help all of them find the answers.

The detective's office was downtown, behind a single plate-glass door in a sea of brick buildings. Steve Walker worked here two days a week, and the other three days at the hospital, with Cheryl.

"I have an appointment to see Mr. Walker," Cheryl told the receptionist, who sat behind a desk in the entryway.

"He's expecting you?" the woman asked.

Cheryl nodded. "Yes."

"Please have a seat," said the woman. Cheryl sat on a leather chair and began reading the latest *People* magazine. But her mind could hardly focus on the words in front of her. Was there any chance that Steve could help her find Dave? She felt brave even asking. A nagging voice in the back of her mind reminded her that she didn't know what kind of person Dave was now. They were so young. He could be married. He could be in trouble. He could be dead.

But she still wanted to find out.

"Cheryl?" said Steve a moment later. She followed him back down a gray wallpapered hall to his office, where he sat behind his desk.

"What can I do for you?" Steve asked pleasantly, a hint of curiosity in his voice.

Cheryl paused. She felt suddenly shy. What would Steve, who knew her only as a coworker, think of her reason for coming here? When his polite smile began to fade, she forced herself to speak. "I'm looking for someone I knew a long time ago. . . ."

"Really?" Steve said pleasantly. "Name?"

"David Lee Patterson."

"Nice that you know a middle name. Helps us verify if we find more than one. Address?"

"Oh, I don't know that."

"Last address you know of."

"He lived next door to my parents . . . when I was thir-teen. . . ."

"Do his parents still live there?"

"No . . ." Cheryl felt herself blush. "I look in the phone book every year . . . and their name is never there . . . his isn't, either."

"You're smart. Lots of people don't think to look in the phone book first. So the last address you have for him would be . . ."

"Five-ten Oak Street. Next door to me."

"Do you have his previous address?"

"It would be a couple of streets away—probably Sumac or Maple. I can't believe I can't remember. . . . You know, I could drive by and find out."

"And how long ago was this?"

She knew her smile revealed embarrassment. "It was thirty years ago. He was my first boyfriend."

"I see." Steve wrote on the pad in front of him, then looked up at her. "You went to school together?"

"He was a year older—and then I got married when I was sixteen and didn't finish school. But there were a couple of years that we were in the same school."

"Do you recall friends from that time who might be in contact with him?"

"No, we weren't in the same year. And he went in the service really young."

"Do you have his military address?"

Cheryl involuntarily remembered the time Gary made her burn Davey's pictures and the letters. But maybe—"I could look," she said.

"Get that to me if you can. What about a birthdate?"

"March 7, 1947."

"Good—we can verify with that, too. Do you have his military service number or Social Security number?"

She shook her head. "No."

"Do you know if his family was from another state before they lived by you?"

"No—"

"Anyone in the neighborhood who might remember him—or his parents?"

It was all so long ago. "Just my family. He was a good friend of ours. He found me in 1966, through my brother."

"Would they still be in contact?"

"My brother moved out of state years ago," Cheryl said. "He said they lost touch . . . just like we did." She smiled ruefully.

"Any line of work he might have pursued?"

"He wanted to work in the oil fields."

Steve sighed and shook his head. "They travel all over. But at least you have a name and a birthdate. I can get started with that. And if you find any other stuff—military address, someone I can call—let me know."

"How long will this take?" Cheryl asked, thinking it was hardly urgent. She only waited thirty years.

"Hard to say. I'll try to have something within a week. Get that other stuff to me as soon as you can."

Cheryl couldn't read the look in Steve's eyes as he stood and shook her hand.

Cheryl decided that she wanted to be thin if Dave ever saw her again. The first day she arrived at work without a bag of mini Three Musketeers bars, she felt as if she might starve to death before her shift was over. Her breaks seemed endless. She drank water, ate a fat-free cookie, and at the end of the night, felt as if she had made a huge sacrifice. At the same time she was elated. She made it through one day. The next day was even harder. Her stomach actually growled on the job. What was the point of starving herself? a voice inside her head asked. But she continued on. Though it seemed as if she had to carve the pounds off her body with a toothpick, they began to drop away. She stood on the scale and looked at it in disbelief.

She was actually losing weight.

She also thought about going to see a plastic surgeon. After Gary died, she'd kept a small part of her savings for herself. Now she planned to ask about eyelid surgery. She almost laughed at her own wishful thinking. If she ever saw Davey, she wanted to look her best.

Chapter Eleven

Two years had passed since she had told Melissa and Brooke about Dave. No one had found him yet. It was a Wednesday afternoon when the phone rang. She was lying on the couch watching TV when she picked up the phone to Melissa's excited voice.

"Mom!!! You won't believe this!" Melissa cried out.

Cheryl sat up straight. She'd never heard her daughter sound like this. She listened as Melissa gulped for air. "Are you all right?" she questioned worriedly.

"Fine, Mom." Melissa was still breathless.

"What about you and Tom?"

"We're fine. Mom, *The Maury Povich Show* just called me! They want you to come to New York and be on TV!"

Cheryl's hand gingerly touched the delicate stitches from the eyelid surgery. "I can't go now! How did they get my name?"

Melissa paused. Cheryl heard her clear her throat. "I can't believe I forgot to tell you. I called them about Dave three weeks ago."

"They called you back? Did they find him?"

"I don't know, Mom. They want you to come Friday. I have to call them back right now and tell them."

Cheryl sighed. The area around the threads still felt raw and sore. "Oh, I can't go now! My stitches are still in—" But could she miss out on her one chance to see Dave?

"They said to call within two hours. What should I say?"

"What am I going to do about my eyes?"

"I've got concealer, Mom. You could use that."

"I'm calling the doctor right now to see if he can take these things out early."

"The plane leaves Friday."

Cheryl closed her eyes, said a silent prayer. "Tell them I'll be there," she said. An attack of nerves struck as soon as she hung up the phone. What could she do now? Fighting to remain calm, she went in the bathroom and looked in the mirror. Didn't the doctor say the stitches could come out in five days? It was already a week and a half by now. He just didn't have an appointment available when she saw him the last time. She would have to convince him this was an emergency.

Drawing a breath, Cheryl sat at the phone.

"Dr. Schaeffer's office—"

"I need an appointment. Today."

She heard the receptionist flipping pages. "Oh—he's all booked up today. We have a late afternoon on Monday."

"It has to be today. Or tomorrow. I'm going on the plane on Friday."

"Could he schedule you in after your trip?"

Cheryl closed her eyes in frustration. "I'm going on *The Maury Povich Show* Friday afternoon. In front of millions of people. If he can't take my stitches out, I'll be tempted to pull them out myself."

There was a long pause. She heard the muted voices of medical personnel conferring with one another. Then the receptionist's voice, as flat as ever.

"We can't promise anything. There just isn't a time slot available. But if you want to come and sit in the waiting room, we'll see if we can work you in. No guarantees."

Cheryl quickly slid on her shoes as she spoke. "I'll be there in twenty minutes."

She felt herself begin to panic after she read three entire magazines, and the waiting room looked as full as when she came in.

Finally, at four-thirty, she stood at the nurse's desk.

"May I help you?"

"They said someone would work me in. I have an emergency. I have to go on national TV and I need my stitches out."

"You were told there were no guarantees. The doctor has a full schedule."

"Could I talk to him? Please?"

The nurse sighed heavily and frowned at her. "All communications go through this desk."

"Tell him I'm going to be on *Maury—The Maury Povich Show*." Cheryl was aware that she was pleading. Her voice was higher and thinner than usual—on the verge of breaking. "Tell him I'm going to see my long-lost boyfriend—that it's been thirty years and this is my only chance—"

The nurse lifted a hand in protest. "You were told he wasn't available. I'll pass the message along, but that's all I can do."

Cheryl's hands were shaking when she picked up a bedraggled copy of *McCall's*. "I'm sitting here until I see him," she said, but her voice sounded weak even to her own ears.

The nurse didn't answer. Cheryl was focusing on an article about missing children when she abruptly became aware of someone standing over her. She cautiously lifted her eyes to see Dr. Schaeffer staring down at her. He peered through his glasses as their eyes met.

"Are you the celebrity?" he asked.

"Uh—I'm going on TV. . . ."

"And you don't want the studio audience to view my gorgeous handiwork?"

"Well, I'm seeing my old boyfriend. I hope. If they found him. I met him when I was twelve."

"And you want to look the same to him now as you did then?"

"Well—" Cheryl was surprised to find herself stifling a laugh. "Not exactly—but I look like a prizefighter now."

"Oh, not the look you were hoping for? Let's see what we can do."

With that, he ushered her back into his office. She cringed as he cut away the stitches, one by one. When he held the mirror in front of her, she gasped. There was now a red scar where each stitch had been.

"Better?" he asked.

"Well—"

"Red marks are better than black stitches, aren't they? A lighter color."

"I can cover them with concealer."

"Stop if it stings or the skin feels raw."

Cheryl nodded.

"And tell Mr. Povich hello for me. He hasn't featured a good plastic surgeon in a long time."

"I'll tell him," Cheryl said gratefully, sliding off the table and putting on her shoes. Was there anything on earth that could stop her now?

It was a lazy Tuesday afternoon. Dinner was cooking in the Crock-Pot. Dave, Cammy, and Scott were watching a talk show on TV. Dave shook his head as a man and woman suddenly grabbed each other in a bone-crushing embrace. The couple screamed, trembled, and even jumped in a circle without letting go of each other.

"Now, isn't that stupid." Dave laughed. "Can you believe people actually go on TV in front of the whole country and do stuff like that?"

Scott and Cammy laughed with him. "I think it's great," said Cammy.

The phone rang. Scott picked it up.

"For you, Dad."

"Hello?" Dave said evenly, his eyes still on the frenetic couple on TV, who still shook and screamed. They stopped for a minute to look into each other's eyes, then hugged again.

"David Patterson, please . . ." The voice sounded fast and foreign. Somebody from back East, Dave thought. Probably selling something.

"This is he—"

"I have reached Mr. David Patterson?"

"You got him." Dave sighed. Definitely a salesman. People who called him David didn't know him.

"David, this is Jason from *The Maury Povich Show*. . . ."

Dave started to laugh. Did someone out there in TV-land hear him say that people who went on talk shows were stupid? Or was somebody just playing a joke on him? "Oh, really?" he said, feeling like joking himself. "Are you sure this isn't Montel or Phil Donahue?"

"This is Jason Kirkland, Mr. Patterson. I'm a producer with *Maury Povich*. . . ."

"Okay . . ." He'd go along with it to see what he said next.

"David—is it okay if I call you David?"

"My friends call me Dave."

"Dave, do you know a Cheryl?"

Suddenly everything stopped. He didn't have an easy answer this time. Could it be that this guy really was who he said he was?

"I did at one time," he said cautiously.

"In Lake Worth, Florida . . ."

Maybe this guy really was for real. "Yeah," he said.

"She wants to find you, Dave."

Dave sat back in his chair and took a deep breath. Could this be a joke? Or could it be the chance to see the woman he'd loved all his life? His mind raced.

"Still there, Dave?"

"Yeah. I'm here. Say . . . if you know where she is, call her back and ask her two questions."

"What are they?"

"Her middle name." Lynn, he thought. "And her oldest brother's name." Kevin, he recalled.

"Okay, Dave. I'll call you right back."

Then the phone didn't ring, though they all sat at the table and waited. Finally Cammy started dinner, and Scott said he better get back to the yard work. They ate, listlessly. None of them could think of anything to say. They cleared the table, washed the dishes, read the newspaper in the living room. Finally they turned on the TV. Sitcoms instead of talk shows by now.

The night wore on. Maybe it was the wrong Cheryl.

Dave was lying awake in bed when the phone rang.

"Hi, Dave. This is Jason from *Maury*. You weren't asleep, were you? Cheryl wasn't home when I first called. Took me this long to get to her. But she gave me the answers to your questions."

Dave was aware that he was holding his breath. "Go ahead. Tell me what she said."

"Her middle name is Lynn, Dave. How does that sound? And the brother's name—it's Kevin."

He thought his heart stopped. It's her, he thought. His mind got all wound up in his memories, and he didn't even think to answer Jason.

"Hey, Dave?" Jason called out to him, as if from a distance away. "Can you fly to New York by Friday?"

Chapter Twelve

Cheryl still couldn't believe she was here. She and Melissa enjoyed what felt like a whirlwind flight to New York. And now they sat here, in the green room, on *The Maury Povich Show.* How many times had she watched reunion stories and cried when the couple saw each other and hugged. Sometimes Cheryl could feel the chemistry between them . . . she knew they were meant to be together. Other times, the two acted as if they had both changed completely. Didn't look or act like the other suspected. Lots of times one or both of them were married.

A man in a classy black suit entered the green room, interrupting her thoughts.

"Listen up," the man said, raising a hand that held a clipboard. "I'm Griff Clark—producer for *Maury.* I need to brief you on a few things before we head to the soundstage."

Cheryl waited.

"You—the deal is, we didn't find your guy," he said, pointing to Cheryl.

"My guy? You didn't find Dave?"

"No, sorry."

At Melissa's aggravated sigh, the man held his clipboard aloft once again.

Melissa protested, "Then why did you make my mom come here? Do you know what she went through? She had to go to the doctor and get off work and—"

"I'm not finished," the man said firmly. "Our search organization—BigHugs.com—feels like they are very close to completing the search. So they asked you here to make a plea—"

"Oh—I've heard this before—" Melissa said. "I've seen this on other shows."

The hand up again. "All you have to do is go out there. Tell the audience you're looking for him. We shoot the photo you sent us up on a big screen. Takes five minutes—tops."

Melissa sighed again.

Cheryl said, "Well, I came all the way here. Guess I might as well do that." A sinking feeling filled her. She couldn't believe she traveled this far for nothing. But maybe she wasn't meant to see him. Maybe she was only supposed to remember the good times in the past. Her nervous excitement gave way to bittersweet disappointment.

Seconds later, she was being ushered out of the room. Cheryl and Melissa followed the man down a long hall filled with many doors. Windows in the walls revealed banks of sound equipment, TV monitors, machines dotted with switches and flashing lights.

The lights were so bright on stage. Cheryl never knew the audience sat so much lower than Maury and the guests. She felt as if she was on display, sitting high above the hundreds of people in the audience.

"Now we bring out two lovely ladies," Maury was saying, his smile revealing bright white teeth. Smile wrinkles hovered at his eyes. He wore a white shirt and a royal blue tie. "Please sit here. Audience, this is Cheryl and Melissa. Melissa, you wanted to give your mother a gift, is that right?"

"Yes," Melissa, said and nodded at Maury, suddenly a bit shy.

"And what was the gift you had in mind for your mom?"

"I wanted her to meet her first boyfriend again."

"They were high school sweethearts, is that right? Or was it college?"

Melissa shook her head. "Before that. They met when she was only twelve. I think he was a year older."

The audience sighed with excitement. "Woo-woo" somebody called out in the first row.

"More like childhood sweethearts, was that it?" Maury's grin widened as he smiled at Melissa again, and she nodded.

"Well, let's see how Mom feels about all this."

Maury tilted his head to the side and gazed at Cheryl.

"Cheryl, you knew this man—uh, Dave—" At that moment someone flashed an enlarged photo of a picture of young Dave on the screen. The only picture Gary didn't find and make me burn, Cheryl thought.

"Oh—" said the women in the audience in a breathless, collective sigh.

"You knew this man since sixth grade?" Maury asked.

"Yeah—" Cheryl squeaked, dabbing at her eyes.

"And he sent you all this army stuff from Germany? A cuckoo clock and some dishes—even some savings bonds, is that right?"

She nodded.

"And the thing is, you used that money he sent you to marry someone else—didn't you?"

"Boo . . . boo . . ." from the audience as Cheryl nodded one more time.

"But still—even though you spent his money—you never forgot this man."

"I didn't," Cheryl said.

"So why do you want to find him now?"

Cheryl stared at Maury, then she stared out into the audience, where she saw women smiling in anticipation. She pointed a shaking finger to the blown-up picture of Dave, then spoke to the women seated in the audience.

"Girls, you can see why I'm looking for this man—look at this picture—he is so handsome."

Voices of agreement erupted from the audience. A ripple of applause.

Maury's voice, gentle and sure, interrupted the commotion. "Cheryl, he's here—"

"Oh—" Her hands flew to her face. She looked up to see Dave, handsome, dark-haired, and smiling, walking down the steps and carrying a huge bouquet of roses and wildflowers. Although she tried to control it, tears began to stream down her cheeks.

"Oh, my God—" she said again and again, quivering and

crying and feeling her heart pounding like a hammer in her chest.

"You look so good," she heard Dave say.

Sure, she thought, with tears all over my face washing off the concealer on my red eyes and my hair all messed up now and . . .

Maury interrupted her frantic thoughts. "Cheryl, is there a question you want to ask Dave?"

She slid her hands slowly off her cheeks, clasped them in her lap and turned to Dave, who was still smiling at her. "Are you married?" she asked tentatively.

"Yes," Dave said, no hitch in his smile.

She couldn't believe it. Her heart sank and an incredible sadness draped like a heavy cape. Yet somehow she couldn't give up quite yet. "Are you happy?" she ventured.

"I've been separated over a year."

"Oh—" she breathed, and her heart rose again, finally settling back in her chest where it was supposed to be.

"So, you two," Maury was saying. "You were childhood sweethearts—both married to someone else—"

"Three someone elses," Dave said, and Cheryl stared.

"Three for him—one for me," she said. When Dave looked at her, she added, "My husband passed away a year ago."

"This is going to work," Dave said.

"We're going to *talk*," Cheryl said back, and the audience laughed.

At least they got to go to the same airport after the show. Luckily, both of their planes headed out from the same spot. There wasn't an evening in a classy New York restaurant, or tickets to a Broadway play. But there was a gift Dave and Cheryl knew they'd use—right down to the second it was used up: long-distance phone cards—160 minutes each.

When Cheryl said they were going to talk, she meant it!

At the airport gate, wind whipped at their hair and rippled their jackets, but they hardly felt it. Dave kept staring at Cheryl, thinking this was just like on the show. When he walked out on the soundstage he didn't see a fifty-year-old woman, he saw the twelve-year-old girl he fell in love with.

He gazed at her now, and kept on feeling the same way.

Catching his look, Cheryl smiled at him, and he grinned back. Dave said, "I want to ask you something."

"You can ask me anything," she answered, a slight frown making her face look as if she was gearing up for a tough question.

"I want to do something—" Dave paused.

"What?" she asked.

"I just want to kiss you."

A lump filled her throat, and she swallowed hard. "You can kiss me," she managed, her voice trembling.

Right there outside the airport gate, with millions of people passing beside them, he kissed her. And although they didn't know it at the time, they both shared the same thought. They weren't at the New York airport, being swarmed by millions of people in drizzling rain and wind. They were all alone, just the two of them, on a warm spring day in the chicken house on Cheryl's dad's farm.

The kiss was exactly the same. The same kiss Dave always thought of as the sweetest-tasting kiss ever. The same kiss that made twelve-year-old Cheryl feel as if she had found the person she wanted to spend the rest of her life with.

And after the kiss they headed to opposite ends of the airport to board planes that would take them thousands of miles away from each other.

But there was still the phone. The minutes sped by.

"You know, we never had sex," Dave said one night.

Cheryl giggled.

"We never were intimate—"

"Nope," she said. "You were a gentleman."

"Oh—I woulda been willing. You coulda talked me into it."

"I didn't know what it was back then." She laughed.

"You were pretty young—"

"You, too."

"Seems like a century ago."

Cheryl sighed.

"No, it doesn't. Way it stayed in my head, seems like it happened last week." Dave laughed.

"Well, you did kiss me last week." Her heart thudded at the thought.

"And it was that same old kiss that hung around in my head for thirty years—gosh, woman, you got some kind of staying power."

"You, too," she said, her voice surprisingly serious. "Really, this is unbelievable that this is you and me talking. After all these years . . ." He could tell she was about to say something big. And then his phone card ran out. No minutes left. The connection between them died, and they were thousands of miles away from each other again.

Days passed. A wistful feeling enveloped Cheryl, and she realized how attached she was to him again, after just this short time. But like before, as she had in past years, she carried on with her work and savoured memories of the kisses they shared—memories that she could call up on dark days.

It was a Saturday when the phone rang. Cheryl was dusting the living room and getting ready to vacuum. Maybe it was Melissa calling, she thought. Or Brooke. Or her mom.

"Hello?" she said.

"Is this warm, sunny Florida?" It was Dave.

Her heart filled. "It sure is. . . ."

"Well, this is cold, rainy Indiana."

She didn't know what to say next. It sounded as if he was in a phone booth.

"You know what Monday is, don't you?"

She actually had to look at the calendar. "Valentine's Day," she said, realizing she felt breathless.

"I want to tell you I'm flying down there."

"That's great." Why couldn't she think of anything to say?

"But there's something I need to ask you. I'm getting down on my knees in here. It's a pretty tight squeeze. But the thing is, I never stopped loving you."

"Or me, you—" she said, her heart pounding now.

"So I need to ask you something." She heard him shifting in the phone booth, then it sounded as if he was out of breath. "Your mama isn't there, is she?"

"No, just me. Did you want to talk to my mother?"

"I really wanted to ask her if this is all right with her. I'm down on my knee now. Will you marry me?"

"Yes," she said, smiling. "I'll marry you."

"Then I'm on the plane Wednesday night. Gets there at eight."

"I'll be there. I'll meet you at the airport."

"And when I get there, I'll ask your mom."

She thought of his mom, who died so long ago, a pale, still-young woman with dark hair, stricken with cancer before her youngest child graduated from elementary school. "I'm still sorry your mom can't be here," she said. "When we were little, I couldn't imagine how hard it must have been for you, to lose your mom so young."

There was a long pause. She heard him clear his throat. "I know she'll be smiling down on us," he said. "She liked you even when you were a kid."

They wanted to marry on his mother's birthday two months away, but that was a weekday, so they decided to get married the weekend after her birthday—April 24, 1999.

Two days later Cheryl was walking out the door to pick him up when the phone rang.

"Cheryl? Griff Clark."

The accent was New York. The name that went with this fast-talking voice didn't ring a bell. "I'm sorry. I don't remember who you are. What company are you with?"

"*Maury Povich.* I'm the producer."

Oh—she thought, surprised. Why would they call her now? Was there any chance they found the earring she lost when she started crying on TV?

"We're inviting you back on the show for an update."

"An update?"

"Yes, to tell our audience what has happened since you were reunited. Are you willing to make another appearance?"

"Uh, yes," she said, smiling.

"And what about"—she heard him shuffling papers—"David Patterson? You are still in contact with him?"

"Yes. In fact, I'll see him in about an hour."

"You'll *see* him? Let's see, he lives in Indiana, is that right?"

"Yes. He's coming here. Arriving at the airport."

"I think we definitely want you back on the show, Cheryl. I'll be calling you."

•   •   •

All during the flight to New York, Dave couldn't imagine what he would say on *Maury Povich*. They were getting married. One sentence. What else would anyone want to know? Try as he might, he couldn't imagine what he could talk about other than that. It would be as if they were saying, "and they lived happily ever after. . . ." So why were they flying there?

In the studio he recognized Ray, the sound technician who was there when they were on *Maury* the first time.

"Hey," said Ray, with a smile. "I remember you guys. Still hanging out, huh?"

"We're getting married," said Dave.

"Married? Really?"

Cheryl nodded at him.

"You guys made my day. Hey, come here—" He led them behind the set, to where a tall, handsome young man in a suit was standing. "You guys need to meet this guy. Troy Dunn. He's from BigHugs.com."

"Oh—" said Dave, "you're the one who found me. . . ."

"I owe you big time," said Cheryl, with a grin that stopped Dave's heart.

Troy shook hands with them. "It looks like you're still friends. We're always glad to see that."

"We're getting married," Dave said, thinking, yes, that is the only sentence I seem to have to say.

"Really—" Troy smiled, and dimples appeared in his cheeks. "Well, that is what we really like to hear. This kind of news makes it all worth it. You made my day."

Well, thought Dave, even if I can't think of what to say, at least I said the right thing.

Then they were out on the soundstage. Since his heart wasn't hammering so hard this time, Dave found he could look around and see what the *Maury* set was like. It was amazing all the machinery it took to operate this place. Cameras. Grips. A sea of floodlights. A stage that looked as if it were built to withstand World War III. More machinery than an oil-drilling rig.

"Today we're featuring an update of our lost loves show. Don't you always wonder what happens to those couples who meet on our show and find a lost love they've been wondering

about for years? Take a look." Maury gestured at the screen.
Dave smiled at the tape of him and Cheryl.

"Well, Cheryl." Maury grinned at the two of them. "We're
glad to see the two of you back on the show with us. It looks
like things are going well." He raised his eyebrows.

Dave was about to say that they were getting married. But
Cheryl spoke first.

"You know, a few minutes ago, when we were sitting waiting to come out here, I sat by him and just rubbed his leg.
For five minutes. Last night I rubbed his back while we were
watching TV. I put my hand on his chest. Then I put both
my hands on his face. It's just a natural thing to do—"

The audience wooed and catcalled. Cheryl raised a hand.
"Not a sexual thing—I just want to touch him, and be close
to him—"

Maury smiled. Waited.

"And I just keep thinking—" Dave looked up in surprise
as Cheryl's voice broke. "That for so many years I could have
been doing this. For so many years I didn't get to hold him
and touch him. I didn't get to walk by him and give him a
kiss—every night or any time I wanted. It's a feeling I can't
explain. The other night there was a car accident on the free-
way while I was driving home from work. And I kept thinking I was losing time—precious time—with him. And I hated
wasting every single minute after that."

There was a hush in the audience. Maury's face, which had
somehow grown thoughtful, now erupted in a grin again. But
it took him a moment to decide what to say. "Well, Cheryl.
We appreciate that. A lot of people in our audience might be
a little jealous of you. Are you, audience?"

Applause, laughter, and some people yelling "Yeah . . ."

"Well"—Maury turned his grin to Dave—"let's ask this
guy. What are your feelings, Dave?"

Dave suddenly thought of Cheryl, and how it felt the last
time they sat together on this stage. "When I was here before,
and I walked out over there"—he pointed off to the right—
"I didn't see a fifty-year-old woman—"

Cheryl jabbed at his side, and laughter peppered the audience.

"I didn't see no fifty-year-old woman at all. I saw the girl

I fell in love with when I was fourteen years old. Her eyes
are the same. She walks the same. Her smile is the same.
She's still the same girl."

Maury shook his head in mock disbelief. "Wow! You're
quite the guy, Dave. What woman wouldn't want to hear a
compliment like that? Do we even need to ask what's in the
future for you guys? Any wedding bells clanging away?"

Dave smiled. "We're getting married—in two weeks." The
audience whooped, roared, and dissolved in a sea of laughter
and applause.

Cheryl, Melissa, Brooke and her family filled her backyard
with flowers and plants, so that it was a riot of color and
sweet spring scents. Melissa, who now had a valid notary
stamp, had received special permission to officiate today. She
stood in front of the two of them. Cheryl looked into her
daughter's big blue eyes and suddenly thought that she didn't
regret her marriage to Gary; she had two precious daughters,
and she'd learned she could take care of herself without anyone's help. But somehow the fact that she knew she could
make it alone made it that much happier for her to be standing
here now.

"I, David, take thee, Cheryl, to be my lawful wedded wife,
to love and to cherish—" Melissa instructed Dave.

"I, David, cherish Cheryl, to love as my lawful wife—"
Dave started out, and everyone started laughing at his mistake. Suddenly the slight formality of this occasion evapo-
rated.

"Okay—Dave—" Melissa said with exaggerated patience
and a brimming smile. "Let's try this one more time. How
about 'I, David—' "

"There's something I have to do first."

Melissa looked at him questioningly. Cheryl's eyebrows
frowned quizzically, though there was no way to vanquish
the smile underneath. Yet everyone gasped as Dave walked
away from Cheryl's side and went to find her mother.

"Dave—" Cheryl called out.

"We need the groom back here," said Melissa with au-
thority.

"Wait." Dave held up a hand. He drew himself up in a straight posture.

"Mrs. Harmon"—he leaned his head to the side and smiled at Cheryl's mother—"I know I didn't ask you before, but I've always wanted to be your daughter's husband. I hope you are going to be okay with this."

Cheryl's mom burst out in surprised laughter. "Me? I'm thrilled. Always thought she should be with you!"

"Okay." Dave nodded, then strode back to where he stood next to Cheryl.

He got the vows right the second time, then took Cheryl in his arms as they danced to "Welcome to My World," by Jim Reeves.

They were walking to cut the cake when Melissa caught up with him. "Smash the cake in her face," she whispered. "Really let her have it—"

Cheryl was thinking how perfect everything about today was. How, during all those long years when her job was her whole life, she would never have believed that a day like this would be possible for her. She was just going to say that her dreams had come true when suddenly a huge piece of chocolate cake with white icing was pressed firmly into her face.

Cake crumbs went up her nose and she couldn't breathe. White icing clung like heavy cold cream to her cheeks. Feeling cake crumbs against her eyelids, she didn't dare open her eyes. But she knew she had to. She couldn't wait one more second. Eyelashes fluttering, she squinted until she caught sight of the cake. Then she grabbed a bigger, more frosting-laden piece than the one that hit her and pressed it firmly against Dave's cheek. She spread the cake across his face as if her hand were a bulldozer, moving her palm in a circular motion to be sure that every single crumb was, indeed, smashed into a creamy goo against his skin. But he wasn't mad—he just kept laughing.

"I'm amazed," she said later, after they'd blown their noses and washed off their faces and danced some more, "after all that has happened, you still love me."

"You can't get rid of me," he said, with a sexy smile. "Never again. I won't leave no matter how many times you tell me to."

"I didn't want you to leave that night," she said. "It was the most romantic moment of my life . . . I couldn't forget it."

"And I told myself that I loved you enough to leave if that's what you wanted—I told myself that again and again for years and years. . . ."

When they set out, it was a lazy Saturday morning. Calm sunshine and flowing breezes bathed the air with soothing warmth. Cheryl and Dave breathed the scent of summer's arrival. They sauntered easily through the old city of St. Augustine, gazing at bright-colored flowers and glancing at clothes, jewelry, and paintings in shops that dotted their path.

Dave was thinking it might be almost time for lunch when Cheryl's pace suddenly slowed.

"There's no one here like us," she said abruptly.

"What?"

Cheryl whispered. "Look around—we're the only ones with our arms around each other."

Dave looked. He saw people, palm trees, and sun settling on the oldest European settlement in the United States. He smiled at her.

"They've got to be married, too." She angled her head at a couple where the woman walked five paces ahead of the man.

"What are you thinking?" Dave frowned a second before flashing her his grin.

"I'm thinking I'm lucky. Look at us. It's like we're out on a date."

He smiled at her again. Waited.

"I just love it that we can be a couple. It's so wonderful to go to bed next to someone whom you look forward to waking up to the next morning. I hate the traffic jams after work because it takes me longer to get home to you—I wish everyone could be like us." She leaned over to kiss him on the cheek, as she had at least a thousand times since the first *Maury* show. "We're together. That's all I need," she said, leaning close and hugging him. "I'm amazed by it all. I'm still amazed—every day."

Cheryl closed her eyes and let out a contented sigh, glad that she and Dave were together again.

The Love She Held in Her Heart

Chapter One

Gulping a burst of fresh air, Amber Lee skated under the mirrored ball. She wove her way through clusters of skaters, trying to catch up with her sister, Mindy. Min skated so fast her whole being seemed to flicker under the fluorescent lights. Her long chestnut curls flapped like a flag, then dipped in a swinging cascade. Min could turn sideways and skate backward and still give Amber a race that left her panting.

Suddenly Amber noticed something was wrong. She watched in horror as a panicked expression gripped her sister's fair-skinned face. Min's knees gave way and her shoulders dipped out of balance. Amber rushed to the other side of the rink where Min now lay crumpled on the hardwood floor. Amber felt her heart beat fast.

"Min! What happened?"

"My leg ... wouldn't work all of a sudden ..." Mindy's eyes widened in fear.

"Here, give me your hand. ..."

Mindy shook her head. "I can't stand up."

"I can help you—" Amber leaned toward her sister.

"No—" Min lifted a hand in protest. "It's really bad. You better get somebody."

"Are you sure?"

"I can't move."

Amber skated off, feeling as if her two legs were traitors to Min, who looked so lifeless. This was Min, who was always one step faster, even though she was just fourteen, one year younger than Amber. What happened to her just now?

Two young men helped Mindy off the rink. At first she was unable to hold herself up, but after a few moments she steadied herself and grabbed on to Amber's arm. The two girls walked slowly home, unable to voice their fears.

"Does it still hurt?" Amber finally asked as they climbed the front steps to their small white frame house.

Min nodded shakily. "It's like needles in there. Really scary."

Mama and Daddy rushed Mindy to the hospital. A doctor took X rays and said her leg and ankle weren't broken. But days later Mindy's leg still throbbed. In the mornings she told Mama she was in pain and couldn't go to school. Mama shouted to Min to get up out of bed, that pretending her leg still hurt wasn't going to keep her out of school. Even though Mama's words were harsh, Amber saw the fear in her mother's eyes and heard the worry in her voice.

So Amber and Mindy trudged the long blocks to Harwood High School, where Amber was in her second year and Mindy was in her first. Each day Amber silently prayed that her sister's leg would stop hurting. She asked God to let them skate again like they did before. She wrote to their brother, Brent, who was in the army in Korea, to ask him to pray for Mindy, too. But what could be wrong if the doctor declared that there were no broken bones—not even a sprain?

As the days passed, Amber tried to thrust aside her nagging worry that Mindy's leg was taking far too long to get better. But one night at Aunt Nona's the fear came crashing down on her. The two girls ate a spaghetti dinner with childless, gentle Aunt Nona, then watched TV late into the night, falling asleep on the hide-a-bed long after dark.

"Amber!" Mindy shook her sister awake too early in the morning. The sky outside was still navy blue.

Amber rolled over, forced her eyes open, and wondered for a moment where the two of them were. Why was her sister whispering to her? Didn't she know this was the middle of the night? "Go back to sleep," she told Mindy.

"My whole side hurts," Mindy said. "And feel this!" She

guided Amber's hand to her small, thin hip, where there was a rounded lump that felt like a buried shell.

"Ooh, that feels weird. What is it?"

Mindy stifled a sob. "I don't know. I just found it now."

"Does it go away when you move? Maybe it's just a bone sticking out . . . the way your leg is bent."

Min held her breath, turned over. "It's still there. And now my whole leg hurts. Clear up to my hip."

"Do you want me to wake Aunt Nona?"

"No. I keep closing my eyes and trying to go back to sleep, but I'm too scared." Mindy turned away, and Amber heard a sob escape her. She reached for her sister's hand and squeezed the small, thin fingers.

As night waned and the sun turned the curtains in Aunt Nona's living room from scarlet to pale pink, the two girls lay in the bed, holding hands and listening to the raspy rustle of their breath on Aunt Nona's soft white pillows.

As a sliver of sun eased across the blankets, Aunt Nona stepped silently into the room, thinking they were still asleep.

"Mindy's leg hurts—" Amber blurted.

Mindy jabbed an elbow in her sister's side.

"There's a lump—" Amber continued, hearing fear in her own voice.

"Oh, honey," said Aunt Nona. "Let me see. . . ."

Mindy turned away angrily as their aunt kneeled beside the bed.

"Come on, Min . . . you showed it to me!" Amber pleaded.

When Aunt Nona gently slid the blankets off her, Mindy stifled a sob.

"I won't hurt you," Aunt Nona insisted.

Mindy reluctantly turned halfway toward Aunt Nona, causing the lump to stand out beneath the leg of her flannel pajamas. Amber would never forget the frightened, pained expression on their aunt's face. "I'll just take a moment to call your mama," said Aunt Nona, standing instantly.

"No!" Mindy protested.

It wasn't long after the phone call, that Mama and Daddy arrived at Aunt Nona's house. Amber watched as Daddy lifted Min out to the car, where Mama had brought a pillow from home and spread a blanket on the backseat.

"Amber may stay here while you go to the clinic," Aunt Nona offered, her hand light on Amber's shoulder.

No, Amber protested silently. Let me stay with Min. But Mama blinked, squeezed Aunt Nona's arm, and said, "That would help me, Nona." Amber felt her heart thud. If it would somehow help for her to stay at Aunt Nona's house, she would do it.

"We'll pick her up on the way back," Daddy said with a dispirited wave.

Aunt Nona and Amber tried to play rummy and checkers, but Amber couldn't keep her mind on the cards or plastic game pieces. Aunt Nona won game after game. It seemed like hours before Amber's parents came to retrieve her. And in the car no one said what happened at the clinic. Amber only glimpsed her mother brushing a tear aside. Her father didn't whistle as he drove, the way he usually did. The car was deadly silent. Although bursting with questions, Amber's voice remained buried in her throat. She didn't dare even glance at Min.

When they arrived home, Daddy held Mindy's arm as she hobbled up the steps and into the house. Amber went to the bedroom the girls usually shared while Daddy helped Min lie down on the couch. There even seemed to be a sadness shrouding the few belongings the two of them shared—the dolls that sat on the shelf and bureau. The few perfume bottles they collected on the dresser. The clothes hanging limp in the closet. Their possessions looked wilted, as if they were all dull and dusty.

It was maybe an hour later—after Mama and Daddy left to go to the store—that Mindy called out to her. "Amber— come talk to me. . . ."

Amber scrambled down the stairs and ran to the living room. "Are you okay, Min?"

Mindy shook her head. "Guess what . . . I have cancer."

Fear thudded in Amber's heart. "No, you do not!"

"I do."

"I'm going to ask Mama!"

"You can't. She doesn't know I heard about it."

"What?"

"After the doctor touched my hip and did all these tests

that really hurt, he took Mama and Daddy out in the hall. But I went and listened at the door. I put my ear right on it."

"And he said you have cancer?"

"First he said another long word. I couldn't hear it very good. Then Mama asked if that was cancer, and he said yes."

"Oh, Min . . . what's going to happen to you?"

"I don't know—" Mindy's face crumpled the way it did the day at the skating rink. Amber rushed over to hug her sister.

"Does it hurt now?" she asked.

Min burst into tears. "It hurts all the time. In my hip . . ."

That night, after everyone else was asleep, Amber sat at the kitchen table. Glancing around to see that no one was looking, she turned on a flashlight and picked up her pen to write to her brother.

March 8, 1961

Dear Brent,
    I wish your leave was next week. I'm really worried about Mindy. What can I do? Mama and Daddy didn't even tell me . . . but Mindy found out she has cancer! Please try to come home quick. We all love you and miss you.

                                        Love,
                                        Amber

Chapter Two

Over the next months Mindy seemed determined to fight for her old life as long as she could. Amber helped her sister dress in the mornings. If they rushed, they could leave earlier for school, in case Mindy was in pain and needed to rest along the way. But even if they left twenty minutes earlier for school, they were almost always late. The Mindy who used to skip and run and jump on the way to school now dragged her leg, one step at a time. The walk from their house to the corner seemed endless, but Amber walked patiently beside Mindy, commenting on the weather and on what would happen at school. Amber knew her sister's leg hurt more and more, even though Mindy seemed determined to make her illness go away simply by not mentioning it. The two of them never went back to the skating rink, even to watch. The two tried to pretend that Mindy's illness happened to someone else, and their own lives were still as uneventful as they always remembered.

Then it was April. Amber slid her dress over her head, combed her hair, and turned to wake Mindy. Somehow a feeling of dread filled her this morning, although Mindy's oval face looked as peaceful as always as she lay on her pillow.

"Min!" Amber shook her sister's shoulder. "Time to get up for school."

Mindy stretched her arms, turned over in bed, and gasped. "Oh . . ." Pain echoed in her voice.

"We only have fifteen minutes," Amber continued, vigorously brushing her long blond hair, although a shiver of fear filled her.

"Amber—" Terror in Mindy's tone made her sister turn. "I can't go to school today."

Amber said, "I'll help you. Don't worry."

"I can't even turn over. It hurts so bad."

"Can I get you a pill?"

Mindy shuddered, struggled to turn on her side to look at her sister. "Get me my pill—but then you go on to school. I can't make it today."

Now a torrent of anguish rushed through Amber. "You'd better try, don't you think? What will the doctor say if you can't go?" Worries raged inside Amber. What did this mean? If she waited long enough, could Min get out of bed and go to school with her?

"I want to, but I can't. Maybe the doctor can help me. I'll go with you tomorrow."

"I can't leave you here. I won't even think about my schoolwork if I know you're still in bed."

"Mama's home, she'll take care of me. You get going now."

Amber sighed and finished dressing. Her clothes felt limp against her skin. The front door seemed to close with a sad groan. She didn't hurry along the streets the way she and Mindy used to before Min got sick. Instead, Amber sauntered slowly, as if Mindy were somehow still beside her. What should she do? Could she have waited for Min's pill to work? Guilt and sadness hovered as she walked the familiar streets.

Mindy never made it to school that day, or the next. The doctor admitted her to the hospital, saying she might need surgery. Amber battled the helpless panic that rose inside her. A year ago Min could skate faster, run harder, and even laugh louder than she did.

Amber forced herself to go to school daily. Yet as soon as she was there, her mind began to drift. All of the homework, grades, and after-school clubs seemed trivial and useless in light of the fact that Mindy was so sick. Amber dragged herself through her seemingly endless days, doing enough schoolwork to get by, although her mind was scarcely on her studies.

The morning that turned out to be one of the darkest days of her life began with a gray, cloud-filled rainstorm that poured buckets on the neighborhood streets. Clasping a plastic rain hat to her head with a hand, Amber dashed through the rain, mindless of whether or not she was on time. The schoolyard, as she approached, was strangely empty. A surge of worry filled Amber with the knowledge that she was late for school, an event that rarely happened to her, even when she walked slow to wait for Mindy. Her wet shoes dripped on the silent floors as she rushed down the halls as noiselessly as she could. Whipping the plastic hat from her head, she eased into her desk at the back of the science classroom. Mr. Staker, the science teacher, was the meanest man she'd ever met. Everyone said the only way to survive his class was to be as invisible as possible. The single hope of avoiding his venom was simply to not call attention to yourself in front of him. Heart thudding rapidly, Amber waited for her breath to ease.

Suddenly she blinked. Why was Mr. Staker looking at her? She wasn't laughing with the girl next to her. Or looking out the window. Or talking. Her assignment paper was finished and placed neatly on the desk in front of her. She held her breath as Mr. Staker walked up to her desk with a big gray tub that looked like a bucket for washing dishes.

He slammed the rectangular tub on her desk. Something heavy inside it shifted.

"This is for you," he said. "Because you're the last student to arrive today."

Her hands trembled in her lap. Amber shook her head slightly.

"Are you saying no to me?"

She sat still. Her eyes closed quickly. Then her voice quavered, "I don't know what that is."

"It's yours. You'll take this apart while all the rest of us watch you. . . ."

Amber slid her chair back and stood. She leaned to peer over the edge. There was a dead cat inside the tub. Big, black, and furry. She shrieked and clapped her hands over her mouth. "Please . . . I love animals. . . . I can't do it," she whispered, shaking her head and shuddering.

"Oh, yes you can," Mr. Staker said menacingly. As she watched, he leaned and pried the cat's eyelid with his fingers. There was a sickening blip before Amber glimpsed a dead yellow eye. Lip quivering, she stood stock-still. Then, as Mr. Staker lifted the tub closer to her face, she knocked her chair aside, screamed, and ran to the back of the classroom.

Mr. Staker's voice thundered, "Get back here!"

Shaking all over, Amber walked, step by step, back to her desk. "Please, sir . . . I love animals. . . ."

"Then you'll know how to find this animal's heart for us, won't you?"

Amber let her eyes drift to the cat in the tub. Her stomach lurched at even the thought of touching its motionless fur. There was no way she could make herself take one more step closer to the plastic tub. But it was even more scary to say no to Mr. Staker. She never talked back to a teacher in her life.

Now Mr. Staker held up a silver knife. Was it called a scalpel? "This is for you to use. . . ." he taunted.

Amber's chin trembled. A tear stung the corner of her eye. She looked down, and her words were almost inaudible. "I won't," she half-whispered.

"I'm afraid you will. . . ."

Mr. Staker lifted the dead cat out of the tub and held it out to her. Fur brushed her skin. She screamed and, gulping a deep breath, she turned and ran out of the classroom, out of the school, across the schoolyard to the street. She stood at the curb, and a sob escaped her throat. Tears ran down her cheeks. Though the rain had stopped, wind yanked her skirt and hair as cars drove by on the street in front of her.

She closed her eyes, counted to twenty, and listened to herself breathe.

Suddenly a car horn blared. Amber's eyes flew open.

"What's the matter, honey? Are you sick?" It was her next door neighbor, Mrs. Rand.

Embarrassed, Amber shook her head. "No," her voice still quavered. "I'm all right."

"You can't stand out here in the street. Are you waiting for someone?"

Amber waited. "No . . . just standing here. . . ."

Mrs. Rand tilted her head. "You look pale. Are you sick or something?"

Amber nodded, gulping. Words burst out of her. "I can't go back." Her lip quivered at the thought. "Mr. Staker . . . he wanted me to cut open a dead cat. I can't do it."

Mrs. Rand shook her head, stared at the sky. "Why they don't fire that man, I'll never know. But you can't just stand here. I'll take you home."

"No." Amber shook her head again. "If you take me home, my mom will make me come back."

"Won't she let you stay home today?" Mrs. Rand's voice was gentle.

"I left my book on the desk. She'd make me come back to get that."

"Well . . ." Mrs. Rand turned to her husband, whispered something. She smiled at Amber. "I'll tell you what. We're going to the drugstore for lunch. Why don't you come with us? That way your mom won't get mad, and you can have a rest."

Limp with relief, Amber climbed inside the Rands' car. Safe and away from Mr. Staker, she stared out the window. Scenes slid by—the school, the houses she passed on her morning walk every day. She began to relax. The warm car seat felt comforting at her back.

Mr. Rand turned in at Mount Jordan Pharmacy. Amber had been here only a few times—she always thought it was too far from home. It took more than half an hour to walk here. She knew the store had a big penny candy section that she loved when she was little. You could get bubble gum for a penny, or a Reese's Peanut Butter Cup for five cents.

The air inside the drugstore smelled like heaven. Perfume, bubble bath, pressed powder. Amber followed Mr. and Mrs. Rand past the cosmetics and the prescription counter to one of the three booths in the back. She fell in a heap on the pillowy, red leather booth.

Mrs. Rand smiled at her. "We usually get the grilled cheese

sandwich. With a root-beer float. Does that sound good to you?"

Amber nodded.

Moments later a waitress handed her a paper-covered straw and a parfait glass filled with fizzy root beer and topped with a rounded scoop of ice cream. Amber dived in, eating the warm sandwich and sweet ice cream without a word or a look at the Rands. As she dipped her spoon into the last drops of the float, fear struck her again. Where would she go now? She couldn't go home and she couldn't go back to school.

"Are you finished?" Mrs. Rand asked gently.

Amber stuck her straw in again, drew on it frantically. But it only vibrated against the bottom of the soda glass. She was staring up at the whirling ceiling fan when she suddenly caught sight of the sign on the front window. Even though the lettering was backward from where she looked, the words seemed to call out to her. HELP WANTED. INQUIRE WITHIN.

"You can leave me here," she said suddenly. "There's something I need to do."

"Oh, no. I couldn't do that. I didn't even ask your mom before I brought you here." Mrs. Rand said quickly. "You probably need to go back to school. Or home. Do you know how long it would take to walk from here?"

"Maybe a half hour. I can make it. I need to stay so I can apply for that job." Amber pointed in the direction of the sign.

Mrs. Rand looked at her. "I feel like I should take you back. I brought you here."

"No—really. I'm okay. Thanks for the lunch. But I can't make you wait."

Mrs. Rand shook her head. Moments later she reached in her purse and took out a dime. "Talk to them about the job. And if you need me to come back and pick you up, I will."

Amber watched the Rands walk out of the drugstore. At the last moment, Mrs. Rand turned and looked at her sympathetically. With a questioning glance, she gestured for Amber to come with them. Amber shook her head. She sat for a long time before she dared leave the booth. She thought about walking out of the store a million times before she approached the girl behind the candy counter.

Could she really do this? Her tongue seemed stuck to the roof of her mouth.

"May I help you?" the girl asked.

Amber didn't answer.

"Do you want some candy?"

"No . . ." Amber said as quickly as she could. "I want the job."

The girl frowned. "Oh! The job here? You'll have to talk to Mr. Sorensen about that."

"Is he here?"

The girl stared into Amber's face for a moment. "I'll get him." She gestured with her chin. "Go sit in the booth."

Waiting for Mr. Sorensen, Amber realized that her hair probably wasn't combed, and her mascara might be smudged, and she wasn't wearing the Sunday dress and gold necklace that she'd wear if she'd set out to apply for a job. But there was no turning back now.

Moments later a balding man with a mustache and glasses sat across from her. He wore a white lab coat as if he were a doctor.

"Clair says you wished to speak with me?" Amber felt as if he were the father of one of her friends. There was definitely the feeling of an adult addressing a child.

"Yes. I want to apply for the job."

"This isn't an after-school job. It's day shifts."

"I need to work days."

The man pursed his lips, then looked at her again. "The hours when I need someone to work would be the time you are in school."

"I quit school. I'm not going back."

"But I would encourage you to go back. You can work all of your life. Finish school now. When you are young."

Amber swallowed. "My family needs me to work. My sister is very sick—she has cancer. My brother is in the army. I am the only one who can work."

"Are you saying your family needs the money?"

Amber nodded.

"I should probably tell you that this is hard work. Especially during the lunch hour. You have to stand on your feet a long time. Do you know how to cook?"

"I have to take care of my sister. Sometimes I cook for her. She's sick in bed."

"Won't your family need you at home?"

"They would want me to work or go to school."

"I need someone on that soda fountain—three thirty-five an hour. But I have to hire someone who wants to stay here and work. I can't have you work a week or two, then decide that school is more fun after all."

"I won't. I promise." Under the table Amber crossed her fingers and pressed her legs together, willing Mr. Sorensen to say yes.

He stared into her face for a long moment. Then he sighed. "I'll let you fill out the application."

He left for a moment, then returned with a long white paper. Though she felt a twinge of anxiousness, when Mr. Sorensen handed it to her she soon saw that the job application wasn't anywhere near as hard as anything in school. Her name. Her address. She even had her Social Security number in her wallet. The back of the paper was filled with spaces where she should list where she worked before. This would be her first job—so she left that part blank. She signed her signature at the bottom and walked to where Mr. Sorenson now stood behind the pill counter.

"I'm finished," she said quietly.

She watched as he read what she wrote. He turned the paper over, saw the back was blank, and turned it to the front again.

He looked up at her with a frown, as if something made him slightly angry. "This isn't just a joke, is it? You really mean this. You're not going back to school," he said accusingly.

"No—I told you—I can't." She swallowed hard, then told him about Mr. Staker.

He shook his head. "I would think you could just ask to be transferred to another class."

"He's the only science teacher this year. I have to have science."

"There is night school. I hate to see anyone quit. But I'll hire you—if you promise to give me a year, at least."

"I promise." Amber unconsciously held her hand up, as if swearing before a judge.

Mr. Sorensen nodded, looked away. "You can start tomorrow if you want. Or you can wait till Monday. Beginning of the pay period."

"Tomorrow's fine. What do I wear?"

"Uniform's not required. Levi's are fine. If, by any chance, you get promoted to the candy counter, then you wear a dress."

"I've got Levi's," said Amber. For the first time a smile crept onto her face. Mr. Sorensen reached across the counter and shook her hand. "See you in the morning," he said with a nod of his chin. When Amber walked out of the store, she glanced back to see that he was still looking at her.

Days passed. Amber dressed in the morning and left at the same time she always left to go to school. Her workday lasted longer than her schooldays did before, but she kept telling her parents that she stopped at a friend's house on the way home.

Yet after a week passed, Amber sensed a thin feeling of dread as she walked up the steps to her front porch. With her hand on the cool front doorknob, she hesitated, feeling an uncharacteristic urge to turn and run. Instead, she quickly opened the front door and scurried into her bedroom. She closed the door and released a long sigh.

"Get out here, young lady!"

Daddy didn't yell like that very often. The words brought chills to her spine, paralyzing her with fear as she sat on the bed.

"I said, get out here now!"

Shaking with fear, Amber slowly walked to the kitchen, where her parents sat at the table with worried looks on their faces.

"Sit down!" Her father pointed to a chair, his finger stabbing the air like a knife.

Amber sat. Chills rushed down her back and legs. "I— should have told you—"

"You lied to us," her mother said suddenly, her words accompanied by her father's furious nod.

"No—I just didn't get to tell—" Amber started.

"You pretended to go to school every day, but they called today and told us you haven't been there—*for a week*," her mother said. "They said they'll let you back in with a note. But what on earth am I going to say—that you lied and played hooky for a whole week?"

Amber breathed. She glanced at the frowning faces before her gaze fell to the floor. "You'll tell them I quit school and I now have a job."

"What?" Her mother's angry face moved closer.

"I'm sorry—but I had to quit," Amber said, furious at her lower lip for quivering at this crucial moment.

"We never said you could do any such thing, young lady." Her father's face leaned in to hers. "And you lied about it, to boot."

Buckets of tears suddenly flooded onto her cheeks. "There wasn't time to tell you . . . I had to run out of the room."

Her father shook his head. "We'll do everything to get you back in—but you've missed five days of classwork! You probably got all F's."

Amber shuddered. "I don't care if I get F's—I can't dissect a cat. . . . I love animals and he said I had to cut that cat in pieces," she said plaintively.

"We'll just write a note," her mother said, shaking her head. "We'll ask that you be excused from that—"

Amber's head shook furiously. "You don't know Mr. Staker. He'll take it out on me some other way . . . especially if you try to get me out of doing what he says. He's the meanest man on earth," she said, finally lifting her eyes to meet her parents' angry scowls.

"Oh, come on—there are other teachers. We'll get you transferred," her father argued.

"Not for science. He's the only one . . . I'm stuck."

"We'll talk to the principal . . . I'll go to the school district if I have to," her father insisted.

"He'll still be mean to me—" Amber insisted.

"You're going back if I get you out of that class," her father insisted, jabbing her shoulder with his finger.

Amber couldn't reply. When her knees began to shake and a fresh wave of tears threatened, she ran in her room. She didn't speak to her parents the rest of the day. And as more days passed, the issue wasn't discussed. She kept working at the pharmacy and didn't dare ask if her father ever talked to the school district.

Chapter Three

The delicious smell and warm, quiet air in the soda fountain always soothed Amber's nerves. In the mornings she pretended that the fountain was her own kitchen and made sure that every counter and dish was spotless and shining. She was busy at noon, when the people who worked in the town offices had their lunch hour, and at four-thirty, when some of them wanted a Coke before going home. A few kids came in after school, but most of them only had a nickel for a piece of candy, rather than twenty-five cents for a Coke or thirty-five cents for a root-beer float. The sameness of the days felt peaceful to her. She knew what to expect when she walked in to work. She thought she could stay here the rest of her life.

Amber swelled with pride the day she received her first paycheck after working one week. Walking up the steps and onto the front porch, she held her breath. What could she say to Mama and Daddy? Her throat closed and tears threatened as she saw Mama folding Mindy's laundry—nightgowns, sheets, underwear. The weight of Mindy's illness on Mama suddenly touched Amber's heart. And it had been so long since she herself did something she thought Mama would approve of.

"Mama?" The word struggled from her throat.

Her mother looked up, caught sight of Amber's quivering

jaw. "What's the matter?" she asked, concern furrowing her brow.

"I got this today—" Amber clumsily held out the check for $47.50 clutched in her fist. She looked down at the floor, then felt her mother gently ease the check from her clenched fingers.

She saw Mama's throat move, and she watched as her mother wiped her eyes. It was a moment before she could speak. "Not all of it, Amber," she said, seconds later. "You earned this money. At least a share of it belongs to you." Mama held the check in her hand a moment. Then she reached in her purse and pressed a ten and a five in Amber's hand. Fifteen dollars.

The next day Amber went to Auerbach's, the department store next to the pharmacy. What did she want to buy? Jewelry, dresses, sheer hose, fancy candies. . . . Her eyes drank in the majesty of the window display. She turned. Wallets, purses, leather boots. Seconds later her eyes settled on a watch with a shiny black band. Abruptly she thought of Min. With a lump in her throat, she walked to the counter.

"I would like to buy two of those watches," she said, pointing.

"Two? Both for yourself? One for day and one for night?" The clerk grinned and laughed at her own joke.

"No—one for me and one for my sister . . ."

"Gift wrap the one for your sister? Only fifty cents more."

How much did the watches cost? How could she forget to look? Didn't she learn anything working with the cash register next door? Amber swallowed. "How much altogether?"

"Twenty-two fifty."

"Oh . . ." How could she admit she didn't look at the price? Slowly Amber took out her wallet and opened the flap. Her money didn't grow overnight. There was still just one ten and one five. "I guess I'd better wait. . . ." she said slowly.

She looked up to see the clerk peering into her wallet. "Do you know about layaway? You could put five down on each watch, then pay on it later."

Amber breathed. "Okay," she said quickly, exhaling with relief. She really did want to buy a watch for Min.

Soon there were lots of items on layaway. The watches. Two navy blue skirts. Two gold bracelets. When her paycheck came, she gave most of it to Mama, then headed for the store.

One night, after work, her mother handed her two letters. "Both from Brent?" Amber asked. Although she recognized her brother's familiar handwriting on the first letter, the second was completely unfamiliar to her. Who else would write her a letter? Could it be from the school? Did they want her to pay for the book she left on the desk? Amber timidly reached for the envelopes. The second letter didn't look like a school letter. The paper was the thinnest she ever felt, and light blue rather than white. It looked like another Army letter—but who besides Brent would write to her? She read words written on the envelope. A Troop—10 Cavalry. 2 Rean. Sqdn. APO 7. West Palm Beach, Florida.

She opened the letter and began to read:

May 10, 1961

Dear Sis,

Your brother, Brent, gave me your address, but not your name. He's my bunk mate. And my buddy. We've been here together three weeks now. He showed me your picture the other night. You were standing on the porch in the picture. (I hope I'm writing to the right person.) He said you like to skate. I do, too. He told me you work at a soda fountain. That sounds like fun to me. I haven't seen a soda fountain in at least two months. He said you help take care of your sister who's sick. I don't know what else to say. I've been in the service six months, and I'm stationed here in Florida with Brent. It's warm here—lots of sunshine. We only had to wear our jackets one night. We may be shipped off to Korea together sometime. Write back if you want.

Brent's buddy,
Ray (well, Raymond actually) Williams

She opened Brent's letter.

May 11, 1961

Dear Amber,
  Sorry to hear you quit school. If I could, I would yell at that teacher for treating my sister like that. Who does he think he is? If there's anything I can do when I get there, I will. I'll be coming home on leave, and might bring my friend Ray with me. He asked if he could write to you. I hope you don't mind.

See you soon.
Love, Brent

The next day, when the lunch rush settled down, Amber read the letter from Ray again and again. How long was it since someone asked how she was? How long was it since someone sent her a letter? A warm, soothing feeling settled around her heart as she reread the words. She smoothed the thin, folded paper, slid the letter back in the envelope, and put it in her purse, where she knew she could take it out to read the next day on her break.

Three days later, pen poised against her notebook on top of the counter, Amber started to write:

May 14, 1961

Dear Ray,
  I received your letter. Be nice to Brent, even if he is a pest. He can drive anybody nuts once in a while. He still teases me all the time. And he beats me at cards, too. Yes, I like to skate. There's a rink by our house that has music and one of those mirror balls that make flashing lights across the rink. I can twirl and go backward. Did Brent tell you I had to quit school? You can ask him about it sometime. It was bad news. And I do work in a soda fountain. If I could, I would make you and Brent a root-beer float and a grilled cheese sandwich and send it special delivery to Florida.

Brent's kid sister,
Amber

She didn't know if she would ever hear from him again.
Then another letter came . . . and another. Soon Amber looked
forward to getting a letter every week. In the letters Ray told
her how hot it was in Florida, about his days as a private,
and what Brent was doing. They wrote more letters. They
talked about radio and TV shows . . . Bob Hope, *The Roy
Rogers Show, Father Knows Best, The Jack Benny Show,* "I
am the only one who can work," she wrote. "My sister, Min,
is in a wheelchair now." She smiled and wrote, "And you
know where my brother, Brent, is." After that, he sent her
thick letters with pictures—he and Brent standing at attention;
another with them posed before a tank; and another with the
two of them seated inside a barracks.

Then, for three weeks, she didn't get a letter. Finally, a
letter arrived that said Headquarters at the top.

November 30, 1961

Dear Amber,
   *Sorry I didn't write sooner, but have been waiting to
see if orders would come in. They finally did. I report
the twentieth of December at Oakland, California, so
Brent and I should be back to visit you around the nine-
teenth or twentieth of November. If you are free on one
of those nights, I'm asking you out on a date. I am
going to the 44th unit, north of Seoul, Korea. Well, I
am going to close and think about seeing you soon.*
                                        Your pen-pal buddy,
                                                  Ray

P.S. Everyone calls me R. J.

Chapter Four

Amber hoped her slip strap didn't show as she nervously adjusted the sleeve of her white piqué summer dress. Would R. J. guess that this was her first date?

"What's taking you so long? Our unit would ship out and leave us at Fort Sill if we dilly-dallied like you!" Brent shouted up the stairs. It felt so good to hear his voice in the house again, even if he was teasing her. Seconds later she heard Brent's familiar giggle along with another natural, boyish laugh. Amber took one more look at her long blond hair and the white dress. She held her breath, smiled at herself in the mirror, and turned to walk downstairs.

She flushed to see Brent and R. J. staring up the stairs to watch her descend. Peggy, Brent's girlfriend, struggled to stifle a yawn. Did I really take that long? Amber wondered. Her nervousness reached a new height before R. J.'s warm, ear-to-ear grin made her instantly grin back. When she reached the bottom of the steps, he took her hand.

"Nice to meet you." He nodded.

"You, too," Amber managed. She felt tongue-tied with shy nervousness. But as they drove out of town and onto the Maryland expressway, she somehow found the courage to ask, "Where are we going?"

"D.C.," R. J. said. He raised his eyebrows at her. "Your brother has the key to the White House—"

Laughter from Peggy and Brent in the front seat. "The FBI's out to get R. J.," Brent called back.

They ended up at the Washington Monument. R. J. held her hand as they walked up what seemed like thousands of steps. When she was out of breath, he stopped and waited. "So can I see this famous soda fountain sometime?"

"Sure," she said, "I'll make you a root-beer float."

"It might be pretty late when we get done here. How about another date tomorrow?" He smiled, reddening her cheeks again.

Moments later, peering out over the panoramic view of the nation's capital for the first time in her life, she felt relaxed as R. J. pointed out landmark after landmark, his hand on her shoulder to guide her. "That over there—that's the National Mall, with the Lincoln Memorial and the one for Jefferson—"

It could be boring, she thought, to listen to someone quietly relate facts about historic sights, but his voice was so soothing, so calming, making her feel that everything was going to be all right. How long was it since she last felt as if life was okay? Not since Mindy got sick. Not since she left school.

The next night they played cards at her house. Hi-Lo, Rich Merchant, Steal a Pile, Hearts. R. J. was the kind of card-player who remembered every card each player played. "That ought to be about your last spade, there, girl," he said once, with a wink that gave her chills. "We'd better watch out, fellas, or Amber's gonna shoot the moon."

Two games later she did just that. Why did it feel this good just to win a card game? A card game shouldn't make her heart rise like this. But was that all this feeling was?

At about ten o'clock, after the last game of Razzle Dazzle, she took his hand gingerly and, along with Brent and Peggy, led him up the back stairs to meet Mindy.

"Hello, Miss Mindy," he said, just as if they were meeting at a restaurant or at least in the living room. It was as if he couldn't feel that Mindy's room was hot and stuffy, and didn't notice that Mindy was dressed in a flannel nightgown with her hair disheveled.

"Hi," said Mindy, with a puzzled look and a trace of her old smile. "Who are you?"

"R. J. Williams, at your service. In the service, too. Home on leave just to beat this sister of yours at cards."

Min giggled. "It's fun to beat Amber. She cries when I win—"

"When I was seven years old!" Amber spat back, mortified.

R. J. laughed. "I better let her win next time." Amber was surprised to feel a tear on her cheek as he grinned at Mindy.

But then all four of them sat in the chairs around Mindy's bed and talked for a long time. Amber sensed she hadn't felt this happy in months, if not years. The next night they went to a movie. But that Friday R. J. and Brent wanted to go to the skating rink. Amber felt chills. Just the thought of the skating rink brought memories of the night Mindy fell.

"I can't go skating," Amber said quietly.

"Why not?" R. J.'s grin again. "You can't kid me. Brent already told me you're a good skater."

Amber paused. "I haven't been for a while."

"Then it's time to give it another shot. I need someone to pick me up when I fall on my face." Another great grin.

"After Mindy got hurt there, I can't make myself go back. I'm not ready yet. Sorry."

Brent shook his head in frustration. He looked at her as if she were insane. "Amber—don't act dumb. It wasn't the rink's fault that Mindy fell."

"I know—I just feel . . . strange . . . going without her."

"Tell you what, Amber. I'll go upstairs right now and ask her if it's all right with her if you skate—"

"No!" She didn't mean to raise her voice. But the last thing she wanted was to remind Mindy of that horrible night. So when R. J. squeezed her fingers and led her out to the car, she went along silently.

Skating with R. J. was completely different from skating with Min—more exciting in a scary way. R. J. wasn't a graceful skater—but he was fearless. He took her hand and the two of them sped down the middle of the rink, her heart in her throat. "Help—we're going to crash!" she shouted. But R. J. just angled in front of her, letting his body ram against the rail before he sat down hard.

Amber battled a laugh, at the same time imagining the pain he felt. "Are you okay?"

He looked up at her, made a cross-eyed face. "Let's do it again. Race you this time. On your mark, get set, go!"

R. J. was faster. Amber glided as speedily as she could to try to catch up, but he remained ahead. Then, just as he reached to grab the rail, he tripped and sprawled across the ice. Giggling, Amber surged past him and gripped the iron bar with her fingers.

"I win!" She watched him pull himself up from the floor. "You're going to be sore tomorrow."

"But you won't see me—will you—" He made another face at her. Her smile froze, and she was surprised at the powerful regret she felt. He was right. Tonight was their last date, maybe forever. All the rest of the night, her feet were on the rink but her mind was on the growing understanding that she didn't want to see him leave.

As her parents dropped Brent and R. J. off at the airport the next day, Amber felt a helpless sadness, knowing that both of them were going so far away, seemingly farther than her imagination could reach. She watched as they walked slowly up the airplane steps, the sight of their green army jackets finally disappearing as they stepped inside the silver plane. When she could no longer see R. J., Amber felt tired and alone. Both she and her parents were silent as they walked to the airport parking lot. The absence of Brent and R. J.'s spirited energy and high-intensity laughter made the silence around them feel barren and sad.

But there were his letters. They continued to arrive, and Amber kept writing back. R. J. continued to send photos— of helicopters, tanks, and jeeps, of R. J. and Brent in uniforms, of places where they were stationed that seemed to contain bare expanses of land and barracks buildings. One thick envelope also felt heavy, yet bendable, puzzling her until she opened it to discover a yellow and green shoulder patch with a black stripe. "This is just like mine—wear it on your swimsuit—ha ha," R. J. wrote. She was surprised to feel a stab of jealousy when she opened one letter and found a photo of a Korean woman. A flood of relief filled her to learn that this woman was just a townsperson he and Brent met. Her relief grew even more when R. J. described the woman's husband and children. Then Amber almost laughed at herself—why should she worry so much what R. J. was doing? There was lots more in her life to think about. There was Min, who seemed to dwindle day by day, spending more hours in bed and lying still once she was there. And Mama, whose despair seemed to almost overtake all of them, as if they shouldn't have any other life past watching Min grow weak. And there was work—Mr. Sorensen hinted that she was doing a good job. He said that when the night candy counter girl went away to college, there might be hope of a promotion.

Mindy was rushed to the hospital one night when the pain in her leg and hip grew unbearable and she cried out with anguish. After sitting in the sad and scary vigil at Mindy's hospital bedside with her parents, Amber somehow forced herself through a nine-hour day at work. Now every muscle in her body screamed with exhaustion. Her legs, shoulders, and back ached. But the sight of another letter waiting for her when she came home made her forget her aching joints and burning eyes. She lay on the bed, relishing a few moments alone before dinner. Her finger eased under the usual pale blue envelope flap. She slid out the letter, unfolded its pages. R. J. always wrote with a cartridge pen with royal blue ink. Now even the ink color and pale blue stationery were like familiar friends, along with the hurried loops and enthusiastically crossed *t*'s that seemed as much a part of him as the words he wrote.

There was the date at the top, like always. And his address—an unfamiliar combination of words and numbers. APO 75. First Army Cav Div. And below that, in R. J.'s familiar handwriting, was a new salutation that made her gasp.

August 8, 1961

"To My Future Wife," the letter began.

My future wife? The words brought self-conscious chills to Amber's spine. What did this mean? She gripped the letter tight between her fingers and began to read.

Was good to hear from you. Hear you have been having quite a bit of hot weather in the states. Brent and I have been getting quite a bit of field duty lately and are due to go again in two more days. You better take it easy during all that hot weather.

Weather? Field duty? Was this what you wrote about once you decided someone was the girl you were supposed to marry? Amber plowed through the letter again, searching for anything that might give a hint as to why he thought of her as his future wife. There. At the end. He signed the letter *"Love, R. J."* instead of "Yours sincerely," or "As ever." But what did that tell her? Nothing. And what should she write back now?

There was no way she was going to write *"To My Future Husband."* She didn't know what she felt, what she wanted him to be. She stared at the stationery a long time before she simply wrote, *Dear R. J.*, like always.

August 10, 1961

Thank you for your letter. I have good news. Mr. Sorensen says I might get promoted to the candy counter someday. When you and Brent come back on leave I could sell you a pack of Lifesavers, or even a box of chocolates. Yes, it is hot here. But the pharmacy is air-conditioned. Let's play cards again when you come to visit. Maybe I'll win—ha!

Amber paused. This letter was awfully short. Should she say something else about the hot weather? About Mindy? Hmm. She left the letter on her bed, went downstairs, ate dinner, and washed a sinkful of dishes. She ironed her blouse for the next day. Then she read the letter again.

An odd feeling like embarrassment filled her as she picked up her pen. She wanted to write "I miss you." Or even "No one else has ever told me I was his future wife." But all of it seemed like too much to say. So finally, summoning all the courage in her being, she simply wrote, "Love, Amber" and folded the letter and slid it in the envelope before she could reconsider. Then she walked to the mailbox instantly—before any doubts could rest in her mind. Once the letter was pushed through the slot, she found some comfort in the knowledge that there was no way she could get it back.

Chapter Five

Mindy was getting sicker; when she finally came home from the hospital, she was weak, pale and a shadow of her former self. This gave Amber little time to think about the fact that R. J. hadn't responded to her last letter. Even as she worried about her sister, Amber wondered what she had done wrong with R. J. Should she have said something about being a future wife? She didn't feel like she could be anyone's wife yet.

Finally a letter arrived. Amber didn't want to read it in front of anyone at work, so she waited to open it until right before she went to bed.

There it was again:

August 31, 1961

To My Future Wife,
   Sorry to take so long to get back to you. I will write to you now that I have stopped traveling for a while. We stopped at Honolulu, Wake Island, and Tachakawa, Japan. I haven't seen much of Korea yet, but will get guard duty about twice a week here. I am waiting to be assigned a job. I was happy that you might get a promotion. Yes, please do save me a seat to play cards with you on our next visit.

Love,
R. J.

She wrote again, and again, now that the letters resumed every week. Neither of them said anything about him calling her his wife. After a while, she decided that maybe R. J. was making a joke, although try as she might, she couldn't find humor in the possibility that they might someday be married. Instead, there was a warm tenderness surrounding her heart with the understanding that this happy, fun, and handsome young man might consider her someone with whom he wanted to spend his life.

The day started with the same serenity she always felt in the pharmacy. There was the soothing calmness of knowing where everything was—the spoons and glasses, the paper placemats, the bottles of root beer, Coke, and 7-Up. She loved the view as the sun rose and poured over the counter in a rounded arc, and the approaching sunset that draped the store with dusty pink when it was nearly time to go home.

There were five customers waiting for lunch right now. The first was Mr. Allen, who owned the electrical supply store, always wore a hat, and read his newspaper while he ate a sandwich and drank a root beer. Two other men in suits sat two stools down from him, discussing business investments, and a woman and her little girl talked happily about the tuna melts they waited for. Then Mr. Sorensen leaned out, gave her the quick grin and nod that told her he was ready for his own lunch. She was just spearing his grilled cheese sandwich with a toothpick when she heard someone laughing outside. The laughter continued as the front door to the pharmacy opened.

"Hey, Amber," she heard an unfamiliar voice call out as she dribbled potato chips onto a plate and handed Mr. Sorensen his sandwich. The next sound was unmistakable. The squeak of wheelchair wheels angling around a corner. Then the same fluid rolling sound she heard on the hardwood floor at home. It sounded like Min—but there was absolutely no way Min could be here.

Thinking her brain was confused, Amber shook her head and focused her gaze on the cheese on the two tuna melts on the grill. She had to capture the moment exactly. Melt the cheese as thin as it could melt before it dribbled off the sandwiches and onto the grill, where it sizzled and burned.

"Amber!" The voice was louder now. As she topped the two bubbling sandwiches with bread, Amber stole a quick look back. Her eyes widened in startled surprise. It *was* Min, sitting up and smiling in her wheelchair, her friend Stacy standing by her. Min's grin was broad, her hair was combed, and her cheeks were pinker than Amber had seen them in a long time. She wanted to capture and save the moment in some way. For just a few seconds it was as if she went back in time, and Min was her old self again.

Then Mr. Allen cleared his throat, folded his newspaper on the counter. "My sandwich please? And a straw?"

"Min! What are you doing here?" Amber placed Mr. Allen's sandwich in front of him, reached across to the other side of the counter for a straw, keeping her eyes on her sister. "How did you get here? Do you know how far this is from home?"

Min's eyes shone with pride. "Stacy walked me—the whole way. Took us an hour. She pushed my chair." Min beamed.

"Ma'am, I'm afraid the bottom of our tuna melts are about to burn." The woman tapped Amber's arm, smiling patronizingly.

"One moment, ma'am." Amber turned back to the grill.

"Another root beer please," said Mr. Allen.

"Amber," Mr. Sorensen's authoritative voice called. "There isn't a pickle on this sandwich today."

She scooped the tuna melts onto plates, dipped into the pickle bottle, rushed for the root beer.

"Amber, you have to read this letter! Right now!" Min was still smiling.

"I can't—look how busy I am."

"My daughter and I need straws," said the woman with the condescending smile.

"Excuse me. We were here before you, ma'am," said one of the two men in suits. "Our roast beef?"

Amber rushed.

"I just know this letter is really important," said Min.

Amber glanced up to see Min waving a blue envelope. A letter from R. J. The envelope did look thicker than usual—

probably more pictures. "I can't read it now," she said help-lessly, piling up roast beef on the bread, making the sand-wiches.

"I came all the way down here. It says 'personal' on the envelope. And there's something sticking out."

Amber shrugged. "What can I do? I'm sorry you came all this way, but—" Two new customers sat at the counter and ordered hamburgers. Amber pummeled the meat, placed the patties on the sizzling grill.

"Just open it quick, please. . . ." Min's voice sounded the way it used to when she was the little sister asking Amber to play checkers or watch cartoons.

Amber wiped off her hands, held them out for the letter.

By now everyone at the counter was watching. What could be inside this envelope? Although Amber wiped her greasy fingers a second time on the dishtowel, somehow the letter was still unwieldy in her hands. She tore off the end of the envelope. As she eased the letter out and unfolded the paper sheets, something slipped from inside. A gold ring with a small, yet incredibly sparkly diamond slid out of the envelope and fell to the floor. Suddenly the restaurant got quiet. To Amber, it seemed like everyone in the world heard the ring hit the linoleum with a thin metallic clink.

"Oh . . ." Amber gasped. Customers at the counter leaned over to look.

"It's a ring," Stacy called out to Mindy, who screamed in delight, then chortled with laughter.

"A ring?" asked the woman who sat with her daughter.

Mr. Allen smiled.

Amber held up the ring so Min could see it, and the other customers gasped along with her.

"How beautiful," said the woman with her daughter. "Con-gratulations."

"You must try it on, miss," said one of the men in suits.

With one more backward glance at the grill, Amber held out her hand, lifted the ring, and slid it on to her finger.

"Fits perfect," said Mr. Allen, taking Amber's hand to look closer at the sparkling stone.

"I think this calls for free ice-cream cones for everybody," said Mr. Sorensen, who came out from behind the pharmacy counter to serve ice creams cones to all the customers who sat at the soda fountain. Amber watched Mindy lick her cone and grin at Stacy. She touched Mr. Sorensen's sleeve.

"Mr. Sorensen, this is my sister, Mindy. She hasn't been out of our house for a long time. For some reason, she just had to bring this letter to me today."

"A good reason, I think," said Mr. Sorensen. He nodded calmly. Blinked. When he made the last cone, he cleared his throat, which Amber knew was a signal to get back to work.

For the next three nights, after everyone else was asleep, she sat at the kitchen table, held her hand out, and watched the ring sparkle. She sighed, picked up a piece of lined paper, and began to write.

Sept. 22, 1961

Dear R. J.,
What a surprise! Thank you for the ring. It is really pretty. It fits me just perfect. I guess this means you are asking me to marry you. Oh . . . so you think you might want to know what my answer is? Maybe I'll tell you in my next letter. Just kidding. Well . . . I'm keeping the ring, so my answer is . . . yes. I will marry you. You didn't say when, but I'll say yes anyway.

Love,
Amber

Amber found herself looking at the ring lots of times during the day. She held out her arm and let the morning sun catch its sparkles. In the afternoon she studied the facets of the diamond in the more subdued light. She studied the ring and thought of Mindy, and how her sister somehow sensed the letter held an important message. Amber hated the realization that the afternoon Mindy brought the ring seemed to be a lull in the storm that raged against her sister's body. Somehow Amber sensed that Mindy might never leave their house again. She vowed to try to remember each sentence her sister said, and set time aside when they could talk together. Some nights she sat, helpless and tired, at the side of Mindy's bed. She gazed at Mindy, so pale and still, and recalled her happy face that day in the pharmacy. How could she be so happy for me when all she has is this bed? Amber wondered, touching the limp red tendrils of hair at Mindy's brow. Was she being selfish to think about getting married? How could she move away and leave Mindy like this? She even felt guilty knowing that R. J. was arriving for a visit next month, meaning she would spend less time at her sister's side.

Her heart swelled when she saw R. J. They shared their first kiss, and Amber experienced a happiness she never knew before. They went to the skating rink. R. J. chased her on the ice, his cheeks reddening, his smile widening as he grew agonizingly closer. She was afraid he'd grab her and she would fall down, but instead, he only took her hand, and they skated together, both gliding fast and sure, like skaters she watched on TV. Her hair whipped her face as they turned corners, weaving in and out of other skaters. Euphoria filled her. R. J. was good at this. They were good at this together. She felt her heart beat in her chest. Finally R. J. eased to a stop, by the railing, and they waited for Brent and Peggy to catch up.

They smiled at each other as they leaned against the rail together, breath flowing in panting gasps.

"R. J.—" she said. Another gasp.

He turned to smile at her. "Race you—" he said, heading off across the ice again. She stared at the ring on her hand, held her fingers high and watched the diamond flash under the lights. Something tore loose in her heart. Her euphoria was haunted by an unspoken despair. She couldn't help thinking of Mindy. Was there any chance that Mindy would live long enough to fall in love, or even long enough to see her own sister's wedding? And how could she get married now and leave Mindy behind when they'd been together their whole lives? She fought to shrug aside the nagging realization that after they were married, R. J. would want her to travel with him to the different military stations. On leave, he would probably want to alternate visiting his family in Florida and hers in Maryland.

Later, she, R. J., Brent, and Peggy went back to her house to play cards. Hi-Lo, Slap Jack, rummy, and the game with jokers. She couldn't laugh with the others. Her cards fell limply on the table, and she didn't care if she won or lost.

Finally they were alone. Brent and Peggy left to go to a movie, and her parents were already at the hospital with Mindy. Amber felt anxious about being here at home while Mindy was suffering at the hospital, so pale, white, and still. Thinking of her sister, she took R. J.'s hand as they sat on the couch watching television.

"R. J.—I need to say something. Right now."

"Just a minute—look at this—" He grinned and squeezed her fingers, then laughed at Bob Hope falling on his face on TV.

"I really do love you," she began, those words finally catching his attention.

He turned and grinned at her. "Love you, too, kid." He laughed again as someone hit Bob Hope's face with a pie.

"Listen, R. J. I love you. But I can't marry you. Not now."

He smiled at her with those twinkling eyes and broad grin that made her heart beat fast. "Sure you can," he said powerfully. "Getting married's easy. You say I do. Takes about three seconds. What's so hard about that?"

"It's hard because I can't leave home right now. Min could go at any time."

"We'll come back and see her—jump on a plane and we're here."

Amber felt a sinking sadness. How could she explain the anxiousness she felt when she was away from Mindy's side? "I don't have time to go and come back. She could die any day. The doctors don't know. . . . I just have to say good-bye to her."

"Your mom and dad will call us. Let us know when it's getting close."

"They might not call in time—"

"Phone call takes ten seconds. Flight's only a couple of hours. We'll go standby. It'll be okay." He patted her hand, leaned to kiss her on the cheek.

"We were always together. Since I was three. The first thing I ever remember was her getting born. . . ."

Even as she was telling him why she couldn't do this, her heart wouldn't stop thudding as she looked into those brown eyes. He was handsome. She loved him.

She'd always remember this moment.

"I know how special Mindy is," he said. "She's like her sister." He grinned at her.

"She's my best friend. She wasn't always sick, you know. She used to skate with me just like we did tonight. When we were little girls, we would hold hands and twirl around. . . ."

With a sigh, R. J. got up, went into the bathroom, and closed the door. When her breathing calmed seconds later, Amber realized he'd given her a minute alone. An aching sadness filled her. She loved them both—R. J. and her sister. Why did she have to choose? But there was no way she could not choose Min now. She held her hand out, let the ring sparkle once more in the lamplight. She stood, went to the mirror over the fireplace, and held her hand up next to her face. She looked at herself with the ring on her finger and smiled. Then she sighed, slid the ring off, and placed it on the arm of the chair where R. J. sat earlier.

She waited. There was no sound of his footsteps. She sensed she couldn't wait another second. Swift and silent, she rushed to the front door and out onto the porch. Then she scurried down the front steps, and headed toward the bus stop. If she ran as fast as she could, she might make it in time to catch the last bus to the hospital. With each step, she expected to feel R. J.'s hand on her arm. She half-waited to hear his voice call out.

But there was only stillness, her own gasping breath. Her pace slowed as she saw the bus drag to a stop. Walking to the curb, she stepped up and reached for the bus handrail. Then she held her breath. She took a cautious look back over her shoulder.

There was only inky black night. Was R. J. still at her house, or did he leave?

"Hey, lady, think I got all night?" She jumped, then looked up into the jowly, florid face of the bus driver. "This is my last run, lady!" the man shouted as she climbed onto the step. "I wanna go home sometime before tomorrow morning."

"Sorry—" Amber put her quarter in the slot, shook her head timidly, and stepped on board. Wanting to get away from the angry driver, she walked to the seats in the back.

As the bus lurched to life, she stared out, looking to catch a glimpse of R. J. or his car somewhere in the distance.

The alcohol and disinfectant smells at the hospital always filled her with anxious worry that heightened into fear. She held her breath as she neared the door of the room where Mindy lay so quiet and still. She always knocked, sensed her heart stop for a second until she heard her sister's faint, "Come in." She knew that someday she would open the door and find Mindy gone.

No matter how many times she visited, the sight of Mindy lying so pale and still always took her breath away. It was like coming face to face with the fragility of her own existence. There was a reverence in the room where her family sat, seemingly waiting for the old Mindy to somehow return. They stared at the frail form and held visions of Mindy rushing down the stairs, speeding and twirling on the skating rink, riding her Schwinn bike and ringing the bell.

Amber clung to those memories during the long hospital visits. But tonight, sitting beside her silent parents, watching her sister sleep restfully, she couldn't get her mind off R. J. What did he think when he found her gone? She held her ringless hand out, the way she did when she used to watch the diamond sparkle. Now her hand looked sadly empty. Was there any chance R. J. didn't see the ring on the arm of the chair? Could he still be at her house?

"I need to go home," she said abruptly to Mama and Daddy.

"She's been asleep a while—probably wake up any time now. We told her you would be here. . . ."

"I'll be back tomorrow."

"How would you get home? You got here on the last bus."

"I'll . . . take a taxi. . . ."

Mama looked at her as if she'd lost her mind. "I don't even know if they run this late. . . . You shouldn't go out alone after dark. Wait and ride home with us."

"It'll be too late . . . please . . . can I borrow five dollars? If the taxis don't run now, I'll come back. . . ."

Daddy shook his head. He looked at her as if she were crazy. "What's the matter with you?"

Amber swallowed. "It's an emergency. I gave my ring back to R. J. tonight. I have to talk to him."

Without a word her father reached in his wallet.

In her hand was a five-dollar bill. She leaned to kiss Mindy on the cheek, then waved good-bye to her parents. Without waiting for the elevator, she dashed to the steps and ran.

A nurse at the admitting desk called a taxi for her. All the way to her house, in the darkened backseat of the taxi, Amber rehearsed what she would say. She would tell R. J. she changed her mind. She would say that they could be engaged now, but couldn't think about getting married and traveling to the different army stations until later, after she knew what would happen with Mindy. Why didn't she think of this before? It seemed so clear in her mind . . . if only she wasn't too late.

She strained to see her house as the taxi turned on to her street. As she paid the man, she saw that the lights were off in her living room. Yet she still hurried up the steps—maybe R. J. was waiting in the kitchen. The front door was locked. Her keys shook in her trembling hands. . . . Maybe . . .

She could tell the house was empty as soon as she stepped into the living room and heard nothing but the ticking of the clock on the mantel. Nevertheless she hurried to turn on the nearest lamp. She gasped when she saw the vacant chair arm. R. J. and the ring were gone.

Distraught, she ran crying to her bedroom. She lay in bed for hours before fitful sleep came. Through the next days Amber longed to contact R. J. and tell him she didn't mean to say no, but she reasoned that nothing had changed. She still loved him—but she couldn't leave Mindy. She felt she did the right thing, but nothing else ever felt so painful. The hopelessness of her plight continued to haunt her, and she was filled with an emptiness like hunger as the long, vacant days moved slowly on.

Chapter Six

Brent didn't have a leave at Christmas, but at least Mindy was home from the hospital. Amber sensed that no one in her family voiced their fears that this could be the last time they would celebrate with Min. It was as if Mindy's illness draped a black cloak of sadness over everyone in their home—but Christmas was one day when all of them at least tried to pretend that life was the same as before Mindy got sick. Beneath the tree were piles of gifts, most of which Amber bought for her sister. A gold bracelet, a blouse, a wallet. Amber's favorite moment was when she received her paycheck and could walk down the street and make a payment on her layaway items. She would always buy one thing for herself and the same thing for Mindy. It was as if buying the same thing for both of them was her way of saying, "See? It's just like when we used to go shopping together." At the same time she sensed deep within that nothing about their lives would ever be like it was before.

What would her Christmas have been like this year if she and R. J. were still engaged? Amber couldn't deny the small, sad ache that hovered over her as she bought gifts for all of her family. Cuff links for her father. A necklace and lipstick for her mother. A shirt she would send to Brent. What would she buy R. J. if he were here? Gloves or a winter hat? A dress shirt to wear when he was off-duty? She kept hoping to receive one of R. J.'s funny letters. A Christmas card. But none ever came. . . .

On Christmas morning Amber found it was impossible not to think of Brent and R. J., so far away. It was the first time anyone from their family was gone on Christmas morning. Mama's voice seemed falsely cheery, as if she were playing the role of a mom in a Christmas movie. Dad carried Mindy down the stairs, the wood creaking under his weight as Mindy clung to his neck. The bright lights on the Christmas tree seemed to mock the sadness that pervaded the house. Part of Amber wished that Christmas would be over, but another part wanted to savor every moment of what could possibly be the last holiday with Mindy.

Mindy loved all of her gifts. The skirt, jewelry, and sweater all sat on her lap as if she planned to don them and walk with Amber to school once again. "Your last present, Amber. Open it!" Mindy said excitedly, pointing to a small silver-wrapped package sitting on a branch near the top of the tree.

Mindy's animated voice caught at Amber's heart and reminded her of Christmas mornings from when she was a little girl. She remembered Mindy tugging at her while she slept, waking her and telling her to hurry, even though it was still dark outside. Filled with chills from her memories of earlier days, Amber sighed and stepped to the tree, wondering who the present could be from.

She slid her fingers under the taped corner of the silver wrapping paper. The paper crackled in the silence of the living room. Her whole family watched.

The wrappings fell off, revealing a small, square box. Amber lifted the lid and gasped to see a pair of gold earrings that she recognized immediately from her shopping outings.

"Who knew I liked these?"

Her parents smiled. Mindy looked at the floor.

"I'm really surprised." Amber stared at the small gold circles. "These were my favorite—"

"You can thank your sister," Mama said softly.

"Mindy?" Amber stared, dumbfounded. "Are these from you?"

Min began to laugh, until her thin, pale face brightened with color. "From me," she said, nodding. "I got them the day Stacy and I brought you the letter with the ring. When you had to go back to work, we went to the store and looked for a present. I wanted to surprise you. . . ."

Amber couldn't speak. She walked across the room to hug Mindy. As her arms circled her sister's neck, Amber squeezed her eyelids together to try to hold back tears. Shoulders shaking, the two girls cried together. "Thank you—they're so pretty. . . ." Amber's words were muffled as she leaned her face into the soft warmth of Mindy's flannel nightgown.

The two girls held each other a long time. "Merry Christmas, Min," Amber managed. "I love you."

"I love you, too," her sister said.

After that Amber wore the gold earrings constantly, and thought of Mindy each time she saw her own face in the mirror and saw the shining gold. It was hard not to grieve over Mindy—to ache for her struggles now and long for the time when they were just two girls with all their lives seemingly ahead of them. Why didn't she sense how priceless each moment with Mindy was?

Now Amber and her parents spent many days at Mindy's bedside. It was a sad, sweet time when each minute indeed seemed both precious and precarious. They all felt helpless as their time together slid past. There were moments when they talked, recalling both girls' younger days. Sometimes Mama wrote to Brent, long letters in blue ink with her curving handwriting. Or she brought piles of sheets and towels for her and Amber to fold and sort. Sometimes they ate on TV trays, studying Mindy's frail, thin face as if their will and attention could somehow help her heal.

After several months Dad moved the television to Mindy's bedroom—yet even if it was on, no one seemed to watch it. The sound and pictures droned away while all of them focused on the small, red-haired girl lying so thin and still in her bed. Mindy's voice always startled Amber when her sister spoke. How could she look so different in her outward appearance and still sound the same when she talked?

Dr. Stevenson came to the house to examine Mindy at least once a month. There was an air of power about the doctor that sent chills of fear through Amber, even though she knew she wasn't the one he came to see. He was a huge man, who seemed to carry the biting smell of winter air on his wool winter coat as he trudged up the stairs to the bedroom where Mindy lay.

Along with her parents, Amber gazed at the doctor's face for any sign of hope or relief, but his features remained forbidding and stonelike as his fingers probed Mindy's thigh and hip. Amber realized she was holding her breath, waiting for a single encouraging word from this man who seemed to hold Mindy's life in his hands. Finally, with a sigh, the doctor turned to face Amber and her parents.

"I have a suggestion for further treatment," he said. "May I recommend we talk in your living room?"

Seated on the living room couch, they all leaned forward, hoping to hear of a medicine that would help.

"The cancer has metastasized from the site on her thigh. Also the sores she has developed may become gangrenous. Amputation of the limb may prevent a degree of the metastasis along with warding off infection."

"No," Mama said slowly. Amber saw a vein twitch in her mother's neck and a section of her cheek began to pulse. "Not my little girl's leg!" Mama shrieked, draped her eyes with her hand, and fell limp against Daddy's shoulder.

Daddy stared at the doctor in horror. "Sir, we—"

"Actually, removing the limb, while it is a drastic form of treatment, may prolong her life. . . ."

Mama sobbed, and clutched at Daddy, who held her as his own tears trailed from his eyes and onto his reddened cheeks.

Her own knees shaking, Amber stood from her place at the far end of the couch. She stepped forward until she stood directly in front of the doctor, who stared over her head at her trembling parents.

"You're not cutting her leg off—" Amber said.

Dr. Stevenson's eyes flickered in a band of light from the venetian blinds as he looked at her for only a second.

"You're not going to touch my sister," Amber said, her voice rising in the thick close air of the tiny room.

He didn't even look this time.

"Daddy, we can't let him do this. It won't help her."

His eyes on her parents, Dr. Stevenson said, "Amputation is a last resort as far as treatment. But her condition is grave."

"That's what I mean! She's not going to live long any-way—you can't hurt her like that."

"Do you often allow your child to address adults this way?" the doctor confronted her parents. Finally Daddy slid Mama's arm off his shoulder and turned to face Dr. Stevenson.

"I'd like you to respond to my daughter. She's spoken to you three times."

The doctor shook his head in pious annoyance.

"Mr. Lee. I am a professional man who has done you a favor by calling on you at your residence and rendering my expert opinion. Your child's emotional outburst should have no place in our discussion."

"If you won't even talk to one of my children, how can I trust you with my other daughter's life?" Daddy took a step toward the doctor and raised a shaking finger.

The doctor shook his head, put his silver instruments back in his bag, one by one, as he spoke with his back to Daddy. "Mr. Lee, that is an insult to my professional integrity. I will not lower myself to your level of thinking at this time. You are obviously carried away by your emotions."

"And you have no feelings at all, Doctor. I don't think I want my daughter operated on by someone who can't see her as a person."

"I won't dignify that with a reply," the doctor said, closing his bag with a snap. "Good day."

None of them moved as the doctor slid on his coat, stormed across the room, and slammed their front door.

No one said any more about the doctor's visit as more days passed. If Mindy returned to the hospital, there would be pain pills—but little else. Each morning before work, Amber went and sat in Mindy's room with her sister and parents. After work she returned to Mindy's side. There was a sad help-lessness in the room along with the sense that this was where each of them belonged, for as long as they could be there. Brent returned home on leave and joined them all at Mindy's bedside, instantly sensing that this vigil belonged to him, too, as Mindy grew weaker day by day.

Mrs. Rand came to visit one night, holding her new grand-daughter. So that her parents could stay with Mindy, Amber went down to the living room to talk to their neighbor, to whom she still felt grateful for rescuing her from that fateful day with Mr. Staker. She was telling Mrs. Rand how happy she was at Mount Jordan Pharmacy when Brent appeared ominously at the top of the stairs.

His voice choked. "She's gone," he mumbled, his hand over his quivering face and his eyes squinting back tears.

Chills, like cold and forbidding thunder, spread over Amber's body. "No! No!" she cried, rushing for the stairs without a word to Mrs. Rand. Did she really miss Mindy's last moment? Was there any chance to say good-bye?

At the top of the stairs Amber hurried into Mindy's room, where her parents sat, crying openly. "Mama, Daddy!" she said, and the three of them joined in a long, tearful hug. After they loosened their embrace, Amber walked slowly to her sister's bed. She touched Mindy's hand, so still. Then her hair. Then her cheek. Then Amber pressed her own cheek against Mindy's.

"Good-bye, Min . . ." she whispered into her sister's lifeless ear. "I'll always miss you. . . ." A sob choked her throat, and she stood and rushed into Daddy's arms. How could they live without Mindy? Why did God take her away?

The days after Mindy's death were bleak and empty. Amber took a second job as a car hop at the drive-in, and work filled her days. Mount Jordan Pharmacy during the day and Hawkins' Drive-in during the late afternoons and evenings. Each time she approached the house after work, she felt the same sense of dread, wondering how Mindy was. Then her mind would suddenly jump to the realization that Mindy was gone now.

Chapter Seven

With Mindy gone, Amber's days were colorless as if the life were drawn out of the earth itself. But one night three weeks after Mindy died, Sue, the girl from the candy counter, came up to her.

"Hey, Amber. I gotta ask ya something."

Amber finished wiping off the counter, thinking Sue would probably order a Coke float or an order of fries. "Yeah?" She poised the pen to her order pad, waiting.

"I'm not going to eat right now. Just had to let you know that my brother thinks you're kinda cute. . . ."

"Your brother?" Amber's mind floundered for a mental picture of Sue's brother.

"Yeah—you know, Mike."

"Do I know him?" Amber asked.

"Says he talks to you all the time—"

Amber mentally considered all of the regular customers. No image came to mind. "I'm thinking," she said.

"He kids with you about your badge and stuff."

"Oh," Amber said suddenly, thinking of the tall, dark young man who told her her badge was upside down lots of times. Then she'd look, and it never was. Or when she reached to pick up the candy he wanted to buy, he'd move it out of her way—two or three times—before he'd let her see the price tag. That guy? He thought she was cute?

Sue smiled at her. "He wants to know if you'll go out with him."

"Me?" The idea was so foreign. She was still recovering—from both Mindy and R. J.

"Yes—Saturday night."

"This Saturday?" Only four days away? With someone she didn't even know?

"Come on—I'm going, too. And Steve. My boyfriend."

Amber sighed. "I guess," she said, because it was easier to say yes than no, and she was still too bewildered to weigh this out.

A date. Could she make it through? As the next four days passed, Amber wallowed in her confusion. Should she try to back out now? What could she say to Sue? Was there any way she—or she and Mike—could actually have fun together?

She was thinking of what it might be like to go on a date with Mike, but all she could think about was R. J. and how she hadn't seen him for nearly five months. A sad longing—coupled with guilt—enveloped her. She shouldn't have left the ring on the chair like that. She should have explained more about why she couldn't leave Mindy. Or she should have said that they could remain engaged, but she couldn't marry him until she knew what would happen with Mindy. But what could she do about all of that now? Did she still have his home address anywhere? R. J. was still overseas, probably transferred by now. Or maybe Brent could tell her where he was. But in his last letter Brent said they were no longer stationed together. And she felt guilty even asking him. He lined her up with R. J. and then she dumped him. What about R. J.'s family? Could she write to them?

Amber stared at the blank sheet of paper before she picked up her pen and tried to think of what she should say. *Dear Mrs. Williams,* she forced her hand to write, all the while wondering if she should just tear up this letter. What if—even the possibility brought an ache to her heart—R. J. was already married to someone else? What if—even sadder—he was killed in the war? She hoped this letter wouldn't hurt anyone. Maybe she shouldn't write. But there was no other way to tell R. J. what she wanted him to know. That she would like to talk to him. That he was her friend. That if she ever had a chance somehow to say yes to his proposal, she would say yes now. Sighing, she wrote the date at the top of the letter.

February 27, 1962

Dear Mrs. Williams,
   I am a friend of your son, Raymond. I called him R. J.—he said you all started calling him that when he was little. I'm writing to ask you to let R. J. know that my sister, Mindy Jane Lee, died last month. She was only sixteen. R. J. knew that Mindy had bone cancer. He was kind to her. Could you please tell him I'd like to hear from him sometime? You have a wonderful son. Thanks for giving him this message from me.
                                        Sincerely,
                                        Amber Lee

Reading it over several times, she thought about crossing out the part where she wrote that R. J. was a wonderful son. Did she want him to think she still loved him? Face it, Amber, she said to herself, you will always be in love with R. J. Gazing at the few sparse words on the seemingly vast expanse of empty page, Amber decided it would call attention to the phrase *wonderful son* if she crossed it out. She read the letter once more, sealed it quickly, then went to the post office.

She grew more and more nervous as Saturday neared. She told no one in her family that she was asked out on a date. That night she worked until five, then hurried home for a shower. Glancing into her room, she thought that going to sleep sounded much more appealing than a date with a boy she didn't know.

Then the doorbell rang. Walking to answer it, she heard laughter on the front porch. She opened the front door and glanced straight into Mike's soulful brown eyes.

"Your badge is upside down," he said, with deadpan seriousness as Steve and Sue hooted with laughter. Amber pretended to look down at her badge.

"Come in—" she said, forcing a smile.

"We left the car running," Steve said, already stepping back to the stairs.

"Come on, Amber," Sue called, turning away to catch up with Steve.

"You don't have to fix your badge—it's okay with us," Mike said. She followed the others out to the car. They went to the movie theater to see a musical.

After the movie, at Mount Jordan Pharmacy, she ordered a root-beer float, keeping her eyes on the ice cream and fizzing root beer.

"Hey, waitress," Mike called out to her once, "is this Hires root beer they serve here?"

Amber nodded shyly, then looked down at her empty glass.

"Hey, waitress, look—my wad of gum floats. . . ." Mike called out. Amber looked up, but saw only his empty water glass. She felt her cheeks redden.

She was silent all the way home in the car.

Sue and Steve stayed in the car together as Mike walked her up to the door. As she reached for the knob, he asked, "Aren't you going to kiss me?"

Her whole body warmed with a blush. She stood completely still.

"I guess not tonight, huh?" he said finally.

She looked up and met his eyes. The porch light silhouetted his features, and she thought he looked like Elvis Presley—tall, masculine, and sexy. She drew in her breath, could not speak. She felt her cheeks flame in the cool night.

"Can't blame a guy for trying. . . ." Mike smiled wistfully at her, gave a floppy wave, and turned to leave.

Amber sighed with relief as her fear began to evaporate. But was that also a touch of regret she felt? Shivers danced at her shoulders. She watched him walk down the porch steps. Then she opened the door—and found Mama waiting for her.

"Where were you?" Mama demanded, angry tears on her face.

"With my friends . . ." Amber answered.

"You went out tonight?"

"Sue—from the candy counter—wanted me to meet her brother."

"You went on a date . . . when your sister just died?"

Amber backed away, confused. She thought about Mindy repeatedly all night long, and wished her sister could accompany the four of them. There was no way she would ever forget Mindy. What was Mama thinking here? And what did she do wrong?

"Answer me—you went out on a date?"

Amber nodded. "I won't lie to you."

"I'm hurt that you have no respect for your sister's memory. . . ."

"You can't say that. I loved Mindy."

"And no respect for me, and my grief—"

"Oh—Mama, I didn't even think—"

"I can't believe you wouldn't think of your sister." Mama's look held horror.

"I did! I still feel sad about her, too."

"So you went out on a date—I can't believe you. I don't even want to see you."

"I'll just go in my room, Mama."

"No—" Mama pointed with a shaking arm. "You need to think about what you did. Get out! Go away until you can come back with some respect."

"You won't even let me in my room?"

Mama held up her hand. "I can't face what you did. . . ."

Stunned, Amber stepped back off the step and onto the porch. Mama slammed the door shut. A second later Amber heard the lock turn. Their door was hardly ever locked. She had no key with her.

She stood in the dark, too wounded even to cry. How could Mama say those things? She guessed that Mama was right—she hadn't stopped to think of Mindy right at the moment Sue asked her to go out. But why couldn't Mama understand that sorrow over the loss of Mindy rode with her every day? That in everything she did, she felt guilty that she lived one more day when Mindy could not. While she worked, when she lay in bed at night, when she ate a candy bar or walked along the street. Her sister was always in her thoughts.

With an enveloping sadness, her heart ached for Mama and for Mindy, for all the pain that seemed to haunt their family. But what would she do tonight? Tomorrow was Saturday. She was supposed to get up early and work at the pharmacy. Now she was locked out of the house without her clothes. She had no bed to sleep in. Her only thought was to call Mr. Sorensen and tell him there was an emergency. She decided to ask him if she could sleep on the cot in the back room of Mount Jordan Pharmacy. Filled with a bleak despair, she walked down the steps to the sidewalk, fighting her fears of being alone in the dark.

With a deep sigh she headed for the gas station, the only place she knew that would be open this late. She prayed that their pay phone would work. Turning the last corner, she sighed with relief as she caught sight of the familiar gas station lights. But then her heart thudded in horror as Mike's car pulled up to one of the pumps.

"Hey, Amber." It was Mike, climbing out of his car and calling out to her, shading his eyes from the gas station lights with his hand.

Amber was speechless. She watched Mike bend and speak to Sue and Steve. Seconds later Sue slid out of the backseat.

"What are you doing?" Sue half smiled.

Amber shook her head, walked a few steps closer. "I just need to use the pay phone," she said, trying to sound calm and logical even as her emotions rushed.

"Phone doesn't work at your house? I called you today. . . ." Sue frowned slightly.

Amber shrugged, headed for the phone without looking at her friends, who were now staring at her.

"Thought you had to be in by eleven-thirty," Mike persisted. "Was our date that boring?"

"No—" Amber said, flustered and blushing. "I just need to call somebody." She reached the pay phone, opened her wallet, and stopped. Her eyes closed briefly in silent desperation. There was no dime in her wallet. Now she had no choice. She turned and walked to Mike's car, even as tears threatened.

She knocked on Sue's window. Rolling the window down, Sue said, "So you're speaking to us now?"

"I'm sorry. I'm just upset—I sort of have an emergency." Sue looked at her.

"I need to call Mr. Sorensen and ask if I can sleep at the pharmacy tonight."

Now Sue's frown knitted her brow. "So now your bed's broken—along with your phone?"

"No—" Amber covered her face with her hands. "My mom threw me out. She locked the door—"

"But we got you home on time. . . ." Mike looked at his watch. "Twenty minutes early."

"She said I did something terrible—"

"What do you mean? You wouldn't even kiss me—" Mike said. Nervous laughs came from Sue and Steve.

"Because I went out so soon after Mindy died—" Amber's voice broke as her resolve gave way, and her lip began to quiver. "I just need a dime. . . ." she said, before a sob closed her throat.

Abruptly Sue opened the back door of the car. She slid sideways on the seat. "Get in," she said.

"I have to call Mr. Sorensen."

"Get in—we're taking you to our place."

"Don't you need to ask your mom before you have a friend over?"

"You were right—it's an emergency. Get in."

Amber reluctantly climbed in the back of the car with Sue and Steve. Later, as she lay awake all night on Sue's couch, Amber cried silently. For Mindy, for Mama, for R. J., and for her own uncertain future that lay too frighteningly ahead.

Feeling exhausted the next morning, she borrowed some clothes from Sue and headed out to work at the pharmacy. She wondered if Sue would tell Mr. Sorensen about her emergency. But the workday wore on without a word from him. For days afterward, her work offered the only haven in her life as she continued to stay with Sue's family. They were very kind and insisted that she stay as long as necessary. Eventually, she shared a bedroom with Sue and was able to stop worrying about waking up early enough to avoid Mike seeing the way she looked in the morning after sleeping on the couch. Yet it felt awkward to suddenly live in the same house with this young man she dated only once. The house was small—only four bedrooms for Mike's grandmother, his parents, and four children. Amber definitely felt like an intruder. She tried to be as quiet and unimposing as possible, but the small space confined them all. She was with Mike whenever she was home. It was as if they were suddenly forced siblings. At the same time Amber knew she would never feel this small house was home. No one invited her to cook in the kitchen, and she felt she had to ask first every time she showered or used the bathroom. She got up early before the rest of the family when she needed to wash the clothes Sue loaned her.

Two weeks after Mama asked her to leave, she approached the house timidly in the early afternoon, searching her troubled mind for the right words to say. She longed for her own clothes, her own bed, the familiar rhythm that was her family. It seemed so unfair to be considered guilty of an offense she knew she could never commit. How could Mama forget all the nights she spent at Mindy's bedside? The tearful hugs, so filled with despair, that all three of them shared?

Amber felt barren and bleak inside as she rang the doorbell. She waited a long time, and realized she was holding her breath. Straining her ears, she heard sounds from inside the house—footsteps, the sound of a cupboard door closing. It was obvious that Mama was home. Yet the door remained as closed to her as the night she left. Was it possible Mama knew the identity of the person who had now rung her doorbell three times?

With a sigh Amber turned to leave, and was startled by the sound of the door opening.

Mama glanced at Amber, then instantly dropped her gaze to the floor. She stood as still as stone in the doorway.

"Mama, I came to get my clothes," Amber ventured. "I need them to go to work."

Mama took one step to the left and waited. She still didn't look up at Amber, or follow her as she slid past the doorway and entered the house. With a sigh Amber trudged up the familiar stairs to the room she used to share with Mindy. She found a suitcase in the hall closet and began to pack her clothes, thinking all the while how much she wished she could just stay here. There was peace in this room that now belonged to her alone, and as kind as Sue's family was, Amber was tired of being a guest in someone else's home. She longed for the freedom to shower whenever she wished, to wear her bathrobe in the living room if she felt like it, to make a grilled cheese sandwich for a snack and to stay up late and read with the light on.

The suitcase was filled. The house around her was silent. While she longed to take a hot shower and fall asleep on her bed for a long nap, there really wasn't any excuse to stay another minute. Exhaling in exasperation, Amber lifted the suitcase and started down the stairs.

She saw that Mama was sitting in the living room. Suddenly something in her heart sank at the sight of her mother's pale, sad face. "Good-bye, Mama," she said.

Mama turned. Her face quivered. "I still can't believe you would hurt me so much . . . and your father . . ."

The words felt like a slap. "What do you mean?"

"We already talked about it. Mindy's funeral less than a month before, and you go out on a date with that boy—"

"It was nothing! It was part of my work. I wanted to be nice to Sue, who works with me and wanted me to meet her brother."

"You couldn't tell her you were grieving your sister's death? She didn't know that from working with you?"

All the tenseness and fatigue of the past weeks gathered in Amber's mind. She didn't intend to raise her voice, but it was like a valve let go. "When Mindy was alive, I visited her every night! Don't you remember *that?*"

Mama sniffed. "How could you put your sister's memory aside like it never happened and go out and have fun? I'll never get over that. . . ."

"You should know I'll never forget her! And I'm sorry, but staying home all the rest of my life won't bring her back. No matter how long I stay by myself."

"You have no respect." Mama sighed. "And you have no idea how much that hurts me."

"And you don't know what I'm going through. I lost her, too."

"And you just went right along with your life."

"No. Never. Part of me died, too. Is that what you want to hear?"

"Don't shout at me!"

"You made me leave my own home!"

Mama stood. "You don't appreciate your parents! Or your home! You need to learn!"

"So you throw me out in the cold."

"I can't face what you did," her mother said, turning and heading for the stairs. She stopped, with her foot on the first step. "It's like you don't even know us," she said. Then she rushed up the stairs, leaving Amber alone in the living room. She didn't know how long she stood before she picked up the suitcase and headed out the front door.

So she went back to Sue's. Mike was attentive and teasing and as months passed, she and Mike played cards, bowled, and went to movies together. She watched him shoot pool, weld metals at his job. She fought the nagging understanding that they were just thrown together haphazardly. How could either of them date anyone else when they lived under the same roof? She didn't know how long this would last but she also didn't know what to do about it. She had nowhere else to go. She already gave Mama another chance to take her back. The sharp sadness over her mother's rejection was a pain she didn't dare face yet again. And she never did get a response to that letter she sent R. J.'s parents. But would he even know where to find her if he wanted to write her back? Amber felt lost. At Mike and Sue's she washed dishes, scrubbed floors, and tried to behave well so that they wouldn't make her leave. During these months, she felt the most at home at Mount Jordan Pharmacy, where at least she had a locker that was truly her own.

Chapter Eight

It was a raw March day, gray and lifeless. Amber and Mike went bowling, then stopped afterward for a soda. As she slid the paper off her straw, Amber looked up to see that Mike held a small velvet box. She reached for it, but he drew it back, the same as he did his candy bar at Mount Jordan Pharmacy.

"Got something to ask you," he said.

"What are you doing?"

"I'm asking you to marry me."

"Marry you?" What? This was a possibility she never considered.

"Yeah—" he said, opening the black box. Her heart skipped a beat as she glimpsed the ring inside. Shining gold with sparkling diamonds. She remembered R. J. and the ring he gave her. She remembered the nagging doubt that kept her from marrying him and the unbearable pain when he left her.

"Well . . ." Mike's foot nudged hers under the table.

"It sure is shiny . . . beautiful," she replied hesitantly.

Mike flashed the ring under the restaurant lights. Sparkles of light flickered on their wood-topped table booth. Could she say no, and still live in the same house with him and Sue? She already knew she couldn't go home.

"Sue told me you were engaged before—" Mike said softly.

"Yes." She nodded. "For just a few days."

"We could get married in just a few days. Get the license, find the pastor. Won't take long."

"But my parents—I want them to be there, and now they won't even talk to me."

Mike sat straighter in the booth. "It'll be okay. I'll go talk to them."

"Oh . . . no," Amber said, a shiver of fear rushing over her at thoughts of what Mama might say. "We'll go together."

"Is that a yes?"

Amber blushed. Her body filled with tingles, accompanied by dread and a sweet, sad feeling. She wasn't certain about wanting to get married, but would she ever be sure? R. J. seemed so perfect, yet she gave his ring back. Maybe she would never be one hundred percent positive.

"Yes," she said, almost inaudibly, the word sticking in her throat.

"What?" Mike said, leaning forward with a smile and cupping his ear. "Say that again."

"Yes," she said, still tentative.

He nodded, as if making a deciding vote. "We'll talk to your parents tonight. We can get the license tomorrow and maybe get married Friday. It's set."

Was it? The quickness of the decision took Amber's breath away.

"Here," he said, handing her the ring. "You better put this on."

The ring shone on her hand. Married. She couldn't believe it was happening to her. Maybe it shouldn't be happening to her. Maybe she should still be grieving R. J. and Mindy—and the loss of her parents. Was this the right thing to do? She felt so unsure, but what could she do about it now? She had no other home, nowhere else to go.

Amber glanced at Mike as he stood under the light on her parents' porch. Was she ever more scared than at this moment? Instead of wondering who might answer the door, she focused her gaze on Mike's shiny, dark hair; crisp, white Sunday shirt; and polished black shoes. His aftershave smelled like spices and limes. As dignified as he looked, she sensed his nervousness by the way his fingers fidgeted as he held her hand. His feet shifted on the porch as he rang the doorbell a second time. Still no answer, and still none five long minutes later.

"No one's home," she said.

He sighed, and she could tell he felt relieved and worried all at once.

"I'll come back tomorrow," she said, sounding braver than she felt. "I'll ask them—don't worry."

The next morning she felt her heart thud as she saw her daddy sitting on the porch in the spring sunshine. He didn't look at her as she walked up the steps and stood in front of him. Amber sighed.

"Daddy—I need to tell you something."

He didn't answer. His sad blue eyes seemed to look through her to the barren, gray-brown lawn in front of the house.

Amber forced a weak smile. "I'm getting married, Daddy."

Now he blinked but didn't respond. He cleared his throat and his feet shifted against the boards of the porch, but no words emerged.

Amber sighed, mustered all the energy she could. "I want to invite you to the wedding—to give me away—"

Daddy shook his head. "Don't think so."

"Come on, Daddy—" Now Amber voice broke. "I'm still your little girl."

A sob gathered in her throat as she saw his lip quiver. "You have my blessing," he said, almost inaudibly.

"Then you'll come?" Amber's hopes rose.

He shook his head, leaned back against his chair. She thought she glimpsed a tear on his cheek. "Can't." He shook his head.

"Oh, please, Daddy!"

Now he shuddered. "Can't come between you and your mama. You're my little girl . . . but she's my wife."

"You can't talk to her . . . tell her I'm sorry?"

"I've tried . . . again and again. . . ."

"Can I ask her myself?"

"Not here, right now."

"But do you think she'd come? This is my wedding day!"

Daddy ran the back of his hand across his lips, then shook

his head. "I can't promise anything. Better not count on it. Better just go on now."

"But you'll tell her at least—"

His nod was dismissing. Amber felt a sob rise inside and felt she couldn't stay here one more moment.

She turned to leave and was on the second step when her father called out.

"Amber?"

"What?" She answered without looking back at him.

"Come here—I have something for you."

She turned and nearly bumped into him. He pressed what felt like a piece of crumpled paper into her hand and folded her fingers over. Then his hand found her chin, which he urged upward so that she would look into his eyes.

"I wish you happiness," he said firmly, as if it were an order. Then he turned and went in the house, closing the door hard behind him. Amber stood still on the porch a long time before she opened her hand and saw that it held two fifty-dollar bills.

"Daddy, I didn't want your money," she said softly, gazing at the front door. But when there was no sound from within the house, she finally turned to leave.

In the days that followed, she mechanically prepared for the wedding as if it wasn't really happening to her. She needed a wedding dress but had no desire to shop for one. She hadn't been back to Auerbach's department store since Mindy died. The thought of never buying another layaway that the two of them could share was another sadness on the pile of inner pain that tormented her. But she forced herself to open the heavy glass door of the department store, telling herself there was no way she could get married without a new dress.

Then she saw it instantly. Short-sleeved, turquoise color, calf length, with a velvet jacket. Not the wedding dress she always imagined, but then she never thought she would get married without her parents. *Face it*, she told herself, *you never thought you would marry Mike*. But what else could she do now?

• • •

The church seemed huge and hollow with no one else in it but the two of them and the pastor. After her parents declined to attend, she and Mike shared an unspoken understanding that his parents, too, might not be happy that Amber would now be a permanent resident at their home. So now they stood alone. Suddenly she heard footsteps at the back of the church. She turned . . . and caught sight of a familiar face that brought tears to her eyes.

"Brent!" she exclaimed, rushing up to hug her brother, who was dressed in his Army uniform and holding hands with Peggy. Stepping back, Amber drank in the sight of her brother as tears flooded her cheeks. "How did you get here?" she exclaimed, her words echoing to the church ceiling.

"Your future hubby here"—Brent elbowed Mike—"passed the word along, then I got a quick flight."

"Now tell her the rest." Mike's smile was wide. Through her tears Amber gazed at his brown suit and white shirt and tie. She thought how handsome he looked as he slugged Brent on the arm.

"What are you talking about?" Brent pasted a fake innocent look on his face—then Peggy slugged him, too.

Now Amber was curious. "What's going on?"

"Well—" Brent raised his eyebrows. "Didn't want to steal your show, Sis. But the thing is—I only had a four-day leave. Didn't want you to know I was here—spoil the surprise and everything. So—Peggy and I beat you to it last night."

"What?" Amber felt a laugh bubble up in her throat. "Do you mean you got married?"

Brent nodded sheepishly as Peggy good-naturedly slugged him again. Peggy and Mike erupted with laughter.

"So you didn't even stop to invite—" Amber staged a mock frown and placed her hands on her hips.

Someone behind them cleared his throat. "If the bride and groom will now step forward . . ." said the minister who had somehow stepped behind the lectern at the front of the church while they had their reunion.

Mike took her hand, his fingers warm and reassuring as he squeezed hers. She sniffed back tears, smelled his aftershave. He was handsome. He was here, and he wanted to marry her. So why did she think of R. J. at this moment, as the two of them solemnly stepped to the front of the church? Her ring felt cold on her finger. She glanced down and saw the diamond flash in the cool afternoon light.

Her mind drifted during the minister's speech about the sanctity of marriage and the family she and Mike would someday have. She fought to pay attention, wondering what she should be feeling now if she were madly in love and absolutely wanted this her whole life.

Abruptly Mike cleared his throat beside her. She looked up, met his glance—and felt chills. A wave of sheer love fell from his brown eyes and dizzyingly caught at her heart. Her throat filled and she blinked. No matter what else happened in her life, this would always be her wedding day.

"You may answer either 'I will' or 'I do,' " the minister was saying, his tone cool and formal.

Mike shifted his weight beside her.

"Do you, Michael David Bentley, take Amber Christine Lee to be your lawful wedded wife?" The minister went on, about richer and poorer, sickness and health, till death did them part.

Amber held her breath in anticipation.

"I do." Mike's voice solemn beside her.

"And do you, Amber Christine Lee, take Michael David Bentley to be your lawful wedded husband . . ."

This was it. It was happening now. Snatches of the minister's words fell between Amber's rushing thoughts.

She was really getting married.

"For richer or poorer . . ."

Without Mama, or Min, or Daddy.

"In sickness and in health . . ."

Or R. J.

"Till death do you part . . ."

The church suddenly seemed mammoth and cavelike, and for a moment Amber felt incredibly small and alone. Then she caught sight of Mike's smile—surer, more comforting than her own confusion.

"I do," she said softly, her voice quavering.

The minister gave her a questioning look, as if to ask, "Are you sure?" He paused. Silence roared around them in the spaciousness of the church before the minister pronounced them man and wife.

She was Mrs. Mike Bentley.

Chapter Nine

She stayed at the pharmacy and he worked as a welder. They lived in two rooms at his parents' house. An army blanket served as the only drapery and a kerosene lamp sat on the floor. No one told Amber to make herself at home. She still felt as if she had to ask permission to use the bathroom, the washer.

But now it should be different. She was a part of the family. She was Mike's wife. One day, after Mike left, Amber crept up the stairs to where her mother-in-law was embroidering a pillowcase.

"I—I'd like to cook once in a while. . . ." she said, surprised at herself for releasing her thoughts so quickly.

"I do the cooking in my home," her mother-in-law said airily.

"But Mike is so tired of chicken from the drive-in. I want to make him a meal. . . ."

An edge crept into her mother-in-law's voice. "You are a guest in my home. You do not take over my kitchen. . . ."

"Just once in a while . . . for a little variety . . . I will make enough for you. . . ." Amber pled. "We're paying rent."

"I still own this home. If you want to cook, get your own place."

Amber knew she would cry if she stayed in the room one more minute.

"Mike, we can't stay here," she said later that night when despair drove her to bravely confront him.

He lifted his arms in a gesture of futility. "This is the only home I can provide now."

"But this isn't our home. I can't even cook."

"So we'll live on love." Mike's smile was forced.

"I'm tired of asking to go to the bathroom."

"Then don't ask. Just go ahead. Anyway, your parents wouldn't even let us in the front door."

"Mike, I'm pregnant. We need our own place."

"You are?" A whisper of a smile crossed his face. He walked over to hug her. Seconds later he looked at his watch. "We'll talk about it, okay?" He raised his eyebrows at her. "I'll see what I can do."

"Where are you going?"

"I've got an appointment."

"With who?"

"The guys. If I'm gonna be a daddy, I gotta celebrate." He lifted a pretend pool cue and expertly shot it at her.

"Not tonight." She shook her head, lip quivering.

"I'll be back in a flash."

"Maybe I won't be here when you come back." It was a hopeless tactic, both of them knew.

"Where else would you go, babe?"

She waited until he left before she started to cry.

By now she was accepting of her life, if not happy. She knew Mike spent too many nights out and loaned too much money to his friends. And his work—both as a welder and as a painter—was sporadic. There could be two hundred dollars one day—then nothing for a week. Yet her mother-in-law's words were the beginning of her dream to find a place of their own. Now, when Mike was off with a friend or painting on a side job, Amber searched for a home of their own. She read newspaper advertisements, walked the neighborhood, and fought not to give up hope. Days at the pharmacy gave her a break from the crowded tension at the house. At about 10:50 every morning, her body felt a natural surge of adrenaline and anticipation with the thought of the lunch crowd. They were, she realized, her social life, now that her parents still were still not speaking to her, Min was dead, and

Brent was stationed far off in Thailand. A faint, yet constant, worry haunted her with the understanding that being married to Mike didn't completely fill her need to talk to other people.

Amber was feeling particularly happy this day. The pharmacy was busy as the regulars came in for lunch, and she was looking forward to tomorrow when she would see Peggy and Brent, who was home on leave.

Why did she notice the girl first? She was blond and graceful, like a thin-necked swan. Blue eyes with corners that crinkled when she smiled. It wasn't until she let loose with a tantalizing giggle that Amber noticed the young man standing next to her.

It was R. J.

Amber's heart thudded in recognition. Chills rushed. He was really here.

The same moment she recognized him, she saw that the blond girl beside R. J. was pregnant. She's his wife, Amber thought. So he's married, too. We're both taken. Both gone. A memory flashed of the night she left the ring on the chair.

"Well, why don't you just stare at me. . . ." R. J. was saying, a grin on his face.

"Hi, R. J." They were the only words her frantic mind could form as thoughts rushed. Your wife is pretty. So very pretty. I always sort of half-thought you would wait for me, even though . . .

He grinned at her, winked. "Looks like you're doing okay."

Amber blushed. Her hand fell to her smock. I look pregnant, she thought.

R. J. effected an efficient, businesslike face. "Got any gum back there? Spearmint? Juicy Fruit? Maybe even Dentyne?"

Amber was grateful for an excuse to turn her back, although their laughter rained on her like rocks.

"How many packs?" she asked, still facing away, dropping her eyes to the brightly colored gum packages.

"Aah . . . give me one of each. Doublemint and Juicy Fruit."

Her hand shook with the gum clasped in her fingers. She forced her mind to add the sum on the cash register. "Would you like a bag for that?" she questioned in her most professional, emotionless manner.

R. J. shook his head and grinned at her. Her heart skipped a beat, and she half-smiled back. For a moment a curtain dropped, and she felt as young as the night they skated together. Then someone in the booth called out, "What does it take to get a Coke over here?"

"I'll be right there—" she called out, feeling her whole body warm with a blush of embarrassment. She was grateful her hair fell in her face, so R. J. couldn't see her red cheeks as she took the woman's lunch order.

When she looked up, R. J. was gone, along with his wife. A thin, sharp sadness filled her. R. J. didn't wait to say goodbye. She might never see him again. But he was married, Amber reminded herself.

And so was she.

Yet she found herself thinking of him—and his beautiful, blond wife—as the rest of the day passed. R. J. stayed on her mind as she made sandwiches and sodas, wiped the counter off again and again, and tallied her cash register drawer that night. Amber found herself looking up, out of the plate-glass pharmacy window, more than usual. She felt sort of happily on edge each time the door to the pharmacy opened, wistfully hoping that R. J. might come back later, thinking she would be less busy.

That night, as she folded clothes and cleaned her and Mike's basement rooms, R. J.'s smile hovered in her mind, and she didn't stop to sit and watch the small TV with Mike, the way she usually would. When Mike gave her a sidelong glance and said he might want to shoot pool for a while with his friend James, Amber felt a surprising relief.

The silence in the apartment felt quick and expectant.

Yet she waited nearly an hour before she called her parents' house. Feeling like a giddy teenager, she simply made her voice lower and flat before she said, "Brent, please," when her father answered the phone.

A long pause. Did her father know who she was? Would he not let her talk to Brent? What would she say if Brent wasn't there? Amber warred against an impulse to hang up, and she had nearly replaced the phone on its cradle before she heard, "Hello?" Brent sounded obviously curious as to who might know he was home on leave.

"It's me," Amber said quickly. "Don't say my name."

"I hate it that you guys haven't made up. If you come over here, I'll tell Mom and Dad you want to talk to them—"

Suddenly, anger rose within Amber. "As far as that goes—how come you get to be there, and I don't. You had a girl-friend—you got married without them. Why aren't they mad at you?"

" 'Cause I'm a man and you're still their little girl."

"That's not fair."

Brent lowered his voice. "I think they figure I was already out of the house and they couldn't say anything to me—but you were still here. And you left the house too soon after Mindy died—or something like that. I don't get it."

"It doesn't make any sense," Amber agreed.

"Maybe if you come over here when I'm here, then—"

"No," Amber said flatly. "I won't put you in the middle. It's not—"

"We should all get together—be a family—while I'm here."

Amber felt a nudge as if someone pushed her. "What about R. J.? Where are he and his wife staying?"

"His wife?"

"I saw her when they came in the pharmacy together."

"What are you talking about?"

"She stood right next to him." Amber hesitated. When Brent didn't respond, she said, "Blond—really pretty." She sighed. "And she was pregnant."

"It wasn't R. J.'s."

"What do you mean?" And why did she feel this odd sense of relief?

"R. J.'s not married. We don't talk about who he goes out with. And I'm not lining him up again after what happened with you. No offense, but he really liked you."

Amber felt a warm glow spread around her heart. She basked in it for a few seconds before she remembered that *she* was definitely married.

"Amber?" Brent asked finally. "Are you still there?"

"Oh—yeah. So who was that girl next to him?"

"I have no idea."

"So you really don't think—he's dating."

Brent sighed. "Haven't heard him talk about anybody. And if she was that good-looking, he'd say something."

Amber took a long breath. She listened to the rooms around her—the water dripping, the hum of the furnace. There was no sound from outside—or upstairs. No noise of Mike quickly darting down the stairs, excited and fast-talking.

Amber closed her eyes quickly. "Please tell R. J. I said good-bye." She was aware that her heart was beating fast. "And wish him luck for me."

"Okay—no big deal." Brent's voice sounded light and casual. "I could do that."

"Thank you."

Brent waited. "Uh—you and Mike—everything okay?"

For a moment the smallness of the basement apartment seemed to squeeze her, as if pressure from upstairs could actually be felt down here, where she sat alone. "Yeah . . ." she said slowly.

"You're sure? You don't sound too good."

"I'm fine," she said. Too quickly.

"I'll tell R. J. for you. Okay? I need to go."

Brent hung up in the middle of her saying, "Okay—"

She went to the corner of the carpet in the bedroom, lifted it, and drew out the pictures of R. J. She ran her finger over his face in one of the pictures, then placed it against her cheek. He was still single. But she was married and about to be a mom. Even so, holding the picture brought back memories of the time she and R. J. spent together.

Mike seemed to be spending more nights out with the boys, leaving her home alone and crying. She found herself looking at the pictures more and more. Lying in bed one day, she realized it was possible to see the place where the edge of the carpet poked upward. After that, she hid the photos in a bag between two pairs of pants she never wore. They were more accessible there, and later, even more readily available underneath the couch cushion. After a while she surreptitiously slid four of the smaller pictures into her wallet, so that she could look at them whenever she wanted without disturbing the others in their hiding place. They were only snapshots, but to Amber, they were the only comfort she had.

That night, alone in the apartment, Amber dialed Aunt Nona, who now lived three streets away.

"This is Amber," she said quietly, bracing herself in case Aunt Nona no longer wanted to talk to her.

"Amber? How are you? Your mother is so worried about you!"

"Mama?" Amber hesitated. "She won't even let me come home."

"Oh . . . I would call her if I were you," Aunt Nona said softly. "She talks about you whenever I see her."

"She *talks* about me? We don't even speak."

"I know you're on her mind. How are you doing?"

"Well . . ." Amber sighed, stared around the apartment.

"You didn't invite me to your wedding—" Aunt Nona broke in.

"I didn't want Mama to get mad at me—"

Aunt Nona clucked. "So you got married—"

"I'm going to have a baby," Amber said softly.

"Does your mama know that?"

Amber shook her head. "I really didn't think she ever wanted to see me again."

"That woman has a temper—" Aunt Nona conceded. "But don't let that stop you. She's just too proud to give in."

Amber shivered at the thought of calling her house again. There was a long silent pause.

"You're pregnant?" Aunt Nona asked suddenly. "I drove by the pharmacy a few weeks ago and saw you standing in the front window."

"I'm still working."

"So you'll quit when the baby comes."

A sudden streak of fear enveloped Amber. She'd been so busy wondering how she would get from day to day that she didn't even think about what would happen in the months ahead. Quit the soda fountain? The only small speck of light in her despair-filled life? "I'm not quitting," she said.

"But what about the baby? Who will look after her?"

"Well . . ." Amber faltered. "Mike's schedule is . . . flexible. And maybe I could hire a high school girl," she finished lamely.

"You can't leave a baby with just anybody," her aunt said firmly.

"I'll—I'll find someone." What on earth would she do?

"I could take the baby sometimes," Aunt Nona volunteered.

Someone from her family coming to her rescue? Amber was a sea of emotion. Tears flooded as her feelings of relief and disbelief spilled over.

"I—wouldn't want to trouble you. I don't know what to say."

"We'd have to work it out—I still sell Beauty Counselor makeup out of my home—"

"I'd pay you—" Amber rushed quickly.

"Do you make enough to pay me?"

"Probably not—" Despair rushed in again. Why hadn't she even stopped to think about the baby? Because she hoped somehow that her life would change before the baby was born. But a sinking sensation within told her that Aunt Nona was right. She needed to find someone to care for the baby *now*.

Aunt Nona sighed. "I can't believe you and your mom aren't talking about this. But bring the baby to me. I couldn't stand to think of her being left with some high school kid you don't even know—"

"It would only be once in a while—" Amber broke in. "Lots of days, I don't start until noon—and Mike's painting and welding is all different shifts—"

"Just bring her here."

"And I'd give you—" Amber racked her brain. How much could she pay of the little salary that fed them and bought the clothes she wore to work?

"Don't worry about all of that. Just do one thing for me . . ."

"What's that?" Amber asked breathlessly.

"Call your mother," Aunt Nona said. "Right after we hang up."

As soon as the phone clicked, Amber realized she was holding her breath.

Chapter Ten

"Mama?" *Amber ventured* cautiously, balancing the phone against her hand as she folded diapers.

"Yes." Her mother's voice was flat, unreadable. Amber waited, listened to her mother breathe. Neither of them spoke, but neither of them hung up.

Finally Amber sighed. "You're a grandma. I had a baby—"

Still her mother's breathing.

"A beautiful baby—" Amber's voice broke.

A long, ragged breath from her mother before she cleared her throat. Then her voice. Tremulous. Tentative. "A boy or a girl?"

Amber closed her eyes. "A girl. She is so tiny."

"And you are all right?"

Somehow, this question brought Amber to tears. This was Mama, who didn't speak to her for so long, now asking if she was okay. She thought of the small cramped rooms, Mike, gone again tonight, and R. J., so far away.

"Amber?" Was that worry in her mother's voice?

"I'm—okay."

"You don't sound very happy."

Amber sighed with exhaustion. "I'm all right," she insisted.

"The baby? Is she all right, too?"

Amber juggled the small bundle on her lap. She felt the weight and warmth of the baby through her jeans. She leaned and pressed her cheek against Amy's small face. "Yes."

"You sound worried. I should probably come to see you."

"Oh—" Amber looked around the small room, at the army blanket over the window, the kerosene lamp on the floor.

"I'll come tomorrow." Mama sounded as if she were writing this down somewhere. "About this same time?"

Amber nodded numbly. "Yes." What did this mean? Why did Mama suddenly change her mind?

"The address? I don't know where you live—"

"Two forty-eight Market Street."

"Oh—just over there."

"Yes." Did Mama wonder where she was all these months?

The next day Amber nervously waited for her mother and was still startled at the knock on the door to their basement quarters. She'd cleaned the two rooms until they were spotless, gave Amy a bath, dressed her in a yellow spring dress, and glued a bow to the top of her head with Karo syrup. She had just placed Amy on a blanket on the floor when she heard the rap at the door.

Amber paused and took a quick breath. She glanced at Amy, lying blissfully on a homemade quilt in the dappled sunlight. Then she opened the door and stared at Mama's familiar face. She saw that the single streak of gray in her hair was wider now than before, the wrinkles around her eyes more pronounced. She felt her own lip quiver under Mama's expressionless gaze.

"Is the baby asleep?" her mother asked, in a near whisper. Amber's throat caught.

"No—she's here. Come see."

She stood back as Mama stepped into the apartment and trudged across the floor. Amber watched as her mother abruptly caught sight of Amy. Her throat filled. She watched Mama's chin quiver before she cupped her face with a hand.

"My gosh—she's beautiful," Mama gasped, leaning over and lifting Amy to her shoulders, wrapping the quilt expertly around her as she did so.

Amber couldn't speak. Somehow, her mother's validation was like watching Amy be born all over again. She stared as her mother traced Amy's tiny eyebrow with a cautious finger, then laid her palm against the baby's round cheek.

"She looks just like you did," her mother said, lifting the

tiny fist, then placing it gingerly back on the quilt. "The same blond hair . . ."

"I love her fat cheeks . . ."

"Yours were like that, too."

A wave of emotion filled Amber, as she thought of her mother and father feeling the same wonder over a new baby that she felt now. Did this mean she was forgiven?

"Mama—" she ventured carefully. "I'm glad to see you. I didn't know when you would talk to me again."

Mama cleared her throat, shook her head.

"I'm sorry I went out on a date that night. . . ." Amber continued. "I just didn't put the two things together—Mindy's funeral and my friend at work. I thought about Mindy all that night—I didn't mean to not think about her. . . . I'm still sorry."

Mama shook her head again. "I was just so upset . . . I knew she was sick, but I never thought I would lose her—then when you went out that night, I thought I might lose you, too."

"Mama, I didn't even want to go with them that bad—it was just easier to say yes than try to say no to my friend."

"And look—if you didn't go, you wouldn't have this beautiful baby," said her mom, gazing at Amy.

If I didn't go, maybe I would have R. J., was Amber's unbidden thought.

Amber was mystified as Mike arrived and her mother greeted him with a smile. After a few awkward moments, they all laughed and talked together as if they'd never been apart. The three of them sat on the small couch and stared at Amy's round, soft face until the baby slept.

As weeks, and then months passed, she and her parents wove a fragile friendship. Short visits grew to longer ones, and after two more daughters, Caroline and Mary, were born, Amber customarily visited Mama and Daddy once a week, to get away from the cramped rooms in the Bentley basement.

She was sitting on Mama's couch when the telegram arrived.

Mama opened the telegram and gasped, the thick, cream-colored paper shaking in her hands. "No!" she screamed, dropping the paper on the floor and running out of the room.

Seconds later Amber heard her bedroom door slam.

Amber picked up the crackly, folded paper telegram. Western Union, it proclaimed at the top. The telegram was addressed to Mr. and Mrs. Harold Lee. The message on the four strips of paper pasted on the telegram bore into Amber's mind, bringing shock and disbelief.

"It is with deep regret that we inform you that your son, SP5 Brent Harold Lee, died on April 20, 1968, in Thailand. Details will be furnished as soon as available."

There was another page that said "preparation of remains" that asked her parents whether they wanted the army to ship the body home or simply take care of the burial. It was this paper that caught at Amber's heart and jarred loose her tears. The thought of Brent—so smiling and full of life—being considered simply as remains brought home the sudden devastation of this loss. Her brother. Her friend. Then, a forbidden thought. Brent was the only person who knew where R. J. was. And now they were both gone.

Chapter Eleven

In the weeks that followed Brent's funeral, a frantic despair enveloped Amber. All the losses in her life—Mindy, R. J., now Brent—converged to form the pain that was almost overwhelming. Yet, in the midst of the agony, Amber realized she had the courage to survive all the losses, and the courage along with her love for her children now propelled her forward.

That night, she went home to another evening of chicken from the drive-in restaurant. Why didn't the bleakness of their life fade Mike's enthusiasm the way it did hers? His life surged on like a fire crackling in a fireplace. He worked hard, played hard, and when he reached for her—sometimes as she lay asleep in the blackness—she clung to him, perhaps in hope that some of his will and fire would become part of her, and she would know how to move on with her life. There were times, though, when she understood that she hardly felt his touch. That in her mind, she was lost and far away, someplace in the past. She stopped herself from hoping that Mike's hands were R. J.'s and told herself that she would someday get rid of the old photos and accept her life the way it was.

Amber gave birth for the fourth time and right after Laura was born she found the house.

"We're taking this place," she said determinedly to Mike, one night when the girls were asleep.

"Can't afford it," he responded, watching the ball game and not looking at her.

"I can't stay here another week. I haven't cooked on a stove in eight years."

"You cook every day at work. All those hamburgers?"

"I want to make meals for my family. I can't stand it any longer. Either we all go—or I take the kids and go."

They moved the next month—to a house she found on one of her long walks through the neighborhood. It was impossible to describe the feelings of peace and relief in finding her own place. A stove, sinks, and a bathroom that she could use whenever she wanted! Before the first rent payment came due, she began to look for a new job, hoping that if life at home were more comfortable, Mike would want to stay there more in the evenings.

When they moved, her mother-in-law informed her that if they no longer lived in her house, she would no longer baby-sit the children. Amber felt a mixture of anger and frustration. She'd worked her hours around Mike's as much as she could, knowing this woman who didn't want to share her sink would hardly be patient if the baby-sitting hours lasted too long. And Aunt Nona still helped sometimes too. But now Mike's mother was actually refusing to help before Amber ever asked. The sting of this rejection haunted her, and she became determined to find the right job to improve their new life in their new home.

Amber approached Mr. Sorensen in his office. Watching him write at his desk, she remembered the first day she applied for the job—how scared she was and how imposing and intimidating he had seemed. Now he looked smaller, thinner, grayer, although his white pharmacy jacket was as starched and snow-white as ever.

"Amber!" He looked up at her over half-glasses. "It's not noon yet, is it?"

"No." She smiled thinly. "I just need to talk to you."

"What about that new girl—is it Sarah? She's not as fast as you were—but do you think she's doing all right?"

"Fine—"

"And the dishwasher—they got it fixed okay?"

"The hot water works better than ever."

"And your raise—came through on your last check, didn't it?"

Amber nodded. "I've decided to resign," she said abruptly. "I'm giving you my two weeks' notice."

Mr. Sorensen seemed to shrink behind his desk as if she had hit him. "Oh, Amber—"

"This has been a good job for me—I'll always be grateful to you for hiring me that day—but I need to move on."

"Your raise wasn't enough? I thought you still liked the candy counter."

Amber was surprised to feel a tear on her cheek. "This is my home. I haven't had a real home of my own since my mom kicked me out. But I need to make more money. And I need a job with night shifts. I don't want to leave my baby with a sitter."

"We used to be open at night—way back when. . . . Do you remember?"

Amber recalled Friday nights when she started working at the pharmacy. Long vacant minutes punctuated by an occasional couple on a date who wanted a root-beer float or a soda.

"Yes," she said. "Those were fun days."

"Well—" Mr Sorensen leaned back. "Fact is, don't know what I could do to make you stay. Been thinking about packing it in myself. You know, I'll be seventy-four next month."

"You will?" Amber truly had no idea. How could she leave him here at the end like this?

"But you go ahead. I'll never find a faster counter girl—but you gave me a lot of good years."

A sorrowful ache hovered around her heart all the rest of the day. For the next two weeks she cherished each moment at the pharmacy—the view out the front window that she loved, the sweet, syrupy taste of root beer and melted ice cream blended together at the bottom of a root-beer float, the customers whose faces, stories, and requests were familiar, and the feeling of satisfaction when she wiped the counter for the last time at the end of the day.

∙   ∙   ∙

Regal Meats had an opening. Packaging meats and waiting on customers. Amber made an appointment for eight A.M. and wore her church dress to the interview.

"Thirteen years in retail." The man who interviewed her seemed to be sizing her up. "That's quite a bit of time."

"Yes—I have references from my supervisor."

"Most of our shifts are days. But we pay good."

"I really need nights. I have four kids. If I have to pay a sitter . . ."

The interviewer stared. "There is one thing. Facilities crew. Most of those shifts are nights—and it pays better than days."

"I'll take it—"

"Wait a minute—let me tell you. We haven't been able to get a woman to accept a position down there yet. There's heavy equipment. You have to scrub huge vats—" He looked at Amber. "It's hard, physical work."

"I'd like to try," she said. "I'd haul rocks all night if I could somehow take care of my kids during the day."

Chapter Twelve

She experienced a surge of nervousness as Mike went to the closet and drew out her purse. Why was she worried? She didn't spend any money yesterday.

"I'll get you some change. . . ." she called out to him, rushing across the living room.

"Just need a couple of bucks," he said, scowling, her wallet in his hand.

"I'll get it for you," she said, reaching, but Mike jerked her hand and flipped the wallet open.

He rifled through the money flap but didn't stop there. Instead, she watched as he slid his finger under the other flap, the inner one where her gas credit card and driver's license were. He pulled out both cards before he found the pictures of R. J., the four pictures she gently eased from the plastic whenever she was sad. They looked foreign and forlorn sitting in Mike's hand. Amber felt her knees shake. Her jaw trembled speechlessly.

"What's this junk?" Mike demanded, fingering the frayed edge of her favorite one, R. J. kneeling in front of the barracks.

Amber fought to keep her hands still and not grab the photos up and away. "Oh . . ." she said, forcibly light. "Just pictures. Old pictures. Didn't know I had them."

"You kidding?" His frown was harsh. "You use this wallet every day."

"Yes—but there's all kinds of old stuff in there. You know. Grocery receipts. Stuff like that."

"But these aren't receipts. They're *another guy*."

"Just didn't think about it . . . never look in that part."

"Never need to cash a check with your driver's license?" He stared into her face, squinted with anger. Then he shrugged. "Never mind . . . I'll get rid of them for you." Amber gasped in silence as Mike headed for the trash can in the kitchen.

"No—" she said helplessly, running ahead and blocking his way with arms outstretched.

"Kinda like that army guy, do you?" he said, shoving her aside, his elbow stabbing her ribs. She was standing in front of the kitchen garbage when he abruptly turned and headed in the opposite direction.

"Give them back—they don't hurt anything—"

"They won't after I'm done with them!" he shouted, running to the bathroom.

She caught up with him in time to see him fold the pictures once, then again and again, and tear them into countless ragged shreds over the toilet. She turned away achingly, heard the toilet flush behind her.

She wanted to tell him the hurt was deeper than he could imagine, and, at the same time, he had no worries. She had no idea where R. J. was now, and no intention of leaving this life they had together. She wanted to let him know that R. J. was just a friend who helped her get through the bleak days when Mindy was dying. But she didn't have the energy to risk telling him and having him not understand. There was dinner to fix, and Amy to drive to her piano lesson, and a stack of laundry in the basement to fold. Besides, Mike would be going out soon. By now she knew the signs. If Mike acted restless at dinner, slamming one fist with the other, then it meant he was headed out somewhere that night. She stopped asking his destinations a long time ago, just like she quit trying to track where his paycheck went. If Mike left the house on one of her nights off, she looked at the photos of R. J. Not every time. But the sweet soulful longing to remember those days caught up with her more often than she was willing to admit.

That night, after everyone else in the house was asleep, she put the remaining larger pictures of R. J. in a brown envelope, and transferred them from her bottom bureau drawer to the loose space under the bedroom carpet that only she knew about. The flap of carpet lifted easily, so that she could draw the photos out whenever she felt the need. At least she still had some comfort to turn to.

One night, she realized that her two oldest girls were now teenagers, the same age as she and Mindy were when they stayed at Aunt Nona's. It was hard to believe—both the fact that they were as old as she and Mindy had been and that Aunt Nona still took care of them some of the nights when Mike went out. She suspected he stayed home more often when she was working late. Was it possible he found comfort in solitude—or at least in her absence—the same as she did with him?

As seven more years passed, she took pride in her work and in her growing girls' achievements. But then there was the day when everything went horribly wrong.

Why did the Pepsi taste strange to her? She had drunk thousands, if not millions, of Pepsis in her life. Pepsi was a comforting taste to her since her soda fountain days. Pepsi was also a taste she knew.

But this Pepsi was different. Amber took another taste, held it in her mouth. She couldn't say how it was different, only that it was. A shiver of fear darted over her with the sudden knowledge that the Pepsi wasn't different. *She* was. Something was wrong with *her*.

But what malady could change the flavor of Pepsi? Amber fought to shrug off her fears, and she succeeded, until the swelling started. It was like the days she felt bloated the week before her period. But this was more swelling, as if she suddenly swallowed an ocean. There was no denying the profound change when she looked at herself in the mirror. Terrified, she called the doctor, who gave her an appointment.

"I'm through with that subdivision job," Mike said, washing his hands that night after dinner. "I can drive you to the doctor. What day is your appointment?"

"Oh—no, thank you. I'll drive myself." She fidgeted, her

hands shaking under the towel as she dried the dishes. Some-how, it seemed her worry would stay smaller if she kept it to herself. She felt the same way she did all those years ago with Mindy, when she tried to make believe her schooldays were just the same after her sister was gone.

"Might have to wait a long time. Could be tired when you're done."

She tried to fake a half-smile. "I don't get to take a drive by myself very often. Thought it might relax me. . . ." Though she knew she could never be anywhere near relaxed.

He shook his head, waved a dismissive hand at her. "I'm just trying to help you. Play the good husband."

"I know—" The dishtowel still masking the shaking of her hands.

Now he shook his head. "Who can figure women out? I'm going to take a shower. Then I'm heading out."

The kitchen was peaceful when she was alone in it. She dried the rest of the dishes carefully, set them each in their places in the cupboard, wiped the counters and cabinets, was even tempted to clean the oven. She didn't tell Mike her ap-pointment was the next day. She knew he would take off work and harangue her until she said yes, he could drive.

She went to her closet and mentally chose her clothes for the next day. Her navy blue Sunday dress. Gold earrings. Maybe if she looked her best, somehow the news wouldn't be so bad.

Mike took forever to leave the next morning, as if he some-how knew this was the day. "Doing some touch-up work," he said finally, heading out in his painting clothes, the beige overalls, white T-shirt, and white cloth hat, all splattered with thousands of drops of an assortment of colors of paint. She nodded.

"Have a good day," she said. She watched to be sure his car actually headed down the street.

Her heart thudded. She was glad the children were all off at school or work. Caroline and Mary were both married now, and even Laura was a teenager. Just last month, she'd told Caroline she would help care for her new baby, the same way Aunt Nona helped her. If only she lived to see that day. Shak-ing aside her thoughts, she rushed to her closet, hurriedly threw the dress over her head, combed her hair with hands that shook the way they did under the dishtowel the night before.

Why was she so afraid? She'd been to doctors dozens of times, given birth to four babies, spent half her teenage years sitting in the hospital with Mindy. It was the Pepsi, she sensed suddenly. It would have to be a serious medical condition to change the taste of Pepsi.

There was a long wait in the doctor's office. She imagined how it would be if Mike were there with her, becoming impatient, putting his hat on and taking it off, picking up a magazine, then slapping it down against its rack five minutes later, muttering under his breath.

She was glad she was alone. Without his rising frustration, she could use this time to relax herself. But the wait didn't soothe her nerves, and when the nurse finally called her name, she nearly jumped out of her chair. There was another long wait after the nurse studied her chart and took her pulse and blood pressure.

Finally the doctor would see her. He looked at her chart, sat in a chair, peered out at her from wire-rimmed glasses. "What are we seeing you for today?"

Amber swallowed. "Swelling. I'm having a lot of swelling."

"Oh." He squinted at her. "Extremities? Your hands and feet?"

In the midst of her tension she almost laughed. In all this staring, wasn't he even looking at her? "No, my stomach. I look like I'm about to have triplets."

His head cocked. "Pregnancy a possibility?"

"No way. I had a partial hysterectomy last year. And I'm too old."

Another frown. "What about eating habits? Consuming additional calories?"

"No. I hardly eat at all. And I'm like a balloon all over. My rings are tight on my fingers. My shoes feel tight at the toes."

"Hmmm—" the doctor said.

Finally all her worries let loose in a wave. "How could I swell so much when I don't have my period anymore and I hardly eat at all?"

This time the doctor didn't have a suggestion of what could be wrong. Instead, over the next three weeks, he ordered tests—blood tests, X rays, and the agonizingly painful procedure where he drained fluid from her stomach. Thinking of all the needles, pains, poking, and prodding she'd been through, she suddenly recalled that long ago day in Mr. Staker's science classroom. I'm like that cat was then, she thought. A specimen. Something to be poked and evaluated. But I'm not dead. And I'm not the girl I was then, either. There is no way I can run away from what's wrong with me now.

The days of waiting after the tests were agony. She was scheduled to return to the doctor's office next week to find out the results. But then the phone call came.

From the first moment the doctor's voice sounded wrong. Why was he calling her at home?

"Amber? This is Dr. Rigby. . . ."

She was too surprised to speak.

"I'm calling about your test results. . . ."

"Am I okay?"

"I'm recommending you go in the hospital for further examination."

Her heart pounded. "What's wrong with me?"

"The results aren't conclusive yet. I'll let you know when the testing is complete. . . ."

"But you suspect something bad! I know you do. . . . Please tell me."

The doctor paused. "There is a tumor on your ovary, Amber. I'm sorry. We think it may be cancer. . . ."

Disbelief draped her in a dark wave when she heard that Mike had had a heart attack at home—while she was in surgery. Lying in her hospital bed, she pictured the scene again and again. Mike—who could do physical work all day, shoot pool half the night, and get up the next morning and do it all again—was suddenly weaker than she was. Each night, she phoned Amy and Laura to make sure they were all right at home. She tried to tell them not to worry, but felt sure she couldn't disguise the concern in her own voice.

Her hospital room was 301 B. Mike was in Room 301 E.

Being three hospital rooms away from him reminded her of that day, so many years ago, when Mama made her leave home and she took refuge at Mike's house.

This was the same feeling. They were together, without intending to be. Thrown into close proximity.

As the nights passed, she weakly walked down to his room, sat at his bedside. Memories of Mindy flooded back as the two of them sat, speaking little. We are the waiting wounded, she thought. Hiding out here in hopes that another attack isn't hovering on the horizon.

One week later she didn't hear the commotion in the hall as the nurse opened the door to enter her room.

"They sent me in to tell you," the nurse began. Amber caught fear and avoidance in the woman's eyes. "It's about your husband."

A molten, sinking feeling spread through Amber. "He's all right, isn't he?"

The nurse shook her head. "It was his heart. I'm sorry to have to tell you—"

"No—" Amber said, her heart beating fast. "Don't tell me." Somehow, she thought God couldn't take anyone else from her. Now Mike—

"He's still alive?" she asked, grasping for a shred of hope.

The nurse shook her head once more. "I'm sorry—"

Amber's voice broke. "How could it happen here? In the hospital . . . I know everyone watched him. . . ."

"He had a second heart attack," the nurse confided. "It happened quickly. There was nothing we could do. . . ."

Amber received special permission from her doctor to attend Mike's funeral. Standing over his casket, she saw that he was handsome to the end of his life. She felt numb as people patted her shoulder, spoke to her, hugged her. This scene wasn't supposed to happen yet. It just seemed so unreal to see Mike lying so still. So silent.

She returned to the hospital to complete her recovery and then went home to the girls. As months passed she went through the motions of life. Work. Home. It was as if her life were happening to someone else.

Chapter Thirteen

Amber's only solace these days were the photos of R. J. With their frayed edges and yellowed backs, the pictures were probably her oldest friends. In the black-and-white photo where he knelt in front of the barracks, R. J. still smiled out at her as he did that night on the skating rink, dimples deepening and white teeth flashing. She sighed, thinking how handsome he looked. She imagined this picture might have been taken the day he sent her the ring—his deep-set eyes seemed to hold a secret that now would probably be kept forever. Amber sat in her rocker, the pictures on her lap, and rocked slowly. It would be impossible to describe the freedom she felt just sitting with the pictures on her lap, not worried that Mike would come in the room, find them, tear them up, and wrench her heart. Mike. She still thought he would come in the room. Her mind couldn't accept the thought that he was gone.

She had a sudden thought that left her with a haunting chill. What would happen to the photographs when she died? She cringed, picturing Caroline or Mary tossing the worn goldenrod-colored envelope out without looking inside. Or Amy or Laura might glance at the pictures and think that R. J. was an old friend of their father's. As soon as they sensed they didn't know the man in the photos, they, too, would see that the pictures landed in the garbage. Now, with all the years that had passed, the pictures seemed more precious than ever in Amber's mind. Even though she still couldn't tell her family about them, she had to see that they were safe.

She had to find R. J. The thought raced through her mind and heart, bringing chills of electricity that raced up her arms to her cheeks.

Or—and she battled this thought even as it rose in her mind—if he was dead, she could give the pictures to his family. As she had all the years before, she fought images of him dying in the service, as Brent did. But if R. J. wasn't alive, she had to find his wife and children, and maybe grandchildren. There was simply no one else who would understand that these pictures were treasures. His children would want them. His grandchildren should be able to find out what a handsome man their grandpa was.

Placing the pictures in the envelope and putting the envelope once more in the corner of her closet, Amber sat and struggled to remember all the places R. J. had mentioned living in his life. The girl she was back then was more interested in who would win the game of Hi-Lo or who could twirl the fastest on roller skates than where her R. J. lived before she knew him. She suddenly realized that, back then, she'd simply thought she and R. J. would go on skating and writing letters and laughing together forever. She shook her head at the boundless faith of youth. But thinking of how fast childhood faded, she concentrated, surprised at the memories that filtered through her head. Suddenly her hand was writing quickly.

There was Seoul, Korea, where R. J. and Brent were together in the army.

Fort Sill, Oklahoma, where they were before that.

Orlando, Florida.

And he always talked about Oregon. Salem and Portland. The address on his last letter. Oakland, California.

And she couldn't forget their first date in Washington, D.C. He knew all the monuments so well. As if he had been there a lot of times. Could he live there now?

Amber wrote, fast and flowing, listing one city after another.

Then she picked up the phone, determined to find as many Raymond Williamses as she could before she grew tired.

She started with Portland, the farthest away from her.

"Raymond Williams, please," she said, as if the operator could simply walk to the next room, tap R. J. on the shoulder, and tell him he had a phone call.

"Address?"

"I can't help you there."

"I have seven of them, ma'am."

Amber hesitated only a second. "Give me all of them, please."

"Can only give you three per phone call."

"But this is an emergency."

"I'll connect you to my supervisor."

A long silence. Amber heard a roomful of telephone operators talking to scores of customers. Would the operator just leave her here? How long should she wait?

"Service Assistant, Mrs. Moran . . ."

"I need to have all the phone numbers of all the Raymond Williamses in Portland. . . ."

"Could we narrow the search—do you know what street he lives on? Or what part of town? Would he have a business that we could locate the number for?"

"I don't know any of those things."

"Might the phone be listed in his wife's name?"

"I have no idea if he has a wife."

A sigh. "The operator said this is an emergency?"

"Yes—" Amber fought back tears as she said the words she only let hover in her head during her darkest hours. "I have cancer. I've had surgery and chemotherapy. I have some valuable belongings of his that I need to give him before I die."

Amber pictured Mrs. Moran weighing the situation in the long pause that followed. Finally she cleared her throat. "I'll instruct the operator to give you all the phone numbers."

"And the addresses—"

"We don't normally supply address information—"

Amber closed her eyes. "This is not a normal situation. I'm very ill."

Mrs. Moran was almost whispering. "I'll tell her to give you those, too."

In the days that followed, Amber collected phone numbers and addresses for nearly a hundred men named Raymond Williams. How could a name for someone so unique be so common?

She sat at her desk and began to write:

She crossed out "Dear" and wrote "To Whom It May Concern."

My name is Amber Bentley. I'm trying to find a Raymond Williams who was in the army from 1958 to 1963. He could have been in the army longer than that. But 1963 was the last year I saw or heard from him. Raymond was a friend of my brother, Brent Lee, who was killed in Thailand in 1968. He was also a very special friend to me.

I am currently battling cancer. My husband, Michael Bentley, passed away last year. The reason I want to find Ray or his family is that I have some pictures of him when he was young. One picture is of his entire family—mother, father, sister, and brothers. I would like to send the pictures to Ray or his family. Now that I am a mother, I know how fast time goes and how precious pictures can be. I would like these photographs to find their way to someone who will treasure them as I have for the past thirty-seven years.

Amber paused. What could she say that would help someone else know that the Raymond they knew was the right one? She began to list facts—the last address where she wrote to him. That his nickname was R. J. That he went to Korea in 1960 and was stationed at Fort Sill before that.

I appreciate your willingness to consider my request. Please feel free to write to me at the following address or call me at the following number.

> Sincerely,
> Amber Bentley

She was writing the letter a second time in longhand before she shook her head in frustration and drove to the copy center.

She wrote envelopes until her hand felt a cramp, then waited an hour and wrote more. It took her three days to address envelopes to all the Raymond Williamses. The stamps cost almost thirty-five dollars.

It was a week before she began to receive responses. Most were quick. Sorry, not the one you are looking for. Not related to my family. No connection to me. I was out of the army long before 1958. Most people dismissed her with a single sentence. Yet others were friendlier.

Jan. 5, 1997

Dear Mrs. Bentley,
The Williams you are looking for would be much younger than my husband was. He died in 1987. He was 62. He was in the service in 1944. He had no sister and was not sent to Korea. My thoughts are with you, though. I sincerely hope you find the person you are looking for.

Sincerely,
Mrs. Raymond T. Williams (Betty)

The army. It seemed as if all the men were in the army. She could write to the army. If anyone should know, it would be them. The next morning she called the army office, who referred her to the Department of Veteran's Affairs in Baltimore.

Dear Department of Veteran's Affairs,
I am looking for a Raymond Williams who was in the Army between 1958 and 1963. After that, I don't know what happened to him. His nickname was R. J. I'm enclosing a copy of one of his pictures when he was in the service. He would be in his early sixties now. He was also a friend of my brother, Brent Lee, who was in the army with him. Brent was killed in Thailand in 1968. My family lived in Annapolis, Maryland, from 1960–1968. I think his family lived in West Palm Beach, Florida, at that time. They may still live there now.

*I am trying to find him because I would like to send
him or his children some pictures that I have of him
when he was younger. I have cancer, and lost my husband in 1994. I hate to think of my daughters finding
the pictures and then throwing them away.*

*If you know where he is or have any idea how I might
find him, please write or call me.*

Sincerely,
Amber Bentley

Three weeks later she received a letter from the Military
Records Department. There was rejection in almost every sentence. "Because of insufficient or inaccurate information, we
cannot identify the proper record," wrote a man named Leo
Carnell, whose title was Veteran's Service Officer, who
added, "If the following information is not furnished, we will
be unable to take further action on your correspondence."

What information did they need about R. J.? Amber's eyes
dipped to the bottom of the page.

Social Security number. Date of Birth. Service Number.
Date Entered Service. Date of Separation. Date of Death.

All the information I don't have, she thought. She folded
the letter and put it with the others sent from people across
the country. She closed the drawer filled with letters and
sighed.

Chapter Fourteen

She knew the routine by now—blood test, X ray, and a long wait. But this time each minute seemed interminable. Dr. Rigby's face looked wooden.

"Amber—" he said, tapping his pen against the examining table where it made a hollow sound. He didn't look at her.

"I'm through with the tests, aren't I?" she asked cautiously.

He sighed. "Technically, yes—"

"But you have to do something else? Is that it? Why aren't you looking at me?" A shiver of fear filled her.

"Sometimes, even when it seems as if everything has been done—we can't predict how the treatment will be received by the body. . . ."

"What do you mean?"

He closed his eyes, wiped them with his hands, then let his hands drop to his knees. "It's back—there's no other way to say it. We found new cancer sites."

"Sites? In more than one place?"

Now he looked at the floor again. "At least two places . . ."

"Oh." Amber covered her face with her hands. "Is there anything left to do?"

The doctor stared into her eyes for the flash of a second. "More chemo."

Dread settled over her like a black, encompassing cloud, and she recalled all too clearly the pain, nausea, and exhaustion. How could she live through it all again? "More chemo?

When it didn't get rid of everything last time? Is there any other choice?"

"None," he said, lips tight, then moments later, "None that will help you heal."

"So it's chemo again—or I die . . ."

"I didn't want to say it that way."

"But that's the truth, isn't it?"

Dr. Rigby nodded.

So she signed up for more chemo. Each week the routine was the same. One day of treatment, at least one more day of feeling weak, and then a woefully shortened week before it was time to go back again. She still worked—one or two days a week. And she babysat for Caroline and Mary, who insisted on paying her.

But in between she wrote letters. Wasn't there someone out there who could help her find R. J.?

It was like carrying a suitcase on each arm—writing and searching helped balance the continuing chemo treatments that left her weak. For the next year she set a goal of writing two letters a week. Joe Culligan, Sally Jessy Raphael, People Finders. She wrote letter after letter. Sometimes two or three to the same place. Usually there was no answer. Still, she kept writing, figuring that she would try as long as she was alive, which couldn't be much longer.

It was Thursday, the day after a chemo treatment. Amber was lazily watching *The Maury Povich Show*. Before the regular commercial a bright, zippy voice advised viewers who wanted to meet their lost loves to call Maury, right then. Amber felt chills. Was R. J. her lost love? They were engaged, if only for a month. You usually weren't engaged to someone unless he was your love.

Reminding herself that she could always hang up if she chickened out, Amber dialed. A voice mail machine answered, then a recording of Maury's voice, friendly, happy, saying that all representatives were busy.

She waited.

"*Maury Povich*—" said the young woman who answered.

Amber breathed quickly, her words a jumble in her mind.

"*Maury Povich*—" A touch of impatience in the woman's voice this time.

"Yes—" Amber waited.

"How may I direct your call?"

"I saw the ad—on TV just now—about lost loves."

"Oh, you are responding to our ad? Looking for your own lost love, by any chance?"

Amber felt chills. "I think so . . . maybe . . ."

"A boyfriend?"

"We were engaged . . . not very long, though."

"Oh . . . a former fiancé?"

"Yes, I guess that would be it."

"You still think about this man. . . ."

"Well . . . see . . . I have these pictures . . ."

"Of this man?"

"Yes . . . I . . . saved them. . . ."

"Since you knew each other? How long ago was that?"

Amber pretended to have to stop and think, even though she knew the answer right away. "Thirty-seven years . . ."

"And you've still got his pictures, huh. . . ."

"Yes . . . I want to give them back to his family. . . ." Amber hesitated.

"Then you don't want to see him. . . ."

"I don't know if he's still alive. . . . He was in the war. . . ."

"But would you want to see him if you could?"

More chills. "I would," Amber said slowly.

"Well, sounds pretty interesting to me. I'll have someone call you back. Why don't you give me some quick facts first. Our staff will see if they think they could do a search."

The dates were all in her head, along with the names. She even recalled the first day they met. She waited while the woman wrote.

"Thanks a lot, Amber. Somebody will probably call you back."

"Okay."

"Bye."

The phone clicked and Amber instantly felt very much alone. The silence in the house roared around her, and she realized she felt anxious with anticipation. The way she felt long ago on the first day of kindergarten. Or on the day she started work at the pharmacy. It was the same sensation she experienced in the hospital when her baby was about to be born. That tingly, not-knowing what-would-happen-next feeling. She sat a long time and waited for the phone to ring, even though she knew she might never hear back. Probably thousands of people called every day. And she didn't absolutely have to see him. She could just send the pictures. The long aching silence in her house was both agonizing and a relief. What did she think would happen here?

Friday passed. The weekend. Monday. She half-forgot that someone would call. Maybe there wasn't much chance, like a sweepstakes. . . .

Then the phone rang Tuesday afternoon, after lunch.

"Amber? Amber Bentley?" Amber recognized a New York accent and chills ran down her spine.

"Yes, this is she. . . ." Amber closed her eyes quickly to try to calm herself.

"Amber, this is Lisa. With *Maury Povich*? We talked the other day?"

"Yes . . . I remember."

"Amber, could you come to New York on Friday?"

"Oh . . ." Her whole body was trembling now. "You found R. J.?"

"Well . . . no. Actually, Amber, we need your help. We're thinking that if you could come and bring those pictures, we could display them on the show, and someone out there—a viewer, say—might know where to find R. J."

"I could just send the pictures to you, and someone there could show them."

"We thought you might like to do that yourself. And you could tell the audience what you remember about R. J."

"But I've never been on a plane."

"Don't worry about any of that, Amber. We'll take care of all the arrangements. The only thing you have to decide is if you want to do this. But you have to let me know right now, during this phone call. We have a space for you on the show, but I need to fill it now. . . ."

What could she lose? She was filled with chills. In total disbelief she said the only answer her mind could form. "I guess I could."

"Is that a yes, Amber?"

"Yes."

"I'll call you back then, in just a few moments. Get those photos ready and start packing your bags."

"But—" Amber said.

But Lisa was already gone. Worry rolled over Amber in waves. What would her kids think, knowing that she really wanted to find this guy she knew before she married their dad? And what about R. J.'s family? His wife and kids? And if he died, did she really want to know about that, too?

Yes, she realized suddenly, terrified as ever. She really did want to know. And whatever happened, she hoped she'd survive it all.

After she left her house the next Friday morning, everything felt like a dream . . . from the plane taking off, the cab ride to the hotel, to her restaurant dinner. Could she sleep, even for five minutes? Could this really be happening to her? She'd never been this nervous before.

The next day in the green room she sat and looked at the photos in the manila folder she held. An ironic laugh erupted in her throat. After all the years of hiding the pictures—under the rug, under the couch, in her closet, between two pairs of pants she never wore—now she was going to show them to millions of people on TV.

She laughed again, silently, until her insides shook. Who would have thought?

Minutes seemed like hours. Or more. She listened to people bustling outside the green room.

Finally Lisa, a gorgeous blond with her hair in a shell-shaped twist atop her head, entered the green room.

"Okay," Lisa said, sitting beside her. "All I need to tell you is that when they ask to see the pictures, hold that largest one up in the direction of the camera—toward your right."

"What do I say?"

"Just answer the questions. It will be easy."

"Do I give them my address? Or my phone number? In case someone wants to tell me how to find R. J.?"

"No." Lisa laughed. "I wouldn't advise you to give out your personal information on national television. Don't worry about that. We'll tell our viewers to contact *The Maury Povich Show*—"

"And they'll let me know? If someone calls?" Why did she feel suddenly desperate? As if finding R. J. were a matter of life and death?

"Yes . . ." Lisa said. "We'll let you know immediately. And, most likely, we'll bring you back on the show for a reunion follow-up."

"Oh." Amber sat back against her chair. The idea of being on TV even once was dizzying. And now she might have to come back.

"Anyway, Amber"—Lisa waved a hand—"someone will be in to get you momentarily."

Momentarily. There was no turning back now. This was it. An electric feeling, like a thousand butterflies.

Then another producer, a handsome young man in a suit, came to get her. Amber walked out with him into a sea of cameras and lights. The sight of the audience took her breath away, but Maury's gentle voice drew her attention back.

"This is Amber Bentley," Maury was saying. "Amber brought a treasure with her today. A priceless memento. Can you show us what you brought with you, Amber?"

She handed him the photo, which he held up in the air. "Pretty ragged edges on this photograph, Amber. I'd say you looked at it a time or two over the years. This is Amber's friend . . . from how long ago, Amber?"

"Thirty-seven years," Amber said quietly, conscious of the microphone around her neck.

"Thirty-seven years. Wow. Let's show the audience what your friend looks like." Maury handed the photo to a production assistant, who instantly projected it onto a screen behind them.

"This is Amber's friend, Raymond."

"I called him R. J.—" she interrupted.

"Amber's friend R. J. And you were engaged, were you?"

"Yes. I gave his ring back because my sister was dying and I didn't think I could move away right then."

"And you thought about him after that?"

"Well, I married someone else. Had four kids."

Maury laughed. "But you still remembered R. J."

Amber nodded tentatively. "I always wondered if he was okay. He was my friend. I wondered if he was all right after the war."

Maury turned to glance quickly at the picture. "Just a friend? He looks like a pretty handsome guy, Amber."

"He was." Amber's smile widened to match Maury's.

"Tell us, Amber. Did he look anything like that man walking down those stairs over there?" Maury pointed over her shoulder, to the right, in back of where she sat.

Amber turned. Her jaw dropped. She shrieked, mindless of the millions of people watching. Her whole body filled with electricity. The man on the stairs was R. J. There was no question in her mind, even though he now had silver hair and wore gold-rimmed glasses. His grin was the same, and he was smiling at her. Suddenly, after all these years, Amber couldn't wait another second. She leaped out of her chair next to Maury and charged toward R. J., who grabbed her in a long hug.

"I'd say they're pretty good friends, wouldn't you?" Maury said to the audience.

She couldn't let go of him. Not now—not after all this time.

"Definitely good friends," Maury said a moment later. "Any way I can talk you two into sitting down with me for a moment?"

Their arms dropped from around each other. R. J. took her hand and led her to two chairs next to Maury.

"Looks like we found your friend, Amber. . . ." Maury's grin again.

"Yes. I was totally shocked," said Amber.

"But now there's still the big question left. . . ." Maury raised his eyebrows.

What did he mean? Amber wondered.

"Amber . . . tell us . . . are you married?"

"My husband died three years ago," Amber said.

"Now, R. J." Maury paused. R. J. grinned, and laughter rippled through the audience.

"R. J.—tell us—you handsome guy. Are you a single man?"

R. J. grinned again, a long grin. Amber realized she was

holding her breath. "Widowed," he said softly.

A gasp from the audience, then boisterous laughter.

"Really. Well, Amber, you might be glad we found this friend of yours."

"I'm glad he's all right."

"Looks like he's more than all right to me, Amber. Why don't we give you two a little bit of time to get to know each other. How about a night on the town, on us?"

Amber and R. J. looked at each other, smiled sheepishly. "Thank you," Amber managed. R. J. shook hands with Maury, and a smiling assistant led them off-stage, then back on again at the end of the show.

"Well, audience, what do you think—what about Amber and R. J.? Anything going to happen here?"

Cheers, catcalls, and more laughter.

Maury patted Amber's shoulder. "It's full speed ahead, guys."

Again, the production assistant, leading them to the exit this time, reminding them about their flights the next day, cab fare, the free dinner, and the hotel costs. They reached an exit at the back of the building.

Finally they were alone. Thirty-seven years since it was just the two of them. Amber found herself feeling as shy as when she walked down the stairs of her parents' house to meet him for the first time. But moments later R. J. slid his arm across her shoulders, and they walked out into the city, which was bathed in a calming, turquoise twilight. Several minutes passed, comfortable and soothing, even though neither of them spoke as they sauntered down the street. "I want to buy you a root-beer float," R. J. said suddenly, catching sight of a hamburger restaurant.

"Then I'll buy you a grilled cheese," she said, her laughter surprising even herself. "But aren't we supposed to have a fancy dinner? Steak and lobster?"

"Maybe later," said R. J.

The restaurant was quiet, reminiscent of her earlier days at the Mount Jordan Pharmacy. Memories flooded her mind as they walked in and sat at a pillowy leather booth.

R. J. angled his chin to where four teenagers cooked in the kitchen behind the counter. "Bet you could step in back there and give 'em all a run for their money."

"I don't know. Been a long time," she said, her eyes abruptly dropping to the Formica tabletop. Truthfully, at that moment, it didn't seem as if any time had passed. She smiled shyly at R. J., feeling suddenly as awkward as a teenager.

The waiter, who couldn't be more than seventeen himself, handed them each a menu. Amber gratefully let her eyes focus on the menu listings. "Some things never change," she murmured. "BLTs, fries, cheeseburgers."

When he didn't respond, she looked up to find R. J. smiling at her. "You haven't changed a bit, either. . . ."

"Oh, yeah. . . . how can I look the same if I'm bald?" She touched her hair, still patchy, growing in now between rounds of chemo.

"What's going to happen now?" R. J. asked.

"With me? Well, my cancer is back, you know."

"But you're having treatment. . . ."

"I had treatment once before . . . and it came back. I don't know how long I have to live. . . ." Suddenly her throat caught, as she saw pain fill his eyes. He reached for her hand, but she shook his hand away, her fingers fluttering with emotion. "I need to tell you. I'm still sorry about the ring. How I just left it on the chair like that—"

R. J. shook his head. "No big deal."

Amber raised her voice. "It was a big deal. I never forgot, and I still need to apologize. . . . I told myself I'd get those pictures back to you if it was the last thing I did—"

"And now I want you to keep them . . . like I kept these. . . ."

She watched as he drew a brown envelope from his briefcase. He reached inside and took out pictures of her, standing on the porch, standing in front of Mrs. Rand's car, sitting on the couch wearing the long-ago engagement ring.

R. J. leaned forward and lowered his voice. After a quick sidelong glance at the teenage cooks in the kitchen, he said, "When I asked what's going to happen now, I didn't mean with your illness." He paused patiently. "I meant with us."

Amber sighed. "Even if nothing happens, I did the one thing I wanted. I saw that the pictures found their way to you."

R. J.'s smile was familiar, accompanied by a few more wrinkles, but just as charming. "I hoped we'd be friends at least. Here we are, both alone. Can't we be friends?"

"R. J.—you don't know. I'm sick a lot. I have chemo one day a week. Then I don't feel good for at least one more day . . . or maybe two days."

"That leaves us four days. Four days isn't bad."

"But—are you still working?"

"I'm a painter. I can work my schedule around yours. I'll come to see you. On your good days."

"My husband was a painter." Amber's eyes widened in surprise. "I never guessed you would be one, too. I sort of imagined you having a job where you worked at a desk. I never imagined what I thought you would be, but I didn't picture you and Mike doing the same work. . . ."

R. J. laughed, rolled his eyes. "You were a painter's wife."

"But when I was his wife, I was doing other things, too. I was a maintenance supervisor. I worked in a restaurant. Mike was full of life, but making money wasn't always what he did best. I had to help pay the bills."

R. J. smiled again. "Always a good worker. Right from the beginning. Old man Sorensen didn't know what he was getting when he hired you. But I knew you were special right away." He touched her cheek, then continued talking as Amber looked away in embarrassment. "The way you were with your sister. You never made excuses about having to leave me to be with her. Her being sick didn't scare me away—it only made me want you more. I wanted you to care about me like you cared about Mindy."

Amber couldn't speak. She draped her forehead with her hand to hide a sudden rush of tears.

R. J. lowered his voice again. "I don't mail engagement rings to just anybody, you know."

When was the last time she blushed? As her cheeks warmed, Amber stifled a nervous laugh. "I'll never forget that day. But I'm not the same girl I was then. I'm pretty boring when I'm sick. I sleep a lot. But I guess you can come visit me. If you get bored, you can leave early," she said hopefully.

"I'm definitely coming to visit. Don't blush again—even

if I ask for your phone number right now." He slid his napkin across the table to her.

Amber fished in her purse for a pen, wrote the number on the napkin. "If I'm sick, I don't answer the phone. But you can leave a message."

"I'm good at that. You won't get rid of me so easy this time."

The lump in her throat came back, but she forced herself to speak past it. "Even if nothing else happens, and we're just friends"—now she reached out and took his hand in hers—"I thank God you are with me today."

Amber was still grasping R. J.'s hand when the teenaged waiter approached with their food. She didn't let go of his fingers until after the waiter set the two grilled cheeses and root-beer floats down on the table. As she lifted the toothpick spear out of her sandwich and bit into the warm melted cheese, her eyes met R. J.'s, and a rising feeling filled her. Somehow she sensed that this was only the first of many root-beer floats and grilled cheese sandwiches that the two of them would share together. The realization filled her with joy and she smiled at him with tear-filled eyes. "I should have written to you—the day after I left the ring on the chair. It only took me twenty minutes to know I'd made a big mistake. As soon as I got to the hospital, I turned around and came back . . . but you were gone."

R. J.'s brown eyes gave her a sympathetic look. "I admit I was surprised. I had no idea you wanted to say no."

"That's just it—" She sighed. "I didn't mean to say no back then. I wanted to say 'not now.' But I never heard of anyone saying 'not now' to an engagement ring. In the movies they always say yes . . . or absolutely not."

R. J. sat back. "I think 'not now' is okay when you're a teenager. When you have lots of years ahead . . . and you're not really sure what you want."

Amber waited.

"But a few years down the line, there are times when 'why not' is probably better than 'not now.' "

Amber blushed and looked down.

"I should have said yes," Amber murmured. "I should have known it would be all right. . . ."

"Water under the bridge," R. J. said suddenly. "We are officially past 'not now' and we're moving on to 'why not?' "

Amber sighed. "I can think of a lot of reasons why not. I'm sick . . . I live in another state . . ."

Now R. J. waited.

When their eyes met, she said, "But after the last time, I wouldn't want to let those things hold me back again. I know I'd be sorry later on. . . ."

R. J.'s smile was patient.

"So, at this late stage of my life, I'm going to be brave and do what I really want to do."

He raised his eyebrows and grinned at her.

She reached out and took his hand. "R. J., why not? Why not be friends now, and see what happens?"

"I can't think of a reason in the world. . . ." R. J. said, smiling at her. Their eyes met and held. They laughed together, a sound as young as they felt inside.

A Bond Beyond Time

Chapter One

Her first day. The orange brick building that was St. Anne's High School seemed to stretch for blocks. She was brave, Sara Montgomery thought, transferring here where she knew no one. Still, the science department received high ratings. Could she really reach her dream of becoming a nurse? Now that more troops were being sent to fight the Vietnam War, Sara sensed her country would need more nurses than ever before.

Feeling suddenly shy, she stared at the groups of students around her, all talking and laughing. No one approached her, or seemed to care that a new student stood here, slightly scared and totally alone. Sara thought of Mama, Daddy, and Grandma at home. They all offered to drive her and help her register this first day. She responded that now that she was starting her second semester of high school, and worked as a candy striper, she should be able to fill out registration cards on her own. But now she wished someone were beside her. She imagined Grandma putting on all her makeup, perfume, and earrings for a visit to the high school. She thought of Daddy, tall and stately, who would be a comforting presence standing beside her. Or Mama, petite and serene, keeping a calm conversation flowing with positive comments—right now she might say the school grounds and students looked clean—or that the school probably had a grand piano for Sara to play. She knew Mama would try to help her feel she made the right choice.

But she was the only one standing here, wishing someone would speak to her. A voice inside seemed to whisper that maybe it wasn't too late to turn back, to return to Skyline High, the neighborhood school where she had friends, knew her way around the halls, and already made good grades. Right now her dream of nursing school seemed light-years away.

Suddenly the bell rang. Everyone rushed for the door. Sara felt as if she were inside her mother's kitchen blender as throngs of students pushed past, some brushing against her and saying "excuse me," as she waited stock-still. After everyone else was in the building, she stood for another long moment. She glanced at the building, the grounds, the cars parked in the teachers' parking lot. With a sigh, she walked up the stairs alone, hearing her new loafers brush against each step. The knob of the glass-paned door felt cold and heavy inside her hand. She shifted her school bag and held her breath. This is it, she thought.

She was looking for the office when someone abruptly tapped her shoulder. She turned to face a frowning woman with gray-beige hair.

"What are you doing out in the hall? You're not supposed to be out of class."

Startled, Sara blurted, "I don't go here—I mean—"

"If you are a visitor, you must report to the office—"

"Well—I'm—not a visitor."

"You *are* a student? Then you're tardy."

Sara stammered, "I haven't—I need to register—"

"For your classes? That should have been complete weeks ago."

"But I'm new—"

"New-student registration was last month."

"I just decided to go to school here. After I read about the school's high science scores." Sara paused. "I'm hoping to go to nursing school at State."

The woman's frown deepened. "Yet you didn't *register*?"

"No—this is my first day."

Shaking her head, the woman sighed. Her hand brushed

Sara's shoulder. "You can't wander in the halls. I'll take you to the office."

Great, Sara thought. My first day and I'm already in big trouble.

But when the stern woman took her to the office and she showed her student identification card from Skyline High the year before, a counselor told her that students often transferred to private schools, like St. Anne's, in the middle of the year. He helped her create a schedule that was hearteningly familiar. English. Science. Choir. Algebra. P.E., Spanish, music. He told her she'd have to try out for choir, but if she'd already been in choir in another school, she had a good chance.

Maybe she'd make it here, after all.

She was walking out of the office when the counselor called her back.

"You have Mr. Steiner second period. That's where you should go now."

"Am I too early for class?"

"No—" He looked at his watch. "Started ten minutes ago."

Great, Sara thought. In trouble in first period, late for second.

She was batting a thousand.

Rick Douglas never felt this way before. Somehow he sensed that for the rest of his life, he would never forget the first moment he saw Sara. It didn't start out to be a life-changing day. He was simply talking to his friend James, who sat behind him in science. When Mr. Steiner spoke and Rick turned to face forward, a tall blond girl stood at the doorway to the classroom. Something about her instantly grabbed his attention. He couldn't look away. Rick stared. His brain hummed with recognition and fascination, though his logical mind told him he'd never seen that gorgeous face before.

"We have a new student," Mr. Steiner announced, smiling and nodding to the tall girl who waited for permission to enter. "Welcome. Please come in and introduce yourself."

The girl skirted across the room and stood at Mr. Steiner's desk. Tall and regal. Blond hair cascading over her shoulders like a cape. Enchanting green eyes. *Enchanting* was a word

Rick had never used before, even in his thoughts. But this time it fit. He—and all the rest of the class—waited for her to speak. She stood silently, shifted her feet. "I know how you feel," Rick wanted to say. "You're shy, like me." His heart went out to her. His own nervousness surged. He knew how it felt to stand in front of the class and feel as if your jaws were glued shut.

Seconds dragged. The class waited. Rick held his breath. Anxiety filled his mind, as if he himself were trying to force out words.

When it seemed as if the tension could stretch no further, Mr. Steiner spoke.

"May we ask your name?"

The girl waited a moment, then looked out into the class. Rick could swear that she caught his eye . . . maybe. In his dreams. He finally released a sigh as the girl spoke.

"Sara Anne—uh, Sara Montgomery." Reciting her name as if it were the answer to a complicated chemistry formula.

"Do you prefer Sara?" Mr. Steiner's encouraging voice.

The girl nodded. Her hair hardly stirred. Rick realized he never knew a girl named Sara before.

"This is your first day here?"

Another nod.

"Where are you from?"

"I live on Osborne Road. I just decided to transfer to St. Anne's."

"We think you made a great choice, don't we, class?" Mr. Steiner turned to smile at the students before looking back at Sara. "We're happy to have you here with us."

Yes, thought Rick, surprised at the assurance he felt. We are very happy.

When the bell rang, Rick stood at the back of the science room, waiting for other students to file out as Sara talked to Mr. Steiner. Unable to stall any longer without looking obvious, he walked out into the hall, and headed for choir.

He finally saw her again, later that day in "A" Hall. She was talking to Hollie, a girl he knew. Now why can't I do that? he thought. Just walk up and introduce myself. Hi, Sara. I'm Rick, he said in his mind. Something tells me I already know you. He felt chills even thinking about it.

• • •

Catching sight of city bus number 20, Sara breathed a sigh
of relief. She'd actually made it to the end of the day after
fumbling through her new school schedule. Shaking her head,
she remembered the crowds of students in the halls, and how
she got lost at first. She'd just gotten so turned around that it
was impossible to find anything. By the time she found the
cafeteria, the lunch lines were so long she only had ten
minutes to eat. She missed her New Testament class because
she didn't know the chapel was a separate building until after
school was over. Thinking back over her day, she recalled
Hollie, the friendly girl who told her she'd like it at St.
Anne's, and Mr. Steiner, who asked what her interests were
and told her he'd make an appointment for her to try out for
choir. And there was that one boy in English. The tall guy
with dark hair and brown eyes. Had she seen him someplace
before? Sara remembered his face clearly. But she had no
idea of his name.

The school was new to her, but she'd already ridden bus
number 20 for a year, once a week to the Joy Estate nursing
home and once a week to Holy Cross Hospital. Sara felt relief
as the familiar pink stucco building appeared in front of her
like an oasis in the desert. Joy Estate. Sara always felt a sadness thinking of the irony of that name and small amount of
joy that existed in what people whispered was God's waiting
room. Finding the rest room, she donned her familiar "pep-
permint stick" pink-and-white candy striper uniform.

She stepped off the elevator, and was walking toward the
nurse's station when someone yelled at her. "Hey, you!
Where you been all day?"

Sara looked around. There was no one else in the hall.

"Yes, you! Where you been?"

Sara stepped closer to the voice. She saw that it belonged
to Mrs. Gessel, a recovering heart attack patient who nurses
suspected had the beginnings of dementia. Sara never saw
Mrs. Gessel get out of bed before. Now she stood barefoot
in the hall in her hospital gown.

Sara forced a calm voice. "How are you, Mrs. Gessel?"

"Well, you weren't here to give me my pill . . ."

Sara glimpsed at the elderly woman's hands knotted in agitation. "I was at school," she admitted. During the summer, she'd arrived earlier, right after lunch. Maybe Mrs. Gessel remembered. As Sara watched, the older woman thrust out her withered chin.

"You didn't get here on time . . ."

"But I'm here now," Sara said wondering if her words registered in the woman's mind at all. "I'll ask the nurse for your medication and bring it to you in just a moment. Let me take you back to your room now." Sara gently placed a hand on Mrs. Gessel's elbow to guide her.

Mrs. Gessel yanked her arm away. "No! I won't go back! When you weren't here, I took my medicine! Now I want to go home!"

A chill of fear darted through Sara. "Show me where you took the medicine," she said.

To her amazement, Mrs. Gessel walked with her behind the nurse's office to the area where pill trays were prepared. She pointed to the medicine cabinet. "There!"

Sara glanced at the rows of pills. "Did you take some pills from here?"

Now Mrs. Gessel wrung her shaking hands together. She stared into Sara's eyes, then looked away as she spoke. "I have to say I did."

"How many? From what bottles?" Sara heard panic rise in her voice.

The old woman's eyes darted from shelf to shelf. She sighed. "I don't remember. I'm ready to go home now. I just need to get the blanket off my bed."

Sara took Mrs. Gessel's arm to lead her back to her room.

"You weren't here," the woman muttered. "You're late again. It's getting dark. I had to take my pill."

Sara knew better than to say it was nowhere near dark at four P.M. She paged the nurse, then waited for her to appear.

"Yes, Sara?"

"Mrs. Gessel says she took pills from the cabinet because I wasn't here when she needed her medication. I rode over right after school."

"Did she take you to the medicine cabinet?"

"Yes."

The nurse sighed, looked at Mrs. Gessel. "Ruth, I gave you

your pill. You are all right." She turned to Sara. "She does this about once a week to get attention. You handled the situation professionally. Don't worry. There is no way she could open a pill bottle."

"I thought I should help her calm down."

"You did the right thing." The nurse's hand grazed Sara's shoulder. A sense of satisfaction filled her. When she was younger, and admired her teacher's handwriting, Sara aspired to be a schoolteacher. But as soon as she turned twelve and started reading the series of novels about Sue Barton, Student Nurse, and her fulfilling career, Sara knew her own fate. The die was cast. Nothing could stop her from becoming a nurse herself someday. She'd finish high school at St. Anne's and then head straight to State University Nursing School. Surviving moments like the one with Mrs. Gessel only made her want to be a nurse more.

In the weeks that followed his first sight of her, Rick felt like an undercover spy as he figured out Sara's schedule. If he left for school half an hour early, he could manage to stand in the main foyer—among thirty or forty other students—when she arrived. He felt a tingling rush of emotion just catching an occasional glimpse of her. He knew he was staring, yet his gaze was riveted. He relished each second. If she happened to glance his way, another rush surged through him, followed by a brief moment of longing. Why couldn't he just say hello? Did she have any idea he waited for her?

After each class, he rushed through the halls to catch up with her. Hurrying didn't look too weird when you were six feet five inches like Rick. After spotting her blond ponytail, he managed to casually saunter along in the same hall where she walked between classes. He still couldn't figure out why she rode on different buses. Two days a week on city bus number 20. The other three days on a regular school bus that traveled the opposite direction from where he lived. Even though it took him farther from home and made him arrive later, Rick sometimes climbed on Sara's bus. He sat in the last seat and rode until the bus made two or three stops. Then he eased silently out the back door. Rick didn't think Sara ever saw him on the bus. He concentrated on looking invisible—or at least not staring too long in case she turned around. And as he left, he always felt a pang of loss. Good-bye, Sara, even though we haven't ever said hello.

"What are you doing here?" The voice startled Rick, rising above the sea of students heading down "B" Hall. Startled, he glanced down at Hollie's familiar, pixieish face. Brown eyes, dimples, and the friendliest grin he ever saw.

There was no way he could help smiling back. "I'm heading to class."

"No, you're not. Class is over there." Hollie's grin widened as she flung a charm-braceleted arm toward "A" Hall.

"Well, I'm going there."

"You're heading the wrong way . . ."

Rick felt his face warm. "I have something to do."

Hollie nodded. Her dimples deepened as she winked. "Looks to me like you go the wrong way every day . . ."

"Well, I go to my locker. Stuff like that."

"Your locker's in 'A' Hall. Like mine. So's your class."

"Well . . ." Rick felt his cheeks flame.

"I think you want to see my friend Sara."

Rick felt his face warm again. He faked a shrug. "Don't know her." He felt color flood his cheeks.

"Listen—anybody with half a brain could see sparks between you two a mile away. Those brown eyes of yours just twinkle when you look at her." Hollie's head fell back in a laugh.

Mortified, Rick turned away, cupped his jaw with his hand. He couldn't compose a response.

"And Sara—if she weren't such a lady, she'd walk up and trip you."

"Really?" Rick shook his head at this dizzying prospect. "I don't think so."

"Anyone can see you have a crush on her—it's written all over your face."

Rick couldn't answer. Were his cheeks ever this hot before?

Shaking his head, he turned and headed back to "A" Hall, Hollie's laughter echoing in his head. Was it totally obvious? Should he stop following Sara? Would Hollie tell her about him? A flood of tingles darted through him at the thought. What if she told him to stop following her? How embarrassed would he be then?

For the next day or two, Rick went directly to class— without his usual Sara detours. But as he sat waiting for each class to begin, he wondered where she was at that exact second. Opening her locker? Combing her hair in the mirror he glimpsed on her locker door? Talking to Hollie in the hall?

That Friday, he could wait no longer. He started to walk his familiar paths to follow Sara again.

Sara listened to Hollie talk as the two of them sauntered down the main hall together after lunch. The day was half over and her mind was veering off with thoughts of her candy striper work after school. Hollie suddenly stopped—stock-still. Without a word of explanation, Hollie took Sara's hand. "Come on," she said, dragging Sara across the hall to where the tall guy from Mr. Steiner's class stood at his locker.

"What are you doing?" Sara protested, as Hollie's charm bracelet jangled against her own wrist.

Hollie groaned. "I'm taking the bull by the horns," she said.

"What bull?" Sara asked, bewildered. At the same time, she wondered what the guy standing across the hall was thinking. Sara secretly watched him in Mr. Steiner's class when she thought no one was looking. She refused to look up at him as Hollie headed straight in his direction, still dragging her arm. When the shorter girl stopped with another jerk to Sara's arm, her first sight was the guy's tennis shoes. Converse. Black and white with the laces tied perfectly. Feeling a ripple of emotion, Sara let her eyes travel up the tall frame until she saw his face. The guy was blushing. He's nervous, like I am, Sara realized.

Now Hollie shook her head. "You two might wonder what I'm doing here."

Sara saw the tall guy shrug. He turned and idly spun the dial on his locker, then shifted back to look at Hollie.

"The deal is—you're both so backward, I have to step up to the plate." Hollie raised her voice.

"Hollie—" The guy shook his head.

Hollie held up a hand to ward him off. "This'll be painless. I *think*."

Both of them kept their eyes on the small, frenetic girl.

"You see—it goes like this." Hollie lifted Sara's hand. "Sara, this is Rick—" Sara stared at the tall guy, who nodded self-consciously at her. She watched as Hollie placed their hands together and moved them in a handshake. Hollie shook her head. "You guys are numbskulls, but maybe you'll catch on before you're a hundred years old."

"Rick, this is Sara," Hollie continued with exaggerated patience before she slapped her own forehead. "Dummy me. I forgot last names."

"Sara Montgomery—Rick Douglas. Rick, Sara, Sara, Rick. I think that covers it."

Now she stared between the two of them, her head turning from one to the other. "Hey—" She waved a hand in front of Sara's face, then Rick's. "Do I have to do everything? Can't either one of you say, 'It's nice to meet you'?"

Rick looked at the floor. "Nice to meet you," he mumbled. Sara nodded, but he wasn't looking at her.

Hollie sighed, left the two of them there. Sara felt her cheeks burn. It was a few moments before she could lift her eyes, look down the hall, and head for class. She didn't know that Rick watched her as she walked away.

Rick would remember the day the rest of his life, partly because it started out wrong. He woke up late, something that happened once a year, if that often. He hurried to shower, ran to catch the last bus. Then he didn't get to school with his usual half hour to spare.

Instead, he heard the first bell ring as he stepped off the bus. He ran for the school, panting and stumbling as he finally reached the heavy glass door. By now there was hardly anyone in the hall. There wasn't time to look for Sara. So he didn't prepare himself to see her.

And when he turned a corner and nearly bumped into her, he was totally stunned. Their eyes met. "Hi," he said, without thinking, nearly tripping over his feet.

He saw her throat swallow. "Hi," she said.

Rick couldn't believe it. She actually spoke *right to him*. He felt dizzy standing this close to her. Yet at the same time, he wanted to drink in the sight of her. He stared, seeing that her eyes were indeed, the green he envisioned since the first day she appeared in Mr. Steiner's class.

Now she stood waiting in front of him, a puzzled look on her breathtaking face, waiting for him to say something.

What could he say? His jaws were clamped closed. Agonizing seconds crawled by. Finally, he managed a nod, headed toward class, and heard the late bell ring just as he reached the door to English.

After that, their eyes always met in the halls. Sometimes they just looked at each other, sometimes they nodded, once in a while they said "hi" again. Rick always felt his heart race with thoughts of seeing her. By the time the school year ended, they still didn't exchange more than a hello. He thought of her all summer. He imagined the two of them going on dates, enjoying long conversations. Once in a while, he dared wonder if she ever thought about him, too.

Chapter Two

The first day of school his junior year, Rick left half an hour early, in hopes of finding out if Sara was back at St. Anne's. A rush of relief poured over him when he caught sight of her blond ponytail, tall frame, and graceful walk as she sauntered down the hall. Now he looked for her every day again. It was a ritual that both comforted and excited him. When he saw her, he felt like all was right with the world, and he was home where he belonged.

Then it was October. Another month of seeing her every day, and feeling that same rush of excitement. Brown- and rust-colored leaves fell on the sidewalk, and the air was crisp and pungent with the scent of approaching winter. The school smelled of chalk dust, books, and floor wax. Rick arrived early one morning, and hung out in the main foyer. Most days, if he arrived early enough, he read the words on all the trophies in the trophy case, scanned each bulletin board announcement, and sometimes walked down the hall and back, talking to his friends, always on the lookout for Sara. But all he could do was look. His tongue felt frozen in his mouth as soon as he caught sight of her.

He could easily talk to anyone in the world except Sara. Just seeing her in the distance caused his throat to close with fear. Squeezing out his usual "hi" took monumental effort. In the back of his mind, his greatest fear was somehow saying the wrong thing to her—and instantly destroying the prospect of their friendship forever.

Sometimes, it seemed like she arrived about the same time he reached the school. Other times, he'd almost give up on seeing her, start to head for his first class, and then he would catch sight of her.

She looked breathtaking, like always, whether she wore her red-and-green plaid skirt or her navy-blue dress, or whether her hair draped her shoulders or was caught up in a ponytail. Her beauty never faltered. The sight of her always gave him the same rush.

There she was—down at the end of the hall. Rust-colored jumper. White blouse. Dazzling as ever. But this time, as Rick watched, Hollie grabbed Sara's wrist and dragged her straight toward him.

Oh, no. Not again. Much as he liked Hollie, this was terrifying. Chills like thunderbolts down his sides. He couldn't turn and walk away, couldn't even move. Sara and Hollie stepped closer and closer. Rick held his breath.

Sara's face looked more helpless and puzzled with each step. Hollie winked at him from three feet away. She abruptly stopped right in front of him.

"Hey, you kids—it's time to move out of the Dark Ages. . . ."

Rick shrugged self-consciously. "What do you mean?"

"You, know. Caveman days. When the girl and guy don't know how to talk to each other. So they just look and grunt and stuff like that."

Rick's cheeks flamed. "I don't know what you—"

"Don't deny it—I see you. Both of you. You've been introduced, so now you're supposed to talk," she continued, turning to Sara, whose gaze abruptly dropped to the floor. "You two stop talking after you say 'hi' to each other. You just give each other goo-goo eyes—like this—" Hollie flung her head back and fluttered her eyes at Rick, then Sara. "And then you don't say two words."

"Well—" Rick started.

"Don't tell me you don't know how to talk. I hear you all the time in class. Now listen to me—"

"Hollie—" It was Sara's first word, but Hollie raised a hand in protest.

"I'm going to introduce you again right now. So there is no excuse for not speaking. Sara Montgomery, may I present Rick Douglas. Rick, this is Sara Montgomery."

They nodded.

"Still not a word?" Hollie looked in each of their faces and shook her head. "I'll tell you the truth. You're supposed to say 'how do you do?' but I'll settle for 'hi, how are you?' this time. And look at each other—you're not talking to the floor."

"Hi," said Rick, half smiling and nodding.

"Hi." Sara's tremulous smile matched his.

Hollie clapped her hands. "Now maybe you could try something really tough . . . like 'How are you today?' Or maybe you're ready for the really big stuff . . . like 'What class do you have next?' Or 'Do you listen to KOBK radio?' or something really complicated like—"

Rick swallowed. "How are you, Sara?" he asked.

"Fine," she answered.

"I'm fine, too," Hollie said all of a sudden. "It wouldn't hurt either one of you to ask about *me*. . . ."

"How are you, Hollie?" They both said at the same time.

"I'm fine, you guys. It's you two that need help. Now do I have to tell you both to go to class or you'll miss the bell? Where would you two be without me?"

Where would she be? Over the next weeks and months until the school year ended, Sara reminded herself she'd have to thank Hollie someday. At first she and Rick just said hi, encouraged by Hollie's second introduction. Then, not giving up, Hollie began her work as their cupid in earnest. She sat between them in the Meditation Chapel on the school grounds, accompanied them to bowling club, walked with them down the halls.

But then, Hollie's intense cupidhood dropped away once they discovered a mutual interest in classical music. Rick began to bring a question to school for Sara each morning. How old was Mozart when he composed his first symphony? What country was Franz Liszt from? Even if she knew the answer, Sara pretended to consider the question long enough for the two of them to walk all the way down "A" Hall together. Then Rick appeared at bowling club on Wednesdays after school, and after that, Sara didn't care if she never rolled another strike. Then he started to walk her to the bus—sometimes he sat on the bus and rode a couple of stops even though Sara now knew he lived in the exact opposite direction.

Rick heard the metallic jangle of Hollie's charm bracelet as she rushed up beside him in "B" Hall. When he kept walking, she grabbed his wrist.

"Hey, Rick," she said, chestnut eyes twinkling above her wide, dimpled smile.

"Hollie." He stopped moving and turned to give her a quizzical look.

"Rick, this is . . . a big emergency . . ." Hollie tapped a painted fingernail on his shoulder. "You need to do something right away."

Rick shrugged. "I'm going to be late. I have to get to class." He sent her a quizzical eyebrow before heading out into the rush of oncoming students. From the corner of his eye, he watch Hollie rearrange her books in her arms so she could keep up with his quicker pace.

"Rick," Hollie gasped breathlessly. "You have to do this *today*."

"Yeah?" he asked, still walking. "Is my shoe untied or something?" He half-smiled down at the pixieish girl.

"Bigger deal than that, Rick. Come back here." Hollie pointed to a bright blue poster on the wall.

Rick stopped walking. He read the words, Spring Fling Senior Prom, on the poster. "Oh yeah?" he said. "Did a friend of yours make that poster, Hollie?" He turned to walk away.

Hollie slapped her forehead as if he were incredibly stupid. "Rick!" she shouted, then rushed after him. "You need to ask Sara to the prom. *Today*."

Waves of shyness draped Rick. What would he say? What if she said no? Sure, they went to bowling club. And talked about music. And ran around together. But a *prom*?

"I've never been to a dance," he said, waving her aside.

"But Sara really wants to go. And this is your only senior prom."

He shrugged. "It's a long way off." He turned as the class bell rang.

"Three weeks, Rick. Today is perfect!"

"Now I'm late! And I have to think about it."

"You don't have time to think."

He shrugged. "Three weeks is almost a month."

"But she has to look for a dress! There's only three Saturdays left!"

Rick stopped. He had no idea it took more than one day to buy a dress. He pictured Sara going to the store the day before the dance, looking at all the dresses on the rack and choosing one. He imagined it would take an hour at the most. But how did he know she was even interested in something like that? "She never said she wanted to go."

Hollie rested her head on her hand in frustration. "Listen. *I* know she really wants to go. She told *me*. All I know is, if you don't ask her today, someone else will . . ." With that, Hollie jangled off down the hall toward the cafeteria.

Even though the bell for classes rang three minutes ago, Rick stood paralyzed next to the prom poster. Was this true? Would Sara go on a date with someone else? He hated the picture that rose in his mind—Sara in a fancy dress, floating across the gym *with some other guy*. What was he supposed to do now? Should he go to the student office and buy tickets? Should he call her on the phone tonight?

Even though he usually took copious notes and raised his hand to contribute to the class, Rick hardly heard his teachers' lectures in English and health. Worry gripped him. How could he ask her? How could he be sure she wanted to go? What if she laughed at him. Or teased him. How would he react?

He saw Hollie in the distance after fourth period. Though he tried to duck down "A" Hall, before he knew it, she was beside him.

"Well?" Hollie asked. Her smile was impish.

"It's a deep subject," Rick said back.

"Have you asked her yet?"

"It's only been two hours."

"Do it today—or you'll be too late. Look, there she is."

Before he could answer, Hollie dashed off down the hall again.

And there was Sara, walking toward him, tall, graceful and smiling—like always.

"Hi, Rick," she said. "Didn't see you this morning."

Usually, he ran like lightning to catch a glimpse of her between English and health. But today, he was stuck staring at a poster with Hollie. "Good to see you," said Rick with a nod, his voice shaking and heart pounding.

Sara frowned. "Are you okay?"

"Sure."

"Aren't you going to history?" She pointed in the opposite direction. He forced a smile.

"I better," he said. "But I wanted to talk to you about something."

Sara smiled, and Rick thought of the sea of students swarming around them. What if someone heard him ask? What if she told him "no" out here in front of everybody?

"What did you need, Rick?" Sara tilted her chin up.

"Handel's composition. Was it 'Messiah' or 'The Messiah'?"

Her face fell. At least he thought it did. He felt his own heart sink as she started to walk away.

"I'll think about it, Rick. That's a tricky one. Let you know after algebra."

But he didn't see her after algebra. Or after gym, either. Then school was over.

Later that night, Rick counted the change in his wallet. Seventy-five cents. He walked down to the drugstore and cashed in two more dollars. Then he sat in the wood-paneled phone booth. Was it too late to call? If he didn't call, it would be too late. Fingers shaking, he dialed the number he'd memorized, though he'd only called her at home a couple of times.

"Hello?" A man's voice. Probably Sara's father.

"May I please speak to Sara?"

"Sara Anne is doing her homework."

"Please, sir. I just have one very quick question." Rick wiped sweat off his face with his hand. He closed his eyes. "I'm doing my homework tonight, too."

"Who is calling, please?"

"Rick Douglas, sir."

Silence. Rick felt his heart hammer. "One moment," said

Sara's father. He heard her father's footsteps. Closed his eyes and ached with hope. More footsteps. Rustling on the phone. "Rick?"

His heart beat at the sound of her voice. "Hi, Sara. I know you're doing your homework, so—"

"It's 'The Messiah,' Rick. I checked. I didn't know the answer until seventh period. How did you?"

Suddenly, he couldn't wait another moment. "I need to ask you something else, Sara—"

"I don't have my music book here. I put it back in my locker. I couldn't check any more answers tonight."

His eyes closed in concentration. "You'll know this answer."

"I will?"

He forced each word out as if it pained him. "Will you go to the prom with me?"

A long pause. "Oh, Rick—"

"Hollie said you want to go." Rick cleared his throat.

"She *said* that? I'll sock her."

Rick shut his eyes in concentration. He forced the words out. "So do you want—"

"Yes, but—"

"But what?"

"I didn't want her to tell you."

"Oh—I'm sorry." There was a long pause. Rick felt his heart hammering. "Well . . ." he said finally.

He heard Sara breathe. "So, thanks for asking," she said.

"You'll go with me?"

"Yes, Rick. And you're right. I didn't have to look it up in my music book."

Hollie grinned at him when he stood at his locker the next day. "Heard ya asked her," she said, raising her eyebrows again and again.

Rick nodded.

Hollie lifted her chin and shrugged. "How're you going to get there? Got your license?"

Floods of panic. "No . . . Probably my dad?"

Hollie shook her head. "Nobody rides with Mommy and Daddy to the senior prom. This isn't nursery school."

"Well . . . we could . . . take the bus . . . or a taxi?"

Hollie sighed noisily at him. She yawned as if he totally lost his mind. "Who's your best friend? Your best friend in the whole world?"

"Bob Gordon."

"Good pick." Hollie grabbed Rick's arm and yanked him around. "He's right over there."

Rick swallowed. What was he supposed to do now? What would Hollie do? Feeling her eyes on him, Rick marched down the hall to where Bob stood at his locker. He tapped Bob's shoulder.

Bob turned. "Hey, man . . ."

Pretending he was as bold as Hollie, Rick kept tapping to punctuate each of his next words. "You are driving us to the senior prom. Me and Sara and you and whoever you ask."

"You kidding? I already asked Marla two weeks ago. Asked my dad for the wheels the same night. Still waitin' for my dad to say yes."

"You're driving us, too, buddy," Rick said again.

Bob backed away, held up both hands to fend Rick off. "You could ask next time. Maybe say pretty please."

"You're driving. That's it."

Bob saluted Rick. "I'll tell my dad you said that. If I can't say no to you, maybe he can't, either. . . ."

Chapter Three

To battle her own nervousness, Sara pictured Rick getting dressed (would he wear a tuxedo?) and picking up Bob a few blocks away. She wondered if anyone would guess that this was her first real date. Her fingers clumsily zipped the aquamarine dress that accented the green in her eyes. (What would her corsage be like—white carnations or daisies? Roses? How would the white carnation boutonniere she bought look on Rick's suit?) Sara already tried on three different pairs of nylons and combed her hair at least five times when she heard a voice from downstairs.

"You just go on in. She's upstairs. I'll tell her you're here."

He was here! And that was Grandma's voice. Seconds later she heard Grandma coming up the stairs. Sara stifled a giggle at the sight of Grandma—Sunday dress, fresh lipstick, gold and pearl earrings, Jungle Gardenia perfume.

"You look like you're the one going to the prom, Grandma," Sara said, forgetting her uneasiness as her grandmother's arms enveloped her.

"He's a handsome young man," Grandma said. "Lucky I didn't steal him. I could have swooped him up, but I saved him for you." She leaned over to kiss Sara's cheek.

Sara and Grandma walked down the stairs to where her father and Rick stood by the fireplace. Sara's breath caught at the sight of him standing there—tall and handsome in a black tuxedo. His dark hair was combed perfectly, and the look in his brown eyes told her he thought she looked nice, too.

"Have a good time—it looks like a beautiful evening out there." Her mother's smile was gently wistful as she stood in the kitchen doorway, dish towel in hand.

"Drive carefully." Sara thought her father's voice sounded a bit too firm, yet she looked over to see him and Rick shake hands.

"Please have Sara Anne home by midnight," her father was saying.

Rick nodded. "I will, sir."

I feel just like Cinderella, Sara thought.

"Let's get the flower for him," Grandma said, heading out to the kitchen.

Grandma opened the refrigerator, and—behind the open refrigerator door—leaned to whisper to Sara. "Did you see how he looked at you—like you were Miss America!"

Sara giggled, her nervousness rising again. Back in the living room her fingers shook as she tried to pin the boutonniere on Rick's lapel. Eventually she stopped, and let Grandma go ahead. She fastened it in a single try.

"You two have a good time now," Grandma said, walking out on the porch, where she had a chair stationed to watch Rick arrive and the two of them leave. She gave a big, parade-style wave as they climbed in the backseat of Bob's father's car.

"Sara, this is Bob," Rick began, suddenly recalling those awkward days in the hall when Hollie introduced the two of them. Now Sara extended a white-gloved hand, and Bob clasped her fingers.

"Nice to meet you." Bob nodded. "Let's get this show on the road."

As Bob sped off in the twilight, Sara felt shy again for the first time in months. While thinking of the right words to say, she listened to the song playing on the car radio, trying to decipher those words through Sam the Sham's energetic whine:

"Matty told Hatty
"About a thing she saw . . ."

• • •

Next to her Rick hoped he was doing everything right. His sister gave him the lecture about the tuxedo, and his brother gave him suggestions on how to treat girls.

The four of them walked into the restaurant—a huge cavernous building that Rick knew could seat four or five hundred people.

"Hey, buddy," Bob said to him. "Where is everybody tonight?"

Rick looked at rows and rows of vacant tables. "Are they closed? But I have a reservation."

Suddenly a white-jacketed waiter with a towel draped over his arm approached them. And Rick discovered that the Prima Pomodoro, the restaurant he picked from the phone book after discovering it was close to the school, could seat the entire faculty and student body of St. Anne's High School, yet they were the only customers. Then the entrée took forever to arrive, so that Bob joked that the chef must have died somewhere back in the kitchen. Then, amazingly, with an audience of only four, a band tuned up and began to play—though the lead singer should have gone into another line of work.

"Good-looking girl, but she can't sing worth a darn," Rick said.

"Good song, though," Bob said.

It was "Woolly Bully" again—which they heard two more times before the night was over.

By the time they got to the dance, the place was packed. The school gym was decorated for spring with pastel-colored paper flowers, and a mirrored ball hung on the ceiling. During the occasional slow dances, Sara quickly discovered that neither she nor Rick possessed flawless dancing skills. Their toes bumped occasionally, and once in a while they had to stop still . . . then agree to start the dance steps over. But even if the rhythm of their steps was a little off, Sara sensed that their hearts might be pounding identically. When the band played the last song, "Good Night, Ladies," she knew she would remember this moment the rest of her life.

Driving home, Bob stopped two houses down from Sara's,

then eased up slowly to the house next to hers. He turned the key, and the engine died with a purr.

Rick sighed beside her. "Be right back—" he said to Bob, reaching to take Sara's hand as he opened the car door beside him.

They walked down the sidewalk hand in hand. Sara felt tingles at the understanding that despite the slow dinner, off-tune accompaniment, and lots of "Woolly Bully," this was one of the best nights of her life so far. She knew she would never forget this moment, right now, as she strolled across her front lawn with Rick, her dress brushing her legs in soft swishes. Together, they walked up to the front porch of the white house, not speaking, listening only to the sounds of the night—their feet against the concrete, the whine of crickets, a whisper of breeze, the simple hum of evening.

"Thank you for inviting me to the dance," she said, each word emerging louder and more formal than she intended in the balmy navy-blue night.

He nodded with dignity, formal, too. She could see the outline of the white carnation at his lapel. "You're welcome," he said.

Then they were standing on the porch, alone. No Hollie. No Bob. The air around them was sweet with the smell of honeysuckle. Suddenly she couldn't think of another word to say. Sara heard her dress rustle in the silent night as she took a step toward the door.

"Wait—" Rick said.

"I had a really good time," said Sara.

Rick drew himself up tall, until Sara saw that the top of his head nearly reached the porch light. She heard him clear his throat. She watched as he shuffled his feet, then stepped toward her. "May I kiss you?" he asked, his voice husky, yet quavering over this seemingly official, yet very personal question.

Sara nodded. Her eyes closed in both fear and bliss as Rick's arms enveloped her waist. He leaned down, and she felt his warm breath caress her cheek before his lips met hers, an incredible warm softness. At the end of the kiss he held her in his arms, her head against his shoulder. Sara knew she could stay here, in his arms, forever. She felt sheltered and safe, cradled and loved.

"Hey, wait a minute." Rick's voice suddenly broke through the darkness. His arms dropped from her sides.

"What?" Sara asked.

"Isn't that your mom?"

"Where?"

Rick pointed to the living room window that looked out on the porch. Through the sheer curtains, Sara glimpsed the lighted floor lamp, and next to it, a shadow that suspiciously resembled her mother's silhouette. "That's her," she agreed, her cheeks warming in the cool spring night. "She's spying. . . ."

They laughed together, then, as they watched, the shadow disappeared.

Rick took her hand. "May I call you?"

"Yes." Sara nodded. "Call me."

Rick squeezed her hand gently, then let go and stepped down off the porch. Sara stood in the night and watched him walk across the lawn. She heard Bob rev the engine of his father's car, then watched it surge past. Rick's wave was a white blur in the darkness.

When Sara stepped inside the house and planned to confront her mother with spying, she discovered an empty living room.

She walked upstairs and peered into her parents' bedroom, where she heard her mother's solemn, even breathing, as if she hadn't been downstairs only moments before.

After their prom date Rick walked to the drugstore every few nights, his pockets filled with change in anticipation of a long conversation with Sara. Though his parents never questioned him or teased him about calling her, Rick sensed that somehow he could speak more freely if he were alone in the calm dark of the phone booth. His voice flowed smoothly, and it was as if he could savor the implication of each single word— both his and Sara's. Although he often exhausted his dimes and quarters, they never ran out of things to say. In the warm blackness of the phone booth, their shyness completely dropped away, and they shared thoughts, feelings, hopes, and dreams.

The thought nagged Rick that he didn't want to lose Sara after high school. He didn't want to go on with his life without her, and couldn't imagine ever not knowing her.

Yet even as this thought registered with him, he also felt doubts that she felt the same way.

"I was thinking about this summer. . . ." Rick ventured one night.

"If it ever gets here," Sara joked.

"I was thinking of places where we could go together—"

"Look, Rick," Sara interrupted him. "I need to go study. Test tomorrow."

"Okay . . . see you later," he said reluctantly, fingering the handful of dimes and quarters that sat coolly in his palm. After Sara hung up, he sat in the warm, silent darkness of the booth, trying not to let the hurt he felt penetrate his consciousness.

After that Rick often left the phone booth with most of his quarters and dimes left. He felt saddened that Sara didn't seem to have as much to say anymore. And at school he didn't see her as often in the halls. Then she told him she couldn't go to his orchestra concerts on school nights—she had to study. Rick told himself that maybe everything was still okay. She was just busy. But he couldn't quell the undercurrent of realization that something was really wrong.

Chapter Four

It was the end of May. The blue sky draped the spring day with cotton-ball clouds. Robins twittered in the trees above the cement ledge where Rick and Sara sat. The warm, pungent air smelled of honeysuckle and new lawn. Dozens of conversations buzzed around them as almost everyone who had first lunch ate on the football stadium grass.

Rick's voice abruptly broke into Sara's mindless relaxation. "The thing is—I don't know how to say this. . . ."

Sara tilted her head, gazed curiously at him. She smiled, thinking back. "Remember when we couldn't talk at all? We just walked past each other in the halls. I'd wait to see you— and then not say anything." She laughed, leaned back on the ledge. Blond hair flowed down her back in a golden cascade. She shook her head. "The first time I said hi, I felt really brave."

Rick paused. "Me, too." He touched her fingers briefly, then moved away. "I'm trying to be brave right now. . . ."

"Huh?" Sara squinted in the sun. "You talk to me every day."

"Only two more weeks of school left."

"You think they'll really let us out? What if they don't?" Sara teased. "We'll have to walk around the halls the rest of our lives."

"The thing is, after we're out, we won't see each other all the time."

"And we'll have a diploma and be through with classes and—"

Rick forced himself to speak. "I don't know when I'll see you. I still want to go out after we graduate."

A pause. Rick's words hung in the air between them. Sara sat straighter. She said, "But I told you. I'm going to nursing school at State."

Rick sighed. "You won't ever get a day off? Like Saturday nights?"

"I'll live in the dorm at school. And I'll have to study a lot."

"You'll need a break."

"I don't know. . . . I've heard the classes are really hard. And I'll probably have to get a lab job at the hospital."

Rick shifted sideways on the bench.

Sara's voice rushed. "I just always knew I could help people by being a nurse. I never wanted any other career."

Now Rick smiled at her. "Did I tell you? I'm going to study something that's really important in the future, too. Electronics. Do you know what a computer is?"

"Not really. I saw one on TV. It filled a whole room. Isn't it some kind of mechanical filing system?"

"It's a new communications industry. Someday all our knowledge will be on computers. There'll be one in every office."

Silence.

Then Rick forced his saddened face into a half-smile. He said, "Nurses might even use computers."

Now Sara sighed, stood, gazed out across the green grass of the schoolyard. "I don't mean to be rude, but . . . working with machines like that . . ."

"They're very technical machines. Do you know why that computer needed its own room?"

Sara held up her hand in frustration. "I know it's complicated. But working with machines sounds like blue-collar work." She sighed. Looking out at the other students gathering their books and brown lunch bags, she said, "I thought that if I study hard enough to become a nurse, I'd get along best with a man who is a doctor . . . or has some kind of professional career. We'd have more in common."

"Clara Barton and Dr. Kildare, huh?"

Sara felt fury, embarrassment—and sadness. But she'd told him the truth.

"Doctors and nurses together," Rick muttered, as if this possibility were a new realization to him. "I know that's how it looks on TV. But in real life there's a world outside the hospital. You're not going to live in the emergency room twenty-four hours a day, are you?"

"No . . ." Sara shook her head in frustration. "But it would be a big part of my life. My husband would have to accept that."

"Would it be that hard to understand? Lots of people work long hours."

"Well . . ." Sara hesitated, feeling as if she had already said too much. "It could be more than long hours. I might need to travel. I really want to be a navy emergency room nurse." She paused. "I'd like to help the soldiers who fight for our country."

Now Rick looked sad, hesitant. "There's a better way to help the country."

"Better than saving lives?"

"I mean—refusing to fight in the first place. If everyone refused to fight, there wouldn't be a war."

"Would *you* refuse?" They'd never talked about this.

"Look how tall I am. . . ." Rick gestured at his six-foot-five frame. "A sniper could hit me in a second. I don't want to get shot. I'd have to keep myself off the battlefield. Maybe I'd rather run off to Canada. . . ." He smiled jokingly, but her frown seemed frozen in place.

Sara inhaled harshly. "Would you refuse to defend your own family? What if someone held a gun to your wife's head?"

"That would be different."

Sara was surprised as fire rose within her. "It's not different at all. War is someone threatening our family's lives the same as if someone came into our houses with a gun. I want to help the men who protect us from that."

Another sigh. "It sounds important to you, Sara." Rick looked off, onto the football field, where students lined up at the garbage cans with their lunch sacks.

Sara waited. Then she reached over and squeezed his fingers even as more anger and sadness surged. Her voice broke. "We had good times together. But I think I'd better just go on to nursing school."

The silence between them was heavy. "Does this count as a fight?" Rick asked, a tremor in his voice.

Sara's hands shook. "Not if I leave now," she said softly. Without looking back, she stood, walked to the garbage, and dropped in her lunch sack. She rushed away before a sob caught in her throat. Tears flowed as she headed across the lawn and past the football field toward the other end of the building.

Her pace slowed as she reached the end of the grassy field. She took shorter steps, paused, waited. Despite her sadness and firm conviction that she had said the right things—the things she believed in her heart—it struck her how strong her bond with Rick was. Even through her anger and tears, she still halfheartedly expected him to run and catch up to her, maybe ask her a music question. She imagined him walking beside her, trying to talk while he was out of breath, the way he did so many times in the school halls. But when she reached the classroom door and dared to look back, she saw that he still sat on the ledge, alone, his hands folded in his lap, his lunch sack beside him.

Chapter Five

Rick sat long past the late bell. His mind ran reruns of their conversation again and again. Where did everything go wrong? He sighed and walked back into the school building. By now it was way too late to rush down Hall A to catch a glimpse of Sara as she walked ahead of him to Mr. Steiner's class. He went into his science class and sat, his hands resting on his book as Mr. Steiner discussed amoebas. Suddenly the teacher caught his eye.

"And it would appear that one of our class members may be moving as slowly as an amoeba today. . . ." Mr. Steiner grinned. "Rick?"

Rick raised his hand.

"Are you our amoeba of the moment?"

How could he explain that his throat was still thick with sadness, his mind frozen with despair? "I'm late," he managed.

"Were you masquerading as an amoeba? Moving a fraction of an inch an hour?" Mr. Steiner was determined to be funny, but Rick couldn't muster a smile.

"I guess so. . . ."

"Well, since you seem to have a personal acquaintance with amoebas, could you please tell us about their cellular composition?" he asked as he walked down the aisle toward Rick's seat. "How many cells and what form of reproduction?"

Rick felt his face redden. He shook his head and stammered. "I-I-don't know. I'll have to look it up—"

"I gave the class the answer five minutes ago. You were here by then."

Heat climbed to his cheeks. He shook his head, then covered his face with his hands. "I'm sorry. I'll bring the answer tomorrow."

"Just be on time. And read the chapter." Mr. Steiner patted Rick's shoulder, then asked, "Can anyone give Rick the correct response to my question?"

Rick tried to concentrate on the lesson but couldn't. His mind kept rushing to Sara, who sat three rows away without looking back. Rick stared at the back of her head as his mind reviewed again the words they exchanged. Why hadn't he said, "Let's not argue. Let's talk about this?" He continued to try to perceive what the next right move would be, and if there was a way he could restore their relationship so that they were dating again. He tried to catch up with her after class, but she hurried down the hall without a backward glance.

Two days later Rick poured the change from his wallet into his hand and walked down to the phone booth at the corner pharmacy. Sitting in the half-light, he fingered the silver quarters and dimes. He studied the coins and the metal pictures on them again and again. Finally he stacked them in a pile, lifted the receiver, took a breath. Seconds later he dialed the number he knew by heart.

"Hello?" Sara's father answered, his voice dignified. Serious.

"May I speak to Sara, sir? This is Rick speaking."

"Just a moment. I'll get her for you."

The moment stretched a long time. Rick waited. He could hear a muted conversation in the background.

"Rick?" Her father's voice.

"Yes?" Rick said.

"Sara Anne says she's finishing her homework now. May I give her a message?"

What could he say? Rick took a deep breath. He shut his eyes briefly and tried to be brave. "Tell her I said I'm sorry."

A moment of silence. "I'll tell her," said Sara's father. "Good-bye, Rick."

Rick kept the phone to his ear long past the time Sara's father hung up. How long was it before he realized he was listening to the dial tone?

For days he felt vacant and haunted with helpless despair. What could he do now? Part of him numbly denied that he'd lost Sara and continued to hope. He'd think of places they'd go in the future—then, painfully, abruptly remember that now there would be no future. And part of him felt frantic, trying to think of the right words to say to somehow win her back. How could this possibly happen? Couldn't she feel the way he felt inside? In a way it was as if he was back to the days of spying on her. He'd follow the usual routine—meeting her after classes and walking her out to the bus—all the while wondering what her thoughts were now. Was there any way she felt the same sharp hurt he felt? The same bleak despair that nothing could ever be the same?

Sara felt a nagging ache about the breakup, but more than that, a sadness that it was unavoidable. She was going to nursing school with hopes of becoming an army or navy nurse. Rick still wanted to work with machines and opposed serving in the military. They were oil and water—okay together in high school, but impossible after that. Sara still felt she'd done the right thing. Yet she knew she'd always remember Rick—the conversations in the halls, the prom, the kiss on her front porch. When she saw him now, she tried to numb the hurt by thinking of their togetherness as visiting a past memory. They walked together in the halls, but the sense of finality hovered, limiting their conversations until they hardly said a word. The last day of school—and probably their last day together—loomed gloomily on the horizon. It was hard to speak of what lay ahead, so the days stretched long and weary. Was there something wrong in what she said to him? Was there any way she should keep her feelings to herself? No matter how Sara racked her brain, their situation didn't change. What else could either of them say?

Even though she felt she did the right thing in breaking off the relationship, it was as if her heart were worn raw. She still thought of him—without meaning to. Music questions she could ask him in the halls popped into her head. Memories of the prom were in her mind often, too. And she wanted to say good-bye to him, to tell him she'd never forget their good times. But if she told him what was in her heart, she'd have to say that she'd always love him even though they couldn't be together. She wanted to say good-bye somehow. But how could she do that without giving him hope?

The last day of school finally arrived.

Sara felt a little thud in her heart as they walked down Hall A for the last time. "Good-bye, Rick," she said, catching sight of her bus in the distance.

"It doesn't have to be—" he said hopefully.

Suddenly her throat caught, and she forced a shrug. "Nursing school and all . . ." Her voice trailed off.

"We could still—"

"We can still remember all of it," Sara interrupted, forcing the words past the sadness inside.

Rick nodded helplessly.

"See you—" Sara said, turning away before he could catch sight of the tears that suddenly threatened. She ran across the lawn and out to the bus. When she looked back at the school, Rick was gone.

Chapter Six

It was six months later, long after Sara started nursing school at State, and he was majoring in electronics at Midwest University, when Rick finally found the courage to call. He told himself that maybe Sara had had time to miss him by now, if she were ever going to. And maybe if she brushed him off this time, he was a little stronger and could take it better. How long had it been since he'd stood in this phone booth? Rick stared down at the handful of pocket change. He ran his fingers over another handful of silver dimes and quarters. Would Sara talk to him long enough to spend all of it? He felt nervous even looking up the number. He read half a column of names of businesses before he found the hospital listing. State University School of Nursing. That was it. He stared at the black letters on the white phone book page. There wasn't a number that said Dormitory. The closest thing was Main Office. What would happen if he called?

"School of Nursing," a crisp voice said.

"Sara Montgomery, please."

He heard the woman flip pages, then, without warning, the phone rang. Was he about to talk to her? Rick held his breath.

"Nursing dorms."

"May I please speak to Sara Montgomery?"

"A student?" asked a woman's voice.

"Yes."

A sigh. Then, moments later, "I have her listed on Four B. May I tell her who's calling?"

Rick hesitated, not sure if Sara would pick up if she knew who was on the phone.

"Who's calling, please?"

"Rick," he said finally. "Rick Douglas."

"One moment."

"House mother," another woman's voice said.

"I'm waiting for Sara Montgomery."

"Hold on. Who's this?"

"Rick Douglas."

A long wait this time. Rick pictured a tiled hall, lots of young women in white uniforms talking quietly, studying. Abruptly he heard a series of clicks, then the phone ringing again. "I'm connecting you, sir," said the woman. This must be a switchboard, Rick thought as the phone rang even as the woman spoke.

"Hello?" Her voice. No mistake. It was Sara. Too bad his own voice wouldn't work.

The receptionist cut in. "I have a phone call for you, Sara. A Rick Douglas."

"Oh. Just tell him I'm not here."

"He's on the line, Sara—"

"Oh. I didn't know. I don't want to be rude."

A sour feeling rose in Rick's throat. "Good-bye, Sara," he said. Numb with shock, he waited for her good-bye, his heart pounding.

No one spoke. He could hear the house mother's breathing, slower than his own. Moments later he heard a click.

"Sara?" His voice choked out.

"I'm afraid she hung up, sir. Do you want me to try to ring her room again?"

Rick cleared this throat. "I guess so."

The phone rang and rang, like a drill boring into silence.

"There's no answer. Do you want me to leave a message?"

Rick didn't answer. He sat still, waited. Then he laid the phone on his desk without saying a word. He sat there until he heard a faint click and knew that the house mother finally hung up.

Through the next ten months he told himself he was crazy

for continuing to drive by Sara's house. But he'd be heading out to the store, or over to Bob's or to work, and his car seemed naturally to slide over to her street. He still felt his anticipation continue to build as street after street brought him closer to where she lived. Then, finally, her street. Osborne Road. Sometimes he paused at the corner and looked down toward her house from a distance. Just the sight of it—an ordinary white house with a rust-colored roof—brought tingles to his insides. Other times he drove by quickly, with just a brief sidelong glance that left his heart pounding. It was a ritual he wasn't ready to give up.

Chapter Seven

Three years later it was her third week as a student nurse, actually working on the hospital floor. Brushing a particle of lint off her fresh white uniform, Sara walked off the elevator at the beginning of a four to eleven P.M. shift. When she reached the nursing station, the floor nurse said, "Miss Montgomery? The patient in three-fifty, bed one. Take his vitals."

Did the nurse stare at her a moment longer than necessary? What was the woman trying to say? Sara sensed something was strange. She felt a prickle of curiosity, then reminded herself that this was why she was here. She headed for Room 350. The door was closed. Sara knocked gently. She knocked again. When there was still no answer, she opened the door and entered.

She recognized the man immediately from making rounds with the nurses during the past two weeks. Mr. Carson, whose wife sat at his bedside each day. Heart attack survivor. Been here at least a week. Maybe two weeks. Probably ready to go home now.

"Mr. Carson?" Sara said, stepping closer to the bed.

No answer. Mr. Carson lay motionless on his back, eyes half-closed.

Sara paused. Then she lifted his wrist, attached a blood-pressure monitor. She waited. The indicator line on the monitor stayed still. Sara unwrapped the monitor, wrapped it again. Still no reading. Sara felt chills at the back of her legs. Mr. Carson had no blood pressure.

She took a deep breath. "Mr. Carson?" she asked, forcing herself to keep her voice quiet. She stared at his face only a second before moving to his wrist. Her fingers fumbled, groped his arm in search of a pulse. Keeping her hand on his arm, she looked away, out the window into the sunny-bright day. She directed her gaze briefly to the well-kept hospital lawn, the parking lot, trying to distract her worries while focusing on what she instinctively knew she should feel now. Where was the tiny drumbeat that should register beneath her fingers? Sara waited.

Nothing.

Mr. Carson didn't react as Sara shifted her hold to a new section of his wrist. Still nothing.

Sara counted silently, then checked again. She tried three times. The chills at the back of her legs grew stronger. The man had no pulse.

Mr. Carson is dead, Sara thought. Now cold chills draped her entire body. She was alone with a dead person for the first time in her life. At the same time her anxiety rose, she understood that this experience would probably happen again and again when she was a nurse. She recalled lectures about death from nursing school. Her professional instincts and natural emotions warred with each other as she stood at Mr. Carson's bedside. She thought of his wife, a tiny gray-haired woman who sat in a straight-backed chair at the end of his bed, patiently waiting all through visiting hours. When visiting hours arrived tonight, someone would tell Mrs. Carson that her husband's life was over. More likely, someone would call her right now. In a quick flash, Sara visualized the wife this man would never see again.

There was nothing more she could do. The realization of her helplessness roared in Sara's mind.

She rushed out into the hall, hurried to the nurse's desk.

"The patient in Room three-fifty—" she said to the floor nurse.

"Yes?" No flicker of friendliness in the nurse's tone.

"He shows no vital signs. . . ."

"No vital signs?" The nurse frowned at her. "You took his temperature, blood pressure, pulse—"

"Yes," said Sara. "All zero."

The nurse stared into Sara's face. "What do you suggest we do now?"

Sara felt her cheeks flush. She thought her report of no vital signs would be enough to send a doctor and possibly two or more nurses into the room immediately. Be professional, she reminded herself. What did she know about hospital procedures?

Sara cleared her throat. "I think the patient should be moved to postmortem care," she said carefully.

The nurse raised her eyebrows. "You do?"

"Yes," Sara said, hating her voice for faltering at that moment. "Please call the doctor—"

"You feel a doctor should be summoned?" The nurse gave her a questioning look as if to give her a chance to change her mind.

Sara swallowed. "Yes."

Still staring at Sara, the nurse paged. "Dr. Bryce, please. Paging Dr. Bryce."

Dressed in blue scrubs, the doctor approached the desk seconds later.

The nurse nodded at Sara. "This nursing student is of the opinion that you need to see the patient in Room three-fifty."

Dr. Bryce strode quickly ahead of Sara, who scrambled to keep up with him. By the time she reached the room, he was already sitting in a chair and filling out a form.

When he didn't offer an explanation, Sara stood at the patient's bedside. Seconds crawled by. The doctor continued writing, then signed his signature with a flourish. Sara angled her head. S. Bryce, the signature read.

She mustered her courage. "What is that form?"

The doctor glanced up at her. "Death certificate." He stood and was nearly to the door before he glanced over his shoulder.

"Please accompany the body to the morgue," he said.

Sara waited, unsure what would happen next.

Minutes later Dr. Bryce returned. Two nurses came and lifted Mr. Carson onto a gurney, pulling the sheet over his head. When they all left the room, Sara followed.

"We'll take it from here," Dr. Bryce said to the other nurses, when they reached the main elevator. Elevator doors parted. Dr. Bryce entered the elevator with the gurney and waited for Sara.

She walked in beside him, watched as he pressed the button for the basement.

The elevator groaned slightly, and Sara felt a dip at her knees. She breathed in, waited. A moment later the elevator jerked slightly. Sara turned her head at a fluid noise beside her. She gasped in horror.

Mr. Carson was no longer dead.

He was sitting up on the gurney beside her.

Sara felt her heart pound. She stifled a scream, then held her breath. Was she seeing things? Her mind agonized as the elevator bell clicked away each floor.

She couldn't look beside her as the elevator landed with a thud.

"Hey, ma'am—you're as white as a sheet," Dr. Bryce said. "This guy bothering you?" Out of the corner of her eye, she watched the doctor tap Mr. Carson on the shoulder.

She couldn't speak. Sara nodded shakily.

"I gotta say, you're the calmest ever. I've had students faint when they pull that old trick of sending in a student nurse to check a corpse's vitals. Then the guy sits up ... and that doesn't even faze you."

"I almost screamed. Why did the nurse send me in like that?"

"Partly to see if you can cut it. Partly for laughs."

"I have to say that it really got me ... when he sat up."

"You mean this guy?" Now Sara swallowed hard as the doctor lowered Mr. Carson to the gurney. "It's just reflexes. Happens every now and then."

"I thought he came back to life."

"Now that's something I haven't seen yet. *I'd* faint myself if that happened." Now the doctor touched Sara's shoulder. "But I have to say, you did great. I've seen student nurses run screaming when the vitals are zero. . . . I even knew a male nurse that ran and hid in the supply closet. But you carried it off like an old pro."

Whistling, Dr. Bryce wheeled the gurney out ahead of her. Sara felt the tension in her shoulders evaporate. She closed her eyes quickly and exhaled. She said, "I wondered why they took so long to accept my postmortem care diagnosis."

"They were testing you. And you passed. Flying colors." The doctor paused, knocked on the morgue door. "Fact is, I think you picked the right career, young lady."

The doctor's words echoed again and again in her head. She repeated them in her mind as days passed. For weeks, Sara studied a little longer each night, paid more attention during the hospital classes during the day. Everything in her life seemed to be moving in the right direction. Then, unexpectedly, Rick popped into her mind, and she thought of him the way she did every once in a while. The sore little ache around her heart seemed to be justified now. I had to break up with him. I had to follow the path that was right for me, she thought to herself. Then why did a sweet sadness hover in her thoughts every time he crossed her mind?

Chapter Eight

It was months later when she saw the obituary. She hardly ever read the newspaper, but this Sunday edition was left on a table in the nursing school cafeteria. After placing her lunch tray on the conveyor belt that led to the dishwasher, Sara idly thumbed through the classified ads. The newspaper fluttered in her hands as she caught sight of the familiar name.

Douglas.

Her heart thudded at just seeing the name in print. A surprising rush of emotion.

Beneath the last name in boldface print was the first name. William Douglas. His father. A streak of sadness shot through her mind as she read the words that stated their conclusion with such firm finality. William Douglas, beloved husband and father, died suddenly, Saturday, following a heart attack. He is survived by his wife, Lucille, his sons, Rick and Don, and his daughter, Marcy Schultz. Funeral services will be held Tuesday at ten A.M. at McDougal Funeral Home.

Tuesday. Her chemistry final. There was no way she could miss school. But the thought of seeing Rick again tantalized her. Would she remain at a distance, and just enjoy the pleasure of watching him? Or would she walk up to him and speak, telling him she was sorry for his loss? She wasn't ready to date anyone now, Sara reminded herself. Nothing about the reasons why they broke up had changed. Sara sighed. Her feelings didn't matter anyway. Permission to miss a test to attend a funeral might be granted for someone in her immediate family. But what could she say about this funeral? I hereby request permission to attend services for the father of someone I thought I could stop loving? The head nurse would say no before she even finished making the request. At the last moment she bought a sympathy card. She stared at the blank space of the card a long time before she wrote her full name, Sara Montgomery.

Opening the envelope addressed to him, Rick stared at the familiar signature on the card a long time. Sara didn't write "sincerely," much less "love." But she thought enough about the pain he felt at this time to send a card. The gesture lifted his heart briefly—but thinking of her and longing to see her only brought more sadness at this time of loss. The bleak emptiness Rick felt at his father's death was indescribable— both for himself and for his mom. Fathers were supposed to last forever. And what was he supposed to do now, when everyone around him was being sent to Vietnam? It seemed as if there was no way he could stay home and comfort his mom now, when she was alone. And staying in this town didn't feel right anyway, without Sara and without his dad. No matter what, he knew it wasn't up to him. The Air Force would tell him where his new destination would be. He only hoped it wasn't 'Nam.

As he walked in the back door, Rick heard his mom answer the phone. "This is his mother," she said a moment later. The tone in her voice reminded him of his school days. He still remembered being scared when the school called, even though he hardly missed a day and almost never got in trouble. But his school days were long past. What was that worried look on his Mom's face? Who could be calling about him now?

He sat at the kitchen table, watched his mom standing stock-still, talking on the wall phone. She turned to face him with another anxious look. "Oh, he did, did he?" she asked. "Well, I can't say it surprises me. . . ." Now her blue eyes gave Rick a resigned look. Her sadness caught at his heart. What did he do to disappoint her like this?

"Yes . . . I'll let him know. . . ." His mother's heavy sigh brought a weight to his shoulders. And more curiosity to his mind. What could this be?

"You want him to call you?" Her shoulders shrugged.

Now Rick stood, mouthed, "What is it?" But his mother waved him away with her hand.

"Yes . . . he'll be here today. . . . Let me get a pencil." Rick watched his mother write down a phone number. Completely unfamiliar. No one he knew. "I'll have him call you." She hung up the phone, shook her head at him. "You're too smart for your own good," she said.

Rick was puzzled. "What are you talking about, Mom?"

His mother started to walk out of the room.

"Aren't you going to tell me who that was?" he asked.

When she came back to face him, he was surprised to see tears in her eyes. "I guess I have to tell you," she said. "It was the Air Force."

His heart sank. "Did I fail the test?"

She shook her head.

"Then why would they call me now?"

"Because"—she forced a smile through her tears—"your test scores were almost perfect. Exceptionally high." Now she wagged her finger at him. "I could have told them how smart you are. But now that they know, they want you more than ever—" Her voice broke. "I don't know if I can take this, Rick."

"High test scores might get me a better assignment."

"But this is the Air Force! You could lose your life!" His mother gave him a hug. "I just lost your dad. I can't lose you, too."

Rick unexpectedly felt his own tears at the thought of his mother missing his father. "Mom . . . high test scores can get me a desk job . . . instead of combat duty."

She wiped her eyes. "I just hope they don't send you overseas."

"That's why I took the test. To get a desk job here in the States. I thought about all that. Face it, Mom. I'm six-feet-five. An easy target . . . a sniper could pick me off in a second . . . easier than those short guys."

"Rick! How can you even talk about that?"

"But I won't be out there now. Not with these test scores."

"But there could be an emergency. In an emergency they take everybody! They don't leave people at their desks."

"Mom, someone has to run the place. And now that's me."

His mother fell into his arms, hugging him. "I still wish you weren't going," she said, releasing her hold and looking into his eyes. Seconds later he heard a single sob as she left the kitchen and went upstairs to her room.

There was no way to change things now, he knew that. The country was at war. He was draft age. And now he had passed the test. Sitting in an easy chair in the front room, he thought of Sara. What would she say if she knew he was about to enter the military? Rick replayed their last argument in his mind. Was there any chance they'd still be together if she knew he was going to fight for his country? What if she was now an Air Force nurse and they happened to meet again? Rick relished the thought of seeing the surprised look on her face. He let his imagination continue. What if he told her about these test scores? How high they were? He blushed even thinking about it. Maybe he still wouldn't be the professional man she was looking for. But it would be close.

Chapter Nine

Carl Parker was good-looking, there was no getting around that. He looked so handsome in his lab coat. Tall, broad shoulders, blond hair, and blue eyes that you couldn't look away from. But why did she feel this sinking feeling when he kept asking her out? The first couple of dates were okay, when she was still going out with other guys. But did she really want to be known as Carl's girlfriend? Now here she was, home for Christmas, and Carl was showing up here, too, at her house. Inwardly Sara tried to shrug aside the feeling that something about Carl made her uncomfortable. But didn't she say she wanted to marry a man in the medical profession? What more could they have in common? And he couldn't be any handsomer. Maybe there was something wrong with *her*, Sara decided. A nagging thought entered her mind that maybe she just needed to get over Rick before she could move on. But that was ridiculous, Sara told herself. In some ways she couldn't believe she still thought of him after all this time. She really just needed to let go.

In an effort to shrug aside her thoughts, Sara tried to imagine a fun evening ahead as she put on her lipstick and combed her hair. Carl was already talking to her dad when she went out in the living room.

"Where are you two headed?" her dad asked. Sara realized that Carl couldn't tell her father's smile was forced.

"To dinner in Mountain View. Hope I got enough gas."

Her dad shrugged. "Well, here. Let me help out the cause a little." He handed Carl his gasoline credit card. Sara was surprised—both at her father's gesture and Carl's acceptance of it. She sat silently in the car as they drove away.

It was after the dinner—when they were nearly back at her house—that Carl drove to the gas station. She still felt strange about his borrowing her father's credit card. She sat in the car while he pumped the gas, then idly watched when he went into the station. Seconds, then minutes, ticked by. Sara waited. And waited longer, shifting nervously on the seat. It was getting late. What was Carl doing in there? Finally she couldn't sit anymore. She got out of the car and rushed into the station.

Surprised, Carl looked at her. His face flamed.

"Will this be all?" the clerk asked Carl.

Sara's eyes fell to the counter. There was candy, a package of cigarettes, a can of motor oil, and a comb.

"That's my dad's credit card—you can't get all this," Sara said.

The clerk looked questioningly, first at her, then Carl. "Cash or credit, sir?"

Carl fumbled wildly in his pockets. "Cash," he said. "All of it."

"The gas, too? I already rang up the gas on credit."

"Switch it to cash," Carl demanded. Seconds later he slammed the credit card into Sara's hand hard enough that the edge scratched her skin.

"I'm sorry," she found herself saying on the way out. "I just knew that my dad only gave us the card to get gas."

Carl strode ahead of her, opened the car door. "I paid for it, didn't I? In cash. Now let's forget about it."

But Sara couldn't. A sick, sad feeling haunted her for weeks after the incident. Somehow, she knew, if Carl suddenly stopped calling, she could never see him again and not regret it. Yet at the same time, she wondered if the fault lay in herself. Was she too rigid? Did she think every man was wrong for her? That she was too good for all of them? Did Carl have a problem she should try to understand rather than a personality trait she felt she could instantly condemn?

Partly because she feared his anger, she numbly continued

to date him, waiting to feel the same fervor he seemed to feel about her. Didn't attraction usually run both ways? What was wrong with her? Did she still think Dr. Perfect was out there somewhere?

Only two days left. Rick climbed in the car and drove. There was a feeling of nervous excitement as he drew closer. Four streets away to Osborne Road. Her street. Now three streets. Two. Reaching the street, he felt a rising feeling inside. He memorized the look of the day—blue sky, crisp air, the scent of summer flowers in a calm breeze. He knew he would look back on this moment—months, probably years from now. Almost there. What if Sara was outside this time? His heart skipped a beat with the memory of a time he saw her sitting on the porch reading a book. If she was out in the yard, he promised himself he'd stop. Just the thought created butterflies in his stomach. He told himself he'd really do it. Even if she was with someone. What was he thinking? He turned onto her street. This time, instead of slowing when he reached the white house, he pulled over to the opposite side of the road, felt the tires brush the gutter. A lump in his throat. He stared at the house a long time, felt as if he knew each rust-colored roof tile, the number of slats in the awnings. His voice worked its way out of his throat. "Good-bye, Sara," he managed, lifting his hand with a wave as a lopsided grin spread across his face. He tried to ignore the pounding he felt in his chest, the nagging thoughts that this could be the very last time, and maybe he should go up to the door and ring the bell. "Good-bye," he said one more time, then forced himself to look ahead to the road. He jerked the car into gear, glanced sideways, and eased on out.

Chapter Ten

A week since she last talked to Carl, Sara answered the phone. "Hello?"

"Hey, Sara! Should we get married in September?"

"Are you kidding?" She forced a laugh. Married? What was this? A sick, sour sensation wound its way down Sara's insides. This wasn't the way this was supposed to feel, was it?

"Yeah, you know . . . at the end of summer?"

Where was the tender kiss she imagined in the marriage proposals in her mind? Where was the absolute certainty she always thought she would feel? The sour sadness stayed. "Really?" she asked.

"Yeah, I figured we could take one of my dad's condos off his hands. Or we could live with your folks until we can afford our own place."

Was this what you were supposed to think about when you wanted to get married? "I guess we could," Sara said, surprising herself with her own words. What was happening here? This was nothing like what she always envisioned.

"Took ya by surprise, didn't I?"

"We never talked about getting married."

"But I knew you wanted to . . . I could tell."

"Well . . . yes . . ." Sometime in the future, when she was madly in love. . . .

"And we've been dating for two years. . . ."

"Yeah . . ." Sara hadn't realized it was that long. Longer

than she ever dated anyone else. Maybe this was the way it happened with everybody. You just dated somebody, and you didn't know how long it lasted, and suddenly it was time to get married. Maybe everyone felt this anxious. Maybe all that "absolutely sure, madly in love" stuff only happened in movies and novels.

"What are you thinking about? Planning your dress and all that stuff?"

"I guess so."

"So should we make it the first weekend in September?" She heard him pull out his pocket calendar. "Nope, that's Labor Day. Better the weekend before. How does August thirty-first sound?"

"Okay," she said.

"I thought you'd be more excited. Guess you're a little stunned, huh?"

"I am," she said.

"What will your folks say?"

A fresh despair blossomed within the dark feeling that hovered inside her. "I don't know. . . ."

"Oldest kid . . . only daughter . . . getting married . . ."

"I wanted to get married before my brother."

"Well, you made it, baby . . . unless he elopes on us." Carl's enigmatic laugh.

"Yeah . . . guess I did. . . ."

"Well, I'll see ya later. Go ahead and spread the good news. Wonder what everyone at work will say?"

Sara forced a laugh. "I don't know."

"Well, catch ya later . . . bye."

The phone clicked in her ear. For a brief, frantic second Sara wished she could withdraw the entire conversation. Declare it null and void. Take it all back. But why did she say yes if she hadn't meant it? She did want to get married before her brother, Ted, she knew that. It was a matter of pride. The first child gets married first. And Ted was pretty serious with Judy. They'd get married soon. No question there. So now she would be the first. She got what she always wanted. So why did the sour sadness still haunt the pit of her stomach?

And her uncertainty intensified to despair as she thought of Rick. The warm peaceful feeling that wrapped around her heart at his memory now felt like a sad loss. She couldn't help but wonder how she would feel if this were Rick asking to marry her. She sensed his proposal would be nothing like Carl's. He wouldn't call on the phone and spell things out. A sweet nostalgia enveloped her as she remembered standing on her porch in the dark after the prom. The way Rick took her hand, held it, and asked gently, "May I kiss you?" She was surprised to feel a tear form at the corner of her eye.

But she quickly rationalized that Rick was nowhere in her life now. He wasn't even going to call her, let alone ask her out or ask her to marry him. He could be married to someone else now. He could have kids. And she had no idea where he was. Probably working with machines now, like he said.

She was just nervous, Sara told herself. Getting married was a big deal. But she waited days before she told anyone. She didn't let anyone else know, until Carl asked who she talked to. Then she knew she had to say something to her parents.

Her dad was watching the news, sitting in his recliner in the living room, one Sunday night when she sat on the couch.

"How's it going?" he asked, with his gentle smile

She started talking about her work. "We spent a long afternoon in the operating room the other day. A man was shot in the head five times."

"And he lived?"

"Lived to tell about it," Sara said. Her voice turned serious, as she recalled the emotions of those days. "Recovered in less than two weeks. His wife says it was a miracle."

"Tell me about your friend Carl," said her father. How did he always know what was really on her mind?

Sara couldn't look in her dad's eyes as she said, "He wants to marry me. . . ."

"Huh?" her dad said. "Which year?"

"This year—this summer." Sara's voice was as flat as her father's.

"Doesn't he want to finish school? Wasn't he talking about medical school?"

"He says he has some nurse's training . . . he plans to go back to school later."

"Sara, you know what Carl is like. If he's what you want, there's nothing I can say. . . ."

"But you wish I'd marry Rick."

"I can't say that. I just never understood why you parted."

"We fought—he's gone now."

"There was just something about him. Solid. Mature. I felt he would take good care of my little girl."

"Your little girl can take care of herself. . . ."

"And I thought he was really in love with you."

"He left, didn't he?"

"After you told him not to come back."

"I told him that if I were going to be a nurse, I might be more compatible with a doctor or a man with a professional career," she said, feeling fresh sadness at the memory.

Her father sat straighter in his chair. "I just remember listening to you two on the phone one night. Your voice. I could tell by your tone of voice that you really were in love with him."

Sara felt herself blush. She remembered, too—and caught herself. "That's all in the past now. . . ."

"Is it?" Her father raised his eyebrows at her.

Her throat suddenly closed.

Unable to speak, Sara left the room.

She was halfway to her bedroom when she heard her dad sigh.

She didn't talk about the wedding with her parents after that. She and Carl—mostly Carl—made all the decisions. Her dress and his tux. The fact that the wedding would be in the church where she and her mother and grandmother were baptized. The date would definitely be August 31, and there would be a catered wedding dinner rather than just refreshments.

Sara felt as if she were in a haze. It was as if she were just visiting her life and could back away at any time and go back to the way things were before—when Carl was just a lab technician that she dated along with other boyfriends. It all seemed as if it wasn't quite real. So when Carl surprised her with an engagement ring, she wore it, but didn't mention it to anyone unless they happened to comment. Somehow, she wondered if it would always belong to her.

Chapter Eleven

Despite what he told Sara, Rick was only eight years old when he decided he wanted to join the Air Force. Now at a career crossroads, he knew that one of the smartest things he ever did was pass those military tests with high scores when he was twenty-one. Now his superiors were asking where they should ship him next. Rick knew he should say he wanted to go anywhere but Vietnam. At least his accounting position gave him the hope of making a choice. He tapped his pen on the desk. Preferred future stations? He began to write. Japan. Florida. England. California.

He received the answer three weeks later. How did that old song go? "California, here I come. Right back where I started from." (Only he'd never been West before.)

Driving past the Rockies in his car, Rick felt an odd sense of being at home. Was it the clear sun? The billowing air? The majesty of the mountains? Rick sensed he'd been here sometime before . . . and somehow knew he wouldn't leave anytime soon.

Two regrets. He was far from his mother. And far from where Sara would think he should be.

Troops on the base in California were in constant rotation. It was like a lottery, Rick decided. Whenever a new group arrived, everyone was given a priority number. High numbers stayed. Low numbers went to Vietnam.

His number changed every two weeks.

1,052 when he first came in.

749 four months later.

502 on his one-year anniversary.

387 at sixteen months.

Then a cascading spiral downward: 340, 268, 109, 87, 54, 23, 2, 1.

Adams, the man at the desk to the right of him, was picked for 'Nam. Rick shook his hand. "I'm next," he said. "Good luck."

"Luck?" Adams shook his head. "Mine ran out."

But Rick's didn't. The lottery stopped there, one desk away.

He was safe. For now.

As the morning sun poured over her bedroom quilt, Sara lay awake in bed, wondering if she would ever feel the excitement this day was supposed to hold. Her wedding day. A once-in-a-lifetime event. The beginning of a new life. Then why was she having a hard time forcing herself out of bed? At least it was a sunny day for this outdoor wedding. Happy is the bride the sun smiles on, Sara read someplace.

Yet her hopes were dashed as soon as she stood by Daddy, seconds away from walking down the aisle. Could anyone else—Mama or Grandma—see the sick sadness that lay in her father's eyes? To Sara, his displeasure seemed accented by the crisp suit and shiny shoes he wore.

Why did Rick cross her mind as her father took her arm, his touch as safe and reassuring as it had been all her life so far? Where was Rick today? How would her life be different if he were the man waiting at the front of the church? Sara glanced ahead. She had to admit that Carl looked incredibly handsome. Blond hair, penetrating blue eyes.

She listened numbly as the pastor read the wedding vows. You could stop this now, a small voice inside her head seemed to say. You could turn and run. But could she really? Look at all the money her parents spent. Look at all the people waiting in the chapel, all smiling and expectant. Still, she looked at the church door and had visions of running outside as the pastor said, "Do you, Sara Anne, take Carl to be your lawful wedded husband . . . in sickness and in health . . .

for richer or poorer . . . till death do you part?"

She had to clear her throat first, and even then her voice wavered. "I-I-I do," Sara said, her voice echoing to the high ceiling of the church.

Later, at the reception in the church basement, she saw that her father still held the pained, struggling expression she noticed earlier. His frown intensified as Carl said, "I don't want this stuff." He pushed away the plate of prime rib, baked potato, asparagus, and rice pilaf that her parents had ordered from the caterer.

"Carl." Sara's voice rose. "My parents paid fourteen dollars a plate for that food."

"Huh?" Carl's incredulous look. "You're going to worry about that today? Every little penny?"

"Fourteen dollars isn't a penny. Do you know what this wedding cost?" Sara was aware that other guests were watching, but she couldn't stop. "My mom and dad saved their whole lives for this wedding."

"And I showed up, didn't I? That's what counts. I didn't ditch you at the church."

An angry sigh escaped her. "You really won't eat your dinner?"

"No." An angry chopping gesture with his hands. "This is my wedding. I'm the groom. I get to say what I'll eat."

Sara felt her blood boil. She couldn't look at her father seated beside her. "So what'll you have, Your Majesty?"

His words hissed between clenched teeth. "Tell a waitress to get over here."

Sara stood, gathered her dress around her. Then she felt her father's hand on her arm. "Sit down, Sara. I'll get someone."

"No—" Sara said, as her father squeezed her hand. "I need a walk. I'll find someone." The waitress she found hardly spoke English. "My—husband would like to order," Sara said.

"Beverages?" The waitress lifted the tasseled wine list.

"No—I need someone to come and talk to him."

"I send someone."

When she returned to the table, Sara dipped into her own prime rib, grateful to be able to focus on something besides her anger toward Carl. She tried not to stare across the table at his perfectly acceptable dinner plate.

"Do you have chicken?" Carl was asking a waitress with an order pad.

"No, sir. The catering order did not include chicken."

"How about steak?"

"No, sir. Prime rib or salmon."

"Caesar salad?"

"I'm sorry, sir. Spring garden or gelatin salad."

"French fries?"

"I'm sorry."

"A hamburger?"

"No."

"What about yogurt? Or cottage cheese?"

The waitress sighed. "There is cottage cheese back there. Would you like a small bowl?"

"A big bowl?" Carl held out his hands.

Sara sighed. Fourteen dollars a plate and Carl ordered cottage cheese. Didn't he care what her parents might think?

Chapter Twelve

Rick couldn't fathom why he felt this way right now. Nothing happened to bring Sara to mind today. He didn't hear "Woolly Bully" on the radio, watch a nurse in a white uniform cross the street, or hear a weather report from the Midwest. No usual triggers. But suddenly there was this overpowering feeling that brought back memories. Like the way he felt when they were together and the warm feeling of being with her hovered after she left. Or the rush when he saw her at a distance and his heart lifted in anticipation. But this sensation was stronger. There was no way he could ignore his thoughts. This wasn't like the usual times when she crossed his mind. He might think of her for several days in a row—then lots of times in a single day. Or days could pass and suddenly she'd be there, stuck in his mind like a recent memory. He'd be sitting or working on a computer program, and Sara would flash through his thoughts. He'd wonder what she was doing, or what she'd think of a movie he saw or a concert he attended. Or he'd see an emergency room nurse on TV and remember how she looked in her candy striper uniform. He'd wonder if she really was a nurse now. Or he'd hear music he knew she played or heard back when they were together. And it was amazing how many times the oldies station played "Woolly Bully." And sometimes there was no explanation. She'd just flash into his mind like a commercial between two other programs that were the rest of his life. So

he'd think of her—wonder where she was, what she was doing. They were quick flashes, not upsetting him, not interrupting his day. Just a reminder that his relationship with Sara
still felt unfinished. He felt that something important was happening in her life today. Graduating from nursing school? A
new job? A wedding? He wished he knew. But what could
he do about it now?

Sara could read Evelyn Boyd's life story in her sixty-five-
year-old face, as well as through the brief conversation she
overheard the night before when Evelyn's husband, Wallace,
was admitted to the hospital. Evelyn's facts were simple: married forty years, husband retired two years earlier, grandkids
still young. Sara knew that Evelyn and Wallace had taken a
couple of scenic trips together, but nothing like the biggest
one that still lay ahead. Sara knew that Evelyn anticipated a
Caribbean cruise with her husband after his recovery. The trip
would be the highlight of forty years of a working life. Everything about Evelyn looked hopeful—her freshly colored
brown hair, dangling earrings, crisp pastel pantsuit.

The head nurse sent Sara to the room where Evelyn waited
for her husband to emerge from recovery.

"Mrs. Boyd?" Sara said gently.

Evelyn smiled. Waiting. Expectant.

"Mrs. Boyd," Sara said as she sat beside Evelyn, "I'm
deeply sorry to have to tell you that Wallace's heart wasn't
strong enough to survive the surgery—"

"What do you mean?" Instant fear.

"As I said, I'm deeply sorry to inform you that Wallace
died on the operating table."

"No!" Evelyn's calm demeanor gave way to emotion. "No!
He was fine. He even mowed the lawn on Sunday, and we
went for a long walk. . . ."

"I'm very sorry."

"He was fine. We already had plans to go to Cancun. . . .
His grandchildren . . ."

Sara reached out, took Evelyn's hand. "Please know that
he died painlessly—"

"But they gave him good chances, the doctor said. . . ."

"His heart didn't survive. Sometimes, Evelyn, it's just a

person's time . . . and the spouse and children and grandchildren are left to mourn. . . ."

Evelyn stopped crying, stared into Sara's face. "Why couldn't I go first?" A sob burst from Evelyn's throat.

"That's up to God, Evelyn. I know that Wallace would want you to go on, for the grandchildren. . . ."

Evelyn sniffed, nodded. "He would." Another sob. "It's all just so unreal, though. . . ."

"It is," Sara agreed. No matter how long she was a nurse, she would never get over the fragility of life. How someone could be here one moment—and then die the next day. It made her see the importance of each moment. There were times in her life when she wished she could go back. Yet now she clung to the hope that at least she and Carl both wanted a baby. Through months of fruitless pregnancy tests, infertility treatments, and the miscarriage last month, it was the first time they worked toward a common goal.

In his twenties, Rick told himself, it didn't matter that he wasn't married. But now that he was almost thirty, it was time to move on. When would he finally face the fact that Sara was gone? When would he accept that no matter how many times he resurrected the memories, the past was over? It was time to start a new life and stop looking back.

Carl didn't expect her to come home for lunch and find the clothes on their bed. "What's all this stuff?" Sara knew she didn't recognize any of these items. Golf shirts, a gym bag, and a pair of shoes.

"Oh"—Carl paused only a second—"I went to the thrift store."

"You went shopping? We don't have any money until payday."

"I only spent a couple of bucks. Did you hear me? The thrift store. Where you can get a shirt for fifty cents."

"We agreed not to spend—"

"You're gonna yell at me for a couple of bucks?"

Sara paused. "But this looks like new stuff."

Carl actually grinned. "I know. I got there just at the right time. They were unloading a new truck. Probably giveaways from some rich neighborhood. Some rich guy was my size and he gave away this stuff . . ."

The taste in Sara's mouth was sour. She didn't see any price tags, but the clothes didn't look worn, either. And she was tired, and would be even tireder unless she relaxed and ate a good lunch before going back to work. So she swallowed her rising anger and rushed out to the car so she would be on time.

Stockings. Late that afternoon, on the way home, she remembered she needed stockings for work the next day. Exhausted as she was, a quick stop at the neighborhood department store was preferable to trying to make it to a store before her early shift the next morning. She was looking for the hosiery aisle when she saw them. The golf shirts. The one hanging as a display was exactly like the one on the bed at home.

The one Carl said he got at the thrift store.

Curious, she sorted through the golf shirts and found another one like one of the shirts on the bed. When she turned to look at the department store clock, she caught sight of the athletic bag. Now there was one more place to look. Men's shoes. The brown loafers like the supposed thrift store cast-offs were the first ones on the display. They weren't even on sale. He'd lied to her, like so many times before. But where did he begin to get the money to pay for these things? Sara felt a sharp sense of panic. They no longer had any savings. Just a little grocery money so they could eat until she got paid. How did he buy the clothes? Was her credit card still in her purse?

Sitting in the front seat of her car, Sara opened her purse with trembling fingers. She fumbled through her wallet. The credit card was there, but in a different slot than she remembered. She couldn't be sure he'd moved it. What could she say? She told herself she was too tired to confront him.

But then, when she got home, he sat in a living room chair, wearing the hunter green golf shirt she'd seen on display.

"I found that shirt," she said firmly.

"What do you mean, you found it?" Was that nervousness or sarcasm in his laugh? "You watched me bring it home."

"I found it at Nordstrom's."

"So they had one like it. I told you it was a great shirt."

"I found the other things there, too. The shoes and the athletic bag."

He shook his head with frustrated anger. "Let me get this straight. You chased all over town until you found some things like mine just to prove—"

"It wasn't on purpose. I needed to buy stockings. And the things were there—right in front of me."

"So—all men's clothes look alike—" He turned to pretend interest in the television.

"Not that much alike. You lied to me."

"Because I needed a few things? What do you care where I got them?"

"I care that we don't have any money to buy clothes until we get paid. The rent's due. We've already been evicted once."

"And you'd be evicted again without me—"

"Carl, I'm seriously worried about you. You'll say anything just to avoid admitting you told me a lie."

"You don't even think about what I need. I needed new clothes. What rigmarole do I have to go through to get a few work clothes?"

"You need to wait a week. Until I get paid. Unless you've already spent that, too."

"What do you mean?"

"I mean I can't trust you with money." The thought rushed to her mind, *Or anything else.*

He shook his head in angry disgust. "You got problems, baby. That's all I can say. Have you ever heard the word paranoid? Fits you to a tee. Hey, listen. You don't trust me with my money? Let's just keep our money to ourselves. You with yours. Me with mine."

For a second, she felt relief. Her own money that she could manage. "But who is going to pay the bills?"

"Ha! You're in control, kid. You work that out."

"We'll have to divide those, too." Her voice was quiet.

"It's up to you. But I'll tell you one thing. If I were you, I wouldn't be arguing with me over pennies. I'd be thinking about that baby we're going to have, and whose money you're going to need if you decide not to go back to work."

"I'm going back after my maternity leave."

"What can I say? You know it all." Carl stood, shoved the chair aside with both hands and left the room. Inside Sara felt an emptiness like hunger.

This time Sara didn't dare hope. Nothing in any medical book ever said how long it would take to recover from a miscarriage *emotionally*. The pain of missing the two babies she'd lost hovered for a long time. It was months before she could walk past the hospital nursery and not feel the ache of loss when she heard a tiny cry or even smelled the scent of newborn skin. She would picture her babies in her mind and wonder if either of them would have had Carl's blond hair or her green eyes. Or if they were boys or girls. She even thought of names for them in her head. Laurel, if one of them was a girl, and Trent, if the other happened to be a boy.

And now she didn't know if she could stand to even think about the possibility of losing another baby. Still, you wouldn't need to be a nurse to diagnose the changes she noticed about herself. The obsession she jokingly called her "seventeen cups of coffee" a night that kept her awake and alert all through the graveyard shift were suddenly accompanied by cravings far weirder than her usual glazed doughnut.

There was the time she wanted a tamale with pizza sauce and Parmesan cheese.

Or the time she ate a pound of shrimp in one sitting. And there were the multiple hotdogs with sauerkraut, chili, mustard, and ketchup.

Maybe all of that could somehow pass as normal. But there was no way she could deny that the way she felt right now was weird. First thing in the morning—before she even had her first cup of coffee—she was already thinking about eating a cheap taco from the Taco King down the street. Cost fifty cents and hot enough to set your mouth on fire.

The first time she drove by, they were closed.

But now it was nine-thirty, and the Open sign was up even though the blinds were still drawn. Sara drove up to the drive-through window and waited. Five minutes. Ten. Yawning, she drove around the side of the building to the parking lot. When she walked inside and stood at the counter, there was no response, although she heard conversations and dishes rattling back in the kitchen.

"Anyone here?" she called out. Waited. "You have a customer. . . ." More waiting.

Finally a short Hispanic woman approached her at the counter. *"Si?"* she asked.

"One—no, make it two—of your Four Alarm Fire Tacos," said Sara.

"To go?"

"No . . . I'll eat them here."

The woman stared for a moment. Smiled. "You'll eat two Four Alarms? Now?" She stared at the clock: 9:45 A.M.

Sara nodded, touched her stomach even as it growled.

"This is the earliest ever," said the woman, returning to the kitchen.

Sara listened as the conversation from the kitchen grew more animated. She was sure she caught the word *pregnant* among the mixed English and Spanish dialogue. Moments later, when her tacos came, she hardly tasted them because she was so filled with excitement. And now she knew she had to rush home before going to work. The diagnosis from the taco restaurant only confirmed what she'd suspected herself these last weeks. It was time to submit a specimen to the lab. She'd have to hurry if she planned to take in her own urine sample and still make it to work on time.

"I can't call," Sara said, turning away from the phone.

"Come on." Carl laughed at her, his grin wide. "It's just a simple yes or no. Positive or negative."

She laughed at the irony of this. "It's not simple at all. All the work we've done, all the doctor's appointments."

"Like it was really hard work—" He laughed and reached out to tickle her.

Backing away, she thrust the phone in his direction. "You do it—you call."

"What?"

"I can't call—they've heard my voice too many times. You call and then let me know what they say."

"Oh, sure." He affected a high voice. "This is Sara Parker . . . I think I might be pregnant. . . ."

When did they ever laugh together this much? "No," Sara said simply. "Just say"—now she put on a deep voice—"I'm calling for my wife's results. She's at work and asked me to call."

"What if they ask for your Social Security number?"

"Right here." Sara handed him her wallet.

Carl shrugged. She handed him the phone and left the room. Seconds later she was back. The grin on his face was her answer.

"No . . ." she said cautiously, even as wings of hope fluttered inside her.

"Yes . . ." Carl said. "Yes. Yes. Yes! They said, 'It's positive, Mr. Parker.' "

Sara giggled in excitement. "I don't believe this. . . . I've got to call them myself."

"Oh, brother."

When the hospital answered, Sara said, "My husband just called. But I had to call back. . . . It just can't say positive next to my name. . . ."

Seconds later she and Carl were hugging and jumping up and down. She still couldn't believe it.

As days passed Sara clung to the reality of her pregnancy as an anchor against an undercurrent of worry about their financial situation. Having a baby would settle Carl down— she hoped. No matter what, Sara vowed she would give this child the best life she could.

Why did she feel this sense of foreboding, even though she was leaving right on time for work? Sara combed her hair, grabbed a five-dollar bill, and headed out the door at three forty-five.

At first she thought the woman's angry voice was calling out to someone else.

"Hey, you!"

She rushed faster, headed for her car.

"Parker!" The voice yelled louder. "Mrs. Parker!"

Sara stopped, her heart thudding, breath coming fast. She

turned to confront the angry, reddened face of Sally Thompson. Her landlady. Sara frowned.

Sally stepped closer. "You moving, Parker? Ya gotta give me notice!"

Moving? What was this? "No—we're not moving. We have five more months on our lease."

"Lease or no lease—you gotta pay your rent."

"It's paid!" Sara felt her fury rise along with the knowledge that precious minutes were ticking by. She glanced around her and saw people stare. She recognized some of them from the corner market and the halls in their apartment building.

"Last time you paid was three months ago. Are you going to make up the money you owe or move out?"

"Money we owe?" Sara's mind frantically scrambled to imagine how they could owe rent money. She still gave her paycheck money to Carl every time, regular as a clock. This shouldn't happen. But she was still torn between not wanting to fight with him and being worried over money. The lady interrupted her thoughts.

"Yes—the rent. You owe eight hundred dollars right now. Next week it will be twelve hundred."

"But—my husband—"

"I tried to talk to him, too. I don't care how you do it. Get the check to me by next week or get out!"

"I'll arrange something—I'm going to be late for work." Sara turned and ran to her car, boiling with rage as adrenaline filled her. Her heart was still pounding with anxious fury when she reached the hospital twenty minutes later. She vomited in the women's room, then smoothed her skirt and got ready for work.

As it usually did, the atmosphere in the hospital felt like home to her. When she arrived, there was no one in the ER, and she began her rounds, calling on her intensive care patients.

A new patient she'd never met before, Mr. Timms, was in Room 300. She filled his water pitcher, closed his blinds.

"I didn't hear anybody say hello. . . ." said a dignified voice from the bed.

Sara looked down, saw that although he looked pale, thin, and weak, the patient in the bed was grinning at her.

"Hello," she said, returning the smile. "How are you to-night, Mr. Timms?"

"Pretty good, for someone who's about to die any minute," he said, with a surprisingly hearty laugh.

Sara found herself momentarily tongue-tied. Then she laughed nervously, too. "All of us will die sometime," she agreed a moment later, feeling her smile waver on her face. "But here in this hospital, we are in the business of prolonging life. We will make every effort to do that for you."

"You like your job, don't you, lady? Know just what to say?"

Now Sara noticed the twinkle in the man's eyes. "I hope so," she admitted. "There are lots of times when it's tough . . . especially when someone says they're about to die!"

The two of them laughed together.

"I know how it goes," said Mr. Timms, struggling to sit up in bed. "I used to like my job, too. Thought I knew the right stuff to say. My kids said I could sell ice to an Eskimo."

"You were a salesman?" Sara could picture this self-assured man with the soothing voice talking all kinds of people out of all kinds of dollars.

"Called myself a designer. Interior design. Really, though, it was sales. Lots of couches, wingback chairs, floor lamps, stuff like that. Truth is, I still have my business. Someone's just baby-sitting it for me . . . until I die. Then my kids will fight over it."

"I bet there's lots of business to fight over," Sara said jok-ingly as she mentally pictured a classy design shop, with Mr. Timms dressed in a crisp, expensive suit rather than the limp, white hospital gown.

"It was my life," Mr. Timms said, in a voice that was proud, sad, and reflective all at once. As he began to describe the contentment he felt in his career, Sara found herself sitting in his bedside chair, letting his calm voice pour over her jag-ged nerves. When was the last time that listening to a man's voice soothed her this way? It didn't take long for her to remember her long conversations with Rick, back at St. Anne's. Hearing Mr. Timms reminded her of the way that hearing Rick's voice made her feel as if everything was going to be all right. The sense that no matter what was happening in her life, she'd be strong enough to face it.

Back then she didn't know how it would be to lose that gentle comfort, that feeling that someone understood her and thought her ideas were okay. Memories washed over her. It had been so long since she felt that way, without the panic of running out of money, of feeling as if the world would give way beneath her at any moment. As Mr. Timms continued relishing his memories, Sara basked in her own thoughts of the way her life used to be. There was no way to deny that she wanted to feel that way again. That there was hope and life could be fun. A daring thought crossed her mind. She would find Rick. Just to thank him, to tell him that she'd never forget. And that she finally appreciated the way he'd made her feel.

Chapter Thirteen

When he first woke, Rick thought the rising feeling inside him was just his awe of the surrounding forest beauty. He slept solidly the night before, and now opened his eyes to an azure sky that bathed the earth like a gentle blanket. He eased out of his sleeping bag, screwed open his thermos, poured a cup of coffee, and stood. He yawned, stretched his arms into the boundless air. There was an impressive high-ceilinged silence, as if he stood inside an empty concert hall. He breathed slowly as his eyes drank in the stillness of lake and trees. He was alone. No bird graced the skyline. No squirrel dashed past his motionless feet.

Rick didn't think anyone would call him a pious person. But he always felt closest to God in nature. He liked to reflect in the silence, feel the majesty of mountains around him. But today something was different. He felt a surge of emotion, a rush of reverence. He swallowed. What could make him feel this way out here—with no one around? There was total silence in the panoramic mountain splendor.

His voice spoke softly. "It's you, Sara. Something's happening with you. I don't know what it is, but it's big. Big event in your life . . ."

He paused, waited as if she might answer.

Her hopeful anticipation for her new baby was Sara's inner strength. The landlord's first warning was the beginning of many turbulent months in which Sara realized she had totally lost control of their budget. Though they paid the rent after the first warning, she had no idea when Carl would add charges to her credit card without telling her, withdraw money from their bank account without saying a word, or seemingly forget to pay bills as promised. Though he continued to work for the same lab tech's wages as always, it was as if he still had no idea their budget had limits.

As she waited for their child's approaching birth, Sara held her breath, fearing that the financial bottom would drop terrifyingly away, leaving them abruptly broke with nowhere to turn but her parents. She ached with despair on the increasing number of occasions when she had to ask her father for money. Yet at the same time she was glad he never said, "I told you so. . . ."

Three weeks before her baby was due, her back and upper thighs began to ache during the last hour of her four to eleven shift. Finally home, Sara sat on the couch, monitoring her own condition. She hoped not to reach the most likely diagnosis—labor. Her due date was three weeks away. She knew—from walking past the nursery each night—how vital each day of growth inside the mother's womb was to a developing baby. Uncomfortable as she felt, her nurse instincts told her to sit still and hope her symptoms would subside. She fought to keep each breath calm and slow. Her eyes followed the second hand on the clock, and she half-listened to the late news. Maybe if she stayed still—

A pain—sharp and stabbing—deep within her belly.

She didn't have to be a nurse to know what that meant.

As if she were in the emergency room, Sara ignored the subsiding cramp and stepped gingerly to the bedroom to wake Carl. Another pain erupted as she reached the side of the bed.

"Carl," she whispered, shaking him gently, "I'm in labor."

Carl turned over in bed. He blinked, then looked at the clock. "It's three weeks away!"

Sara inhaled sharply. "It's right now—we have to get to the hospital."

"Now? Do we have time to get there?"

"It's the baby's only chance—if they can stop the labor before it progresses—" Sara left her sentence unfinished.

The two of them threw their clothes on as if they were hurrying to a medical emergency at work. Only this time, it's us, Sara thought. They dashed out into the parking lot. Carl held the car door, and Sara slid across the seat. She realized her forehead was wet with sweat.

They drove through the black and satiny darkness, and it seemed like only seconds before Carl wheeled her into the hospital.

"Hey, what are you guys doing? Is this a joke?" called a paramedic who recognized them. "Don't you have another month?" He stepped in front of the gurney, but Carl waved him aside, steered the gurney into the elevator, pushed the button. They surged upstairs to labor and delivery.

"The monitor," Sara called out from where she lay on her back. "Get me on the monitor right away." Another nurse rushed into the room, and she felt someone strap a belt around her middle. Another nurse started an IV, then felt between Sara's legs with a gloved hand. "You're dilated three centimeters," she said. "I'll notify the doctor."

Now it's my turn to be the emergency patient, Sara thought.

Another jarring pain.

"Carl!" Sara called out. "I just had another contraction!"

She watched the monitor, with its graph of peaks and valleys. Another pain was about to rack her body.

"Carl, look!" Sara called out. "The baby's heart rate is dropping!"

Sara's own heart leaped with fear. Her eyes glued to the monitor screen as she watched her baby's struggling heartbeat. She felt each tiny thud as if her own heart floundered: 94, the monitor registered. . . . 90. At least ten beats slower per minute than it should be.

"Can't you stop my labor?" she asked Jane, a nurse she knew.

"I don't like those dips," Jane said. She pointed to the monitor printout with a pencil. "Can't take a chance with that heart rate."

The monitor registered 89.

"When will you give me the medication?" Sara asked.

The nurse didn't answer. She watched the monitor, wrote on a clipboard, then left the room.

The monitor registered 88.

Sara held her breath. She felt more helpless at this moment than at any other time in her life. No procedure she had learned as a nurse could help her now.

Another pain coursed through her body.

The monitor registered 87.

Dressed in green scrubs, Dr. Thomas strode into the room.

Sara sighed with relief that her doctor was there. "The heart rate's dropping. I need medication right away."

"I think we're approaching delivery," Carl said, sounding professional.

"What about medication?" Sara pleaded again.

Another pain. Then another.

"If you're going to deliver, when are you going to give me the anesthetic?"

The doctor said, "We're not. We can't. You know why. We have to administer the anesthetic between contractions. And they're coming too fast. There isn't time to anesthetize you. You're going to have your baby."

"But I'm three weeks early."

"There's risk of fetal arrest," the doctor told Carl without looking down at Sara.

"Then it's an emergency delivery—" Carl agreed, helping the doctor wheel the gurney over to the delivery room. "It's going to be okay Sara," he said.

Sara steeled herself. There was no turning back now. Sweat swam on her body, and tears of excitement mingled with the pain. After all these years of waiting, she was really going to have a baby. Here. Now. A splash of white light in the delivery room. Pain, racking her insides. Worry, more powerful than the pain.

Then she saw the lowest heart rate reading yet—85.

The nurse checked her again. "Dilation at five centimeters," she said to the doctor.

Almost here. The heart rate registered 83.

A nurse placed an oxygen mask on her face.

Then the baby's heart stopped. No bleeps on the monitor. No red numbers indicating heartbeats. Just a black square. The longest single second of Sara's life. She held her breath as her own heart seemed to cease in panic.

Then the monitor registered 82.

Sara exhaled in relief.

Another 82.

Then Sara stared at the ceiling as Carl and the doctor rushed the gurney into the delivery room.

"I want to push," she realized suddenly, thinking of all the times she'd seen this happen.

The doctor checked her, then said, "Push now."

With flagging strength, Sara grabbed the hospital bedrails, closed her eyes in concentration, and gave every ounce of force she could muster.

"Again," said the doctor.

Exhaling with a shuddering sigh, Sara geared up, summoned her remaining strength, and pushed. Then her body sagged in exhaustion.

"One more time," said the doctor.

Sara grasped the rails, forced what felt like barely a tremor. Sweat beaded on her forehead, and she drank in a long breath, sensing her energy was gone.

A pause. The only sound in the room was the fetal monitor. Then Sara heard a high, thin cry.

"There he is!" the doctor said excitedly, holding the baby up high. Sara caught a glimpse of peach-pink skin, a rounded head. Seconds later the doctor pressed a warm, blue-blanketed bundle in Sara's arms. Tears rushed down her cheeks as she drank in the long-awaited beauty of her baby's face. She stared, knowing she would remember this moment forever. A rosebud mouth with prominent upper lip. His parents' fair complexion and a shock of fine hair. A face she felt she'd always known.

Her son. Patrick.

In the recovery room she lay calm, sated. A sense of success filled her. It was all worth it, she thought. And worth everything else I have to do from here on out.

It was the next morning, after the hospital breakfast, when her father, caring a delicate vase filled with pink roses, came to see her.

After he kissed her cheek and set the flowers on her breakfast tray, he said the words that made her laugh. Words that, years later, she would always remember with a smile. "You did good work," he said, causing the warmth that a compliment from him always brought. "But I can see you any time. Right now I'm going to go see my grandson."

He squeezed her hand, and she felt the touch of his fingers a long time after she heard his footsteps die away out in the hall.

Chapter Fourteen

Every time he got another promotion, Rick stayed grateful he didn't go to 'Nam. His GS number kept rising, and his salary grew. Weekends, he camped. Not a bad life, but the feeling never left that something was missing.

What could it be? He didn't have to think hard. He had no family, no wife. He pictured Sara, a nurse married to a doctor. Probably a big house, nice cars. Two kids . . . maybe three. His heart caught, and he forced himself to focus on the computer screen in front of him.

Why couldn't she guess how tired she'd be—working and taking care of a baby? Her six-month maternity leave passed in no time. And now she was back at work—Patrick still seemed so fragile and tiny.

"It just feels like too much sometimes—but I can't imagine doing anything else," Sara said as she flopped on the couch after settling Patrick in his crib. "A stabbing and a gunshot wound tonight . . ." She sighed. "While I'm there, at work, I'm okay. But when I get home, I feel dead."

"A crazy day for me," said Carl, somehow unconvincingly. When their eyes met, Sara suddenly remembered. She sat up straighter on the kitchen chair. "The landlady called today. She said our rent check is late again. It didn't get there yet."

"I'll talk to her."

Sara shook her head. "I don't see how that could be. We budgeted—and I wrote the check. . . ."

"Maybe she made a mistake."

"And I gave it to you to mail—what day was it?" Sara leaped off the couch, dashed to the kitchen calendar. "Thursday . . . no way does it take five days."

"I'll talk to her. . . ."

"Maybe I should call right now. . . ."

"Sara. It's almost ten o'clock. The woman's probably about to go to bed. Let me handle it."

"I just can't figure out. . . ." She stared at the calendar and counted again.

"Here," Carl said suddenly. "This is what you need." Beside her, he opened the fridge, took out the bottle of Jim Beam left from New Year's Eve. "Just a little bit to relax you . . ."

"Oh, I don't know. . . ."

"Sara—" He squeezed her arm. "Take my word for it. You're agitated. You just need a little to relax so you can sleep. You have to work again tomorrow, don't you?"

"Yes, but—"

Carl poured an inch of whiskey in the glass, added a little water. "This is medicine for you. You're too keyed up to sleep. And Patrick's already out like a light. This is when you should get some rest so you can make it through tomorrow."

She couldn't argue with that. Sara numbly accepted the glass. Later, she had to admit that the drink relaxed her. She felt rested when she woke in the morning and got up to get Patrick ready for day care. But what had happened to the rent check?

It was months before she saw that night as the beginning of a downward spiral in which Carl gave her a drink every time she became upset. Jim Beam and I are friends, she thought, though doubts nagged as her drinking progressed. She never drank before work—always at the end of the day when Patrick was already asleep. When doubts nagged, she went for a checkup, where the doctor diagnosed her as having clinical depression and prescribed Xanax. Though she had her doubts about his pronouncement, there was no denying that she was unhappy.

On her day off she was sitting at the kitchen table with a

glass in her hand when a loud knock sounded at the door.

She opened the door to greet her landlady, red-faced and agitated. The woman held up a hand before Sara could even say hello. "One week—you're out."

"What?!" Sara frowned even as anxiety rose inside her. "But I gave my husband the check—"

"The check never reached me. I can't wait any longer. You're four months past due."

"Why didn't you talk to me before?"

"I talked to him—gave me some spiel about a check coming in. It never made it. I can't afford to listen to any more excuses."

"We'll get it to you—"

"No. I won't accept another late check. I'm giving you one week's notice to vacate."

"But I promise—"

"You're out!" The landlady stabbed her finger in Sara's face. "One week or I call the police."

Chapter Fifteen

Rick told himself he knew this wasn't the same. Paula wasn't Sara. She would never be Sara. He didn't look at her across the room and feel the same zing of electricity he felt in the halls back at St. Anne's.

But they did get along working in the same room at the Department of the Army, and she was single and pretty, and maybe he needed to give her a chance. He reasoned that by now, he'd spent so many years building up Sara in his mind that probably no one else could compete with her. The contest wasn't fair. And he was thirty now. Time to get on with building a life for himself.

As if reading his thoughts, Paula glanced up across the room and caught him looking at her. She smiled, a quick businesslike smile. "Need anything, Rick?" she asked, dark eyebrows raised in her fair-skinned forehead.

"Yes." Rick swallowed. Had it really been twelve years since the last time he did something like this?

"I've almost got the protocol finished," Paula said, turning to her typewriter.

"I need to ask you something." Rick forced a smile.

"Yes?" Paula looked up. Those raised eyebrows again.

By now he felt his heart thud. Maybe he was back at St. Anne's. "Are you busy Saturday?"

"Do they need somebody to work overtime?"

"No."

"I show my horses on Saturdays, but if they need somebody . . ."

"That's not it." All right. Here goes. "I wanted to ask you
to have dinner with me."

A quick nod. "I could—after the horse show." Immediately
back to her work. Not a blush or even a hesitation in words.

But what had he done?

After they were evicted from their apartment, the next ten
years inched by, with Sara always worried about where their
money went. She shooed her anxiety aside so she could be a
good nurse and a good mom. But one day, she thought of a
way to check out Carl's changing stories about his past.

Sara decided to make the telephone call after she dropped
Patrick off at school. Her son was in fifth grade now. Trying
to forget her nervousness, she studied the miracle that was
Patrick. Without a pause, Patrick carefully assembled all his
math papers and geography reports from the night before,
filed them in his school folder, and put it in his schoolbag.
Then he went to the refrigerator, grabbed his sack lunch, and
inserted it in the schoolbag. "Come on, Mom," he said automatically. Steady as a clock. The rudder in their lives. They
climbed into the car, and Sara drove. She pulled into the
schoolyard, waited for Patrick to get out. Instead of driving
off right away, Sara watched as Patrick, head held high,
walked proudly into the school without looking back. No matter what happens now, Sara thought, I'm proud of my son.
No matter what happens in my marriage, it was all worth it
to get him.

She sighed, drove home. She took a deep breath before
dialing the number she'd looked up earlier. Why did Carl
never guess she might do something like this? She rehearsed
once more what she planned to say.

"Iowa State University," said a switchboard operator.

"Transcripts, please . . ."

"You need a transcript?"

"Yes."

A pause. Then another voice. "Records."

"I need a transcript for Carl Parker."

"This doesn't sound like Carl Parker."

"I'm his wife."

"Due to the privacy act, I can't give out transcripts for another individual."

"He's out of town. On a job interview. Didn't know he'd need one."

"Well, I'm—"

"I have all his numbers. Social Security. Driver's license. Birthdate." Sara waited and breathed.

"Well—"

"I really just need to know his grade-point average at the time of graduation. And his chemistry grades . . ." Sara's voice rushed. "He's applying for a supervisory position at a lab."

A sigh. "Just a moment."

Sara waited, fingered the paper with the numbers she wrote down after borrowing Carl's wallet while he slept. Now she would find out. Once and for all.

"My supervisor says this is a one-time exception. If you have the correct numbers. Tell your husband that next time he'll need to call me himself."

"Thank you. I'll tell him. Okay—his driver's license number is—"

"Stop right there. It was probably different when he went to school here. Give me the Social Security number."

Sara read the number. Waited. Could hear the woman in records opening files.

A bigger sigh. "Nothing here. Are you sure you gave me the right number?"

Sara read the number again.

"That's the one I tried before. Not here."

"What do you mean?"

"We have no records of a student with that Social Security number attending the university."

"Do you mean the chemistry department?"

"No. I mean the university."

"This is for Carl J. Parker."

"Give me his birthdate."

"Eight-eighteen-forty-eight," said Sara.

"No Carl J. Parker. With that Social Security number, or

birthdate or even middle initial. He never went to school here, ma'am."

Stunned, Sara waited.

"Ma'am?" the receptionist prodded.

"Could you check again, please?"

"I already looked twice. Take my word for it. It's not here. Carl J. Parker never attended Iowa State University."

Sara hung up the phone, drummed her pencil on the desk. What should I do now? she thought. Unbidden, she realized her body was screaming for the Jim Beam. She got up from the table and went to the refrigerator. Then she swallowed her drink with a Xanax. Carl got the pills from his HMO— a month's worth had begun to disappear in a couple of weeks. But they couldn't numb the knowledge Sara had now. Ever since they started dating, Carl had told her he had a few credits toward nursing. At the beginning he'd mentioned a few missions in 'Nam when he was a medic. But Sara would have to be totally dense not to see how he embellished and added to the stories as the years passed. At first she thought his false bravado only extended to his military career. But now she knew he didn't even have his college degree. And what was it Patrick said the other night that gave her chills? Sara recalled Patrick's words with clarity. "Mom, why is it that every time someone tells Daddy a story, that story turns out to be part of his story, too?"

Sara shuddered with the knowledge she had discovered today. What should she do now?

Chapter Sixteen

The part of him that loved the outdoors also enjoyed the horse shows. Rick was certain of that. And once they started going out, Paula was happily willing to see him again and again. As they dated more than a year, something inside him nagged that he wasn't in love with her the way he was with Sara—but then there couldn't be another Sara. He told himself he couldn't rationally expect another woman to measure up. He probably wasn't being fair to Paula, who was slim, attractive, dark-haired, and savvy. She loved the outdoors as much as he did.

And there was one thing he knew: He was ready to stop being alone for a while. How could he expect another Sara to come along? She was obviously the love of his life. Who said you got more than one?

Paula's face was flushed, her hair disheveled, and her smile as broad as the open California sky the day her horse won the big trophy. Rick had to admire her dedication to the horses—it took money, lots of time, and lots of physical work. He'd been with her when she went to muck out the stalls.

He smiled. "Gimme five," he said good-naturedly, and seconds later her hand smacked his.

Glancing from side to side quickly, he abruptly said, "Now, I have something else to ask you." He paused, felt his heart thump. Then his voice wavered with the words. "Will you marry me?"

"Sure." Her grin still the same.

"Did you hear what I said?"

"Sure."

"And you will?"

"I said sure. Sure means yes."

"And you mean it?"

"Did you want me to say no?"

Did he? Abruptly his mind flooded with memories of the day Sara told him she'd be better off with a professional man, a doctor. And now Paula didn't hesitate at all about saying yes. Maybe she knew something he didn't. Wasn't it said that sometimes events that were destined fell into place easily? Maybe he just didn't appreciate Paula enough. Possibly theirs was a love that would deepen with time. When he had some memories with her the way he did with Sara.

He hoped so. Right now he was feeling the loss of Sara more strongly than Paula's acceptance. It was a sweet sadness, and he forced his logical mind to remember that Sara was probably married to Dr. Somebody someplace. She was half of a Dr. and Mrs. Pair. Maybe she didn't even remember him.

The thought of Sara forgetting what they had together heightened his sadness and firmed his resolve.

Sara was gone.

Paula was here.

It was time to move ahead.

Trying to distract her mind from the rising anxiety she felt, Sara remembered the time, three years ago, when she took her first Xanax prescription. For the short-term relief of symptoms of anxiety, said a flier that came with the bottle of pills. That was my trouble, Sara thought. My anxiety wasn't short-term. And she knew, even back then, that taking Xanax could lead to "dependency," as the medical profession called it, or addiction, as everyone else knew it. I'm like any other patient, Sara realized. I thought I could stop in time. But there was no way she could ignore the nagging persistent longing for another pill. It was as if her body was screaming for relief that only the pills could bring. As much as she knew she was addicted, she couldn't ignore the urge.

Now Sara was about to go against everything she stood for—as a nurse, as a person, as a mother. The small paper fluttered in her hands. It looked weak and flimsy compared with the enormity of the deed she was about to commit.

Lincoln General Pharmacy, the prescription form said at the top. Pharmacy, Suite 202. How many thousands of these passed through her hands as a nurse? She knew exactly what to write, so that the prescription would state she should take the antidepressants twice a day, and so that the bottle would say six refills. Enough pills to last her a month. Trying not to think of the magnitude of what she was doing, Sara wrote herself a prescription for the pills even as her body screamed for them. Dispense as written, the form stated.

She hesitated only a second before she wrote the doctor's name.

M. K. Bronson, the way he always signed it. Sara unfolded the prescription she found in the hospital garbage and compared the signature she forged with the doctor's original.

The letters she wrote were slightly bigger. More straight up and down rather than the doctor's usual slant. But didn't everyone say you couldn't read a doctor's handwriting? Besides, the urgency inside her was rising faster than her worry about the way the signature looked.

She got in the car and drove to a pharmacy fifteen minutes away, instead of using the one around the corner.

Trying to seem as casual as possible, she walked up to the pharmacy counter.

"Need to have this filled," she said, handing him the prescription she'd folded in half.

"Be twenty minutes," the pharmacist said, without looking at the form.

Sara walked the aisles of the grocery store where the pharmacy was located, looking back every few seconds to see if she could tell what the pharmacist was doing. Ten minutes passed. Fifteen. A chill of fear crossed her mind, making her shiver in the sunshiny spring morning. What if the pharmacist could tell the prescription was forged? What if he called Dr. Bronson? What if he called the police? What if they told the pharmacist to stall until they could get here to arrest her?

Her heart pounded, breath quickened. She almost ran out of the store.

But the urge for the pills was stronger than her will to leave.

Twenty minutes. Twenty-five.

She walked back toward the pharmacy counter, saw the pharmacist on the phone.

He caught sight of her.

"Mrs. Parker?"

She nodded.

"There's something odd about this prescription."

Oh, no. She forced a confused expression. "What do you mean?"

"It says thirty pills, and six refills. That's more than the legal limit for a single prescription. This is a controlled substance."

She didn't think. How could she make a mistake like this?

Catching her look, the pharmacist said, "Take me just a second to check with Dr. Bronson's office."

"No—" Sara raised a hand. "I'm in a hurry," she added lamely.

"Don't think I can fill it, then. . . ."

"Just give me one prescription—forget about the refills."

"Supposed to indicate whether refills are available on the bottle. . . . just take me a minute to call. . . ."

"No . . ." Sara was surprised at the fervor in her own voice. "I have another appointment next week. I'll ask him about it then. He can write me another one."

The pharmacist stopped to consider. "Sorry about that. But better have him write you a new one. I'd feel better about it."

He handed her the paper, and she put it in her pocket without looking at it.

"I'll come back," she said, even as she knew she would never set foot in this store again. She rushed out the door, gulped in a gasp of fresh air, and literally ran to her car. There was no way anyone could prove anything. She had the prescription form in her hand. She was safe.

But her body still screamed. The urge was irresistible.

In the weeks to come, each time she forged a prescription,

she promised herself it was the last. She was a nurse—her logical mind reasoned that she should admit to herself that she was addicted and seek appropriate treatment. But at the same time she felt she was sinking—in a sea of despair, of debt. The pills and Jim Beam were her only relief. And the more she tried to make her marriage with Carl work, the less she really wanted to endure even one more day in it.

"I just can't do this anymore," she told Carl, in a rare confrontive moment.

"What?" A pained, half-tolerant look on Carl's face.

Sara sighed. "I feel like my life is crashing down. I can't work fifty hours a week, have creditors calling constantly, and wonder what lie you're going to tell me next."

"I never lie to you."

"That is the biggest lie ever. There are always mysterious charges. You took the money I gave you for rent and spent it. I give you my check to pay the bills and they don't get paid."

"How much does your liquor cost?"

She wanted to slap him—but that would mean getting close to him. "If I'm an alcoholic, you made me that way."

"Huh!" Carl's bitter, sarcastic laugh. "That's what they all say. You're in Denial City. Get out one of your nursing textbooks. Alcoholics always blame their addiction on anything but themselves."

Sara cleared her throat. She'd never felt more sure of herself than at this moment. "I could get better if I weren't married to you."

"Huh! You'd be dead in a week."

"No—I could start over."

"You couldn't. You'd lose Patrick."

"I wouldn't lose anything. He'd stay with me. He knows about you—"

"I'll declare you unfit. They'll never let Patrick see you."

The horror of this was too great even to imagine. Sara caught her breath. Then it was as if the venom inside her overflowed. "I'd tell them what you did to me first. It started way back with my dad . . . that night with his credit card . . ." There was a small amount of relief as the words poured from her throat.

"He said I could use it!"

"He wanted me to see what you were . . . and I did see . . . but I was too dumb to stop myself."

"I'm the best thing that ever happened to you. I stayed with you through everything—even though you're a drunk."

"If I'm a drunk, you're nothing but a liar. All that crap about how you had a degree—"

"I've had years of medical training. And experience—"

"And *no* college degree. I found out, Carl. I called."

"And you don't even trust me!"

"It isn't just me. Patrick knows, too. Do you know what he said the other night? 'How come every time Daddy talks to somebody, their story turns into part of his story?' He can tell. All those missions in Vietnam. They're all fake."

She jerked, narrowly missing the dictionary he threw at her head.

Carl's voice held anger and disgust. "I'm calling AA. I've had enough of this. It's the whiskey talking. But I don't care. I've put up with it too long. I'm having you committed."

"Over my dead body."

He nodded, gave a sick smile. "It just might be that. Who knows what you'll do to yourself next."

Chapter Seventeen

Rick fought feelings of panic. Where was the church? He drove around again and again, sure he was in the right area of town. Rows of houses, brick, stucco, and wood. The right slant of sun. Trees the right height. How could he get lost in this neighborhood, after driving past Sara's house at least a thousand times? And even after he moved away, he saw the house in his mind. White, with those rust-colored shutters and rust-tile roof. So why couldn't he find the house now?

Did they change the name of her street? Or did all the streets always start with O? Overland, Oliphant, Olivia, O'Hara, Olney, O'Keefe. Nothing sounded familiar. And all he remembered now was that her street started with O. And everything else looked different. More traffic. A shopping center. Office buildings at the edge of the subdivision, instead of an endless even skyline of houses. Turn lanes in the streets, and three lanes on the main drag that led in here.

But this had to be it—didn't it? Was he completely off base?

Rick drove, weaving along streets that all looked the same. Oscar Avenue. Osteen Circle. How many O's could there be? He squelched a nagging feeling that maybe he should ask directions. As much as he wanted to find Sara, he balked at the thought that she might resent him searching through her neighborhood. Perhaps she might prefer a phone call—an appointment. If Sara was married to a doctor, she might be used to appointments. And what would he say? And how could he find her? He didn't even know what her married name was.

It was safer to keep driving. He drove around and around the streets, stopping once at a curb, any curb. It was strange how the street looked completely familiar—yet totally anonymous. No house caught his eye as even possibly the right one. Rick shook his head at the futility of his obsession. Then he laughed in exaggerated frustration.

He couldn't even drive by her house like he used to.

In the depths of her own despair Sara looked in the phone book again, as she had at least twenty—or maybe fifty—times before. It was as if she thought it might somehow change before her eyes as she turned to the D's.

She even had the page number memorized: 148.

She felt the same sinking feeling she always did, looking through the D's. First there was Donaldson. Then Donatello. After that were other Doo names—like Dooley, Doolittle and Doom. Finally, there there were the Douglases. Don. Gordon. Hugh. Kevin, Merrill, Paul. But then it jumped to Roger. There was never a Rick in her hometown phone book. Ever. She had lost her chance, back during those years when she could look in this book anytime she wanted. Now Rick was gone.

Whatever was different about today didn't have anything to do with the horse show. This show was like all the others that took a thousand hours a year out of their lives during each of the ten years they'd been married. Rick walked to where Paula sat at her desk. Piled around her were forms, lists, planners, and accounting books for the shows. She didn't even look up when he walked in.

Suddenly all the exhaustion and loneliness of the past years fell on him like a shower of stones. "Would you even notice if I never came back home?" Though the words formed a question, his tone was accusatory.

Paula abruptly glanced up and stared at him. A fleeting frown crossed her fair-skinned face before she turned back to the filing cabinet filled with all the documents relating to horse shows.

This time Rick emphasized his words with an angry gesture toward the papers on her desk. "I don't want to do this anymore."

This time Paula shrugged. "Then don't. . . ." she said simply, filling out a purchase request and signing her name.

"I can't work full-time and spend every night getting ready for shows."

"I never said you have to. I thought you liked going with me."

Rick stared at her indifferent face. "I'm tired"—he hesitated before another flood of anger released—"and I can't drive that far to work anymore."

Finally Paula carefully set her pen on top of a document. She turned to look at him. "What are you talking about?"

"I need my own life. I need my own friends, my own interests."

"So?" Another shrug punctuated her words. Did she understand how much her complacency hurt? That even though she always displayed a calm demeanor, he was talking about discontent that tainted all of the ten years of their life together?

"So I'm filing for divorce—"

"Just like that?" She snapped her fingers noiselessly, glared at him in annoyance.

"No, not just like that." Rick's voice raised in anger. "We haven't been happy in a long time."

Now she held completely still. "I don't know what I could do any different. I worked hard—ever since you met me. And you knew I was big on horse shows from our first date. . . . Seemed fine back then." This time her shrug was sharp with anger, and he heard bitterness in her words.

"Maybe I—" He waited. "Look, we don't even like the same parts of the show—don't even hang out together—"

"I thought that's what you wanted." Sarcasm dripped over her voice. "Fine for you—you always thought being alone was more fun anyway." She sniffed. "Like you're so entertaining."

"You don't even like me," Rick spat. "I'm just a piece of furniture. You don't care what I think—"

She sighed in exasperation. "All this because I wanted to

live closer to my work and you have to drive five more minutes to the office."

"That's not it—I just can't take one show after another. I'd like to relax, enjoy what I have. Running from one show to the next is craziness."

"Okay." Her chin jutted with determination. "You told me. Do what you have to do. I won't stop you."

"But—"

"I need to finish this right now," she said, holding up a hand in his direction. "You make your decision and let me know."

"And you'll just be at your desk or the horse show no matter what." The bile in his throat surprised him.

"Listen"—her hand formed a fist on the form—"I'm not the one who's talking about leaving. I'm not back in high school stuck on somebody I knew twenty years ago. I work hard for what I have. If you can't appreciate that, that's your problem."

Her fingers trembled slightly for a moment, but then she turned the ledger pages smoothly. He sensed that no matter how long he stood there, she wouldn't look up.

With a dull ache inside, he left the room. Sitting in the living room, he sensed that both of them knew—from the first—that this was a partnership, not a romance. How did she find out about Sara? He realized she'd always throw that at him now, no matter what he said. Was he acting like a kid to still hold his feelings inside? No, he told himself. He felt what he felt. It was that simple.

He and Paula hardly spoke as weeks passed. It was as if once they confronted their barren marriage, they couldn't go back to pretending there was a relationship left to save. He filed for divorce—then she filed, too.

Chapter Eighteen

The note was taped to her locker when she reported for the night shift. Sara read it. Her heart plummeted with a sick, dead feeling.

Only five words.

Jane wants to see you.

Jane. The head nurse. Her boss.

Not the usual friendly phone call or even a message on her pager. Just this note, its few words carrying a heavy message of dread.

Sara looked at herself in the mirror, combed her hair with a shaking hand. She straightened her skirt, then walked out into the hall. Each step seemed endless until she reached Jane's office.

Emily, Jane's secretary, looked up at her with a distinct expression of pity before her eyes fell back to her computer. "I'll tell her you're here," she said.

What was going on?

Jane was writing on a pad. "Sit down, Sara," she said, without looking up. "The others will be here any time now."

What others? What was this?

Sara sat at a chair facing Jane's desk. She pressed her sweaty palms together, smoothed her skirt over her knees. Moments later the floor nurse entered, accompanied by other members of the nursing board. No one looked at her.

"We need to talk to you, Sara . . . about something very serious."

Why was Jane's familiar voice so ominous? "All right," Sara managed.

Finally Jane looked up at her. "We obtained information that gave us reason to believe you suffer from chemical dependency."

"What do you mean, information?"

"The evidence arrived only recently, but it proved highly significant."

"What are you saying?" Sara's voice sounded thin and hollow in the silent room.

"We have documentation to prove that your chemical dependency could interfere with your work and the safe operations of this hospital."

"What? I have never endangered a patient in my care."

"We believe the seriousness of your dependency could lead to impairment at any time. We can't risk that."

"I have twenty years of high recommendations. Being a nurse is my life. . . ."

"There are hundreds of patients whose lives depend on you. As you know, in the ER, a split second means life or death."

"I always—"

"We feel we can't risk the patients or the integrity of this hospital. If there is a mistake and a patient proves you are impaired, a lawsuit could run into millions of dollars."

"I still don't know how you—"

"How we found out? That isn't as important as the fact that we can't continue taking this chance. We have no choice but to terminate you immediately."

"I'm losing my job?"

"I'm afraid so. There will be a hearing soon to determine the status of your license."

"My license? You're questioning my competency to *practice* as a nurse?"

"That's not up to us. There will be a state hearing to make that determination. We only know we can't keep you here, at Lincoln General. Please clean out your locker within the hour. Turn in your keys to security."

"This is so unfair! I always perform my duties perfectly!"

Without a word, Jane flipped open a folder. Her hand shaking with anger, she held up one of the forged prescriptions. Sara gasped. The handwriting that looked so much like Dr. Bronson's now seemed so obviously her own.

"So someone in the pharmacy—"

"It isn't important who, Sara. I must say that I am totally surprised at your actions. I always placed my trust in you and so did patient after patient. We regret that we can no longer trust you to serve as a nurse. You are a talented, capable person. Your care and compassion is well-documented. But you've gone the wrong way—your behavior is unprofessional and out of control, to say the least."

Sara sat stunned and silent. From her first day as a candy striper, she never imagined that anything like this would ever happen to her. She thought of all the years of work in the emergency room, all of the lives that she had touched. The thousands of people she helped heal. The ones who phoned, or wrote notes to thank her for the care she gave.

Staring at the floor, she was vaguely aware of all the nurses filing out of the room around her. Someone touched her shoulder, but she didn't look up. Instead, she sat in the empty room alone a long time. At first she numbly repeated Jane's words in her head. *No longer trust you as a nurse. Gone the wrong way. Can't keep you here at Lincoln General.*

Both anger and relief filled her. She wanted to know who told on her, but moments later decided it didn't matter. All her worries about getting caught, about somehow endangering a patient, were now over. But so, it seemed, was her life. She sighed and dragged herself down to the nursing floor to her locker. There were the notes from grateful patients—they no longer mattered now. The extra uniform in case she spilled something or needed to change clothes. The quotes and thoughts she taped to the door to buoy herself up on dark days. A few old phone numbers from families who told her to call them sometime. And even one or two numbers from families she'd notified about a family member's death. It wasn't a messy locker, but it represented a full and fulfilling career. After she lifted out all her belongings, the emptiness of the locker haunted her. Like her bereft marriage. Her worn-thin nerves. Her empty life. She handed her keys to security, changed into her street clothes in a rest room, and walked out into the darkening twilight. She sighed with bleak despair, which contrasted sharply with her usual walk down these stairs, when she felt satisfied that her day's work as a nurse was complete.

Even though she saw the light on in the living room, she prayed Carl wouldn't be home.

"That you, Sara?" Carl called out as she opened the front door. "Thought I heard a car door shut."

"It's me," she said, keeping her voice even and matter-of-fact.

"Home early, aren't you?"

"Yes," she said, her heart pounding.

He stepped closer, stared into her face. "Are you sick?"

Sara paused. She could lie. She could be like him. But as more and more time passed, she knew how opposite the two of them were, and how different they always would be. "No. I'm not sick," she said finally.

"Just tired—they let you off a little early?"

"No." She walked down the hall, but he followed her.

"Then what are you doing home," he persisted.

Sara closed her eyes quickly, trying to somehow draw inner strength. "I lost my job," she said softly.

"What?"

"You heard me—" She sighed.

"You didn't just up and quit—you really . . ."

"They fired me," she said.

"But how could they fire you? You have seniority and everything—"

"Not anymore."

Was that actually a smile on his face? "Don't tell me. Don't tell me Little Miss Perfect actually screwed up."

Fury filled her, but she couldn't answer.

"But they fired you? Don't you get warnings and stuff like that?"

"Not this time."

"What did you do, exactly . . ."

Sara took a deep breath. "They found a prescription I forged . . ."

"What? . . . You're kidding . . . after all these years of accusing me of being dishonest . . ."

"That's why I have to tell you the truth now," she said, an amazing peace suddenly filling her. "They found out I'm addicted. They said I could be a risk to patients. So they fired me."

"Just like that?" Carl snapped his fingers.

"Yes," Sara agreed. "Just like that."

Carl picked up the phone. "They can't do that to you. I'll call them and straighten this out."

"No," Sara said simply. "I can't lie to them or to you. They have the prescription. It's proof, in my own handwriting."

"Then what are you going to do?"

"I have to think," Sara said flatly. "I never thought this would happen."

"I have to ask," Carl said acidly. "How are we going to pay the rent? And the bills? They're all coming due at the end of the month."

"I'll have to find another job. But I don't know what I'll do. A nurse is all I ever wanted to be . . ."

"Can't you call them? Tell them you really need your job and you'll never do it again."

"No." She sighed. "They're not just firing me. They're taking my license away."

"And you say I make dumb mistakes. You call me a liar. Look at what you did! You're lucky they didn't have you arrested."

"Shh!! You'll wake Patrick! He doesn't need to hear about this."

"Maybe he does . . ." Carl said evenly. "Maybe it's time he knew his mother isn't a saint."

Sara wanted to hit him, but she couldn't stand to be in the same room with him another minute. She went in the bedroom, changed into her robe, and lay awake all night in the dark.

As weeks passed, all of Sara's problems weighed on her mind, seemingly without hope of release. Her life's work was gone while their debts steadily rose. She despaired for the patients she thought she would never see or help again. She knew now that she wanted to separate from Carl—but how could she ask for that when Carl promised to declare her an unfit mother? The thought of her marriage left such a vacant emptiness within her that she forced herself to think back to her memories in search of solace and comfort rather than facing the dire impossibility of today.

She thought of Rick, so far away—in years and probably miles, too. She wished she could turn back both time and distance. Why didn't she realize, way back then, how her life might have been if she and Rick stayed together? Why didn't she cherish each moment that they had? Because no one did, she told herself, until it was too late to recreate the bliss of what was now so painfully and irretrievably gone.

The sheer, bleak austerity of her life haunted her as she dragged through day after endless day. No money. No hope. No love for her husband. No trust in his fake sincerity. She'd start to feel as if somehow she'd rise above all of this—then realize she'd already lost hours that day in a drunken fog. Carl's insurance plan still paid for the pills and he kept the liquor cabinet stocked with Jim Beam. The pills and Jim Beam were always there—friends who became enemies as the workless afternoons wore long and her anxious thoughts loomed menacingly in her mind.

Another night when her body screamed for the pills and the drinks. Sitting in her living room chair, Sara tried to think of something happy that could happen in her life. As minutes passed her hope dribbled away. Her life's work was gone. Her relationship with Carl was based on lies. Her father was dead. And she couldn't be a mother to Patrick when she could hardly stand to be herself.

This time she would decide how their fight would end. And this time Carl would have to face the landlord and the creditors . . . and her mother. She wouldn't be there to straighten things out . . . and try to cover for his lies. Numb with sadness, she took a fresh bottle of antidepressants out of its pharmacy sack and found the sleeping pills in the medicine cabinet. Then she got a six-pack of beer from the refrigerator. She sat on the couch, pills and drink beside her. She swallowed each pill with a swig of beer, waiting in between at first . . . and then just rushing on. The sky outside darkened from charcoal to ebony . . . the blackest black she'd ever seen.

Like coming out of a fog. The way she always imagined general anesthetic would feel. Or time travel. You went on a journey outside yourself, and then eased back within your own consciousness a little at a time. She felt the bedsheet beneath her, and first imagined that she was home, waking up in the morning. But what was this groggy, grainy, terribly nauseated feeling? She felt dizzy. And there was a stabbing ache in her throat. And the walls here, above her head. Not white, but pale green. Chills racked her from within as she understood she was at the hospital. What was she doing lying down at work?

Reality came rushing back. She was no longer working. She was a patient. And she was supposed to be dead now. The realization hit like a thunderbolt, bringing chills of terror and sadness, then waves of tremulous relief, like the soothing warmth of a long bath.

She was alive. She felt herself breathe, listening to the whistle of her breath against the crisp fabric of the pillowcase. She shifted against the mattress beneath her and felt she could lie there and stare at the ceiling forever, grateful for every moment.

But what happened? How did she get here?

When she tried to turn to look at the clock, her legs wouldn't move. Fear jarred her with the understanding that she was bound to the bed in leg restraints. The pain in her throat was a feeding tube.

I tried to kill myself, she thought. I'm a nurse. I know how to succeed. I shouldn't be here. What did I do?

As her initial relief subsided, paralyzing despair set in. Beyond being bound to a bed in the hospital, the reality of losing her job, then receiving a letter that she'd lost her license, weighed on her like a stone. Not being a nurse was like being told she couldn't talk anymore, could no longer be herself. She tried to imagine never wearing her uniform again, never assisting in another emergency surgery, never seeing relief on another face while feeling that same inner solace when a patient's life was spared.

Images of herself as a candy striper rose in her mind. Memories of her days as a young girl with dreams of saving lives now brought heartfelt pain. She literally could not imagine what lay ahead. She thought of Rick, of that past carefree time.

A hand on hers. She looked up to see Carl staring at her. That analytical look in his wide blue eyes. He stared at her, then let go of her hand and turned away. He paced in the small, silent hospital room. She watched as he half-shrugged helplessly. "Sara, I'm sorrier than you'll ever believe . . . really."

"Me, too." Sara managed to force her words out past the tube in her throat. She pressed her lips together. "It's strange. . . ." She paused. "I thought I'd be sad that I didn't die . . . but I'm not. . . ." She looked away, gazing out through the venetian blinds, where she caught a glimpse of green leaves. So it was daytime.

Carl inhaled deeply. He sighed. He turned toward the window, where slats of sunlight striped his profile with gold. Another shrug. "I guess I'd have to say I saw it coming. . . ." Now he looked at her. "I knew you were unhappy, babe, but not this bad."

"How did I get here? Did you put me here?" Sara shifted on the bed. She felt a shiver of panic and wanted to sit up to confront him.

Carl shook his head. "Patrick," he said slowly.

"Patrick! What are you saying?"

"Your son found you. . . ."

"No!" Sara thought of all the nights she worried over money, worked as hard as she could, quelled the rising tide of anger and despair within her so that Patrick would not find out . . . and now to think of Patrick coming home and finding . . . Sara shook her head fiercely.

Carl nodded. "He thought you were dead, Sara."

Sara closed her eyes, held back tears. Felt a flash of anger—at herself, at Carl, at life in general.

"He felt for your pulse, like we taught him . . . and then he called the ambulance."

"Oh . . . I never would have . . . but I couldn't even think. . . ."

"He did the right thing. He saved your life." Carl's voice grew quiet. "You wouldn't be here without him."

Sara shook her head, felt sweat and tears swim on her face. Then she looked up and read pity in Carl's eyes. She felt a surge of anger and swallowed hard. "Carl, you have to listen to me. I want a divorce. I need to go on with my life."

He shook his head. "Sara—you don't mean that. The booze is talking."

"It's not. I'm clear-headed for the first time in years. I know what I want."

"I can't believe you're so selfish. I stayed with you all these years. You can't throw me away now."

"It took me a while." Sara leveled her gaze at him in the waning afternoon light. "But you enable me. You give me drinks and put pills in them."

Carl shook his head in disgusted fury. "You're lying. Addicts always blame everyone else."

"Who handed me my first drink?"

"One drink didn't make you a drunk. You did it yourself. It's your problem, not mine. You're lucky I stayed with you."

"Not anymore," Sara said softly. "I'm getting a divorce as soon as I'm strong enough to climb out of this bed."

Carl swore, then threw his half-empty paper water cup against the wall of the hospital room. "Sara, promise me. Don't do anything until we talk to a counselor."

"You aren't telling me what to do. Ever again. I promise that," Sara spat.

Swearing under his breath, Carl yanked himself off the bed and rushed out of her room. He slammed the door with a cracking noise. Sara took a tentative breath before her fears and doubts rushed. How dare she fight with him while restrained to the bed? Did she really know her own mind when she was so out of it?

Feeling her adrenaline gradually subside, Sara rested, watched TV, thought. As the afternoon waned and the sun fell, she decided life couldn't get any lower. She lost her job. Lost her nursing license. Was about to lose her marriage. What was left?

A timid knock at the door. "Come in," she said, knowing that Carl would never announce his presence so timidly.

There was a pause. Then she heard the knob turn, caught sight of Patrick's panicked face, his brown eyes huge and troubled. Sara's throat caught and tears rushed. "Oh, Patrick—" She held out her arms and took her fourteen-year-old son in a welcoming embrace.

When the hug ended, Patrick stood at the end of the bed, hands clasped behind him. "We love you, Mom. We want you back."

Sara reached her hand out, stretching as far as the leg restraints would let her. "I'm here, honey. I'm glad to be here."

"Mom—" Patrick took a deep breath. "I love you. I have to ask you . . . please stop drinking. It's killing you."

Sara felt her heart thud. "I thought I wanted to die. But I never imagined you would find me. Believe me, if I had any—"

A sob from Patrick. "I thought you *were* dead, Mom."

Sara's tears flowed. "I'm so sorry you had to go through this—I wish I could just erase it from your mind—"

Patrick sobbed, then walked over to bury his head against Sara's shoulder. "I was so scared, Mom. I tried to remember what you and Dad told me to do—in emergencies—but then I just called 911."

"You saved my life. Plain and simple." Sara leaned back to gaze at her son's face. "And now I promise I won't ever put you through that again."

"Dad says you want a divorce."

"That might happen," Sara admitted. How could Carl dump this weight on their son? "Part of my problem is my problem with him."

Patrick sat up on the hospital bed, looked away. "Just get better right now, okay?"

Sara breathed.

"Then you can come home," Patrick said.

Sara touched her son's hand. She said, "We'll see."

Rick would look back as months passed and recall that there was no shouting, no accusations, no messy litigation. Everything split down the middle as neatly as a candy bar broken in half. In the end there was a lingering sadness over failing at something he'd worked at for ten years. Wasted time, empty months. But nothing he could change now. At least he kept rising at work. The raises, promotions, and accolades were steady. Maybe he wasn't cut out for a romantic relationship anyway.

Then why did he still remember Sara? What was it about her that kept hovering in his brain, year after year? "You got to quit torturing yourself, buddy," he said, alone in the mountains, kicking at ashes and stones to put out the campfire where he'd cooked himself dinner moments earlier. Smoke drifted up into his face, his eyes, making him cough. What was it about Sara that wouldn't leave his mind? Maybe if he found her—just saw her at a distance, the way he used to back in school—he could finally let her go. If he saw where she was now, maybe he'd know it was finally over.

Chapter Nineteen

Squaring her shoulders and telling herself this was no scarier than facing Patrick earlier today, Sara walked up to the admitting desk.

"Sara? What are you doing here?" the admitting nurse said, glancing at Sara's everyday clothes. She lowered her voice and leaned closer. "Are you here to see somebody? One of your patients?"

Sara shook her head. Her lip quivered.

"Busman's holiday?" The nurse smiled.

"Worse than that." Sara waited. "They fired me."

"You? No way!" The nurse shook her head.

"Yes—my last day was Monday." Sara took a deep breath. "Now I need to be admitted."

"To the hospital? What do you mean?"

"I need treatment."

The nurse frowned. "In this unit?"

"Yes." Sara sighed. "I'll tell you before you hear it from someone else. I suffer from chemical dependency. They fired me and then they took away my license. There's no way I can work again until I prove I'm clean. Maybe not even then." Sara shrugged painfully.

"Sara, I can't believe—" Shaking her head, the nurse drew a form out of a drawer and gestured for Sara to enter a conference room. Moments later she didn't look at Sara as she asked the routine questions. Age, Social Security number. "Nature of your dependency."

"Alcohol and narcotics." Sara said.

The nurse stared at her.

"I know I need help," Sara said simply. "Now everyone else will know."

The nurse's hand abruptly folded over hers. "You're not the first," she said simply. She stood, went to a calendar chart on the wall. "I think I can get you in today or tomorrow. We'll call you—" She paused. "I'll need your home number."

First there were the talking geese. Even as her body screamed for Xanax and Jim Beam, Sara watched the mother goose and six babies walk around her hospital bed. She sensed they planned to swim in the pool in front of the hospital. But when she looked out her window, she saw a horse-drawn carriage pulling up to the hospital door, and a husband and wife in old-fashioned clothes presenting their daughter to the hospital management. Then she watched a baseball game. Then she had front-row seats at a Rolling Stones concert—Mick Jagger gyrating in frenetic rhythm as he stood in front of her hospital window on the locked psychiatric floor.

She knew she could ask for Valium if the hallucinations became unbearable, but somehow it seemed best to ride this out. Eight days passed. On the ninth day, bored and exhausted, Sara dragged herself out of bed and began to pack items in her suitcase. She'd made it this far and sensed she could make it the rest of the way on her own.

As she walked past Sara's room, the floor nurse stopped abruptly. "What are you doing, ma'am?"

Folding her robe and setting it in her suitcase, Sara said, "I'm going home today."

The nurse yanked her chart from the clipboard at the bottom of her bed. "There's no discharge listed. Your treatment is not complete."

Sara kept her voice calm. "It's complete as far as my medical provider is concerned. They only pay nine days."

"But we can't sign off on unfinished treatment."

"I'm a nurse—I know what needs to be done. And you've detoxed me. I'm clean."

"The psychiatrist hasn't issued a release—"

"Then send him in here—I can't stay another day."

With an angry sigh, the nurse said. "When you signed yourself in for treatment, you agreed to abide by the judgment of the treatment personnel."

"And I've done everything they told me so far—I know I can recover at home."

The nurse shook her head and left the room. Sara finished packing—her underwear, her nightgown, her toothpaste and toothbrush. She was trying to snap the suitcase shut when the psychiatrist entered the room.

He sat in the visitor's chair, leaving her to sit on the bed. She waited, then said, "I'd like to be discharged today."

"Mrs. Parker. As a nurse, you know it could be dangerous—even life-threatening—to leave before your chemical dependency is regulated."

"I can't pay for another day—it's that simple."

"You can talk to your insurance company."

"My husband is out of work—we're in debt. And I can't work while I'm in here. The only coverage I could get was Medicare disability—Workman's comp—because of my addiction. They pay for nine days."

The psychiatrist looked at his watch, then at her chart. "Today is the ninth day. If you don't plan to stay here, what were your plans for continuing treatment? Surely you understand the risks of—"

"I could monitor myself. I monitored hundreds of patients."

"And did you manage your own alcohol intake at the same time? Surely you know that the inability to restrict one's own intake leads to further addiction—"

"I won't get into that trap again."

"You feel certain of this?"

"Yes . . . I was in an unhealthy relationship—my husband encouraged—if not forced—the dependency. We are still married legally, but I'm filing for divorce. I'll be staying with friends from work after the treatment."

"You know that's what they all say. Any cause but the addict himself."

"I know that. I'm determined to change the pattern."

"And your husband—he won't influence you further?"

"Never again," said Sara, with a determination that surprised even herself.

"It's for your own good that the treatment is the length that it is." The psychiatrist sighed. "I would hate to think that a relapse resulted from a prematurely shortened stay."

"Believe me. I don't want to suffer those hallucinations again. But even if I did, it wouldn't pay my bill."

He sighed again, wrote on a prescription form, handed it to her.

"Tranquilizers," she said, after the doctor left the room. "Same dirt, different shovel." As soon as she heard his footsteps die away, she tore the prescription form in half.

They decided to have lunch when they reached the airport ninety minutes ahead of takeoff. After they sat in the light blue booth, Rick's sister, Marcy, smiled at him. "Did you know Becky is getting married?"

"Our niece?" Rick raised his eyebrows at her.

Marcy rolled her eyes. "You really need to visit more often." She laughed.

Rick waited, tried to judge Marcy's easy grin. After a moment's wavering, he decided to go for it. He said, "This is the year for me, too."

Marcy tilted her head quizzically. "What year is that? *You're getting married?*"

"No. I'm going to find out what happened to Sara *this year.*"

Marcy patted his hand. "Sure you will." She smirked.

"Really—this year. Maybe I'll find her next week when I go home."

Marcy leaned closer, looked around to see who might be listening. "Haven't you tried already? Lots and lots of times?"

"So I've got to be close—it'll happen soon. Maybe before Becky's wedding."

"But you told me you looked in all the phone books and stuff like that."

"I've done more research . . . it's got to pay off. . . ."

"Didn't you used to drive by her house?"

"I did . . . but I can't find it anymore."

Marcy's hearty laugh rose above the conversational buzz

in the restaurant. "You didn't just lose her . . . you lost her *house*." Her head leaned back with laughter. "Listen, Rick. I'll buy your lunch today—you buy mine when you find her—or her house."

"I'll buy yours today. You can buy mine and Sara's next time." Rick smiled at his sister.

"Deal." Marcy shook his hand gleefully before she laughed again.

On the plane Rick fought the rising logic that Marcy was right. It should be simple. Like two plus two, or A follows B. He knew her name. Sara Montgomery, the name everyone called her. Sara Anne Montgomery, her full name. He knew her city. Southbridge, a suburb of Detroit. So what was the problem? Why was it that every time he looked in the phone book, none of the Montgomerys seemed like the right one? And when he tried to drive by, street after street passed with no familiar house? How could he explain it?

He couldn't. He had to find her. This had to be the year.

He had four weeks' leave. Almost a month. Enough time to drive down all the streets he thought were in the right area. And he would actually stop at houses this time. He could call every Montgomery in the book in hopes that he could find the right one.

But what if her parents had moved away and no one knew exactly where?

The possibility was unthinkable.

At least the sun was shining. Sara took a last look at herself in the mirror. She looked pale and tired, but there was a serenity in her green eyes that she hadn't seen in months—maybe years. She combed her hair one more time and smoothed the eyeshadow on her eyelids. This was one day when it wouldn't hurt to look absolutely perfect. It wouldn't carry her through the ordeal that lay ahead, but it would help.

Jane's secretary looked at her with undisguised curiosity as she entered the office.

"I have an appointment," Sara said coolly, hoping her voice sounded calm and unruffled.

"Yes, some of them are already back there," said the secretary.

Some of them? Who did she have to talk to? Sara smoothed her skirt. She licked her lips as a shot of fear and adrenaline surged through her.

"You can go on in." Was that mockery in the secretary's voice?

No turning back now. Remembering her nights as a nurse when she had to tell a mother her baby died, or needed to let a family know their father was never coming home, Sara stepped down the hall. She could hear people talking behind the closed door to Jane's office. For a moment she stood stock-still. She raised her hand and knocked softly.

Silence from the other side of the door. Then muffled words. A man clearing his throat.

"Come in," someone said.

Sara's hand shook as she turned the knob. There was a hush in the room, and she knew everyone was looking at her. The office light seemed unnaturally bright, almost as if a spotlight were trained on her.

Her eyes fanned the room until they found one empty chair. She stared at it and felt everyone's eyes still on her. Finally someone said, "Sit down, Sara."

Sara sat.

Everyone stared. Sara felt herself swallow. She shifted against the hard wooden chair.

Jane said, "Sara? You wished to address the board?"

Sara cleared her throat. "I'm here to request that you reinstate my full-time employment as an emergency room nurse at Lincoln General, based on—"

Jane interrupted, "Considering the circumstances of your termination—"

"The circumstances have changed—they no longer exist."

Jane raised her eyebrows. "And the fact that your nursing license was revoked—for forgery, for which there could have been criminal charges."

"I've gone through rehab and retraining—I have the papers right here."

"Still, it's quite a stretch to imagine that you could perform to full capacity, considering the extent of the problem before."

"I never had any problem carrying out my duties before and I won't now. My evaluations were always excellent—"

"But a substance abuse violation—the extent of your addiction would indicate obvious impairment—"

"I'm completely clean." Sara raised her hands for emphasis. "And my training is fresh, too. Here's my retraining certificate." Sara hated her hands for shaking as she handed the paper to Jane. She took a deep breath, then paused. "You're getting a good deal with me—twenty years of experience."

The director, sitting next to Jane, said, "She'll go somewhere else if we don't take her here—"

"And they're short in the ER—you know they are, Jane," said the floor supervisor.

"I can start next week—or tomorrow night, if you need me," Sara implored.

Jane appeared to evaluate her. "You'll be drug-tested without warning."

"I'm not worried. Test me now. This minute."

"And if there's any indication that the previous illegal activities are continuing, you'll be fired immediately—and this time we'll contact law enforcement."

"I understand that."

"No warnings or temporary suspensions. No hope of ever coming back."

Sara paused. "Believe me—if anyone ever found out how bad things can get, I did. I've been to the lowest point I'll ever go, and I'd never go back there again."

What else could she say?

"Excuse us, please, Sara," Jane said. "We'll confer briefly. You may wait outside."

Sara sat on the bench outside Jane's office, racking her brain. Did she say something wrong? What were they about to do to her now?

Minutes ticked by. She got a drink of water, idly thumbed through magazines on a table. Her stomach growled with hunger.

Finally the door opened.

"Come in, Sara," said Jane.

She walked in. She remained standing, unsure whether to sit again.

"Sara," Jane said. "We have decided to reinstate your employment, contingent on our examination of the papers you have presented today. If we find your information satisfactory in our investigation, we will rehire you."

Relief, pouring over her in waves. Best not to show that she felt like jumping up and down. "Thank you," she said simply.

"If the papers are satisfactory, we will call to tell you when to report for work."

Yes, Sara thought to herself. Her life wasn't over after all.

Chapter Twenty

"*I'm leaving, Carl.* I can't stay here another day."

Could he really be as stunned as he looked? "Come on. Just because you got your job back—now you think you can get rid of me."

"That's not it—we haven't been happy for a long time. For years."

"That was just you—I was never good enough for you. I couldn't be a surgeon general like you wanted."

"It wasn't that—" But what was it? Sara wondered if she could ever distill all her unhappiness with Carl into just a few words.

"Yes it was. You wanted a rich doctor, and when I wasn't it, you wouldn't give me a chance."

"I gave you plenty of chances. Let's not argue about—"

"And I lived with you when you were so drunk you couldn't see straight."

Sara caught her breath. "What caused me to be an alcoholic?"

"See—you never stopped blaming me—"

Sara held up her hand. "I'm not saying we'll divorce. I'm saying I need my space."

"Like I ever had any space in this house."

"Look. I was almost dead two years ago. Just give me some breathing room."

"What about your son? How will you explain this to him?"

"I'll just tell him, Carl. He'll be in high school next year. He knows the score. I'll tell him everything straight out. I'll just go—and after a few days I'll see if he wants to come stay with me."

"No. I'll go," Carl said suddenly.

"So you can tell everyone I threw you out?"

"It's true, isn't it? I stayed with you through everything, and now you're getting rid of me."

"I need my own life," Sara said firmly. "And so do you."

Though Carl slammed the bedroom door with a crack as he went to pack his things, Sara hardly heard the sound.

Sara sifted through her mail while watching TV on her day off. It was amazing how good a day off felt now that she could work as a nurse again. There was no relief like putting on her nurse's uniform and heading out for the night shift. When all her knowledge and experience seemed to come back, she felt like she regained her identity while losing the blackest years of her life. Yet at the same time there was nothing as soothing as a long afternoon at home on the couch after four nights on her feet. She picked up her mail while halfheartedly watching *The Sally Jessy Raphael Show*. There were letters and Christmas cards. She saved the small brown box from her mother until last. This was her mom's first Christmas alone, and Sara's first without her dad. Seeing the familiar home address in her mom's handwriting brought an ache to her heart. She wondered how her mom could even think of buying Christmas gifts this year.

A commercial on the TV. The show was almost over. Sara slid her fingers under the tape holding the brown paper together. She tore it off to discover a small red-and-white striped box. Curious, she lifted the lid.

It was a necklace; a gold heart with a guardian angel on it. Sara instantly felt tears, knowing her mother sent her this to remember her dad—the guardian angel who now watched her from Heaven. Sara took the heart from the box and held it in her hands. She ran her fingers over the shiny, smooth gold surface of the heart and felt the rougher edge of the guardian angel. Suddenly she looked up, the necklace still in her hands. Something drew her attention to the TV.

"Is there someone in your past that you never forgot? Maybe a high school sweetheart? A high school crush that you thought might be the real thing? Are you someone who would like to find your lost love?" Sally asked the TV audience. "If you are, call us at 55-SALLY."

Sara looked at the screen, then down at the necklace in her hands. A current of emotion filled her. What would the dad who was her guardian angel want for her now? Was he trying to tell her something? There was no question in her mind. She picked up the phone and dialed. When a receptionist answered, Sara said she was calling in response to Sally's question on the current show. Seconds later Sara heard the phone ring in another department.

"Producer's desk," someone said.

"I'm calling about the lost love show," Sara said.

"Oh, would you like to be a guest?"

Sara swallowed. "I lost the man who was the love of my life . . . and I want him back."

"Was he someone you knew a long time ago?"

"Yes . . ." Sara felt her heart beat. "Thirty-three years ago . . . at St. Anne's High School . . ." Once she started talking, the memories flowed, and she sensed how hard it had been to hold them back all these years, when they were still as real in her mind as yesterday. She kept talking until the producer's assistant interrupted her.

"Ma'am, before you go any further, I need to get all of your information and talk to Miranda, my producer, about all of this. I really think she would be interested in your story."

"Okay," Sara said. "Thank you for listening to me."

"She'll call you back if she's interested in pursuing the story."

A warm feeling filled Sara as she hung up the phone. But maybe they got hundreds of calls. And maybe the stories had to be approved by editors, managers, advertisers, lawyers. Probably about as much chance as winning the Publisher's Clearing House giveaway. During the next hour, she finished opening her mail, put a load of laundry in the washer, wrote her grocery list. She was heading out to run errands when the phone rang. There was no way, she told herself. No way.

"Sara Parker?" A friendly voice. Sara could hear lots of muted conversations in the background. Probably a telephone salesman.

"Yes," she said.

"Sara, this is Miranda, a producer from the *Sally* show. You have a lost love story to tell me?"

It was his annual December visit. Rick had been at his mother's house a couple of hours when the phone rang. While he waited, deciding whether to pick it up, a recorded voice from his mother's bedroom clicked to life. When did she get an answering machine? As if he were home, Rick rushed to hear the message in case it was important.

He recognized a New York accent. Someone talking fast. He could only catch snatches of the hurried message. His name. Rick Douglas. The words "wants to meet you" and a phone number at the end. He played the message back again and again. Nothing about it struck a familiar chord, but the person was definitely asking for him. If it's important, they'll call back, Rick reasoned.

Half an hour later the phone rang.

"Rick Douglas? This is Miranda Bennett. I have something to ask you."

"Excuse me," said Rick. "Who are you? What is this all about?"

"I'm a producer with *The Sally Jessy Raphael Show*. Let me ask you, Rick. Did you ever know someone named Sara?"

Total shock. Chills rushed through him. He felt seconds pass before he could even consider an answer. Floods of emotion poured over him. Amazement. Euphoria. Relief. Then a wave of frightened caution. He'd waited too long and hoped too hard. Somehow, he sensed he couldn't survive a mistake. Or a joke. Or a con. Even a harmless error. What if he traveled a thousand miles and Sara Sullivan or Sara O'Rourke came walking out on the sound stage. After all these years, could there be any greater disappointment? He absolutely couldn't survive it, could he?

"I've known a lot of people in the last half century." Rick faked a laugh, realized his palms were sweating.

"Anyone named Sara?"

"There are lots of Saras and lots of Ricks in this world."
Another unconvincing chuckle.

"What about Sara Parker?"

Wrong name. She could be married, of course. And if she
was married, why was Miranda the producer calling him? If
her doctor husband was there on the stage with her, could he
still tell her he never forgot her? That he was still in love,
hopelessly, absolutely, after all this time? But if this was
somehow a chance, could he pass it up? He knew that if there
was any possibility, he needed to really make sure.

"Did she go to St. Anne's High School? Was she from
Southbridge?"

He heard the woman scrawling as he spoke.

"Was her maiden name Montgomery? Sara Anne Montgomery?"

When Miranda didn't answer, he asked, "What year did
she graduate from high school?"

"I'll get back to you," Miranda said, hanging up.

By now, Sara knew Miranda's voice. This was the third day
in a row that they'd talked.

"I have to tell you. We're having a hard time finding him,"
Miranda said.

Sara's heart sank at the doubtful tone in the producer's
words. "I never could track him down myself," she admitted.

"We don't do it ourselves," Miranda said. "We use
BigHugs.com, a search agency. They look all over the world.
Do a great job."

"And you told them about Rick?"

"We did."

"What did they say?"

"No luck so far. Tell me—" Miranda paused. "Was there
another name that he knew you by?"

Another name? Sara subconsciously shook her head. Rick
never called her anything but Sara. She couldn't remember
anyone except her father ever calling her Sara Anne. That
name appeared only on her birth certificate.

"No," she said sadly. "I really can't think of any other
name."

"It would give BigHugs.com more to work with on their

databases if there happened to be a nickname or any other name to check."

Sara shook her head. "I'll keep thinking."

"Let me know," Miranda said. "Call me back if something comes to your mind."

"I will," Sara said.

It was three days later when Miranda called again. "Sara, could you fly to Chicago to be on the show next week?"

"You found him?"

"No. Not yet. We're still hoping. If we don't find him by then, BigHugs.com is thinking that if you appear on the show and make a plea, maybe someone who knows him will contact us."

His sister, Marcy. Would she see the show? His mom? People he worked with?

His wife. Sara felt a chill of fear and sadness. Rick probably had a wife. A woman who was smart enough to see what a wonderful husband he would be. Genuine. Honest. Romantic. Fair.

Was it fair of her to ask him to meet her after all this time? He could always say no. Maybe then, if she knew that he was happily married or no longer interested in seeing her, then she could stop wondering.

"I-I'll do it," she said to Miranda. "I'm scared, but I'll do it."

"I appreciate that, Sara."

"You're in group B," the producer said.

In the green room Miranda, who Sara now discovered was a young woman with an auburn pageboy dressed in a royal blue suit, held a paper in front of her, her hands shaking with frenetic energy.

"I have something to tell this group," she said.

"Come on," said Sue, a smiling woman beside Sara. "Tell us where you're hiding them—or we'll tear this studio down looking."

Miranda held up a hand. "Wait," she said.

"We already waited thirty years," said Sara.

"Twenty for me," Sue added.

"Fifteen," said a man who was the other member of this group.

"Well—how do I say this—your wait is going to be just a bit longer."

"Are you telling us we're last on the show—don't make us be last!" Sue shouted.

Again, Miranda held up her hand. "It's not quite like that. I need your attention," she added. "I need to explain something."

"What's to explain? Just let us at 'em. We know what to do. We're not teenagers anymore." Sue leaned back and roared with laughter, slapped a hand against her thigh. Sara giggled nervously.

"Please—" a sudden seriousness in Miranda's voice. "I need to tell you that while we were able to find the past love partners for those in Group A, you are now in Group B. Group B includes those we will not be able to reunite today."

Sue stood. "Aw, you gotta be kidding. I took off work and flew all the way here for—"

"This is still an important day for you." Miranda held up both hands now. "We need your help. We need you to go on the air and make a plea—"

Sue shook her head in disgust. "No. Don't tell me—"

"To everyone in our audience—millions of people—and someone out there may know how to find your lost love. . . ."

Groans from Group B. Sue stamping her feet in anguish.

"We're sorry we could not find them yet—we will try again after you make these pleas. There are so many people out there—this is a very important chance for you—"

"Meet Sara," Sally Jessy Raphael said. "Sara would like to be reunited with a man she met more than thirty years ago, am I right, Sara?"

Sara nodded. "I think of Rick every day of my life," she began, fighting to ignore the tremor in her voice. "I'm not obsessed. But I never forgot him. I just want to know what happened to him, and if he's all right."

Sally nodded, then asked, "You still have feelings for this man, although you haven't seen him in thirty years?"

Sara nodded, half-smiled. "As I got older, I discovered that you don't always appreciate what you have until you lose it. I lost my father a few months ago. My father always said he couldn't understand why I parted from Rick . . . and I think he would want me to—"

"You met at a very young age—"

"Yes . . . it was the last half of our second year of high school. Back then, I didn't know how to cope with my feelings. . . ."

"So you fell in love way back then?"

Sara nodded. "We knew each other for two years. Our feelings were getting stronger. The relationship was deepening and I didn't know how to handle it. Since then, I've learned that sometimes you can trust your first instincts—it's possible to fall in love when you are young."

"And to have that love last the rest of your life?"

Sara's smile wavered. Suddenly she couldn't speak.

"So could you say that you are still in love with Rick?"

Sara nodded. She felt tears threaten. She leaned to dab at her eyes, looked to the right—and saw him. Electricity streaked through her body, and she leaped to her feet. She screamed, "Oh, my God, *Rick!*" She rushed at him. Recalling his formal, "May I kiss you?" thirty-three years before, she grabbed him in a bone-crushing hug and gave him a passionate kiss. Gazing into his face, she glimpsed the warm brown eyes she remembered so well. Her right hand traced his cheek as his left hand stroked hers. "Sara," he said, in a warm, loving tone that made her heart skip a beat. "It's been so long . . . we have so many stories to tell and share. . . ." He paused. "You are so beautiful. . . ."

Sally's voice reminded them both that they were, after all, on television in front of millions of viewers. "Sara and Rick— after thirty years—do you think the two of you can rekindle a romance?"

Still overcome with emotion, they looked into each other's eyes—and shrugged simultaneously as if to say, "Well?" Then Sara glimpsed tears on Rick's cheek, leaned over, and kissed him again. "Do you think you can?" Sally asked again, laughing. Sara nodded as she led Rick back to their sound-stage chairs—and started to laugh along with millions of viewers. Rick reached to take her hand, and their two hands clasped tightly, as if they would never let go.

It seemed like seconds later that Sally said, "Thank you for being with us today. We're going to give our couples an evening in New York as time to get to know each other. We promise to follow up on these possible romances at a later date. Keep us posted, will you?" She tilted her head at Rick and Sara and the other couples.

A warm rush of relief flooded Sara's mind as she and Rick walked off the soundstage hand in hand. They were actually together again, at last. He hailed a cab. "I guess you're at the Wilshire, too?" he asked Sara.

"I think they gave us this night in New York. . . ."

"I always hoped I'd see you again. I just never guessed it would be under these circumstances."

They laughed together.

"Just a few more people than we used to see in the halls back at St. Anne's," said Rick.

Sara ventured, "I hope you don't mind that I brought you on national television. I just had to know if you were okay."

"If Miranda hadn't called when she did, I would have found you anyway."

"Really?" Sara was genuinely surprised.

"I promised myself it would be this year. I went home on a visit with the goal of finding you. I arrived at my mother's house—and Miranda was on the answering machine."

Sara was speechless. Overcome with emotion, she stared out the window as the cab drove past scores of buildings.

"Wilshire," said the cabdriver from the front seat. He pulled the cab up to the curb and stopped.

Rick approached the desk clerk at the Wilshire and gave their names. "We're guests of Sally Jessy Raphael," he said.

"Just a moment." The clerk sat at a computer screen, frowned. Her fingers clicked furiously on the keys. She frowned again.

"Can't find our names?" Sara asked. "Rick Douglas and Sara Montgomery?"

"It's not that." The clerk shook her head. She stood, faced the two of them. "You're not going to believe this. I know this sounds strange, but there are . . . budget problems. . . ."

Her glance drifted to Rick and Sara's clasped hands. "Would the two of you mind sharing a room?"

They all laughed together.

"Well," said Sara. "If he's the same gentleman I knew thirty years ago . . . I'm completely safe."

They followed the bellman up to the fourteenth floor, waited as he unlocked the door with a plastic electronic key.

Sara was stunned to see the room had a single king-size bed. She stopped short, fumbled to find words. She looked at Rick, and the two of them laughed together. She turned to the bellman. "Uh . . . when I said I'd share a room, I didn't mean . . ." She paused. "I need to tell you that we've just been reunited. I just saw him for the first time after thirty years, and I'm not quite ready for this."

"Do you have a similar room with twin beds?" Rick asked, saving the moment.

Later that night, as they watched TV with a nightstand between them, Rick smiled at her. "It feels so good to gaze into those beautiful eyes. I've waited thirty years to look at them again."

Sara squeezed his hand, then reached into the bowl of popcorn they'd bought from a street vendor.

It was about three weeks later when Rick flew east for the second time in a month. His mom was remarried now, and she hinted that it was about time he did the same thing. Rick glimpsed happy surprise on Sara's face when she held out her hand to his mother—who promptly leaned in to give Sara a long hug. "It's about time," his mom said simply.

"If you're going out on a date, seems like you might need a car," his stepfather said, jiggling the keys to the Crown Victoria before placing them in Rick's hand with a smile.

Rick and Sara gave his mother another hug before they climbed in the car. After he turned the key and the engine spun to life, Rick and Sara sped off to Prima Pomodoro.

"We can't go anywhere else," Rick said. "It's a tradition. They probably still have our reservations. Not another customer since prom night."

"And that singer," Sara added. "Who else in the world would hire her?"

"Speaking of singers," Rick said, turning on the radio and trying to find a station here in this town where he hadn't listened to a radio for years. They heard radio static for a few moments as Rick turned the channel knob, trying to find any kind of music. He gave up with a sigh—then suddenly a station crackled to life. When Rick lifted his hand back to the steering wheel to make a right turn, the lyrics on the unknown radio station instantly were hauntingly familiar and brought back a flood of memories.

Even though this was the beginning of the third verse, neither of them had forgotten a single word. For the first time in more than thirty years, his baritone and her soprano blended as they sang the lyrics they remembered perfectly from so long ago.

Together, they sang the words that they could remember, and felt as young as when they heard them the first time. Rick smiled at Sara, and she felt comfortable and companionable with him at this moment, as if they had never been apart.

"Did you know that the *Sally* show will air on our anniversary?" he asked, taking her hand in his, and feeling an appreciative return squeeze from her fingers.

She frowned, that same quizzical, gorgeous frown he fell in love with all those years ago. "Our anniversary? Did I miss something? Do we have an anniversary?"

"Yes, we do. The show airs on our thirty-fourth anniversary. . . ."

Sara smiled at him. "Really? Now when is that?"

"Hah! Don't tell me you forgot. I never forget our anniversary."

Sara grinned mischievously. "I won't forget if you tell me when it is."

Rick's voice turned solemn. "It's February fifth—thirty-four years ago, on February fifth, I first saw you. . . ."

Sara felt herself blush as memories flooded. She felt a rush of tingles at her spine.

"—you stood in the doorway of Mr. Steiner's classroom, and right then I knew I was in love with you. I felt a connection and thought I might love you the rest of my life. . . ." Rick paused, and his voice grew thick. "And now the show